THE CRY

On the streng
scriptwriter in t
the navy to devote his time to writing, since when
he has written six successful novels: *The River
Running By*, *The Raging of the Sea*, *The Believer*, *Armada*,
The Fighting Spirit and *The Crying of the Wind*.

He lives with the artist Susan Keeble and they
divide their time between their flintstone cottage
in Hampshire and their seventeenth-century farmhouse in France.

CHARLES GIDLEY

The Crying of the Wind

Fontana
An Imprint of HarperCollins*Publishers*

Fontana
An Imprint of HarperCollins*Publishers*,
77–85 Fulham Palace Road,
Hammersmith, London W6 8JB

Published by Fontana 1993
9 8 7 6 5 4 3 2 1

First published in Great Britain by
HarperCollins*Publishers* 1992

ISBN 0 00 617810 3

Set in Linotron Baskerville

Printed in Great Britain by
HarperCollinsManufacturing Glasgow

Only if someone writes this as fiction will it last, will it be believed. Journalism expires within twenty-fours hours, and it is so easy to forget.

ANDREW GRAHAM-YOOLL,
A State of Fear, 1986

To a Child Dancing in the Wind

Dance there upon the shore;
What need have you to care
For wind or water's roar?
And tumble out your hair
That the salt drops have wet;
Being young you have not known
The fool's triumph, nor yet
Love lost as soon as won,
Nor the best labourer dead
And all the sheaves to bind.
What need have you to dread
The monstrous crying of wind?

W. B. YEATS

Part One
ANNA

I

THE NEW MISSIONARIES, Dr Timothy McGeoch and his wife Ursula, came to Misión Yuchán in the October spring of 1938. They had arrived at Buenos Aires by steamer two weeks before and had made the long journey through the pampa northwards to the Chaco, the wilderness on the Paraguayan border.

They had seen much on their way, and by the time they dismounted from the ponies upon which they had made the last lap of their journey from Embarcación, both had undergone the shock that every European experiences on first visiting South America.

But neither the young doctor nor his wife was prepared for the further shock of arrival at Misión Yuchán – 'Bottle tree Mission'. From the moment she set foot in the village, Ursula in particular was appalled at the living conditions of the Matacos Indians. She was appalled at the superstition among the people and at the shrines to the Virgin Mary they kept in their shacks. She was appalled at the number of infant deaths. She was appalled at the number of suicides among young girls and the custom of executing married women for adultery. She was appalled at the prostitution, the alcoholism, the cheapness of life, the despair, the fatalism, the blindness, loss of teeth, venereal disease, Chagas' and tuberculosis.

Above all, she was appalled at the number and status of the village dogs.

The dogs at Misión Yuchán were everywhere. They lay in the shade of the bottle tree by the well, fouling the muddy puddle where black swine wallowed to keep cool. They gathered in dozens whenever a steer was slaughtered and skinned. They gnawed and pulled at the hides that were pegged out to dry in the sun. They scratched and licked themselves under the benches of the village store where an old hag sold pod alcohol and the menfolk sat about drinking yerba maté.

There was no need for latrines at Misión Yuchán because the dogs, which were never fed, ate every scrap of human faeces and licked clean the babies who lay among rags and the toddlers who played in the dust.

1

In their first weeks at the mission, the McGeochs spoke frequently about the problem of the dogs. It was impossible to ignore it: they could not sit on the verandah of their bungalow in the evenings without witnessing the village dogs taking it in turn to mount a bitch or fighting over a scrap of meat. Wherever you looked they were licking or scratching or fighting or fouling or copulating. Ursula said that they could hardly expect to minister to the spiritual needs of people who were sunk in such physical degradation.

Following the death of the previous missionary, Misión Yuchán had been abandoned for nearly two years and in that time the witch doctor, a wealthy young Indian called Anselmo, had established a strong hold on the people. Anselmo made Ursula and Tim feel tolerated rather than welcomed, and a series of little accidents and incidents focused this effect on Ursula in particular.

Though she never admitted it to a soul, Ursula was not happy at Misión Yuchán and secretly regretted coming to the Argentine. Sensing her revulsion to their ways, Anselmo made sure that she was confronted with as much as possible that would revolt her. Soon after the villagers witnessed her shock at seeing a steer being slaughtered, the severed head was sent round to the McGeochs' bungalow as a gift. It was hung by the nose on a hook outside the missionaries' front door so that the blood dribbled down onto the wooden planks of the verandah.

When Ursula first visited the village store the old criollo woman gave her a spoonful of añapa to taste. Añapa is the raw mixture of carob pods and water from which pod alcohol is made. It was not explained to Ursula that one should chew and spit out the carob husks, so when she tried to swallow them, she vomited in the middle of the village with the women turning away and covering their smiles with their hands.

On New Year's Day, soon after Dr McGeoch had allowed it to be known in the village that his wife was pregnant, Ursula found a dead bird in the mission hall. Its innards had been replaced by the severed penis of a recently dead infant.

The discovery of such a bestial thing would probably have broken the spirit of many women, but Ursula had dedicated her life to the battle against the powers of darkness and was convinced that with God's help she would win it.

'We must show them that God is not mocked,' she said. 'We must prove to them that nothing they can do will frighten us or drive us away.'

Dr McGeoch promised to have a word with Anselmo, but Ursula said he might as well go and talk to the vizcachas.

'Then what do you suggest, my dear?'

'We have to do something positive, Timothy. And I know at least one way in which we can make a start.'

McGeoch was a slightly built young man, fresh-faced and dedicated to the Lord's service. He was somewhat under his wife's thumb, and knew what she had in mind. 'You mean we should do something about the dogs?'

'Yes, I do.'

'You want me to start shooting them?'

'The diseased ones, at any rate. You said that was needed on the very first day we arrived here.'

The last thing McGeoch wanted was to start a feud between himself and the witch doctor. That was almost certainly what Anselmo would want; and while he loved and admired his wife and acknowledged the fact that she was the driving force in their new marriage, he regarded his own role as that of a steadying influence, the gentle rein on a courageous but sometimes impulsive mare.

'I seem to remember that it was you who persuaded me to wait before doing anything rash,' he said. 'And I think you were right. You know how superstitious these people are about killing their domestic animals. Don't you think we should persevere a little longer?' He took her hand and gave it an encouraging squeeze.

She turned to him. 'Let's pray about it, Timothy. Let's lay it before the Lord.'

They went into their spartan little bedroom and knelt side by side to ask God's guidance. McGeoch knew that much of the strain that Ursula was undergoing was because of her pregnancy. When they got up from their knees he tried to cheer her up.

'It's only a few weeks now before Anna arrives. You'll feel so much happier once you have her for company.'

Anna was Dr McGeoch's younger sister. She had agreed to come out to Misión Yuchán for six months to look after Ursula and the baby. Although she had never voiced her reservations about the idea, Ursula was not as enthusiastic about it as her husband. She had only met Tim's younger sister a couple of times, but the impression she had gained had been of a girl who was too young, too impulsive and too flighty to be well suited to the Lord's service.

Anna McGeoch could never in her twenty-one years have been accused of indecision. She was the youngest of four and the brightest. As a little girl, she had adored her elder brother. As a teenager, she had somehow survived a strict evangelical upbringing with her sense

3

of humour and her independence of mind intact. Now, having come of age, she had leapt at the idea of a sea voyage and a stay in Argentina. For years she had been itching to break free of the dour atmosphere of her home under the shadow of the Pentland Hills, and although her trip to South America was being funded by the Free Church assembly to which she belonged in Colinton, she was honest enough with herself to see that this might be a stepping stone out into the world where she knew, instinctively, that she belonged.

Her father was pleased and proud of her. Her mother was full of advice and family sayings. Her elder sisters envied her sense of adventure as they had envied everything else about her from her earliest years. A letter from Tim had arrived to say that she would have a bungalow to herself, that there was more than enough work for her to do and that her presence at Misión Yuchán was eagerly awaited.

Then, one leaf-spattered day in Morningside, Anna met Lieutenant Angus McNairne of the Midlothian Fusiliers and all her enthusiasm for Argentina evaporated into thin air like steam from a railway engine on a dry day.

Angus was a softly spoken giant who was more attractive to Anna than South America. She was working as a child's nurse at the time, and spent several afternoons pushing a pram with Angus walking at her side. Neither could believe their good fortune. Against her father's wishes, she accepted Angus's invitation to a Halloween ball in the officers' mess at the Redford Barracks. It was her first dance and when she arrived home in the taxi soon after midnight she knew that she was in love.

A few weeks later she told her mother that she was having second thoughts about going to Argentina. Janet McGeoch was an obedient wife and she told her husband everything. Arthur McGeoch rued the day he had given his permission for Anna to go to the ball. There was a family rumpus.

It was a rumpus that lasted. There were tears over the porridge and silences at tea. The minister came to talk sense into McGeoch's wayward daughter. While November and December easterlies blew icily through Edinburgh, Anna stuck to her guns. But the money had been spent on her passage and was not recoverable. There seemed no way out. She told Angus as much on New Year's Day.

'There is a way out,' he said.

'There is not.'

'There is, Anna.' He put his hand on her shoulders and forced her to look at him. There was snow on the ground. She had a Fair Isle

4

scarf wrapped round her neck, and her cheeks and nose were red with the cold. 'Marry me,' he said.

She said she needed time to think. He thought she meant a day or two, but Anna needed only half an hour.

They went by bus back to Colinton and climbed the hill to Pentland Neuk. It was already dark. Before going into the house, Anna gave Angus her instructions. 'Wait a little way down the road, and when you see my bedroom light come on, knock at the front door and ask to speak to my father.'

He looked blank. 'What about?'

'To tell him you want to marry me, of course!'

'So the answer's yes?'

'What do you think? I only want to give father time to get his jacket and tie on.' She went round the house and in by the back door.

He strolled down the road for a few yards. When he turned back the upstairs window was open, the light was on and Anna was looking out at him. 'What are you waiting for?' she whispered.

'So you really will marry me?'

'I told you! Yes!'

He went up to the front door and a minute later he was in the dank front room, trying to break it gently to Mr McGeoch that he wanted Anna for a wife.

Anna's father was the headmaster of Oxgangs Grammar School and a pillar of the Wee Free. He was suspicious of gentry and of army officers in particular. He had viewed the rapid progress of Anna's friendship with a man who held the King's commission with alarm. Quite apart from her commitment to go to Argentina, he would far rather see his elder daughters, Evelyn and Harriet, married first.

'And when would you be thinking of wedding her?' he asked.

McNairne braced his powerful shoulders. 'As soon as convenient, sir. Perhaps April or May?'

'You're – what – a lieutenant?'

'That's correct, sir. I have a small private income and a part share in a farm at Howgate. I shall be a captain within eighteen months. I undertake to take good care of your daughter.'

'That may be so,' said the headmaster. 'But are you a practising Christian?'

'I was baptized into the Church of Scotland.'

'I said, are you a practising Christian? Have you repented of your sins? Have you proclaimed Christ as your Lord and Saviour?'

'I think that's my business, sir.'

5

'And so it may be, young man. But if you're to marry my daughter it's mine as well.'

'I see,' said McNairne, and there was a very long silence.

Mrs McGeoch and her three daughters were in the back room toasting scones at a small coal fire. They heard Angus being shown out by the front door and a moment later Mr McGeoch came in and beckoned to Anna to follow him into the front room.

'You have promised your service to the Lord,' he told her. 'And what's more, you're too young, the both of you. You've only known him a couple of months. And he's not a Christian. Och yes, I know you're twenty-one, Anna. I know you can wed him if you're so minded. But I'll tell you this: if you insist on having your way, you'll break your mother's heart. Do you want that on your conscience for the rest of your life?'

A dry, dusty wind had been blowing for several weeks, putting everyone at Misión Yuchán on edge. Ursula was being sick in the mornings and had pains in her legs. Tim was sleeping badly and suffering from headaches.

One morning in March, not long before Anna was due to arrive at the mission, there was another crisis. Just before dawn Ursula was woken by noises, and when she went to investigate found a dog and a bitch locked together under the kitchen table. When Tim arrived, rubbing the sleep from his eyes, she was in hysterics. 'I can't go on like this! I can't go on! I don't care what you do, Timothy, but you must do something. Shoot them! I don't care! I don't care!'

When he had got rid of the dogs, he calmed Ursula and persuaded her to take a light sedative. Having dressed, he unlocked a cupboard where a small-bore hunting rifle was kept. He had inherited the weapon from the previous missionary, along with a box of soft-nosed ammunition, which he put in his pocket. With a heavy heart, he slung the weapon over his shoulder, looked into the bedroom to make sure that Ursula was settled, and left the bungalow.

He walked out of the compound through the mission cemetery where wooden crosses marked the resting places of the converted Indians who had died in Christ. Among these was that of the last missionary, who had suffered a stroke less than a week after completing a translation of the New Testament into the Wichi dialect of the local Matacos Indians. His grave and that of a young woman who had come out in the early twenties and had died in a riding accident were the only two foreign ones: all the rest were of Indians with Spanish names like Lopez and Pereyra and Rosas. Many of the graves were of infants. Branches had

6

been strewn across them to keep the vizcachas from burrowing among the corpses.

He stopped. Fifty yards away a bitch with a litter of puppies had seen him. The bitch had stood up from her nest with her puppies still hanging on her teats. She was barking at him. Not yapping or baying, but barking one defiant bark at a time like the regular firing of a light field gun.

It was still early. The sun's white light splintered through the saplings at the edge of the cemetery. He was a doctor, not a hunter. He had never willingly killed a living creature in his life.

He took the box of ammunition from the side pocket of his alpaca jacket and opened it. The original invoice was folded inside. It was dated 1913. Forty-eight rounds remained. If he fired now, this would probably be only the third gunshot to have been heard at Misión Yuchán since before the Great War.

The bitch continued to bark defiantly. She was not going to run away, so he could take his time. He might even go closer, but the thought of shooting her at point-blank was in some way despicable.

His hands shook. The bullet refused to go into the breech and dropped at his feet. He picked it up and this time it went in. He closed up the rifle with a click. It was a lady's hunting rifle. He wondered whether he should sight on the animal's chest or its head. There was a better chance of hitting it in the body, but he didn't want only to wound it and have it escape back into the village.

He could feel his heart thumping and he was cold and wet under his arms and down his back. The dog was still barking and one of the puppies still hung from a teat.

He came down from his aim and forced himself to think again about what he was doing. He thought about Ursula sobbing in his arms only half an hour ago. He had to do something, if only for her sake. If he didn't take positive action now he would probably have to take Ursula away from Yuchán, and if they could not work at Yuchán he wouldn't want to remain in the Argentine. They would have to return to Britain and face the congregation in Colinton who had raised the money to send them out here. It would be a personal as well as a spiritual defeat. In the space of six months Satan would have sent them packing. What would he do with the rest of his life? How would he explain to the son or daughter that Ursula was carrying how he had been defeated by the influence of a witch doctor?

He raised the gun again and sighted directly on the bitch's head. As he did so the animal began to bark more ferociously and rapidly. He held the foresight as steady as he could on her head but at the last moment changed his mind and lowered the point of aim to the chest. The gun went off sooner than he had expected. The wind was not yet up and the sound of the report seemed to hang in the air for a long time.

It took him a moment or two to realize that the bitch was no longer barking. Shaking all over, he went nearer. She was stretched out, quite dead, not even twitching, a glob of blood in place of an eye.

He felt cold and sick. The puppies were crawling about at his feet. Their eyes were not yet open. He had no sack so he could not take them back to drown them. Dimly he realized that in killing the bitch he had been changed in a fundamental way. He had lost something that could never be regained.

Hardly knowing what he was doing, he stamped on the heads of the eight squeaking puppies one by one. It was a relief when they were silent. But as he straightened he caught a glimpse of one of the village boys running back through the cemetery to the village and all his apprehension returned.

He started back to the bungalow. On any other day at that hour the village would have been full of movement and noise. There would have been women chattering at the well, men passing the maté round outside the huts, children playing in the dust. That morning there were no women at the well, no children playing. It was as if the sun had not risen.

He walked along the path that led under the eucalyptus trees to his bungalow. There would normally have been people waiting outside the clinic by now. Women helpers would have been lighting a fire outside the school to make the thin vegetable soup with pieces of boiled meat in it that was served every day to the children who attended class. But the clearing was deserted. The only sound was the repeated call of the 'ben–te–veo' bird, the great kiskadee who says, 'I–see–you–well.'

Ursula was sitting up in bed. She was drowsy from the sedative but had heard the shot and was unable to sleep. He sat down beside her and told her what he had done, and that he was sure the whole village must know about it.

'I'm such a fool,' he muttered. 'They'll never forgive me for this. Never.'

'We're both fools,' she whispered. 'God's fools.' She stroked the back of his head.

When she had dressed and plaited her hair they went to the mission and knelt down side by side, their hands linked tightly together.

The wind was getting up. It blew the dead eucalyptus leaves into whispering eddies and hummed in the lattice wires that served in place

8

of window panes. There was a notion in the village that the sound the wind made in the mission hall windows was the spirit-voices of the Wichi ancestors mourning their lost children.

When they came out, Tim said, 'It's as if I know something but don't yet know what I know.'

Ursula shivered. Apart from the birdsong and the wind's sighing, the village was still very quiet.

'Will you go and talk to Anselmo?'

'I shall have to.'

'Don't make any compromises, Timothy. You did what had to be done. I would rather we leave altogether – shake the dust of this place off our feet – than strike hands with the Devil.'

The witch doctor lived in a shack on the far side of the compound near the bottle tree from which the village took its name. When Tim arrived he was wearing a black wide-awake hat and pleated bombachas – the baggy trousers worn by horsemen in Argentina. The outfit marked him out from the rest of the villagers and gave him an air of authority.

It was midday. Anselmo was eating at a table under a cane awning with his back to the visitor. Three tabby kittens picked their way about the table round his plate. A dozen or so dogs and puppies lay about, panting in the dry heat of the day. A little way off a girl was spit-roasting a chicken over an open fire. Inside the shack one of Anselmo's wives lay suckling a baby.

McGeoch greeted the witch doctor in the Wichi dialect. 'Good day to you, Anselmo.'

Anselmo went on eating without bothering to acknowledge the missionary's presence.

'I suppose you heard the rifle shot this morning?'

Anselmo spat.

'And I think you know why it was fired. Yes?'

The witch doctor beckoned to his daughter to bring him the kettle and the maté gourd. He waited while she put a quantity of the pale green herb into the gourd, added cane sugar and poured in hot water. Then he accepted the gourd from her and sucked at it through the bombilla, appearing to forget completely that the missionary was standing behind him.

McGeoch tried again. 'There is no need for us to be enemies, Anselmo. We both want the same thing for the people of Yuchán. We want them to be healthy. We want the boys to have strong legs and good eyes for hunting. We want the girls to have clean, fragrant bodies that will bear healthy children to the menfolk. Isn't that so?'

Anselmo shovelled another spoonful of yerba into the gourd, added more sugar, more water from the kettle.

'We are medical men,' McGeoch continued. 'We know the dangers of allowing dogs to breed unchecked. We know that they cause diseases – worms, syphilis, tick fever, infant blindness. We know that all these can be spread by contact with their filth. What I did this morning was the first step in a battle we must fight together. It is a battle that I shall not win without your help. All that is needed is for you to tell the people of this village that –'

He was interrupted by the breathless arrival of a man from the neighbouring village of Carboncito. Ignoring McGeoch completely he told the witch doctor that his daughter was in a high fever and close to death. Her skin was burning hot and her eyes had disappeared into her head. In the past hour she had suffered convulsions that had shaken her so that her teeth rattled. His wife had put the warmest egg from the nest of a sitting hen up her vagina, but all the strength had gone from her and she was 'stretching out her muzzle', an Indian euphemism for dying. His excellency the curandero was her only hope. If he did not attend her, she would certainly die – indeed, it was quite possible that she was already dead.

Anselmo sighed and made as if to get to his feet. But then he appeared to change his mind and sank back onto the bench. For the first time, he acknowledged the presence of Dr McGeoch. 'What's your opinion? Is it necessary to attend to this child?'

'Of course it's necessary!'

Anselmo showed his teeth. 'But the people here have told me a story they heard from you about a healer who can heal without going to the sick person, isn't that so? Didn't a soldier, a man of authority like this man here, ask him to heal his servant? And didn't the healer do so without going to the sick person's hut?' Anselmo took another suck of maté before resuming. 'Do you mean to say that you can't do the same as the curandero of whom you tell so many stories, doctor?'

McGeoch turned to the man who stood waiting for an answer. 'I shall come and see your daughter immediately,' he told him.

Anselmo began to laugh. He rocked about on his bench, tittering to himself and shaking his head. 'No, no, no! There's no need for that!' He spat in the dust. 'There! She's cured! I am telling you – she is sitting up and asking for food and drink.' He waved expansively to the storyteller. 'Go home, man. Your daughter is cured. Go home and celebrate, and bring me a gift tomorrow. Go! Hurry!'

The man ran off. As he went, McGeoch called after him, 'I will come and attend your daughter straight away.'

10

'I do not advise it,' Anselmo said, and all trace of humour left him. 'The girl is cured. It is not good to question what the spirits have done. Nor is it good to kill the animals of the village, for they have spirits just as we do and those spirits will be angered by what you have done. In your heart you know this. If you have any wisdom, you will go back to your house and stay indoors for three days, you and your wife and the baby inside her belly. That is my advice to you, doctor.'

McGeoch found Anselmo's words frighteningly persuasive. He did indeed feel a sense of guilt over the killing of the bitch and her litter. All his instincts were to return to Ursula, to comfort and be comforted by her – and to forget for just a few days the spiritual and physical ills of Misión Yuchán.

But he had promised to attend to the girl and he could not go back on his word. That would be just what Anselmo wanted.

'And what if I decline to follow your advice?'

Anselmo shrugged. 'Who can say what will happen? Who can say?'

There was a silence. The bird went, 'I–see–you–well! I–see–you–well!'

McGeoch shook his head and turned to go. 'I'm already bound by a promise I made when I became a doctor, Anselmo. I have sworn never to withhold my services from the sick. So I shall go to Carboncito, and pray that God will deliver me from evil.'

'Pray hard, doctor!' Anselmo tittered. 'Pray hard!'

He collected his medical bag from the clinic before setting out. The road – which was no more than an earth track leading through the scrub – was a lonely one and he made the journey in the fiercest heat of the day.

When he reached the village it was still the hour of siesta. He went to the shack of the headman and announced himself. A minute later, the old Indian came out looking cross at having his afternoon sleep interrupted.

He asked where the sick girl lived. The old man said there was no sick girl. 'All in Carboncito are healthy.'

'Was there not a girl close to death this morning?'

The elder shrugged dismissively. 'Yes – but she is cured. Her father went to the curandero in Yuchán and he worked a cure. There's the girl now, sitting over there by the well with her mother.'

No wonder Anselmo had laughed. He had been made a fool of. Not by any miraculous cure worked by witchcraft but by a piece of simple play-acting. The child had not been ill at all. Anselmo had merely employed her father to make a fool of him.

'I thank God that the child is well,' he said. 'Is there anyone else in the village who needs medical attention before I return to Yuchán?'

The elder waved his hand. 'There is no sickness in Carboncito,' he said. 'We are all healthy.'

He set out back along the parched earth road that cut through scrubland and forest. He had not eaten properly that day and had drunk little. His head began to throb painfully and there was singing in his ears. The sun beat down. After a while he walked as if in a dream, his thoughts eight thousand miles away in Colinton, Edinburgh.

What were his parents doing now? His father had worked as a schoolmaster for thirty years. He had scraped and saved all his life and had little to show for it but the terraced house with a narrow garden that ran down to a stream. It would be about seven in the evening over there: his father would be home from school and they would be sitting down for their evening meal.

Anna would arrive at Buenos Aires any day now. She would be met off the boat by Miss Jowett, a lady Tim had never met who was a supporter and benefactor of Misión Yuchán. Miss Jowett would put Anna on the train for Salta where she would be met by the missionaries. From Salta she would travel by train to Embarcación, where he would meet her personally and accompany her on horseback to Misión Yuchán.

Everything would change for the better as soon as Anna arrived. Her sense of fun would provide a much-needed relief from Ursula's intense spirituality. She would take over the school and teach the children anything and everything, from drawing and singing to the three Rs.

Everyone loved Anna. He could almost hear her voice now. She talked rather fast and had an infectious enthusiasm for life. He remembered the rambles they used to have as children on the Pentland Hills behind the house. He remembered snowy afternoons dragging branches back for the fire, and magical family Christmases and Hogmanays.

He was still daydreaming about home when a mirage appeared in the distance ahead. It seemed to float a foot or two above the surface of the earth road. As he got nearer, the mirage materialized: twenty or thirty dogs were lying panting in the sun, their ears pricked, watching as he approached.

This was not a mirage. They were shaking the dust from their

12

quarters, stretching and scratching and barking. It was as if they had made an appointment to meet him and were relieved that he had finally turned up.

He told himself that he had never been afraid of dogs and that there was no need to be frightened of them now. These animals were excited, but they were not hostile. The worst thing to do would be to show any sort of fear.

He walked briskly on, deafened by the noise of their barking as they surrounded him. He ignored the first nip on the ankle, but when a larger dog bit his leg he whirled round and swung his medical bag at them, scattering them momentarily. But they came back and he was again surrounded. He resisted the temptation to run. He turned this way and that, swinging his bag at them to make them keep their distance.

He whirled the bag round again. Two of them seized it and started a tug-of-war with him and with each other.

Immediately, others attacked him from behind. He felt his trousers rip and a tug at his shirt-tail. He lost hold of his medical bag. It burst open and the contents scattered on the cracked earth road. One of the larger animals leapt at his throat. He staggered backwards, protecting himself with crossed arms, but as he did so teeth clamped on his crutch and he doubled up with a shriek of agony.

After that, they brought him to the ground very quickly. They began jerking and tugging at his flesh. They ripped open the stomach and tore out the intestine. The body took on a different sort of life. It jerked this way and that like a rag doll.

When the sun went down the dogs were still gorging themselves on the flesh and gnawing the bones. By dawn the next day all that was left was the medical bag and its scattered contents, a few scraps of clothing and a dark stain of blood upon the sun-baked earth.

2

CECI JOWETT SAT IN HER CAR on the quayside at Buenos Aires city docks and tried to guess which of the passengers who had disembarked from the *Highland Princess* and were now emerging from the customs shed was Miss Anna McGeoch. It was a rather severe-sounding name, so when she saw a mournful-looking young woman in a grey nanny's uniform she jumped, as Ceci was prone to do, to a wrong conclusion.

'Miss McGeoch?' she asked and held out her hand. 'Welcome to Argentina!'

The girl, who was a Norlands Nanny on her way to take up a position with a family in the Chubut, looked taken aback.

'Mrs Cunningham?'

'No,' said Ceci. 'Miss Jowett.'

'I don't understand,' the girl said. 'I was told I would be met by Mr Gotto.'

'You are Anna, aren't you?'

'No, *I'm* Anna.'

Ceci looked round to see a girl in a yellow cotton dress and a straw hat. She was instantly captivated. 'My dear,' she said. 'How lovely to meet you. Now where's your luggage?'

Anna indicated a porter with three suitcases on a barrow. 'He seems determined to put me into a taxi. I can't get rid of him –'

'That is not an uncommon experience for a woman in this part of the world!' Ceci laughed and having directed the porter to load the luggage into the back of her Ford coupé, tipped him and sent him on his way.

Ceci was not at all the sort of person Anna had expected to be a supporter of a Christian mission. She was some years older than herself – about thirty, with pale skin and auburn hair; expensively dressed in a print frock with outsize shoulder pads and shoes that matched her lizard-skin bag.

'How are you feeling? You're looking very bronzed, I must say. So did you have a good voyage? Lots of parties, I bet?'

14

Her questions poured forth and Anna was never able to answer with more than a few words before another one tumbled out. They got into the car, started up, stalled, started again, made a seven-point turn and finally set out through the docks, bumping over railway lines, finding themselves in dead ends, reversing, trying again and finally, after much nervous laughter and apology from Ceci, emerging triumphant on the Avenida del Libertador.

'I hope you don't mind if we don't talk while I drive,' Ceci said. 'The traffic here requires all one's attention.'

Anna saw why. From either side, private cars and taxis hurtled past, cutting in, hooting, swerving and jamming on their brakes at the last moment as they arrived at each set of traffic lights, which were invariably at red.

'This is Palermo Park,' Ceci said while they waited at lights. 'My house is in Belgrano, which is a couple of miles further out.'

The lights changed and the traffic roared off ahead of them.

'Zoo on the left!' Ceci shouted, and a little later on, 'Racecourse on the right!'

They turned right three times round a block and shot back across the Avenida del Libertador and into a leafy suburb. The convertible bumped over cobbles. Anna said, 'This could almost be part of Edinburgh.'

'Lovely, isn't it? French influence. Here we are. This is us.'

Ceci led the way up steps to the front door.

'What about the luggage?' Anna asked.

'My gardener will see to that. Come on in. I don't know about you, but I could do with a cup of tea.' She called through to the maid in the kitchen then took Anna into a sitting room that was lined with books and tapestries and overlooked a small garden. She threw open the French windows then turned back to face Anna.

'What a lovely room!' Anna said.

Ceci looked distraught. 'I think we'd better sit down, my dear. I – I have some bad news for you. I didn't want to tell you before we arrived here because I couldn't trust myself to drive properly if –'

She stopped. Anna said, 'What sort of bad news?'

Ceci took her hands and led her to the sofa and they sat down together.

'It's about your brother. I heard two days ago from Ursula. You must be very brave. He had an accident. He's dead.'

The colour seemed to go out of the room. The deep reds and blues of the Persian carpet that Anna had admired moments before changed to black and grey. It was like a waking nightmare.

'What sort of accident?'

'I had a telephone call from Ursula the day before yesterday. From Salta – that's up in the north. They think he must have been attacked by a puma or a wild cat. He was on his way back from a neighbouring village and failed to return.'

'But hasn't he been found? I mean – if he just disappeared surely there's a possibility that he's still alive?'

'No. Ursula said they found . . . evidence. I'm afraid there's no doubt. You will have to accept it.'

There was a tap on the door and the housemaid brought tea in on a tray. For a while, Anna was not aware of what she said or did. She heard Ceci say something about a memorial service that had been held in Salta and Ursula's time of arrival in Buenos Aires.

'Ursula?' she said.

'Yes. She's on her way south. She arrives tomorrow by train.'

'Why?'

'Well . . . presumably to meet you.'

'I don't understand. I was going up there.'

'My dear – it's not safe for women to be on their own up in the Chaco.'

'Has she abandoned the mission then?'

'I don't think she had any alternative. She is pregnant, after all. I've invited her to stay here.'

'I think I would like to go up to Misión Yuchán, all the same. I would like to see it.'

'Well let's wait and see what Ursula thinks,' Ceci suggested.

'No! Why should we? Why shouldn't I go and see my brother – see where my brother –' She stopped herself. 'I'm sorry.'

'Perhaps I should have waited before telling you,' said Ceci.

'No. I had to know. I'm so sorry about this, Miss Jowett. It must be very difficult for you.'

'My dear – please do call me Ceci. Everybody does. And please don't apologize for anything at all.'

Anna stood up and went to the open French window. She looked out at the potted geraniums, the lemon tree, the hibiscus. In a tree nearby a bird was repeating the same four notes over and over again. In the distance the traffic roared and a tram bell clanged. There was a strange surreal beauty in Argentina. It was a fascinating, alluring beauty that she found both attractive and repellent at the same time.

* * *

Ursula seemed to be bearing up surprisingly well when they met her at the station the following morning. She embraced Ceci and Anna and accepted their sympathy with the comment that one could not question the Lord's will.

Over lunch, Ceci asked her to go into more detail about what had happened. Ursula launched into the story she had obviously told several times before.

'I wasn't feeling too grand that day and Timothy had had a contretemps with the local curandero. Quite what passed between them I don't know, but there is a lot of black magic and evil superstition in that village. When Timothy didn't get back that night I thought that he had stayed at Carboncito to be with his patient, because he had done that once or twice before. But of course he hadn't.' Ursula put on a brave smile and turned to Anna. 'I'm afraid these things happen in the monte.'

'But are you saying that Tim died because of black magic?'

'Not at all! Though of course the Wichi said that was the cause. This is the trouble, you see, Anna. These people are so firmly in Satan's grip that they can only see events from a Satanic point of view.'

'But I still don't understand why his body was never found.'

'Well, if it was a puma, as I think it must have been, the body would probably have been dragged away into the monte. There is also a large rodent called a vizcacha up in the Chaco. Nothing ever gets left, you know.'

Anna shuddered.

'Try not to think about it,' Ceci whispered.

There was a silence. Anna asked, 'So when will you go back?'

'The day after tomorrow if the boat leaves on time.'

'The boat?' Ceci said. 'You're surely not thinking of taking a boat up the Paraná are you?'

'Of course not! I mean the Highland boat.'

'You're going back to England?' Anna asked.

'God willing, yes.'

'I see.'

'What about you, Anna?' Ceci asked. 'What do you feel about this?'

Ursula said, 'Unless you have a real vocation for some specific work I would urge you not to remain here. Without wishing to offend you in any way, Cecily, I have to say that I believe this country to be spiritually corrupt. It is no place for a young lady on her own.'

'But Anna won't be on her own. She'll be with me.'

Anna put a fishbone on the side of her plate. 'Have you already booked the passage?'

'Yes. Aboard the *Highland Princess*. She sails on Tuesday. I got the agent up in Salta to telegraph ahead and reserve a double cabin as I presumed you would wish to accompany me. I'm certain that is what Timothy would have advised.'

Anna was equally certain that her brother would have advised the exact opposite. She took a quick decision. 'No. I shall stay on for a few weeks at least. I'm sure you understand, Ursula. I couldn't possibly turn round and go straight back.'

Ceci put her hand over Anna's and gripped it tightly. 'I think you are quite quite right, my dear. Argentina is a most wonderful country when you get to know it. You would miss so much. I'm sure we'll have no difficulty finding you a suitable position in Buenos Aires, and you can stay here with me for as long as you like.'

Outside in the street there was a squeal of brakes followed by shouted insults.

'Well,' sniffed Ursula, 'never say I didn't warn you.'

Soon after Easter, Ceci took Anna out to the Hurlingham Club for lunch.

On their way out of the city Anna caught her first glimpse of the tin shacks where the poor lived.

'My dear, this is nothing,' Ceci said when Anna gasped at the squalor. 'These people are positively wealthy by comparison with the indios up north.'

'It makes me feel guilty to be wearing these clothes.'

'I know exactly how you feel. That was one of the reasons why I began supporting Misión Yuchán.'

'How did you get to hear about it?'

'Friends of mine own a sugar plantation up at Tabacal. I went up there on a visit. I heard that a new missionary was needed but that the church was desperately short of money so I agreed to help.'

'So was it you who made it possible for my brother to come out in the first place?'

'Let's say I contributed. I would have liked to work there myself but it's virtually impossible to achieve anything in this country if you're a woman on your own.' Ceci sighed. 'On second thoughts I don't expect I would have actually worked as a missionary. I'm too lazy. I don't know about you, Anna, but I haven't got Ursula's zeal.'

'Oh – nor have I! I was only going to look after her baby for a few months. I'm . . . unofficially engaged, you see.'

'Oh are you? My dear – do tell me all about him.'

While they drove on to Hurlingham, Anna told Ceci about how she had agreed to go to Argentina on the condition that her father make no objection to her marriage to Angus on her return.

'Anna, how wonderfully romantic! I'm sure I would have married him on the spot.'

'I very nearly did.'

'Well I think you've been tremendously brave these last weeks. It's been such a delight having you – no, I really mean it, Anna. I feel we've known each other for years, don't you?' Ceci laughed in her nervous way and patted Anna's knee. 'It's all right, you needn't answer that. Anyway – here we are. This is Hurlingham now.'

The clubhouse was an imposing building of red brick that looked like an Edwardian millionaire's castle. The tennis courts were surrounded by well-trimmed privet hedges and beyond them were the stables, polo pitches and a golf course.

Ceci led the way into the anteroom where out of date copies of *Punch*, *John Bull* and *Blackwood's Magazine* were laid out on a huge round table. While their sons and husbands fought it out on the polo pitches and tennis courts, the ladies were taking morning coffee.

The introductions began. 'Anna, this is Betty Jowett my sister-in-law. This is Mr and Mrs Rathbone who live out at Cadoret . . . Mrs Dalligan, Mrs Harrison, Mrs Delmar-Jones, Mrs de Basili, Mrs Duggan, Mrs La Rivière, Mrs Deane, Mrs Campbell, Mrs Santamaria . . .'

'I can't possibly hope to remember all these names,' Anna confided.

'*Pierda cuidado*,' said a mannish voice behind her. 'There are only two names worth remembering here. One's Cadoret and the other's Jowett. Isn't that right, Ceci?'

Anna was introduced to Mrs Annelise Cadoret, a lavishly dressed lady of sixty, with several strings of beads round her neck, several bracelets on each wrist, heavily pencilled eyebrows and dyed hair.

'Where did you find this little beauty?' Annelise rasped, but gave Ceci no time to reply. 'What are you doing out here, sweetheart? Looking for a husband, I suppose. Well it won't take you very long. You've come to the right place. You're knee-deep in handsome bucks in Argentina.'

'Anna came out to work at Misión Yuchán,' Ceci said.

'Oh – wait a minute, wait a minute! Was your husband that poor devil who was eaten alive?'

'He was my brother,' Anna said very quietly.

19

'Your brother? I see. Well – lovely to meet you, dear. Make the most of your time out here, won't you?'

'Don't take any notice of her,' Ceci said when Mrs Cadoret had swept on. 'She's a wicked old woman.'

After taking coffee, they strolled past the tennis courts to the stables.

'The ponies are even more beautiful than the people,' Anna said, watching six polo ponies cantering round and round an enclosure.

'Aren't they wonderful? If you're going to stay for any length of time you'll have to learn to ride, Anna. Would you like me to teach you? It would be the easiest thing in the world to organize and it would give me tremendous pleasure.'

'I couldn't possibly afford it!'

'Anna,' said Ceci. 'How many times do I have to tell you? You don't have to worry about money.'

'It's my Scottish blood. I hate having to accept charity.'

'Listen. How many hectares of land do you think I own? Just have a guess.'

'Ceci, I don't even know what a hectare is. I have no idea. Five hundred? A thousand?'

'Thirty thousand. That's more than sixty thousand acres. I'm a wealthy woman, Anna, and until you stepped off that ship I was a very unhappy one as well. There's no question of charity in my having you to stay. You're giving me far more in the way of companionship than I'm giving you.'

'I don't understand.'

Ceci sighed heavily. 'No. I don't suppose you would.'

They walked along in silence towards the polo pitch. Suddenly Ceci said, 'You may as well know. You're bound to find out sooner or later. I was crossed in love. The usual thing. That old witch you met just now was going to be my mother-in-law.'

'What happened?'

Ceci gave her high-tension laugh. 'What didn't happen! Well, let me see, how can I keep it as brief as possible? I was engaged to my childhood sweetheart, Tito Cadoret, who grew up on a neighbouring estancia. Tito is a Catholic and I was too. Was, please note.

The share-out of property in that part of the camp is complicated to say the least so I won't even try to explain that side of it. Anyway, for reasons of her own, Tito's mother – that's Annelise – didn't like the idea of her precious son marrying a Jowett, even though it would have meant doubling the size of his property from thirty thousand to sixty thousand hectares. A case of cutting the nose off to spite the face if ever there was one. At the same time dear old Annelise – at the age of fifty-eight, mark you – was having an affair with her husband's lawyer, an old rascal called Hugo de Rosslare who has his fingers in just about every single pie in the Argentine. And while Annelise and de Rosslare were pressurizing Tito to break off his engagement to me, poor old Johnny Cadoret – that's Annelise's long-suffering husband – found out about his wife's affair and blew his brains out early one morning out at La Calandria.'

'Where's that?'

'It's the name of their estancia, which is near a railway station and village called Cadoret, just to confuse you. The Cadorets have been out here since about 1850. They used to own an enormous chunk of land at one time, but it was all gambled away or sold or split up among the progeny. Where was I? Well, as you can imagine, his father's suicide threw Tito off-balance more than a little and he took up with a nightclub dancer called Magdalena Salgado and made her pregnant. She then sued him. Tito told me, I broke off the engagement and he was then married to the said Magdalena at a high nuptial Mass before many witnesses.'

Anna shook her head. 'I don't know what to say.'

Ceci laughed piercingly. 'Don't say anything, darling. It's much safer.'

'How long ago did all this happen?'

'Over the last year or two. Magdalena had the baby last November, since when she and Tito have split up because he discovered – *after* they got married, mark you – that she already had a four-year-old daughter, who incidentally is almost completely unmanageable and burnt down the nursery of La Calandria. So now Tito's spending half his time here at Hurlingham with his mother and half out in the camp on his estancia, while the irresistible Magdalena lives in luxury with her two children on Quintana.'

'Who's he?'

Ceci laughed again, but this time out of genuine amusement. 'The Avenida Quintana. It's a street in one of the more fashionable districts of Buenos Aires.'

'What about you? Didn't it hurt you terribly?'

'Yes. To be quite frank with you, it did. I had something the trick cyclist called a nervous breakdown. I lapsed, you know.'

'Lapsed?'

'As a Catholic. I went and shut myself in a room for a month. Then I decided I had to do something with my life and went up north to stay with the friends I mentioned, the ones who own a sugar plantation at

Tabacal, and while I was there I met some Protestant missionaries, which prompted me to support Misión Yuchán, which in turn brought me into contact with you. So I suppose one might say that God moves in a mysterious way his wonders to perform, mightn't one? Ah. You hear that bell? They're just about to start the next chukka.'

The pitch was much bigger and the teams much smaller than Anna had imagined. There was a lot of riding about with sticks held vertically and a great deal of shouting and swearing in Spanish.

'Kipling called it a game of dust and bad language which always takes place on the far side of the pitch,' Ceci said as two riders raced neck and neck for the ball. 'Now – you see that? He's riding the other one off. That's Stiffy Rathbone, you met his mother having coffee. You see? He gets his knee up behind the other chap's thigh and pushes him off the line of the ball. It's a frightfully rough sport, you know. Ah – now you see that chap, the sweaty one with the big nose wearing a red shirt? That's Tito.'

'Your ex-fiancé.'

'*Sí, señorita.*'

The game veered suddenly across the pitch towards them, the players shouting to each other. Hooves thundered and turf flew; and from the middle of the mêlée, pursuing the ball at full gallop, the player with the Roman nose emerged in the lead, whirling his polo stick and hitting the ball a tremendous crack, which sent it clean between the goal posts.

'Typical Tito,' Ceci sighed. 'Always wins at everything, the beastly man. I don't know about you, Anna, but my tummy's rumbling. Shall we go back to the clubhouse and have some lunch?'

3

TITO CADORET HAD SCORED five of the seven goals in the match against the cavalry officers of Campo de Mayo, and when he entered the men's shower he felt like a man in a million.

He stripped off and joined the steamy throng. He soaped himself all over and as the water sprayed down and the soap suds made a flood because the drain was partially blocked with hair, he joined in that particular style of cross-talk that is often to be heard in all-male company after sport or battle.

'That was a bloody good little mare you were on in the third chukka, Stiffy! Where'd you get her?'

'One of Renown's cria. My pony boy wanted to sell her but I wouldn't have it.'

'You did right there . . .'

'. . . a good big arse and bags of guts. Turns on a bloody tanner. Unlike that little palomino queer. Hanging about like a fart in a four-poster . . .'

'I'd put the bugger in a gag-snaffle.'

'Who was that little cutie with Ceci?'

'Never seen her before in my life . . .'

'I wasn't paying too much attention to the talent at the time. Was she any good?'

'Was she! Quite a cracker.'

'Probably one of Ceci's holy-bloody-Joannas.'

'Well I wouldn't have chucked her out of bed on a cold night.'

'Who's for a night on the town, then? TC?'

'Count me out.'

Stiffy Rathbone rubbed his freckled back and shoulders vigorously with a towel. 'You're turning into a dull old sod, Cadoret. When are you going to sort yourself out and bring Magdalena to heel?'

'Wish I knew!'

'I don't see why you don't dump her,' Randy Jowett said. 'Go to Uruguay and buy a divorce.'

'And kiss half my estancia goodbye?'

'Who said anything about that?'

'De Rosslare seems to think I'd have to.'

'You've got the wrong lawyer, old son. These things can be fixed.'

'Maybe so, but I don't want to wind up with some gaucho who takes me to the cleaners.'

Cadoret sat down on a wooden bench to powder his feet. He put on a clean shirt, silk square, hacking jacket and cavalry twills. By the time he had dressed only one other person – a young cavalry officer from the opposing team – was in the shower room. Cadoret was just about to leave when he introduced himself.

'José Ocampo,' he said and insisted on shaking hands. 'Can you spare a moment, Señor Cadoret?'

Cadoret paused at the door.

Ocampo smiled, showing his teeth. 'I couldn't help overhearing what you were saying just now. About finding a good lawyer.'

'Oh yes?'

Ocampo went to the hook where his jacket hung and took out a wallet. 'May I suggest you approach my cousin, Rui Botta? He's an extremely able attorney with impeccable references and very good contacts with both the Army and the Church. Here's his card. Do get in touch with him, Señor Cadoret. I know you won't regret it.'

Cadoret pocketed the card and went along the corridor to the bar where Stiffy Rathbone, Paddy Dalligan and Randy Jowett had a pint of bitter waiting for him.

'What a bloody diabolical liberty!' he said, wiping the froth off his mouth with the back of his hand.

'What's that, Tito?'

Cadoret took the card Ocampo had given him from his pocket. 'Chap can't even take a shower at his club without being pestered by touts these days. Look what that little tyke slipped me in the shower.'

'If you're talking about José Ocampo, he's no tyke. Comes from a bloody good family.'

'Dr Rui Botta,' said Rathbone, reading the card. 'Half a minute – isn't that the bloke who represented Uriburu against Obersky?'

Jowett took the card from him. 'I think you might be right for once, Stiffy.'

'Of course I'm damn well right! And I reckon it's a chance not to be missed, Tito. If anyone's going to get that wife of yours off your back, it'll be Botta.'

*   *   *

The train clanked its way through the suburbs of Chacarita and Palermo and arrived, panting, in the echoing vault of Retiro station. The passengers spilled out of the carriages and surged along the platform, the businessmen dressed in dark suits and polished boots, the office girls looking as if they were due to take part in a fashion show. Some of the faces looked Latin, some Indian, some Celtic, some Jewish, some Teutonic, some Slav. All looked indefinably Argentine.

Distinctive in a coffee-cream suit of immaculate cut and with his hair smeared back off his forehead with brilliantine, Cadoret strode out of the station past the beggars, the chocolate vendors and the newspaper stands. He joined the crowd waiting to cross the Avenida del Libertador and, having successfully avoided death under the iron wheels of a tram that appeared to have gone out of control, strode purposefully up the hill beside the Plaza San Martín.

He was a little early for his appointment with Botta so he sat down on a bench, glanced at the *Buenos Aires Herald* and mused for a while about grain yields, bovine foot-rot and the price of Hereford steers. When the clock in the British clock tower showed five to ten he folded up the newspaper, threw it in a litter bin and walked two blocks along the Calle Maipú, entering at a door upon which a brass plate announced, DR RUI BOTTA, ABOGADO.

On the ground floor there was a crowd of people all talking at once. He elbowed his way through them towards the lift.

'What the devil's going on here?' he asked of no one in particular.

'Señor,' explained a perspiring woman. 'An old man has fallen down the shaft.'

'Well he's a bloody fool,' said Cadoret, and went up the stairs three at a time.

Botta did not keep him waiting. Suave in a pugilistic way, he was heavily built with restless, vigilant eyes. He was smoking a cigar and wore a large gold signet ring on the little finger of his right hand. He shook Cadoret by the hand and bade his prospective client sit down in a deep leather armchair. Then he called to Consuela to bring in two black coffees.

'You mind if we speak in Spanish, Señor Cadoret?'

'Not at all,' said Cadoret in that language. 'I'm as Argentine as you are, Dr Botta.'

'Good. I understand you have been playing polo with my cousin José. He's a good boy, José. So what can I do for you?'

Cadoret joined his fists under his chin. 'I want to divorce my wife.'

'*Divorce* your wife?'

'That's what I said.'

25

Consuela entered with the coffee. Botta waited for the distraction to pass before resuming.

'There's no divorce in Argentina, Señor Cadoret. The only way a marriage can be dissolved is by death. Surely you know that?'

Tito Cadoret had fair hair that was bleached by the sun and brushed straight back from his forehead. His moustache was a neatly trimmed rectangle of flaxen bristle. His blue eyes looked out from under a brow that was nothing if not well chiselled, and his aquiline nose gave him an air of considerable authority.

'Your cousin recommended you to me, Dr Botta. That's the only reason I'm sitting here. I understand that there are ways – legal ways – round the law. But if you don't think you can help –'

Botta raised a hand to stop Cadoret going further. 'Perhaps we should be more precise in our terms, señor. Correct me if I'm wrong, but I think what you want is not a divorce, but an annulment, which is a pronouncement by the Church that your marriage was invalid or has been since invalidated. Am I right?'

Cadoret took a sip of coffee. 'I'm sure you are.'

'In which case we shall have to apply to the Bishop.'

'I'm quite prepared to do that.'

'Also, before we can proceed, I must have a detailed knowledge of the circumstances leading up to your marriage, the events since the wedding and the extent of your estate.'

'Why do you need to know so much?'

'Annulment's not a matter to be taken lightly. I have excellent relations with the Bishop's secretariat and with certain officials in Rome. If I find the slightest reason to suspect that you are acting with a view to financial gain, I shall have to disappoint you.' Botta carefully deposited a cylinder of cigar ash into a brass tray. 'I have my reputation to consider as well as yours.'

'But ... presumably there are ways of ensuring that suspicion doesn't arise in the first place?'

The traffic surged noisily outside. Cadoret glanced quickly at Botta, who happened to be glancing quickly at Cadoret at the same moment.

'Are there grounds for such suspicion?'

'None to my knowledge.'

'I think we must be completely open with each other,' Botta said quietly. 'Until I can be assured of your complete confidence in me, I shall not be willing to take up your case.'

'That goes without saying. But I'm not entirely new to this business. I came to you because I'd reached a dead end with my family

26

lawyer. I heard you could arrange things. Everything has a price. Isn't that so?'

Botta blew a smoke ring and waited for Cadoret to continue.

'I want to be rid of my wife, Dr Botta. I want to be *unmarried*. Provided we act within the law, I'm willing to pay. So can we come to the point? Can you or can you not fix an annulment?'

Botta smiled as if at a private joke. 'Yes,' he said quietly, 'I can fix it.'

'Legally?'

'Of course.'

'How much will it cost?'

Botta gazed up at the slowly rotating fan above his desk. 'It is not exactly a question of cost so much as what you are prepared to give, Señor Cadoret. Application for an annulment is a delicate matter. There is no doubt that the wheels can be oiled and the process speeded if the applicant is prepared to offer a voluntary donation to the Church.'

'So what are we talking about? Five thousand pesos?'

Botta laughed. 'I think it will be more than that, don't you? But as I say, I must first have a clear idea of your personal and financial situation. So perhaps you would like to start by explaining how you came to be married to Magdalena Salgado in the first place?'

Cadoret launched into the whole ghastly story. 'The problem is,' he concluded, 'that she knows that it's in her interest to delay a settlement until after my father's probate has been granted.'

'She's got her eye on your estancia.'

'Right.'

Botta was silent for a few moments. The fan slapped slowly round overhead. 'So if we are to apply for an annulment, we would say that the grounds are what?'

'You're the expert, Dr Botta. What do you suggest?'

Botta inhaled deeply and blew the smoke upward. 'How old is your wife?'

'Nineteen.'

'So might it be said that she was too young to know what she was doing when she entered into matrimony?'

'I suppose if one stretched a point –'

'Or that she made her vows lightly, without any intention of keeping them?'

'Yes, that would be better.'

'Or even that she married solely in the hope of personal gain?'

'Very probable.'

27

'And . . . she's refusing you conjugal rights?'

'Yes.'

'Now as to your financial position.' Botta reached for a pad and began to jot down notes.

'Not very good.'

Botta frowned. 'But you're a wealthy man, Señor Cadoret. Everyone knows that.'

'And everyone's mistaken. My mother holds the purse strings. I'm given an allowance, but I have very little capital of my own.'

'How much could you raise at short notice?'

Cadoret blew his cheeks out and thought. 'Perhaps twenty thousand pesos at a week's notice and a further forty or fifty thousand at a month's.'

Botta frowned. 'As little as that?'

'Well . . . maybe a bit more. I would have to check.'

'What about the livestock?'

'It's not mine to sell.'

'But you have control of the estancia . . . what's it called?'

'La Calandria. Yes, I have control of the day-to-day running of it, but I don't hold the title deeds. Every major financial decision has to be cleared with my attorney.'

'You could sell stock.'

'Perhaps. But only if – if I did it a bit at a time.'

Botta glanced quickly in his direction. 'You own some fine polo ponies, I believe?'

'I would be most reluctant to part with any of them.'

'I'm not suggesting that you do, but I must include their value for the purposes of calculating your potential collateral.' Botta added a column of figures. 'So if we take into account the land value of the estancia together with the stock and the buildings, we are talking about an estate worth something in the region of four million pesos, would you agree with that?'

'I think you're being rather over-optimistic,' Cadoret said quickly. 'And I must emphasize that it's not mine.'

'But you have a limited power of attorney, and will inherit when your mother dies.'

'Once my father's probate is sorted out, yes, but –'

'So the land and the money are yours, to all intents and purposes. And, of course, we have not included foreign investments and bank deposits abroad. I think . . . potentially you are a very wealthy man, Señor Cadoret. We would have to offer a very substantial donation to the Church to have any hope of success. I would be reluctant to make

28

any approach to the Vatican without being able to offer a donation of at least quarter of a million pesos.'

'Quarter of a million!'

Botta opened his hands. 'You want a quick resolution. There's no question of doing this sort of thing on the cheap.'

'All the same –'

'And of course it would not be necessary for you to realize assets to raise the money in cash if you don't wish to.'

'How else am I going to raise it?'

'By means of a bank loan.'

'But I would have to use the estate as security on the loan, and my bank would be bound to refer the application to my mother's lawyer. And he wouldn't hear of it.'

Botta ejected the stub end of his cheroot from the holder and inserted another. 'There's no reason why he should know anything about it. I can give you an introduction to a bank where your request will be treated with complete confidentiality.'

'Quarter of a million,' Cadoret repeated. 'Is that inclusive of your fee?'

Botta laughed drily. 'I have to earn a living too, my friend.'

'And what guarantee have I that I get the annulment?'

'Every guarantee.'

'You mean here and now? Without consulting the Bishop?'

Botta smiled his crooked smile. 'The Church does not run entirely on Hail Marys, you know. Do you understand what I'm saying?'

'It still seems one hell of a lot to pay.'

'Not pay. Donate. I could propose a lower sum of course, but in that case I would be able to offer no guarantee of success. It's really up to you. If you want to end your marriage badly enough, you will have to dip into your pocket.'

'I suppose there's no other alternative? I mean – legal alternative?'

'None that I know of.'

'And can you guarantee that this will cancel all my obligations towards Magdalena? What about the child, for instance?'

'As far as the child is concerned, you will have no obligation at all. But if she retains custody of your son she will have a legal claim on you for maintenance.'

'In that case I want custody. Can you get that?'

'I think I shall have to.'

Cadoret was finding the whole business thoroughly distasteful and was sure there were other questions he should be asking. But he had checked Botta out carefully and it was unlikely that another

29

opportunity to rid himself of Magdalena would present itself. 'So what's the next step?'

Botta reached for the telephone and dialled. 'I'll fix an appointment for you at the Banco Pergamino. He spoke on the telephone in Italian that was too rapid for Cadoret to understand and a few moments later said '*Ciao*' and hung up.

'My friend will see you in half an hour. You know the Banco Pergamino? It's on Corrientes between Maipú and Esmeralda. I'll give you my card. Show it to the security guard and ask to see Toni Lambretti. He's a personal friend of mine. You can deal with him in complete confidence. He will open a loan account in your name, a draft can then be signed and we can take your case straight to the Nuncio.'

Toni Lambretti was a lean man in rimless spectacles with a habit of licking his lips. He required Cadoret to sign a statement of his mother's assets and when this had been done and Cadoret had signed an undertaking to pay interest at double the London bank rate, Lambretti opened a loan account in his name. Afterwards, walking along among the bustling crowds on Corrientes, Cadoret felt an enormous sense of relief. It really had been a good morning's work, and he was particularly pleased with himself at having concealed from Botta and Lambretti the existence of a bank account in his name with Coutts of London.

He turned down the Calle 25 de Mayo and went along to the English Club, where he found some city acquaintances who had made a start on the day's drinking and were keen for him to join them in a game of bidou.

They played until two o'clock and then went in for lunch. Before the soup arrived they helped themselves to fairy toast which they buttered thickly and ate with a liberal sprinkling of Wilde's savoury sauce. Tito Cadoret entertained them with a joke about a monkey that made love to an elephant. Everyone at the table laughed, and Tito, feeling encouraged and pleasantly tight, proceeded to tell several other stories, most of which he had told once or twice before.

4

IT WAS BLANCA SALGADO'S BIRTHDAY; she was five years old and her
mother had given her a doll called Mimi. Mimi was just like Blanca
because she had glossy black hair and a dimple in each cheek and
long eyelashes which closed when you tilted her head back. She had
her own pram which was just like the one baby Luis went in, only
smaller. Blanca had a media luna with dulce de leche for breakfast and
afterwards her mother said they could go for a walk in the park and
take Mimi in the pram. But first her mother had to make sure her hair
was just right and put on her lipstick and file her nails and decide what
to wear. Blanca always watched her mother getting dressed. She had
things made of black lace which she put on first and when she put
on her stockings Blanca had to say if her seams were straight. On her
mother's dressing table there were little bottles and boxes, and her
mother put a dab of something on the back of Blanca's hand so that
she could smell it. This morning, because it was Blanca's birthday,
her mother painted Blanca's nails. Blanca's nails didn't look as pretty
as her mother's even with red nail varnish, but her mother said that
one day she would have lovely hair and long legs, straight seams in her
stockings and high-heeled shoes. Blanca put her feet into her mother's
shoes before her mother put them on and then her mother had to find
her keys and her purse. Teresa, the nurse, had to be told to look after
Luis properly and Mimi had to be put into her pram and tucked up.
They went out of the apartment and into the cranky lift. They went
down to the vestibule and out into the street, her mother showing her
how to let the pram go gently down over the steps onto the pavement.
When they got to the end of the road, they crossed over into the
park in front of the church with the yellow front where the ladies
were gathering to show off their hats before they went into Sunday
Mass. In the park was a huge ombu tree with branches that swept
low over the ground. There were other ladies with prams and some
people with dogs. Mimi was very good and didn't cry once. Blanca
pushed her along in the pram and then they sat outside at a table
and Blanca had a chocolate ice cream because it was her birthday.

Her mother told the waiter about it and he asked Blanca for a little kiss and called her his pretty chinita. Then it was time to go back, and as they were leaving a car came up with four gentlemen in it and one of them leaned out of the window and asked Mama if she would like to go for a ride. Her mother said she didn't want to but the gentleman said it would be a good thing if she did so she agreed. She took Blanca's hand and told her to bring Mimi and leave the pram because they could always buy another one later. They all got in and the car drove very fast and her mother asked the men what the hurry was. Blanca thought it was a special surprise for her birthday. The men were laughing and joking with her mother and one of them tickled Blanca under the chin and asked her Mimi's name. The car went on and on until they left the big buildings behind and then it went faster, straight on, with sometimes trees and sometimes houses flashing past on either side. Then it turned off the main road and bumped along much more slowly until it stopped. The men stopped joking and pulled her mother out of the car. Blanca tried not to let go of her hand but the men made her. One man put his hand over her mother's mouth to stop her making a noise and another helped pull her away from the car. Blanca wanted to go to help her mother but one of the men stopped her. His hand was like a tight iron ring round her arm. She sat in the car with the door open and saw what the men did to her mother. Blanca saw everything and it was her birthday. She was five years old today and she saw everything that the men did to her mother.

Annelise Cadoret was having her customary glass of whisky before Sunday supper when the telephone rang. She was sitting in the large drawing room of her villa at Hurlingham, throwing biscuits to her sealyhams and saying 'One for Poppy . . . and one for Rags' and the two dogs were yapping and begging and falling over backwards in their attempts to catch each morsel as it was thrown.

Luisa, the maid, came in and said the call was for the Señor. 'Then go and find him, imbecile,' Annelise said, so Luisa went upstairs to fetch him.

Tito had been very moody ever since the trouble started with that little bitch Magdalena, but in the last week he had appeared particularly difficult and bad tempered. Annelise wondered if it might be polo, not Magdalena, that was the cause of Tito's bad temper.

The trouble with polo was that it was like an addictive drug. Johnny had forbidden his cadet managers to play because it could take over a young man's life and wreck his career. Annelise hoped very much that it had not taken over Tito's life. It had been splendid for him when he was in his teens and twenties. It had made a man of him. But he was thirty now and his father was dead. It was time he faced up to the responsibility of running La Calandria even if that meant forgoing his weekly game of polo at Hurlingham.

She was pouring herself another whisky when Tito came in from the hall followed by a police officer.

'Who is this? What on earth's the matter?'

'This is Comisario Perez, mother. Magdalena's been abducted.'

Annelise's pencilled eyebrows went up. 'Abducted? What do you mean, abducted?'

'She and Blanca were seen being driven off in a car from Recoleta this morning. One of the waiters reported it.'

Mrs Cadoret threw another biscuit to Poppy and Rags. 'Well you can talk to them out in the hall, Tito. I'm not having his clodhoppers on my best Persian carpet, thank you very much.'

The press arrived unbidden within the hour. Tito held them at bay at the front door.

'Have you any idea who can be behind this abduction, Mr Cadoret?'

'Absolutely none.'

'Have you received a ransom demand?'

'No.'

'Will the fact that you and your wife were living apart affect your decision if it comes to paying a ransom?'

'I have nothing more to tell you! Now will you please leave!'

'What about the child, Mr Cadoret? Is it correct that she's your stepdaughter and that you were not aware that she was your wife's child until after your marriage?'

'No more comment –'

'How long have you and your wife been separated, Mr Cadoret?'

'No comment.'

'Any truth in the rumour that you were seeking a legal separation before your wife and stepdaughter were kidnapped?'

'Look – we don't know for sure if they've been kidnapped.'

'Any idea who the father of your stepdaughter is, Mr Cadoret?'

'Can you confirm that your wife worked as a striptease artiste before her marriage to you?'

'Mr Cadoret, what sort of price would you be prepared to pay to get them back? Would you go to half a million?'

'I won't go to a half of anything!' he declared, and slammed the door in their faces.

*   *   *

33

Tito remained at his mother's house in Hurlingham instead of returning to La Calandria as originally intended. When he rang Botta for advice, Botta said that this sort of thing was right outside his province and that he would have to act as he thought best.

His mother's lawyer, Hugo de Rosslare, was more positive. Cadoret lunched with him at the club on Wednesday and over brandy and cigars the lawyer pointed out that a woman with Magdalena's background might have contacts in the underworld, in which case it was not beyond the bounds of possibility that she had agreed to her own kidnap in order to extort money from him.

'I hadn't thought of that,' Cadoret admitted.

De Rosslare regarded him with bloodshot eyes. 'What else haven't you thought about? You're not keeping anything from me are you, Tito?'

Cadoret played with the ash on the end of his cigar. 'I don't know what the hell you're talking about.'

'What about the baby?'

'The nurse is looking after it.'

'At Recoleta?'

'Yes.'

'Well that's a stupid arrangement for a start. Next thing we'll hear is that they've been kidnapped as well. I'd advise you to bring them to your mother's as soon as possible.'

He took de Rosslare's advice. Teresa and the baby and all the nursery paraphernalia were moved to Hurlingham and the whole household was disrupted by the baby's almost incessant crying. Cadoret waited for a ransom demand but none came. He gave an interview to the *Buenos Aires Herald* in which he appealed to the kidnappers to release his wife or make their demands known. The article appeared in the Saturday edition and on Sunday morning when Cadoret was halfway through the fourth chukka the police turned up at the Hurlingham Club.

Police Comisario Juan Perez wore riding boots and leather gloves. He watched the last two chukkas of the game before strolling over to the far side of the pitch where the ponies were tethered in the shade of the eucalyptus trees.

Cadoret had had his worst game in years. His face was flushed and his vest was soaked in sweat. Perez waited for him to dismount before approaching him.

'What can I do for you, officer?'

Perez patted Cadoret's chestnut mare. 'You have some fine ponies,

34

Señor Cadoret. I admire this one particularly. How much would she fetch at sale, I wonder?'

'I'm sure you didn't come here to ask me the value of my ponies,' Cadoret said.

'No, that's true,' said Perez.

'So why did you come here?'

'We've found your wife.'

He sat in the back of the Ford between the sergeant and the police officer. The car sped out of Hurlingham, going past the military airfield at El Palomar and on towards Ciudadela and Vila Madero before taking the road south towards Ezeiza airport. After a while they turned off the road and took an earth track to a wooded area where a police van was drawn up at the edge of the tree line. They parked alongside it and Perez invited Cadoret to get out and accompany him. Perez led the way in silence a short distance into the trees where armed police were standing about, smoking. He pointed at the ground and Cadoret saw Magdalena.

He stared for a few moments, then turned away.

'Well?' asked Perez.

'Yes. That's her.'

They went back to the car and Perez got him to sign a certificate of identification. He borrowed a pen for the purpose and used the car roof as a rest. 'By the way,' Perez remarked, fanning the ink dry. 'We picked the kid up in the park at Recoleta this morning.'

They got back into the car. Perez ordered the driver to hand round the last of his cigarettes before they drove off. 'We know who was responsible,' he said in English as they turned onto the main road. Cadoret was glad he spoke in English. He had no wish to discuss the case in Spanish with the sergeant and driver present.

'You know?'

Perez laughed. 'Of course we know!'

'So when will you arrest them?'

'You want that?'

'Why shouldn't I?'

Perez snorted. 'I think you know why, Señor Cadoret.'

Cadoret remembered a remark Botta had made about marriage in Argentina being dissoluble only by death. He was clammy with sweat from his game of polo and now he felt fresh sweat break out under his arms.

'What are you suggesting?'

Perez smoked his cigarette and said nothing. He looked at Cadoret then looked away and shook his head, laughing. The car hurtled through a village with its horn blaring.

'A good pony can make a big difference to a man's game of polo, isn't that so?' Perez asked.

Cadoret ignored him.

'Well? It's true isn't it?'

'I'm not inclined to discuss polo at this moment, officer.'

'That's a pity. I'm keen to improve my game, you understand? That was a nice mare you were riding in the last chukka. Strong.' Perez laughed again. 'A big arse. That's good in a pony, yes? You are a fortunate man, señor. You have everything you want. And when you want to get rid of rubbish, you get rid of it, right? *Bueno*. Let me make you a proposition. You've got what you wanted, so can I have what I want also? What do you say? Make me a present of the pony with the big arse and I will make everything good for you.'

The car stopped at the Hurlingham level crossing. While they waited, Perez said, 'Please. Don't say you want time to think, Señor Cadoret. I must have your decision now. We can go to your club or we can go to the police station. I can make things easy or you can make things difficult. It's with you. It's with you to choose.'

The train went through and the level-crossing gates were opened. The car bumped over the lines.

'All right,' said Cadoret. 'You can have the pony.'

The family vault at Recoleta was set back against the far wall of the cemetery. Behind a glass front, the heavy coffins containing the remains of three generations of Cadorets were stacked one above the other and a ladder went down to a lower level where the coffins of the less illustrious members of the family were kept out of sight. It was in this lower chamber that a space had been made for the butchered remains of Magdalena.

Annelise had opposed having her daughter-in-law buried in the family vault and de Rosslare had agreed with her, but Tito had insisted that she be buried with the rest of the family, giving the reason that as Magdalena was the mother of his son it would seem very odd to later generations if she were to be the only Cadoret to be buried in the city cemetery at Chacarita.

So the funeral Mass was said in the old Pilar church of Recoleta and afterwards the coffin was wheeled on a chromed trolley with rubber wheels past the resting places of the dead generals, politicians and millionaires of the republic. The burial party consisted of the priest, the undertakers and Cadoret. While the priest was saying the last prayers and sprinkling holy water on the coffin, a sash window flew up with a screech and a woman in a scanty dressing gown looked out from one of the apartments on the far side of the road that were used by call girls and prostitutes.

'Murderer!' she screamed, and immediately the sash window came down again with a crash.

Cadoret called on Botta the following morning. The lawyer offered his condolences. 'A most unfortunate business, Señor Cadoret. But when all things are considered, perhaps for the best.' He spread his hands. 'Now. You wished to discuss another matter I believe?'

'Yes. The money.'

Botta turned his bullet-shaped head. 'What money is that?'

'The loan. For the annulment.'

'What about it?'

'Well – I'd like it back. That is – I'd like the loan cancelled.'

Botta frowned and smiled at the same time. 'But that's out of the question! It was transferred over a week ago.'

'Maybe so, but the money was paid over so that I could obtain an annulment.'

'No. It was not paid.'

'What do you mean, you know damn well it was paid!'

'Given, Señor Cadoret. Given, not paid. It was a gift that was given to the Church of your own free will. In law, it had nothing to do with your application for an annulment, so there can be no question of asking for the Church to give it back.'

'And where does that leave me?' Cadoret muttered.

Botta leant back in his revolving chair. 'You got what you wanted. You're a free man. You're unmarried just as you wanted to be. My advice to you is to put all this behind you and forget about it.'

'Forget about it! Forget about an outstanding loan of quarter of a million pesos!'

Botta waved his hand in the air. 'Don't try to fight it, Señor Cadoret. You will only get hurt.'

'Is that a threat?'

Botta waved his cigar. 'I never make threats. No, it's a piece of advice. That's what I am here for. To give you good, professional advice as your lawyer.'

'Well I've got news for you, *Señor* Botta. You're not my lawyer any more. Let's be quite clear on that.'

Botta stopped lolling in his chair and stood up. He went to the window, lifted a slat of the venetian blind and looked down into the road below.

'I think there's something you should know before you decide to dispense with my services. I had a police officer here making enquiries about you last week. He said they did not rule out the possibility that you might have had something to do with your wife's disappearance. They wanted to know if at any time you had asked me to get rid of your wife for you. Of course, I told them no. But if you now choose to go to another attorney, I think I would have to reconsider what I told the police, don't you? What was it you said to me two weeks ago? You wanted to be rid of your wife, wasn't that it? I think you said you wanted her "off your back". Yes, I understand completely what you meant.' Botta turned back from the window. 'But will the authorities understand? Would a jury understand?' He crossed the room and held out his hand. 'I think you and I can get along very well together. I know I can help you, if you will let me. I want to help you. It's in my interests to help you, after all. So let's have no further talk about going to another attorney, agree?'

Later that day he left Blanca and Luis with his mother and Teresa at Hurlingham and set out by car for the camp.

Darkness fell and it began to rain. He drove through Junin and Rufino, paused for a snack at Laboulaye and forked left onto an earth road to complete the last forty kilometres to Estancia La Calandria.

The rain slashed down and the Mercedes slithered about from side to side, the mud spattering up over the windscreen like brown sleet. The last ten kilometres seemed endless, with the wire fences on either side going away to a vanishing point ahead, the car bounding and sliding, the mud and rain splattering on the windscreen.

It was after two in the morning when the headlight beams turned into the tunnel of paraiso trees that led to the house. It was still raining. The wipers could only just keep up with the splatter of drops and leaves on the windscreen.

He went into the house and roused Catarina, the Russian-Argentine housekeeper he had taken on after the servants had walked out in protest over the fire caused by Blanca. The woman waddled in with an oil lamp and busied herself with lighting the boiler for his bath; but by the time the water was hot, Tito had drunk himself into a stupor, so Catarina kindled the log fire in the sitting room and left him to sleep it off in an armchair with the light of the fire flickering on the beamed ceiling and the portraits of his grandparents looking down at him with Victorian severity from either end of the room.

5

CECI SAID THAT IT GAVE HER every bit as much pleasure to teach Anna to ride as it gave Anna to learn. She took Anna into town and fitted her out with jodhpurs, boots and riding jacket at Smarts. She chose the mildest-tempered pony in the stables and ensured that her pupil cultivated only the best habits. She told Anna that she was a joy to teach and refused to accept any sort of payment. She corrected Anna's posture and taught her to grip with the knees. She explained how to make friends with a horse and taught that the essence of riding was an understanding of horses in general, and how gentle but firm action applied in the right way always won over tugging or kicking.

'Never let anyone tell you that men make better riders than women,' she said, 'because they simply don't. A woman's touch is always more sensitive and, while horses are incredibly stupid on occasion, they always react better to patience and sensitivity.'

One evening in May, when the days were drawing in and the weather getting colder, they arrived back quite late from Hurlingham having spent nearly three hours in the saddle. Anna thought she might have a cold coming on as she had a slight sore throat, so Ceci insisted that she have a hot bath and go early to bed.

Ceci's bathroom was large and magnificently tiled in blue and white. While Anna was wallowing happily in the tub and adding hot water from time to time by turning the brass tap on with her toes, there was a knock at the door and Ceci came in with a hot drink of lemon and honey.

'For your throat, my dear,' she said in her conspiratorial way. 'I always think it tastes nicer when you're in the bath.' She sat down in a wicker armchair. 'You don't mind, do you? My coming in while you're having your bath?'

'No!'

'I always think a hot bath is greatly improved by lively conversation, don't you?'

'Never having tried it, I really couldn't say!'

'Anna!' Ceci sighed. 'You're such a delightful person. You will never

39

know what a difference you have made to my life. I am so very, very pleased you came here to stay with me. And can I say one other thing which will really embarrass you?'

'I can't really stop you, Ceci –'

'Never, never be ashamed of your body, because you have the loveliest figure I have ever seen.'

And then – mercifully, as far as Anna was concerned – the telephone rang and Ceci went to answer it. Anna was out of the bath and into her robe by the time she got back.

They went to *La Bohème* at the Colón opera house when Anna's cold was better and a few nights after that Ceci took her out to dinner at the English Club. 'I'm determined that when you go back to Scotland it will be with a good impression of Argentina,' she said. 'I want you to prove Ursula wrong. I so admired you that day. The way you decided to stay. It was very brave of you.'

'As a matter of fact, it wasn't at all brave. The real reason I didn't want to go back with Ursula was because I didn't want to get involved with the Chief Officer of the *Highland Princess*.'

'Had he made a pass or something?'

'Well . . . there was a party on the last night at sea –'

'Champagne cocktails and dancing? Sweet nothings under a starry sky?'

Anna blushed. 'It was a bit like that.'

Ceci tut-tutted and laughed. 'You're quite a naughty girl really, aren't you, Anna? Well I don't blame you one little bit. Quite honestly I don't know why we bother about men. They simply aren't worth one's time, let alone one's affection.'

'I hope they are. At least, I hope Angus is.'

'But he's not much of a letter writer is he? How many times have you heard from him so far? Three letters is it?'

'No, four and a postcard. And he is *very* busy.'

'Busy having the time of his life, more than likely.'

'Well I can't complain, can I? Here I am living in the lap of luxury, dashing off to the opera. I've never had such a long holiday in my life. I really ought to start looking for a job.'

'Well, all in good time. I haven't even begun to show you Argentina.'

When they got home, Ceci brought in two cups of hot chocolate and put a record on the gramophone. 'I'm going to teach you to tango,' she said. 'Come on, don't be shy. I'll be the man. No, we have to dance quite close. Otherwise I can't lead properly. Don't look at your feet, darling. Look straight into my eyes, that's the way. Now. I'll keep it simple. All you have to do is follow. Ready? Here we go!'

They danced to 'Mi Buenos Aires Querido', sung by Carlos Gardel.

'Whoopsa-daisy!' Ceci laughed. 'You must relax, darling. You're all stiff. That's better! But don't look at your feet. I tell you what, just touch my forehead with yours. That's the way. Now then, try again . . .'

Ceci's hand was firm in her back, pulling her closer.

'Do we have to dance so close, Ceci?'

'Of course we do. Tango is the most sensuous dance ever invented. In Argentina we say that when tango was born, morality died in childbirth, did you know that?'

Ceci was in the garden when the telephone rang the next morning, so Anna answered it.

A grating voice said, 'Who's that? Ceci?'

'No, this is Anna McGeoch speaking.'

'Just the person I want to talk to. Annelise Cadoret here. Now – do you want the job or don't you?'

'I don't understand, Mrs Cadoret. What job is that?'

'The job I rang Ceci about last week. Hasn't she told you? I need a nanny for my son's two brats.'

'I don't know anything about any job, Mrs Cadoret –'

'Well you know now. Ring me back with an answer today, will you? If you can't do it I'll have to start looking elsewhere.'

Ceci came in from the garden with a basket of flowers for the house.

'Did I hear the telephone?'

'Yes. It was Mrs Cadoret. She wanted to know if I wanted a job as a nanny. Did she ring up last week?'

Ceci took off her gardening gloves, spread out a newspaper on the floor and put the flowers on it.

'Yes, she did as a matter of fact.'

Anna watched her arranging the flowers in a brass vase. 'Why didn't you mention it?'

Ceci sank back on her haunches and pushed a stray lock of hair aside. 'Because I know the Cadoret family, darling. They're the last people you should work for. You met Annelise. You know what she's like. And anyway, looking after that child of Magdalena's would not be at all what you're after. Blanca's a delinquent, did you know that? I told you she burnt down a wing of the house at La Calandria, didn't I?'

'Being delinquent may not be entirely her fault.'

'No, but it doesn't make her any easier to cope with either. It's not the sort of job for you, believe me. I'm sure that once we start looking we'll have no difficulty in finding you a good family and a nice new baby to look after. That's what you were trained to do, isn't it?'

Anna sat down on the sofa and looked at the flowers spread out on the newspaper. 'I don't want to appear ungrateful, Ceci, but I really feel I ought to think seriously about this offer. I didn't come out to the Argentine for a holiday. I came to work.'

'You've got all the time in the world to work, my dear.'

'But I haven't. I'm going back to England in November at the latest. That's barely six months.

Ceci put her hand in Anna's lap. 'Aren't you happy here with me?'

'Of course I am. You've been terribly kind.'

Ceci's thumb began going nervously back and forth, stroking the back of Anna's hand. She shook her head and gave a little sob.

'Ceci – what on earth's the matter?'

'I haven't been kind at all, Anna. I – I've just been selfish, that's all. Don't you understand? I just want you to myself. It's not kindness at all. I just want you to myself.' She looked up at Anna with tear-filled eyes. 'The fact of the matter is I – I've become tremendously fond of you. I simply can't bear the thought of losing you.'

Anna began to feel distinctly uncomfortable. 'I can't just go on and on having a holiday, Ceci. My church paid for me to come out, quite apart from anything else.'

Ceci closed her eyes and heaved a sigh. 'Well. I suppose that will have to be that, won't it? I mean – if you're unwilling to accept my friendship –'

'That's not the case at all. It's just –'

'Just that you're frightened out of your wits, aren't you? Frightened of your own emotions.'

'No,' Anna whispered. 'No!'

Ceci released Anna's hand and stood up. 'It's perfectly obvious you don't want to stay on here. You can't have it both ways, Anna. You can't allow someone to get close to you and then insist on holding them at arm's length at the same time. It doesn't wash. Not with me, at any rate.' She picked up the brass vase in which she had started the flower arrangement. 'Do you know why I picked these flowers? For you. Do you know why I'm wearing these things? This scarf? These shoes? For you. That's what affection is, Anna. There's nothing wrong with it. Nothing sinful about it. So why be afraid of it?'

'I am not afraid of it, Ceci, I told you –'

Ceci went to the French window and threw the vase onto the rockery.

42

'I've been wasting my time, haven't I? No, don't look like that. It's your choice, not mine. If this is the way you want it, I suggest you pick up that telephone and tell the blessed Annelise right away that you would be only too delighted to accept the position she's so kindly offered you. Go on! I'm sure you'll find her company far more congenial than mine. I can guarantee that there won't be any affection to embarrass you in *that* household.'

It was cold and drizzly when Anna went by train to Hurlingham to call on Mrs Cadoret.

Annelise received her in a drawing room full of fading photographs and glass-fronted trophy cabinets. She wore a diaphanous dress, with quantities of rings, necklaces, bracelets and other jewellery. Her hair was kept very short and tinted an unnatural shade of red. The line of her lipstick encroached well beyond the boundaries of her upper lip.

'You're not a bad looker, are you?' she said. 'When were you born?'

'I'm twenty-one, Mrs Cadoret.'

'Answer the question, will you? What was your birthdate?'

'The twenty-ninth of December, 1917.'

'So you're a Capricorn. Very interesting. How did you get on with Ceci?'

'Extremely well.'

'Of course you did. She's a Pisces. So. When can you start?'

'Could you tell me a bit more about the job before I make a decision?'

'What is there to tell? Two kids, one five, the other six months. You know what happened to their mother, of course. You'll have to be more than a nanny to them. More like a foster mother.'

'In that case I ought to tell you that I shall only be in Argentina for another five or six months at the most. I shall be returning in November at the very latest.'

Annelise lit a cigarette, coughed and then laughed shortly. 'Oh, you'll stay a lot longer than that. I can see it written all over you. But that's neither here nor there. Do you want the job or don't you?'

'May I meet the children before I make a decision?'

Annelise rang a small brass bell and when Luisa came in directed her to take Anna up to the nursery.

She followed the maid upstairs and was shown first into a prettily decorated nursery where a teenage maid was watching over a baby that was asleep in a cot.

'This is Luis,' Luisa whispered. 'Isn't he a fine baby? Just like his father, of course.'

Anna looked down at the infant. 'Well there doesn't seem anything wrong with you, my wee bairn,' she whispered, and tiptoed out.

She was then shown into a bleakly furnished little bedroom on the second floor. The room appeared to be empty until they discovered Blanca hiding behind the door with her face to the wall. Luisa shrugged and shook her head.

'Is she always like this?' Anna asked.

'More or less.'

Anna crouched down beside the little girl, who wore a dirty white dress and shoes that looked as though they were pinching her toes. 'Hello, Blanca. My name's Anna. I've been asked to come and look after you. Would you like that?'

Blanca remained in the same position, crouching like a frightened animal, her face to the corner.

'You know her mother was murdered?' the maid said. 'She's hardly spoken more than three words in a day since.'

Anna crouched beside Blanca and put her hand lightly on the child's arm. She had picked up enough Spanish to make herself understood, so she spoke in Spanish.

'Listen, Blanca. Do you want me to come and look after you? If not, please tell me, will you? I'll understand. But I want to know first if you want me to come and live here or not. Can you tell me? Can you just nod your head to tell me yes? Can you do that for me?'

'It's no good,' said Luisa. 'She never speaks, that one.'

Anna summoned her patience. 'Just nod your head, Blanca. Can you do that for me? I want very much to come and look after you. We could be friends. I want that. Will you nod your head for me to say yes?'

Blanca's reply was unexpected: she wet her knickers.

Luisa cuffed her over the head. 'You see? That's what she's like. Dirty little bitch!'

But Anna wasn't listening, because although Blanca was still facing into the corner and the pool of urine was spreading out on the floor, the little girl's head was nodding vigorously up and down.

Anna returned to Belgrano that evening and told Ceci that she would move out the following morning. Ceci accepted the news with bitter resignation, saying that she only hoped that all went well for Anna and that she would emerge unscathed from the experience of working for the Cadorets. When she offered to drive Anna out to Hurlingham,

Anna accepted. They had a silent last supper together before Anna went to her room to pack before going early to bed.

They were at breakfast the following morning when the maid brought in the post. There was a letter from Angus. Anna had never opened a letter with such a sense of relief and happiness.

Angus was not a man to waste words: his letters seldom ran to more than three sides. Nor was he good at expressing himself romantically on paper, filling his letters with stories of mess life and the practical jokes he and his fellow subalterns played on one another. 'In spite of all the ragging I'm getting at the hands of certain of my fellow officers, I am counting the days until you come back and we can be married. As you may have gathered, things are hotting up over there, and we shall be on manoeuvres for the next six weeks, so if you don't hear from me for a while, don't worry. Will you be back in time for the Tattoo this year? I do hope so, because the battalion will be taking part and they might even entrust yours truly with the Colours. Glad you're making the most of your time out there. I am missing you and thinking of you *every day* . . .'

'Nice letter from nice man?' Ceci asked brightly.

'Yes thank you.'

'Well that's all right then. Now. When would you like to depart? Shall we say about ten?'

'I would be quite happy to take a taxi to the station and go by train, Ceci.'

'Nonsense. Much easier for me to run you straight there. I've got nothing else to do, after all.'

'Ceci – I do hope we can remain friends.'

'Oh I'm sure we shall! Now. What was I just about to do? I know. Get the car out of the garage, that's the next item on the agenda. Give me a shout when you're ready, and I'll help you load up.'

'One other thing,' Anna said as Ceci was about to leave the room. 'I thought I wouldn't pack my riding things. They cost so much – I think you ought to have them.'

'Oh no,' Ceci retorted quickly. 'That really would be adding insult to injury, wouldn't it? No, you can damn well take them and be thankful, Anna. You've already thrown my friendship back in my face. I'm not going to let you throw your cast-off jodhpurs at me as well, thank you very much.'

Anna went to the bedroom and packed the riding gear. She closed up her cases and put Angus's letter in her bag. When she caught sight of her face in the mirror she looked the other way.

6

'YOUR DUTIES ARE SIMPLE,' Annelise said to Anna on her first day. 'You are to act as nanny to my grandson and you are to keep the other child out of my sight and out of my hearing. I don't care how you do it – tie the little beggar up and gag her if you have to. I don't want to see her or hear her. Take your meals in the nursery and use the back stairs and tradesmen's entrance. You may have Sunday afternoons off provided the children are properly supervised while you are out of the house. Have you a uniform?'

'No, Mrs Cadoret.'

'Purchase one. Cook will tell you where you can get one made. There are any number of seamstresses in the village. Blue and white.'

'Blue and white?'

'Your uniform, the colour of your uniform! As to religious education, Blanca is to attend Mass once a week and is to be taught to say her night and morning prayers. In English. Do you have a missal?'

'I'm not a Catholic, Mrs Cadoret. I'm a member of the Free Church of Scotland.'

'I said, do you have a missal?'

'No, I don't.'

'Buy one. There's a shop in the village.'

'Who will take Blanca to Mass?'

'You will. What are you looking like that for, girl?'

'I've never been to a Catholic Mass, Mrs Cadoret.'

'Now's the time to start.'

'Is there a Protestant church in Hurlingham I can go to?'

'I have no idea. You won't have time to go to church. You're not bound to do so, are you?'

'No, but –'

'No buts! Now: what you see or hear in this household is not to be discussed with any person – inside or outside these walls, do you understand? If I have reason to believe that you have passed on any sort of tittle-tattle about me or my friends, you will be out on your neck, pronto. Payment will be weekly. Do you have any questions?'

Anna was strongly tempted to walk out then and there but decided to stick it out for a month and if necessary bring forward her return date to Britain.

She had little time to think of home that first week. At least twice a day, in spite of all her efforts, Blanca suffered a complete breakdown of control – crying, punching, throwing things and deliberately wetting herself. There was a deep, dark anger that seemed to possess her. When she went out of control she gained in physical strength and would use anything that came to hand as a weapon. By the end of the first week Anna had a black eye and a deeply scratched arm and felt close to physical and mental exhaustion.

Custodia, the cook, advised Anna that the only way to get Blanca through Mass without a major rebellion was to get her up at five thirty in the morning and go with the servants to the six o'clock, at which the priest gabbled away as fast as he possibly could, reducing the whole service to a bare fifteen minutes. Anna sat right at the back holding Blanca's hand to make sure she stayed put, and the necessity of doing so caused her to make the discovery that Blanca responded well to physical contact.

It was as if she needed someone to keep hold of her – as if she might be afraid of herself. Anna extended the practice: whenever she was with Blanca, whether playing with her or bathing her or giving her meals, she made a point of holding her hand or touching her.

'Why do you always hold my hand?' Blanca demanded one morning when they were telling Blanca's doll a story.

'Because we're friends,' Anna said.

Blanca fixed her grape-black eyes on Anna. 'You're not my friend.'

'How do you know I'm not?'

'I don't have friends.'

'Do you think we might be friends one day?'

'No.'

'Why not?'

'Because I don't want friends.'

'Well I do, Blanca. That's why I like holding your hand.'

Quite without warning, Blanca put her head down and bit her on the arm.

Luis was easier to deal with, though he seldom slept through the night between his ten o'clock and six o'clock feeds. Anna found that she hardly had a minute in the day to herself and even when the children were asleep she was continually listening for a cry from Luis or the thump of furniture from Blanca's room.

At the beginning of Anna's fourth week at Hurlingham, Annelise

47

sent for her and calmly dropped a bombshell. 'I heard from my son today that the repairs to the nursery are now complete and that you can therefore move out to the camp immediately. Well? What are you looking at me like that for?'

'This is the first I've heard about moving to the camp, Mrs Cadoret.'

'Nonsense. I made it quite clear from the start that you would go to live at La Calandria as soon as the nursery wing had been rebuilt.'

'I don't wish to contradict you, Mrs Cadoret, but nothing was said to me about this at all.'

'Yes it was. I explained it the very first time I rang Ceci. Ah! That's what it is: she never told you, did she? I might have known it. Well I can't be responsible for Ceci Jowett's infantile jealousy. You've been booked on the sleeper the day after tomorrow. I suggest you start packing your bags.'

The overnight train arrived at Cadoret station soon after dawn and when Anna, the children and their luggage had been deposited on the single platform the train let out a mournful hoot and went on its way.

No one else had alighted at Cadoret and there was no one to meet them. A bitter southerly wind moaned in the telegraph wires. Broken here and there by copses on the skyline, the pampa stretched away as if to eternity in every direction.

Luis had slept through the journey but was now hungry and fretful. Blanca had been sick twice in the night. Anna was tired and chilled by the wind, which seemed to blow straight through her.

The ticket collector examined the tickets officiously before accepting them. She enquired if it was possible to take a taxi to La Calandria.

'No taxis in this part of the world, señorita,' he said cheerfully. 'But lose care. Señor Cadoret will to send someone to pick you up soon enough.'

'But when? I've got two children with me, as you can see.'

'Somebody'll be along. They may have had a puncture.' He looked at Blanca. 'That's Señora Magdalena's little girl, isn't it? That was a bad business, eh?' He glanced along the earth road which ran dead straight into the distance. A car had just come into sight. 'This looks like your man now.'

The black Buick drew slowly nearer but then went straight past the station. Its driver gave her a wave and shouted something in Spanish which she didn't catch.

'He's going into the village,' the official explained. 'He'll be back

48

in half an hour. Come in out of the wind, señorita. Can I offer you some maté?'

It was hot and very sweet. Blanca insisted on having some too. Anna thought this unwise in view of her sickness in the night but the last thing she wanted was a tantrum, so she allowed her to have a little. When Anna had sucked some of it through the bombilla the official took the gourd back, topped it up with more yerba, more cane sugar and more hot water and after taking a drink himself passed it back. Anna didn't like having to use the same tube to drink from as he had, but felt that it might insult him to wipe it with her handkerchief.

After forty minutes the Buick returned. The driver got out and strode over to where Anna and the children were waiting. Anna was aware of a reddish face, beaky nose, plastered-back flaxen hair and a trimmed moustache; of dark blue eyes, boots, baggy bombachas and a superb belt of silver coins.

'Miss McGeoch,' he said, and gripped her hand so firmly she almost cried out. 'Tito Cadoret. Delighted.'

Driving along at a steady fifteen miles an hour with the back wheels skidding in the mud, he made attempts at conversation that dried up as soon as they started.

'What do you think of the camp, then? Bit flat after bonny Scotland I should imagine?'

Yes, she agreed. It was very flat.

'Well, it has its compensations. You'll not regret coming to Cadoret, I can assure you of that.'

A faint smile; no answer.

'Did you have a good journey out?'

Not at all bad, she said.

'That's one of the many things this country can be proud of – its railway system. British-built of course.'

Yes, she'd gathered that.

'You were staying with Ceci Jowett I believe?'

Yes, that was correct.

'See that copse over there? That's La Ventolera. Belongs to Ceci's brother Randy. Used to belong to my grandfather, as did Ceci's place and a few other estancias in the Cadoret district besides. All been split up now, of course.'

He lapsed into silence and the car bumped and slid steadily onward.

'Anna,' growled Blanca, who was sharing the front seat with her, 'I want to go pichi.'

49

Miss McGeoch came to life.

'Could we stop please, Mr Cadoret?'

'Can't she hold it until we get there? It's only another five minutes.'

'I'd much rather we stopped. Please. It is quite important.'

As he drew to a halt in the centre of the road, she said, 'I'm afraid I'm going to have to ask you to take Luis for a moment,' and without waiting for a reply handed the baby over. She opened her door but did not get out.

'Mr Cadoret, could we possibly draw into the side so that we can get out onto the grass? This mud's about a foot thick.'

He shook his head. 'No can do. If I leave the crown of the road we'll go in over our axles. It'll take six Clydesdales to pull us out.'

'But we'll get absolutely filthy!'

'You'll get a lot filthier if we get stuck, Miss McGeoch.'

Blanca said, 'I want to go pichi *now*!'

Anna got out into the mud and held out her hands for Blanca. She lifted her out of the car and waded in mud over her ankles to the grass verge. The business over, Blanca refused to allow herself to be carried back.

'Come on, Blanca, look at my shoes! Do you want to get all dirty like that?'

'Yes,' said Blanca and threw Mimi into the mud. Anna contained her impatience and went to retrieve the doll, which gave Blanca the opportunity to make her own way back to the car, sinking up to her knees and losing one shoe in the process.

They set off again, Blanca clutching her muddy doll to her chest.

'Well done for asking,' Anna said to her quietly, and took her by the hand. 'Good girl.'

'Very bad girl, if you ask me,' Cadoret remarked.

'Perhaps I could have a word with you about that later, Mr Cadoret.'

He grunted. A minute later he swung the car left into the avenue and Anna caught her first glimpse of La Calandria.

It was a mixture of the predictable and the unexpected. Set in its own landscaped park, the house looked imposing as one approached it along the tunnel of trees, but at closer quarters gave the impression of going to seed. Along the front verandah geraniums straggled in cracked earthenware pots. The whitewash was streaked and peeling and the vegetable garden was overgrown with weeds. To the side of the house part of the netting round the two tennis courts had blown down.

The building was flat-roofed and whitewashed with a pseudo-classical pillared colonnade running round it, bow-fronted railed balconies outside every first-floor window and the name, 'LA CALANDRIA, 1878' moulded into the cement façade over the front door. At the back of the house, a flagpole protruded from a squat rectangular tower. At either end the house was extended by a ground floor wing, one end for the nursery and schoolroom, the other for the kitchens and servants' quarters.

As the car drew up, two boxers came bounding round the side of the house, one biting the other's neck. They wagged and barked round the newcomers and knocked Blanca over. Tito roared at them, 'Sancho! Ralda!' and they calmed down immediately.

Catarina appeared. She was a comfortable body with greying hair and dimpled cheeks. She tutted at the state Anna and Blanca had got into, relieved Anna of Luis and led the way up a wide, solid staircase and along a tiled corridor.

'Blanca's room,' she announced, then, 'Luis's room,' and finally, 'Nanna's room.'

'No – please don't call me Nanna. My name is Anna.'

'Anna? Anna is good Russian name.'

'Are you Russian, then?'

'Of course!'

'When did you come to Argentina?'

The housekeeper sighed. 'Sixteen years. Is a long time.'

'Where was your home?'

'In the province of Tula.'

'Why did you leave?'

'Because things were not good for us. Here is bathroom.'

The work started immediately: Anna changed her shoes and stockings and set about cleaning up Blanca and feeding Luis. Catarina showed her where everything was kept and then took her and Blanca down to the rebuilt nursery, which was decorated with a frieze of gauchos fighting Indians. The windows faced out over the park. Tall eucalyptus trees were swaying in the wind and in the distance, at the end of a ride, black steers could be glimpsed grazing.

'This is my eldest daughter, Marga,' Catarina said as a girl of fourteen or fifteen entered the nursery with breakfast for Anna and Blanca on a tray. 'Marga help me in the house and my husband Piotr does the man's work. Marga want very much to speak English.'

The girl put the tray down on the table and curtsied.

Anna protested, 'Please – there's no need for that. I'm a servant in this household as well!'

Catarina shook her head. 'No. Don Tito say we treat you with respect.'

'But I think we should all treat each other with equal respect, Catarina, don't you?'

Tears came to the housekeeper's eyes. 'I think you are a good person, Miss Anna,' she said softly. 'And I hope you are happy here always. Come, Marga. Let Miss Anna have breakfast in peace.'

Cadoret sent for her that evening. He received her in the drawing room where a newly lit log fire was crackling in the hearth. He had bathed and changed and was looking crisp and scrubbed in twills, blazer and square. At his feet lay the pelt of a puma, its head snarling upward at the ceiling. Cut glass decanters of gin, whisky, brandy, port and sherry stood on the sideboard. An original Stubbs hung over the fireplace. There were silver-framed family photographs and a pile of old magazines on the grand piano.

He stood up to welcome her. He couldn't help noticing things about her: her straight back and steady eyes, her chestnut hair, her Scottish lilt that conjured up visions of brisk walks over grouse moors or the sun shining through peat smoke on a chill winter evening.

'Will you have something to drink, Miss McGeoch? A glass of sherry, perhaps? Or a whisky?'

She settled for sherry.

'Argentine,' he said, pouring from the decanter. 'It comes from San Juan, in the foothills of the Andes.'

When she accepted the glass from him he noticed that she wore no rings or bracelets.

'Well then. Here's to your stay at La Calandria. May it be a long and happy one.'

They sat down on opposite sides of the fire, he in his father's chair, she in his mother's.

'So,' he said. 'Tell me all about yourself.'

'I think you probably know enough already.'

'Hardly! If you're going to be nanny to Blanca and Luis I'll want to know more about you than my mother told me.'

'Well . . . I'm a trained child's nurse as you probably know.'

'Where did you do your training?'

'In Edinburgh.'

He nodded. 'A Scottish nanny. One can hardly better that.'

She smiled faintly. 'I think you ought to know that I don't intend to stay long in Argentina, Mr Cadoret. Certainly not beyond the autumn.'

'Autumn next year?'

'No, this autumn.'

'Ah. You mean the English autumn. We've just had ours. Why must you go so soon?'

She looked down at her glass. 'For personal reasons.'

He nodded. 'Understood. Believe you had a bereavement recently? Your brother, wasn't it?'

'Yes.'

'Expect you – er – know all about my background. I mean . . . what happened to my wife?'

'I think I know as much as I need to know, yes.'

'How did you get on with my mother?'

'Your mother is a most unusual lady, Mr Cadoret.'

He laughed, then laughed a little more. 'Good answer, very good answer! No – don't apologize. I know what my mother's like. Didn't envy you having to cope with her these past few weeks. Sheer bloody murder, I should think, wasn't it?'

She relaxed a little, and for the first time since meeting her at the station he felt he was making headway.

'It wasn't always easy.'

'All right. So how can I make things easier for you here?'

'Would you really like to know?'

'Wouldn't have asked otherwise.'

'Well first of all, I would rather not wear uniform. What your children need at this moment – particularly Blanca – is love, Mr Cadoret, and it is very much more difficult for them to accept love from a nurse in a starched apron.'

He inclined his head. 'All right. No uniform.'

She looked surprised. He had the impression that she had come prepared to do battle.

'Secondly, I think it would be a good idea if you could spend a little time with your children yourself every day, even if only for ten minutes. Would that be possible?'

That caught him slightly on the hop. 'Well – don't know about that. Not every day. But – er – see what we can do.'

'Thank you. I'm sure you appreciate that Blanca has been badly hurt by recent events, Mr Cadoret. She's not an easy child. I've discovered that she doesn't respond to traditional nursery discipline. You saw what happened in the car this morning – and I think you disapproved of the way I dealt with her. But I must ask you to give me a free hand with her and to be very patient with her. I think I have her trust now, but it's a very fragile trust and could be easily broken. The difficulty is that every time her trust is broken it becomes all the harder to re-establish. I do hope you understand.'

53

He looked at her and shook his head. 'Where did you learn all this, Miss McGeoch?'

'Isn't it common sense?'

'It sounds like sense, certainly, but I wouldn't call it very common.'

Marga came to the door to say that niña Blanca wouldn't settle and was demanding to see Anna.

'That damn child,' Tito muttered.

'I think I ought to go,' Anna said. 'It is her first night back, after all.'

'Very well. But kindly bear in mind that I have not employed you to spoil her. Right?'

'Of course,' she replied, and the moment she was gone from the room, he wanted her back.

For some while after that first interview, Anna saw little of Cadoret. He was up at six every morning, spent the entire day riding about his estancia, returned for a solitary supper and, providing there was no emergency with the livestock, was usually in bed by nine. On Saturday afternoons Victorio, the pony boy, trooped a dozen polo ponies to the local polo club and the following morning Tito would ride into Cadoret for seven o'clock Mass before going on to the Laguna Blanca club for polo and lunch with the local landowners.

Apart from the occasional visit to the drawing room with the children, Anna's routine had nothing in common with his. Though Blanca had made some progress, she still suffered tantrums once or twice a day during which Anna was the only person able to bring her back under control. The only time Anna had to herself was when Blanca and Luis were asleep, but Luis was teething and giving her sleepless nights. She knew that looking after two children should not be such a strain, but it was nevertheless. The days turned into weeks and she heard nothing more from Angus. Thrust in on herself for most of the day, she longed for company. She began to look back on the weeks spent with Ceci with nostalgia and remembered what Ursula had said: 'Never say I didn't warn you.'

One night she gave up trying to get to sleep after being woken by Luis and at two in the morning sat down to finish a letter to Angus. There was a freak summer in the middle of winter that year and it was an airless night with the insects making a racket outside the window.

The words wouldn't come. She could no longer bring herself to simulate that cheerful optimism which she believed should set the tone

54

of every letter, however miserable one was feeling. In the solitude of the early hours, she put her head in her hands and admitted to herself that she was lonely – hopelessly, desperately lonely.

After a while she abandoned the letter and went to the window. A nearly full moon was blazing down sending long shadows creeping across the lawns at the back of the house. Beyond the eucalyptus windbreak, the pampa stretched out under a sparkling bowl of stars. Far away, a dog was howling.

A movement caught her eye. Something was coming towards the house along the ride bordered by eucalyptus trees. It was a man on a horse. He came trotting out of the shadows and across the lawn. When he was halfway across the lawn he reined in the horse and looked up at her. It was Tito.

She let the curtain fall quickly back, realizing too late that she was wearing only a flimsy nightdress and was standing in front of the light.

June and July should have brought a season of frosts, clear days and cold winds, but that winter of '39 the weather in the camp was quite unpredictable, with spells of wind and rain giving way suddenly to summery weather and temperatures in the high seventies. Cadoret had lost a third of his maize crop the previous year and was having to buy in fodder. He was having to sell steers underweight to keep up with his interest payments to Lambretti, and the sacking of his manager had not added to his popularity among the peons at La Calandria. With every consignment of steers sent by train to Cadoret his morale slipped further.

On Sundays at Laguna Blanca when he met the Jowetts or the Rathbones or the Dalligans or the Harrisons, he felt obliged to keep up appearances. He had to be his usual ebullient self. He had to put on the old Tito Cadoret mask for the benefit of Randy and Stiffy and Paddy and Teddy. No one must know that sometimes he went through a night without a wink of sleep. No one must suspect that he went for solitary night rides about his estancia – rides on which he wrestled with his conscience, going over and over in his mind exactly what he had said to Botta and what Botta had said in return.

Always he came back to the same undeniable conclusion. He had agreed to pay money to get rid of his wife, and she had been subsequently murdered. He had parted with his best polo pony to forestall a police inquiry. He had committed no crime, but felt as guilty as if he had murdered Magdalena himself.

And now he had seen Anna at the window and he was longing for her more than he had ever longed for Ceci or Magdalena. He needed a woman. There was no denying it. But not any woman, no, he had learnt his lesson in that respect. He needed the love and the trust of a woman as well as the warmth of her body. That was what had gone wrong with Ceci: he had enjoyed her company but not her body, whereas with Magdalena it had been the other way round.

He wondered if Anna might have deliberately waited up for him, deliberately shown herself at the window. Was she as desperately in need of company as himself? Which was the better course: to take the Buick to Laboulaye and seek a temporary satisfaction with a whore, or to seek a more permanent satisfaction by taking the first step with Anna and inviting her to take her evening meals with him in the dining room instead of by herself in the nursery?

7

THE INVITATION WAS DELIVERED by Marga two days later when Anna was in the nursery with the children. It was scrawled on a sheet of headed notepaper:

Request the pleasure of your company at dinner this evening. 7.45 for 8.00 p.m.

She put on her only smart dress, which was not at all fashionable, black with a V-neck, three-quarter sleeves and unpadded shoulders. She only had one piece of jewellery to wear, and that was a single string of pearls – small but real – which had belonged to her grandmother. She brushed her hair briskly before the mirror and added a touch of lipstick, silencing the voice of her conscience which kept asking why she was taking so much trouble over her appearance.

Tito was an excellent host. Without appearing inquisitive he drew her out about her family, her home, her brother, why she had come out to Argentina and what her likes and dislikes were. Then he told her about his own childhood at La Calandria and of his earliest memories. She was surprised to learn that he was the youngest of four. His elder brother had served with the British Army in India and had been killed in a skirmish on the North West Frontier in '22. Both his elder sisters were married, one to a sheep farmer in Australia, the other to a doctor in Ireland. Furthermore, his mother's mother had been a Jowett, so that he and Ceci were distant cousins.

'Ceci never told me that,' Anna said.

'She wouldn't. The Jowett family is a very large one and very divided as well. Fifty years ago La Ventolera was one of the biggest estancias in the Argentine. It included all the land of La Calandria and La Tijerita – that's Ceci's estancia – as well as most of the Rathbone, Dalligan and Harrison land.'

'Why did it get so split up?'

'Partly Argentina's crazy inheritance laws, partly human weakness. My grandfather gambled away half his inheritance and had to sell land to pay his debts, and my father spent so much time in Europe that his administrator took him to the cleaners. He sold Ventolera and Tijerita to the Jowett family, so their land now surrounds Calandria on three sides. My father inherited ninety thousand hectares and left thirty.' Cadoret laughed, then shook his head bitterly.

'That's still an awful lot though, isn't it?'

'Not by Argentine standards.'

'Do you like it?'

'Do I like what?'

'Living in the camp.'

He looked away and laughed again. 'Now there's a question. The answer's yes and the answer's no. The weather this winter hasn't been too bad so far. Been able to get out most days. Keep busy. But sometimes we have week after week of wind and rain and all you can do is sit and watch it. Shall we take coffee in the drawing room?'

He ushered her from the room.

'Expect you wondered a bit when you got my invitation to dine,' he remarked when Catarina had brought in the coffee. 'Not normally done, of course. For el patrón to invite the nursery nurse to dinner. But our circumstances aren't exactly typical, are they?'

Behind the smooth exterior lay a mixture of bluff jocularity and gruff melancholy. As if he were hiding something. As if he needed a bit of tender loving care . . .

'You realize that Catarina never stops singing your praises, I suppose? From what I can gather, you've done wonders with those two children. Especially Blanca. Most grateful to you.' He frowned and looked at the ceiling, bit his lip and then shot another glance in her direction. 'Look, I'm no good at wrapping things up, and I don't think you're the sort of person who wants them to be, are you? So let me ask you a straight question. Are you happy here at La Calandria?'

'Well,' she began, 'not exactly happy. But –'

'Didn't think you were. To be perfectly frank with you, nor am I.' He smiled and glanced twice at her in order to catch her eye. 'Chaps don't go hacking round the pampa in the middle of the night when they're blissfully content, do they?' He looked at her again, smiling. 'Any more than young ladies stand at their windows at two in the morning.'

He turned his head on one side to make his statement into a question.

'Well? Do they?'

'I suppose not.'

'Of course they don't! That's what prompted me to invite you this evening. Decided it was damn stupid to go on living at opposite ends of the house like this. Don't see why you and I can't be on more friendly terms, Anna. Don't see why we shouldn't take an evening meal together from time to time. Do you?'

'I don't think it's really my decision, Mr Cadoret.'

'And that's another thing. Why don't we drop the formalities? I'd much rather you called me Tito.'

She was very still and quiet. He couldn't begin to imagine what was going on inside her head.

'You don't mind if I call you Anna, do you?'

'Is it wise?'

He laughed again. She thought, Why is there so much unhappiness in the way he laughs?

'Find it rather boring being wise all the time, Anna. Don't you?'

'I was just thinking that if Catarina or Marga hear that we're on first name terms, well –'

'What?'

She looked down at the snarling puma. 'I'm sure you know what I mean.'

He chuckled. 'You realize the domestic staff have been watching us like hawks since the day you arrived?'

'Isn't that all the more reason for giving them nothing to talk about?'

He regarded her with lazy, laughing eyes. 'You mean . . . go on pretending that we don't find each other attractive?'

She looked at the Stubbs over the fireplace and tried to think what she should say.

'Now you're angry with me.'

'No I'm not.'

'What, then?'

'I suppose . . . angry with myself.'

'Is there any good reason why you should be?'

'Well, I was unofficially engaged before I left Scotland.'

'And are you still?'

'Yes, but –'

'But what?'

She shook her head. 'Nothing.'

'Does he write to you?'

'Oh – yes.'

'But not very often, eh?'

'They keep the subalterns very busy, you know.'

'All the same. Can't be all that keen, can he?'

'I think he is.'

'Oh – come on, Anna! He must have been off his chump to let you go off halfway round the world on your own! I wouldn't have let you go if you'd been my fiancée – whether we were officially or unofficially engaged.'

'He's only twenty-three. My parents thought we should wait.'

'Glad you were such a dutiful daughter.'

She finished her coffee and stood up. 'I really ought to be getting to bed, Mr Cadoret.'

'Hold your horses. Don't go just yet. I want to see more of you. I tell you what, I'll get Victorio to look you out a pony tomorrow morning so that you can get a bit of riding. There's a mare called Jemima that would suit you. Mouth like butter and gentle as they come. Leave the kids with Catarina and take an hour or two off. You deserve it. I'll be revising the herds in seventeen-south tomorrow afternoon – that's just beyond the polo pitch. I could do with a bit of company.'

'It's very kind of you, Mr Cadoret –'

'Tito. Go on, Anna. Be a devil. Say it.'

She coloured. 'Well – good night – Tito.'

He caught her hand, drew her to him and kissed her lightly on the cheek. '*Pierda cuidado*,' he whispered. 'I'm not being forward. We always kiss good night in Argentina.'

When she had departed, he went to the sideboard and poured himself a nightcap. He went to the window and looked out at the racing clouds, touching his lip with the rim of the whisky glass and smiling at his thoughts.

There was a storm in the night and when Anna woke in the morning the wind was screaming in the eaves and the eucalyptus trees were swaying and creaking and small branches were being tumbled across the lawns behind the house.

She went about her usual routine: changing Luis, getting Blanca washed and dressed, taking them both down to the nursery for breakfast.

Catarina bustled in with a big smile on her face. 'Ah, you look so beautiful last night, niña Anna. You are like a countess! And Don Tito, well – I think he like you more than not much!'

After breakfast Anna put Luis in his pram and took him and Blanca for a walk to look at the storm damage. There was a tree down in the drive and one of the covered wagons belonging to the ploughing contractors had been blown onto its side. They watched a couple of

Clydesdales pull it upright and walked on past the farm buildings to the outbuildings where the peons lived. On their way back to the house they were met by the pony boy. Victorio was a bronzed man of forty with the build of a jockey, flared nostrils and a lascivious grin. He rode a palomino gelding which he had taught to bow respectfully on being told to say 'buenos días'.

He said Don Tito had directed him to make a suitable pony available for Miss Anna to ride that afternoon. Would she come and approve his choice of pony, so that he could have it saddled up for her?

Anna said that she would have to take the children back to the house first, but Blanca objected. She was gazing up at the palomino with an expression of wonder on her face.

'I want to go on the horse,' she said.

'Well you can't just yet, Blanca. Another day.'

'I want to go now.'

Victorio said, 'She will be safe with me, Miss Anna,' so Anna left Blanca to gaze up at the pony while she took Luis back to the house, leaving him in his pram outside the kitchen under the eye of Catarina, who was scrubbing the flag stones.

Victorio looked down at the little girl. 'You like my pony, niñita? Blanca nodded.

'You want to come up here with me?'

She nodded again. Victorio leant down, put his arm round her waist and scooped her up to sit in front of him on the sheepskin saddle.

His arm was a bar across her tummy, keeping her from falling off and making her feel completely safe. Sitting up there with him, looking down on Anna as she came running across the grass towards them gave Blanca the best feeling she had ever had in her life.

'All right up there?' Anna asked as if nothing unusual had happened.

'Yes,' Blanca said in her strange contralto. 'I like it.'

They walked over to the fifty hectare paddock where thirty polo ponies were kept. At their approach the ponies came across the field like children crowding to meet a popular schoolteacher.

Victorio dismounted and lifted Blanca down. They went into the paddock and Anna was introduced to Jemima, a pretty bay mare with a perfect white heart on her forehead.

'What you think of her?' Victorio asked, smiling slyly and flaring his nostrils.

'She's lovely!'

'Don Tito say she is yours.'

'Yes, he said he would choose a pony for me to ride this afternoon.'

Victorio shook his head. 'Not for this afternoon. For keeps.'

'I'm quite sure he didn't mean that, Victorio.'

'*Vamos a ver*,' Victorio said, and shot an intense, brown-eyed look at her. They went out of the paddock. Blanca announced that she wanted to go 'up there' again.

'She's safe with me,' Victorio said. 'Up you come, niñita.'

And again that strong arm was holding her and the sheepskin was warm and soft under her legs, the pony's movement was like magic underneath her and it was as if she were flying: the trees going by on either side and the hooves thudding and the wind in her face; and all too soon she was coming back to where Miss Anna was waiting and it was over.

The hours of work at La Calandria were marked by the ringing of a bell. In the winter, the men worked from seven to eleven in the morning and from three to seven in the afternoon. The midday meal was from noon until one and siesta from one until three. On wet days the cattlemen 'revised the rain', which meant that they stayed under cover and watched it pelt down. These lost hours were regained when cattle were being dipped or de-horned or trooped to the railhead at Cadoret on their way to the slaughter houses in Buenos Aires.

Tito took his lunch in the house. It was always the same: a couple of beef steaks washed down by hot maté. It was the diet the gauchos had lived on a hundred years ago and which still sustained most working men in the camp.

Today there was a slight alteration in his routine. When the foreman rang the three o'clock bell after siesta, instead of going straight out to the field to watch the peons parting blacks, he swung himself into the saddle and trotted over to the stables to meet Anna.

Victorio was on hand to assist. Jemima had been saddled and was waiting impatiently, her ears going back and forth as the men talked, her rear offside hoof tipped provocatively on edge. Anna turned up a minute later, wearing the riding boots, jodhpurs and the houndstooth hacking jacket Ceci had insisted that she keep. Victorio held Jemima's head while she mounted and Tito led the way out of the paddock and along the eucalyptus ride to the field.

'How does it feel?' he asked.

'Wonderful!'

He smiled broadly. 'Like to canter?'

'Do you think I can?'

'Of course. Jemima'll look after you.'

'Wonderful!' she said when they reached the end of the ride. 'So exhilarating!'

He showed her how to open the gate and close it without dismounting.

'Golden rule number one,' he said. 'Never leave a gate open behind you.'

They went across a huge field and into another where three cattlemen were working on horseback.

'What are they doing?'

'Parting.'

'What's that?'

'Separating the steers for sale. Have to corral them first.'

They rode in a wide sweep round the back of the herd. The peons had positioned themselves behind and on either wing of the steers. From time to time when a steer broke away from the main body one of the men would ride out to chase it back. There was a lot of whistling and shouting and the occasional crack of hide on hide as the men wielded short, flat thongs of raw leather.

The corral was in the corner of the field by a fenced-off mill square where a wind pump raised water that was piped via a cistern to four troughs, one in the corner of each adjoining field. The steers were herded into a large corral and made to pass one by one through a narrow corridor at the end of which was a weighing platform and a two-way gate used to separate out those steers to be sent for market.

They were joined by Cruz Navarro, the foreman. Cadoret talked to him for some time and, by the way Navarro shook his white head and shrugged and looked away and spat in the mud, it appeared to Anna that he was not at all pleased with what the patrón had to say.

Two of the cattlemen were in the corral with the steers. One of them had a hooked nose, high cheekbones and straight black hair. He sat right back in the saddle, steering the horse left and right with the weight of his body and trumpeting through pursed lips at the steers to urge them forward.

The work of parting went ahead with Tito doing the choosing and Navarro looking disapprovingly on. Every so often a steer would be weighed, and the capataz wrote the weight in a notebook.

'Why did you weigh some and not the others?' Anna asked when the operation was complete and they were trotting side by side.

'It's a sample. We can average out their gain in weight to calculate the overall average gain of the herd.'

'So you always weigh the same ones?'

'Right.'

'How did you know which ones to weigh?'

'Ear tags. Don't really need them though. You saw that Indian-looking peon? Knows every steer by sight. Can't read or write, but he can tell you the birth date of every bull, cow, steer and heifer on the property.'

'And the ones you parted were all going off to market were they? They looked awfully small.'

Cadoret snorted. 'Yes. They were.'

They rode half a league to a field where two teams of Clydesdales were pulling disc harrows and a dozen or more were tethered nearby.

'How many shire horses have you got altogether?'

'About eighty. We used to have over three hundred when I was a boy.'

'How on earth do you manage to keep so many horses groomed and looked after?'

'Each peon has his own animals to see to. They live in the open, and all that's needed at the end of the day is a bucket of water over their backs and a scrape down with the blunt edge of a knife.'

They visited the campamento – a circle of covered wagons and tents made of hides that looked as if they had come straight off a Hollywood western. In the centre of the circle, women in shawls were cooking over an open fire. The contractor came over and talked to Cadoret. He was a wizened man with a boozer's complexion and bloodshot eyes. He shouted to his son, who dived into one of the tents and came out carrying a stone ball which he handed up to Anna for inspection.

'Part of an Indian bolas,' Cadoret explained. 'They turned it up when they were ploughing yesterday. We find them from time to time.'

'What were they used for?'

'Hunting and fighting. See the groove round it? That took a leather thong, and three balls were attached to a long line. The Indians used to whirl them round their heads and throw them at ostriches or cattle. Or their enemies. Known as the Three Marias.'

He turned to the contractor and spoke in Spanish that was too idiomatic and quick for Anna to understand. Anna moved away, aware of the curious looks of the women round the fire. While she waited, two of the men entered a small enclosure of sheep, caught one and dragged it out. They threw it on its back and one of them took a knife from his belt and pierced its throat. The animal gave a groan and quickly died. The men began skinning it. Incisions were made at the feet and the fleece was peeled cleanly away from the body in one piece. The operation was so swiftly and skilfully done that after the first slight shock Anna felt no revulsion.

'Think you can make your own way back?' Tito said behind her. 'You know the way from here – across this field here, through the gate at the far corner, over the polo cancha and then you're at the end of the ride. Just hand Jemima over to the pony boy – he'll do everything. Don't forget to close the gates.'

Riding back on her own with the wind in her hair and a flock of geese flying overhead, she felt a wonderful sense of liberation. There was something about these distant horizons and high skies that lifted her spirits. She felt that she was in the right place at the right time. For the time being at any rate, this was where she belonged. It was an instinctive, irrational feeling but very powerful. High, white clouds were skidding along in the sky. Jemima's hooves made a soft thudding sound on the damp earth track. The thought occurred to her suddenly that she was *happy*.

'The post's arrived,' Catarina said when she came into the kitchen and sat down to take off her boots. 'Some for you. I put in your room.'

There were two letters: one from her mother and one from Angus. She opened her mother's first.

Folded inside the letter was a newspaper cutting. It was a clipping from the *Scotsman*. At first she couldn't understand why her mother had sent it because it was part of an advertisement for oatcakes. But when she turned it over she understood it very well because it said that a marriage had been arranged, and would take place shortly, between Lieutenant Angus Dairmid McNairne and Miss Constance Drane.

Frowning in disbelief, she read the announcement for a second time then turned it over and looked again at the oatcake advertisement. She scanned her mother's letter. 'Your father saw the enclosed announcement in the paper this morning. We have had no word from Angus in over a month . . .' – she skipped a line or two – '. . . we are so relieved, now that he has been shown in his true colours, that you had the sense not to bind yourself by any promise to marry. Father sends you his love and blessings and says to tell you that the Lord will surely show you the way forward. Cast all your care upon Him, for He careth for you . . . I know this will come as a terrible shock to you, Anna, but you are a sensible girl, and we are sure that you will see that what has happened is for the best and that you will accept what is God's plan for you, whatever it may be . . .'

She sat on her bed and let the truth sink in. She knew that she should burst into tears, but all she felt was a little sickened. She picked up Angus's letter.

Did she really want to read it? Either it would be another of his well-spaced efforts full of regimental news and cricket scores or it would be a carefully worded 'Dear Mary' to tell her that their unofficial engagement was at an end. But what was done was done, and nothing Angus could write could undo it. Besides, why should she read his apologies or rationalisations? Why should she allow him the luxury of explaining? Why should she allow him to hurt her with hollow regrets?

Sadly but deliberately, she tore it up in its envelope and dropped the pieces into the waste-paper basket.

8

TITO PLAYED POLO at Laguna Blanca the following Sunday and who should he see in the bar before lunch but Ceci. They had not met socially since breaking off their engagement two years before. Now, by the look of her, Ceci was intent upon burying the hatchet, though Tito could not be sure that it would not end up buried between his shoulder blades.

'Tito!' she cried with what seemed to him synthetic joy, and offered her cheek to be kissed.

'Hello, Ceci. Surprised to see you in the camp at this time of year.'

'My dear – I'm running away from the *Buenos Aires Herald*. Not even a camp winter could be more bleak than the headlines these days.'

'When did you arrive?'

'Crack of dawn this morning. I'm staying at Ventolera with Betty and Randy. Couldn't be bothered to open up Tijerita just for a week. But now tell me, Tito – how are you? How's life at La Calandria these days? You're not having a torrid affair with a bottle of whisky, I hope?'

Tito suspected that Ceci might be fishing for information about Anna, but refused to rise to the bait.

'Not quite as bad as that. Mind you, I could be tempted if we get another maize crop like last year's.'

Ceci was saved further agricultural details by the arrival of Stiffy Rathbone, who managed his father's estancia, El Palenque.

Stiffy was a tall, wiry man, very smooth-skinned, with pale blue eyes and lips that turned outwards when he smiled, giving him the look of a stallion baring its teeth. He and Tito had gone to Quilmes school together and had played polo together here at Laguna Blanca since the age of twelve.

There were more exclamations as others joined the group. It was the first time Ceci had appeared at Laguna Blanca since breaking off her engagement and everyone agreed that it felt like old times. Stiffy was joined by the lovely Emelda Dalligan and the group then enlarged further when Teddy Harrison and Emelda's brother Paddy rolled up, along with a few hangers-on and polo addicts. The English stood in the middle of the bar eating nuts, clutching drinks and roaring with laughter as if they owned the place, which they did. The last member of the team to show up was Ceci's brother Randolph, a barrel-chested, balding man in his mid thirties who was known as Randy. He announced that his wife Betty was pregnant for the second time in eighteen months. Stiffy said that called for a celebration, and when three bottles of champagne had been consumed the whole group of sixteen trooped into the dining room, pushed three tables together and fell upon the fairy toast while the waiters shouted instructions to the chef on how the Anglos wanted their beefsteaks.

No one remarked (but everyone noticed) that Ceci had contrived to sit opposite Tito; and after lunch when the men had gone out to get ready for the first chukka and Ceci had gone to powder her nose, Betty confided to the other camp ladies that she thought it would be a jolly good thing if Tito and Ceci got together again.

'It must be coming up to the second anniversary of their engagement isn't it?' Emelda remarked.

'That's right,' Louise Harrison put in. 'They announced it on Tito's birthday. I remember because Annelise and Johnny had that awful scene right in the middle of the asado.'

'The fourth of August,' said Betty. 'Isn't that next Saturday? I say, girls, I've just had the most ripping idea!'

She was not the only one: trotting along the earth road that evening, with Victorio and his troop of polo ponies coming along behind and a crimson lake sun slipping away beneath the horizon, Tito also had an idea.

Anna had just finished bathing Blanca when Marga came up with the message that Don Tito would like to see her with the children before she put them to bed.

She put Blanca into her dressing gown and slippers and took the two children downstairs and along the corridor to the sitting room where Tito was standing in front of the fire in his damp riding things, the steam rising off him.

Luis was now nearly nine months old. He was going to have Magdalena's Indian looks and black hair.

Cadoret sat down and held out his hands to Blanca. 'Now, Blanca,' he said. 'Tell Daddy something. Do you like surprises?'

Blanca held Mimi behind her back with one hand and put her spare thumb in her mouth. She stared up at him and shook her head.

'It depends on the surprise, doesn't it? So I'll tell you part of the surprise but not all of it. We're all going out for the day next week. You, me, Luis and Anna. And Mimi too. We're going to drive in the car all the way to Laboulaye and we're going to buy you a great big special present, something you'll like a lot. But I'm not going to tell you what it is because that would spoil the surprise, wouldn't it?'

Anna had never seen him so affectionate towards the children. He bounced Luis up and down on his knee and sang 'The Grand Old Duke of York' and he pleaded so persuasively with Blanca that she agreed to sit on his knee and play 'This is the way the ladies ride' and sang it with him in a growly voice.

'Going to buy her a pony,' he told Anna when Blanca had been allowed to run up to her room. 'We can go to the feria. Have a bit of a day out. What do you say?'

'I think it's a lovely idea.'

'And – er – might I have the pleasure of your company at dinner after we get back?' He smiled his most devastating smile. 'Small celebration, you see. My birthday.'

The weather was kind to them. The sun shone and the temperature rose into the seventies. Marga came along to look after Luis, and Blanca was allowed to ride on the front seat with Anna.

They went to the fair. Watching Anna ride with Blanca on the dodgems, Cadoret realized that she was everything he was looking for. He could not take his eyes off her. And what a thing it would be to give her children! What a wonderful mother she would make!

Blanca was not quite as thrilled with the pony – a skewbald mare called Chocolata – as he had hoped, but as Anna remarked, she was not a demonstrative child and it was never easy to know what was going on inside her mind.

After a chaotic restaurant lunch at which Blanca spilled a full glass of red wine over Anna's lap, they called back at the stables to say hasta luego to Chocolata, who was to be delivered by horsebox on Monday, and set off back to La Calandria.

But it was the evening that was the most important part of the day, and as far as Cadoret was concerned the whole of the rest of the day had been a preparation for it.

Anna was wearing the same black dress she had worn a few weeks before and when she came down for dinner looked so fresh and young and defenceless that he was tempted to sweep her into his arms and ask her to be his wife then and there.

Instead, he opened a bottle of champagne.

'Here's to you. And thank you for everything.'

'Oh,' she said. 'I don't think I've done anything of great significance.'

'What about Blanca? You've transformed her. Think she'll take to her new steed?'

'Oh – I'm sure she will. And it'll be good for her, too. That was a real inspiration, Tito.'

It was the first time she had called him Tito in so natural a way.

'What about Jemima? You still happy with her?'

'I think she's much too good for me. I'm terrified of spoiling her mouth.'

'In that case there's little chance that you will.'

'I was wondering – can I take her out before breakfast occasionally?'

He touched her arm. 'My dear – you can ride her whenever you like. She's your pony. She's my first present to you.'

'I still can't regard her as mine.'

'You must. Ponies are like people. They like to feel they belong. Like you and me.'

He went to the glass-fronted bookcase from which he took an old leather-bound photograph album and went and sat on the arm of her chair. 'Here you are,' he said, opening the album. 'That's how we used to break horses when I was Blanca's age. They still do on some estancias.'

Anna saw a faded sepia photograph of a stallion using every muscle in its body to strain backwards against the halter rope, which had been taken round a heavy stake in the ground.

'We used to tire them out on a palenque first, then use a woman's silk stocking as a bit and ride them to exhaustion. Not any more. You must watch Victorio horsebreaking one of these days. Spends days talking to a pony before he tries to get on its back.'

He was about to close the album when she said, 'Can I see?' so they sat down side by side and he opened the album at the first page, which bore a picture of a huge country mansion with the family and all the staff standing outside in their Sunday best.

'That's the old country seat in Sussex. My grandfather was brought up there. Came out via Chile in the fifties and crossed the Andes on a mule.' He turned a few pages, all filled with faded ladies and gentlemen, their expressions frozen by the requirement to hold still and concentrate on the camera lens.

'Here we are. That's me, first time on horseback, aged two. That's my brother. Me again, learning to walk. That's my father playing polo at Laguna Blanca. This is me in polo gear for the first time. And here I am on my sixth birthday. Twenty-five years ago today.'

'So the war had just started.'

'Right. Yours truly knew precious little about it though.' He looked up. There were headlights in the drive. 'Damn. Who the hell's this?'

It was Stiffy Rathbone. He came thundering in bellowing, 'Cadoret? Where the hell are you, you old stick-in-the-mud?' but stopped short when he saw Anna. 'Ah. Didn't realize you had company.'

Cadoret introduced them. Rathbone looked Anna up and down then turned back to Tito.

'Orders from high command. 'Your presence required at the big house.'

'Much regret unable,' Cadoret said. 'For obvious reasons.'

'*¡La gran puta!*' said Stiffy. 'That's a blow.'

'Why?'

'Not supposed to tell you, am I? Thing is, Betty's pushing the boat out. They've laid on a do. Asado criollo and all that. Surprise, surprise. You know the sort of thing.' He glanced again at Anna. 'If I go back without him they'll tear me limb from limb.'

Anna tried not to laugh. Stiffy was such a gross caricature with his neighing laugh and horse teeth that one could scarcely believe he was real.

'If it would help at all, I don't mind dropping out,' she offered.

'Not on your life,' said Cadoret.

Rathbone balanced on his heels and looked at his toecaps. 'Going to be damned embarrassing if you don't show up, Tito.'

'Why?'

'Don't be so bloody obtuse, man! You were at Laguna Blanca on Sunday. You saw who was there. Put two and two together, for God's sake!'

'I did that when I saw you coming up the drive.'

Rathbone shook his head in desperation. If Anna had not been present he could have explained that Betty had organized the whole thing in the hopes of getting Tito and Ceci together again. But with this lovely sylph-like creature at Cadoret's elbow, the whole point of the party looked like a non-starter.

'Tell you what, why don't you both come along?'

Tito turned to Anna. 'What do you think?'

'I really don't mind staying behind –'

'If you stay, I stay. I've never stood a girl up in my life, and I don't intend to start now.'

Rathbone's eyebrows went up so far that they practically disappeared over the top of his head. 'Yes, well . . . what do you say, Miss McGeoch? You'll do me the greatest favour by accepting and that's the honest truth.'

So she accepted.

'Splendid!' said Stiffy. 'We'll go in my car.'

'No,' countered Cadoret, 'Anna and I will follow you in mine.'

'But the whole idea was —'

'Don't give a toss what the idea was. We'll follow you when we're good and ready.'

They watched the tail-lights go away down the drive.

'Well, Anna,' Tito said. 'It looks as though you're going to meet the gang.'

'One thing before we arrive,' he said as they drove along the featureless earth road. 'My ex-fiancée is almost bound to be there. Ceci Jowett. You know her, of course, but I doubt if you know her as well as I do. I just — I just want to make it clear that you're my guest tonight, not her, and there's absolutely no question of my changing horses in mid-stream. I'd much rather be having dinner at home with you, Anna. So if you feel like pushing off at any time, just give me the nod and we'll hop it. Right?'

They came up with Rathbone a little further on. He was changing a wheel. 'Puncture!' he shouted. 'You go on ahead!'

The approach to La Ventolera was much more grandiose than the drive up to La Calandria. The 'big house', as Tito referred to it, was something of a fin-de-siècle monstrosity with mock-Tudor beams, lookout towers, parapets and balconies. Every light in the building was on when they arrived and a band was playing on the verandah. A glittering crowd was milling about, chattering, laughing, smoking and drinking cocktails.

Cadoret drove straight up and stopped on the lawn in front of the house. As he held the door open for Anna, there was a shriek of, 'He's here, everybody!' and Betty Jowett came tripping (almost literally because of the croquet hoops) across the lawn.

A cheer went up and everyone came outside. The band played 'Happy Birthday', and Anna had no option but to stand with Tito as everyone sang it to the guest of honour. When the singing stopped there was a brief lull, during which Paddy Dalligan drawled, 'Who's the floozy he's picked up this time?' Then they were swallowed up in the throng and Tito was swept away by a tide of hugs and kisses. Gifts wrapped in shiny paper were thrust upon him. He was

72

shaken by the hand, patted on the back and punched playfully in the stomach.

Anna was not so much ignored as inspected. People came up to her – Jowetts, Dalligans, Rathbones, Harrisons – and said, 'You're his new governess, are you?' or 'Are you the one Ceci had staying with her?' – and having given her the once-over drifted away.

When the band started again, Tito came straight over and asked her to dance. It was 'Mi Buenos Aires Querido', the same tune Ceci had played on her gramophone the evening she had tried to teach Anna to tango. 'We won't try anything complicated,' he reassured her as they took the floor. 'Don't look at your feet, look at me.'

He was a superb dancer. She relaxed in his arms and allowed him to pull her closer. The guitars sighed and wept; she began to feel something for Tito that she had not felt before. She wondered what her parents would say if they could see their little Anna now, dancing like a harlot in a rich man's castle.

Tito felt her relax and knew at that moment that provided he didn't try to rush things she was as good as his. They stayed on and danced while the band played 'El Dia Que Me Quieras' and 'Volvio Una Noche' and when he took her hand and escorted her from the floor he knew that in the space of ten minutes their relationship had shot ahead – that they were now more than good friends and that she was longing to dance again just as fiercely as he was.

Servants in white coats brought in the asado: whole carcasses of lamb that had been roasted on vertical frames before a huge log fire in the hall. Anna had never seen so much roast meat in her life.

'What are you thinking?' he asked.

'I was comparing this with our Sunday joint at home.'

Betty Jowett joined them and began engaging Tito in conversation about people and events of which Anna had no knowledge. A little while later, Tito turned to her and said, 'Will you excuse me if I dance with my hostess, Anna?' and the moment they had gone, Ceci came over.

'Do you mind if I plonk myself down?'

'Not at all.'

Ceci did so. She looked quizzically at Anna. 'Well! We do seem to have got our feet under the table, don't we?' She glanced round as if to see that the coast was clear. 'How are you? Looking even more irresistible than ever, I'd say. If that's possible, of course. So I presume the job has proved a resounding success?'

'It has turned out well, yes.'

'You certainly seem to have done the trick with Tito, I must say.

Never seen him looking more attentive. If I didn't know you weren't already promised to another, I'd say what everyone else is saying this evening. You know what that is? No, of course you don't, you're far too innocent, aren't you? Well I'll tell you. They're saying that you're angling for a very big fish indeed, my poppet.'

Anna felt her pulse begin to race. She wanted to hit back but knew that was exactly what Ceci wanted. It also dawned on her that Ceci was fiendishly jealous. She was a woman scorned. She wants to see me run from the room in tears, she realized. Well, I won't give her that satisfaction.

'I may say I would agree with them if I didn't know you better, Anna. But you're not an angler are you? That's not your way at all, is it? Oh no! Just having a little flirt, aren't we? And as soon as poor Tito takes the bait no doubt you'll chuck him back into the river with his emotional guts ripped out and dangling on the crook of your little finger, mmm? Oh yes, I'm sure you'll be able to get a really good run for your money out of Tito before you go back to Scotland. Then you can do the same with Angus, can't you? And if they have this war everyone's talking about you may even be able to break his heart for him before he goes off to fight. That would be really something, wouldn't it? Notch up another one, so to speak. Well. I won't prattle on. Nice to talk to you, dear. Enjoy the rest of the party, won't you? Right up to the hilt, what?'

She watched the couples dancing. Tito was now partnering the elderly Mrs Rathbone, whose horsy features were every bit as exaggerated as her son's. Suddenly Anna saw that she was not among fellow countrymen but foreigners. These people were not English but Argentine – however closely their accents echoed those of the home counties, however precisely their clothes followed the latest London fashion. They belonged to a different world. How could she possibly have believed that Tito might be taking a serious interest in her?

Like acid, Ceci's words burnt deeper.

Is she right? she wondered. Am I a flirt? Why did I give in to my parents over Angus? Was it because I wanted to see a bit of life first, wanted to have a fling before settling down?

Suddenly she realized that she was dangerously close to tears. She had never allowed herself to cry, that was the trouble. First she had kept a stiff upper lip over Tim and now she had bottled up all the hurt of being thrown over. Suddenly the force of it hit her and she realized what had happened, what she had lost.

She was grimly determined not to give Ceci the satisfaction of seeing her depart in tears. She looked across the floor and caught Tito's eye. He excused himself to Emelda and came across to her.

'Would you like to go?' he asked.

'Please.'

He took her arm and escorted her outside, along the verandah and across the grass. He held the door of the car for her and got straight in behind the wheel. Within moments the car was bumping away over the grass.

'I'm so sorry, Tito. I'm afraid I've made a fool of myself.'

'Not a bit of it. I'm the one who should be sorry. I should never have brought you here in the first place. It was Ceci, wasn't it? I saw her talking to you. Saw your face. Damn the woman. I might have known it. I wouldn't have had this happen for worlds.'

'I don't think it was entirely her fault –'

'I do. I know Ceci. I know how poisonous she can be when she can't have what she wants.'

They went down the long, straight avenue and out onto the pampa, with the earth road stretching away ahead and the sky bursting with stars. A mile or so on, Tito stopped the car and switched off the engine.

'What was she saying?'

'It really doesn't matter –'

'It matters a lot to me.'

She looked straight ahead, unable to give him an answer. He took her hand and held it between his own. She felt her eyes fill with tears but did not try to fight them back.

'It wasn't just Ceci that upset you, was it? You haven't been happy for the last fortnight. Are you homesick?'

She shook her head.

'I want to help you but I can't if you won't tell me what's wrong.'

She used her handkerchief. He said, 'Let's get out of this damn car.'

They stood together on the grass verge with the dark shapes of grazing steers just visible in the adjoining field and an idle windpump squeaking as the vane turned it back and forth in the night breeze. How long they were silent she never knew. Perhaps it was five minutes, perhaps half an hour. Nor could she later remember what she thought during that long stillness with him under the stars. But eventually, when he spoke, his words came as both a surprise and yet not a surprise, a revelation and yet something that she had half expected.

'I love you, Anna. Did you know that?'

She whispered, 'Yes, I think I did.'

75

'Do you . . . feel anything in return?'

She couldn't trust herself to speak, so she simply nodded her head.

He said, 'I . . . know that you've been through a lot these last few months. Goes for me, too, you know.' Then he put his arms round her. 'All of us need love, isn't that right? All of us need someone to lean on. I'm no exception. I need you. Blanca and Luis need you, too. We all do.'

They were silent again. Later, he said, 'Do you love – what was his name – Angus – very much?'

Did she? Yes, she did love him, that was the trouble. She still loved Angus and would always love him. She loved him in spite of his one-minute letters, his inability to be romantic on paper. She loved him in spite of Miss Constance Drane.

'Well?' he asked.

'I don't know any more.'

'In that case, you don't. If you don't know whether you love him you can't possibly love him. I know I love you. And I know I want you to be my wife. I've never been more positive about anything in my life. You know that I've made mistakes in the past. You know that. Well, you're the one person in the world who can help me put those mistakes behind me.'

She looked away, wondering, wondering.

'I'm not a Catholic,' she said eventually.

'Doesn't matter a scrap.'

She turned back to him. 'Doesn't it?'

He kissed her on the lips. When she returned his kiss she knew that she was severing her last links with Angus, with Scotland, with her parents and her former life.

'Will you then? Will you marry me?'

She whispered 'Yes,' and the tears came again. He kissed her and held her, and she became aware that he was crying too.

They got back into the car and with one hand on the steering wheel and the other arm round Anna, Tito Cadoret drove slowly back to La Calandria.

They kissed on the verandah and they kissed in the hall under the portrait of a Grand Champion bull.

'I never felt happier than I do at this moment,' Tito said between kisses.

She nodded and smiled. 'Me too.'

'Now you're quite sure, aren't you? Not going to have cold feet on me?'

76

She shook her head. 'I never get cold feet, Tito.'

'No regrets about your fiancé?'

She smiled a tight little smile. 'No.'

'What'll you do? Send him a telegram?'

'There's no need. He broke it off. He's engaged to somebody else.'

He frowned. 'I didn't know that. When did you hear?'

'Two weeks ago.'

He pulled his head back from her. 'Why didn't you say anything?'

She shrugged. 'There was no need, was there? Does it make any difference?'

'No,' he said quickly. 'Of course not. I just – well, I was a bit surprised that you didn't say anything at the time, that's all. Oh – what the hell! We love each other and we're going to be married. That's all that matters, isn't it?'

9

IN THE MORNING he brought his diary to the breakfast table. 'No point in having a long engagement is there? Agree?'

'I'm still trying to convince myself that we're engaged, Tito.'

'Must buy you an engagement ring. We'll get one in BA next week. An emerald to go with your eyes. Would you like that? Where were we? Short engagement, agree?'

'All right. Agree.'

'Little mosca,' he said affectionately. 'When did I last tell you I loved you?'

'About two minutes ago.'

He gazed into her eyes. 'Never thought I was a romantic, did you?'

'I wasn't sure.'

'Just goes to show. Hidden depths, you see. Now then. Concentrate, Cadoret. When may I marry you? How about this afternoon? No. Seriously. How about the first Saturday in September?'

'That only gives us three weeks. I'll have to get a wedding dress from somewhere.'

'Then what about the second Saturday. The ninth. Spring wedding. What could be better? We'll move to BA next week and stay there for the Palermo show and the Hurlingham Ball. Sort out your wedding dress and all the other nonsense. Better send some telegrams, pronto. Let's go into the village this morning and fix it right away.'

They sent four cables from the local store in Cadoret: one to the *Buenos Aires Herald*, one to the Edinburgh *Scotsman*, one to her parents and one to Annelise.

The entry in both newspapers read:

The engagement is announced between Martin George Cadoret of Estancia La Calandria, Cadoret, Province of Buenos Aires, and Miss Anna McGeoch of Pentland Neuk, Colinton, Edinburgh. The wedding will take place at the Basilica de Nuestra Señora del Socorro, Buenos Aires, on Saturday 9th September 1939.

Two days later Victorio came back from Cadoret village with a cable for Anna.

DEEPLY SHOCKED BY ANNOUNCEMENT OF YOUR PROPOSED WEDDING BY ROMAN CATHOLIC RITE. IMPLORE YOU TO THINK AGAIN. LETTER FOLLOWS. FATHER.

The Catholic question had seemed insignificant when Tito proposed to her; now she felt a qualm at the prospect of marrying into the Church. But in a way that qualm was exciting in itself: perhaps it was because she was defying her father and uprooting everything she had been taught from her earliest childhood. Perhaps it was because she tasted a sweet revenge on Angus for jilting her so abruptly and mercilessly.

She showed the cable to Tito when they met for lunch.

'Doesn't make any difference, does it?'

'No. I gave in to my father once. I'm not going to give in again.'

'Expect it hurts, all the same.'

'Yes, it does a bit.'

'Want to send a cable back?'

'I don't know what I should say.'

He shrugged. 'Ask for their blessing. Tell 'em how happy you are. You are happy, aren't you?'

She nodded.

'Would you like me to do it for you?'

'No. I'll do it.'

'You're a very independent person, aren't you, Anna?'

'Am I? I hadn't thought about it.'

'Well you are. It's one of the things I like about you.'

'Can I ask a favour, Tito?'

'Of course. Anything you like.'

'I'd like to call you Martin. That is your proper name, isn't it?'

'Yes, but I've been called Tito since I was a baby.'

'Why Tito?'

'Oh – I was always asking to be carried and Nurse was always saying "momentito". Something like that.'

'I think Martin's so much nicer than Tito.'

'Because it sounds less Spanish?'

'Perhaps.'

He leant across the table and kissed her.

'Honestly, Martin! I can see I'm going to have my hands full with you!'

'Christ!' he said. 'You make me feel like a schoolboy. It's got to be Tito, Anna. Martin just isn't me.'

He sent for paper and pencil and helped her compose the reply to her father. 'Let's get it over and done with,' he said. 'The sooner they have a reply, the sooner they'll see it your way.'

The cable went off that day:

> HAVE KNOWN MARTIN LONGER THAN I KNEW ANGUS. WE ARE VERY
> MUCH IN LOVE. HE IS A CHRISTIAN. PLEASE DO NOT WITHHOLD THE
> ASSURANCE OF YOUR LOVE AND BLESSING ON OUR UNION. WITH
> LOVE. ANNA.

Her father's reply arrived within thirty-six hours. She found it perplexing:

> UNABLE TO GIVE BLESSING TO MARRIAGE WHICH DEFIES HOLY
> SCRIPTURE. BE YE NOT UNEQUALLY YOKED TOGETHER. ANGUS ALSO
> BEWILDERED AND SHOCKED. DID YOU NOT RECEIVE HIS LETTER?
> FATHER.

'Bit strong,' Tito commented. 'And what's this about a letter?'

'I think he means the one Angus wrote to me when he broke off our engagement.'

'Have you still got it?'

'No, I tore it up.'

'What did it say?'

'I don't know.'

'What d'you mean? You must know!'

She shook her head. 'I tore it up without reading it. I – I just didn't want to read his excuses. I don't know why my father should be referring to it now though. He's probably grasping at straws. He's virulently anti-Catholic. He'd do almost anything to stop me marrying one.'

'Question is, will he succeed?'

'No.'

'Sure?'

'Quite sure. Tito –'

'What?'

'Thank you for being so understanding.'

'My little mosca! It's nothing!'

'Can I ask another favour?'

'What's that?'

'Not to call me "mosca". I don't feel like a fly.'

He pursed his lips, smiling. 'I'll try and remember that.'

Later that day, she sent one last cable:

SADDENED NOT TO HAVE YOUR BLESSING BUT CONFIDENT THAT THIS
IS WHAT IS RIGHT FOR US BOTH. OUR MINDS ARE MADE UP. LETTER
WAS RECEIVED FROM ANGUS BUT NOT READ. POINTLESS NOW AS
WEDDING ARRANGEMENTS HAVE BEEN CONFIRMED. ALL LOVE. ANNA.

The following morning they packed up the Buick and set off for Buenos Aires with Marga and the two children. As they left the avenue and turned onto the earth road towards Laboulaye there was a shout behind them and when Anna looked back she saw Victorio riding along at full gallop behind the car, waving them goodbye.

Tito put his arm out of the window and waved back.

'Well,' he said as they accelerated away and Victorio dropped behind, 'when we come back, we'll be man and wife, Anna. Think of that.'

That year's Palermo cattle show was the best attended for over a decade. Encouraged by an unusually hot spell, breeders and cattlemen from all over the camp flocked to Buenos Aires.

While estancieros in plus-fours and bowler hats muttered in envy as Bernard Duggan's 'Sittyton' shorthorns carried off prize after prize, their wives and mistresses went on shopping sprees, sipped coffee in the expensive confiterias and gossiped about who was wearing what, who was being bedded by whom and whether padded shoulders would remain in fashion much beyond Christmas.

The hot spell broke suddenly and dramatically. Traffic in the city was interrupted by freak storms and torrential rain. Houses were unroofed at La Plata. Telephone lines were disrupted. It was as if Nature herself were trying to warn that a catastrophe was at hand.

But if Nature was speaking, few in Buenos Aires were listening, and the social life in South America's most sophisticated capital whirled merrily on. The Irish Argentine Cultural Society held its cocktail party, the British Hospital its Charity Ball, the Rural Society its luncheon and, on the last Friday of August, the Hurlingham Club its annual Winter Ball.

Tito had cancelled his room at the Hurlingham Club and had

instead booked a suite at the Plaza, putting himself in one room, Anna in the second and Marga and the children in the third and smallest. On their first day in town, he bought Anna a large emerald set between diamonds. He then sent her off to the main shopping centre on Calle Florida, giving her unlimited credit to fit herself out with a wedding dress, ball dress, going-away outfit and a complete wardrobe of summer clothes.

'Don't stint yourself,' he said. 'We shan't be back in BA for quite a while after the honeymoon, so make the most of it.' She took him at his word and bought a magnificent saffron yellow ball dress with sequins and a plunging neckline that made her feel like an heiress.

She designed the wedding dress herself, keeping it on very simple, classic lines with a tailored bodice, high neck and white satin buttons all the way down the back; and to make sure that Blanca did not feel left out had a bridesmaid's frock made for her in pale blue.

At the hotel, the register read like an Argentine *Who's Who*. Hardly a meal went by without Anna being introduced to more of Tito's friends or relations. There seemed to be an unending convoy of Bobbies and Eddies and Mickies and Jimmies, and each of them invariably had a Dot or a Bet or a Bun in tow.

'Been invited to share a table with Betty and Randy and Stiffy and Emelda at the Ball,' Tito told Anna one evening at dinner. 'Paddy'll be there too. And Ceci. Thought it might be an idea if the two of you made your peace. I've invited the whole party to champagne in my suite beforehand. All right by you?'

She shrugged. 'It'll have to be, won't it?'

''Fraid it will, Anna. Can't afford to let old wounds fester. If we did, no one would speak to anyone else from one end of the year to the next. If it's any consolation, yours truly still finds Ceci heavy going. But that's the way things are in these parts. Chaps just have to make the effort.'

Anna had the impression something similar had been said to Ceci, because when they met in Tito's suite before the ball, Ceci took her to one side, kissed her on both cheeks and apologized. 'It was very cruel of me,' she whispered, then, glancing from side to side to make sure no one would overhear, added, 'Let's forget all about it, can we? From now on I'd like you to look on me as your closest friend and ally. And I mean that.' Then in a louder voice she went on, 'My dear what a simply gorgeous, lovely ring. Do look everybody! Do look at Anna's ring! Isn't it just divine?'

Stiffy opened the champagne and the cork shattered an electric light bulb. Anna was then kissed on both cheeks by Randy, who had appalling breath, Betty, whose lipstick left its mark, Paddy, whose moustache scratched, Emelda, who touched cheeks and kissed the air, and Stiffy, who made such a meal of it that Tito had to pull him away.

'No need to eat the poor girl, Rathbone! She's *my* intended, not yours!'

Betty, who was inclined to be bossy, took charge. 'Now come along, Tito. Stop fooling and tell me all about the wedding plans. Who's giving the bride away? Where are you going on your honeymoon? Who's going to look after the children?' She turned to Anna. 'Typical man. Absolutely hopeless when it comes to practicalities. Have you thought about bridesmaids?'

'Well Blanca must be one.'

'Bit of a risk isn't it? I mean – isn't she rather a handful?'

'Not with Anna,' Tito said. 'She's worked wonders, haven't you, darling?'

'I think there ought to be some older bridesmaids to look after Blanca,' Anna said. 'I was wondering' – she looked at Ceci and Emelda – 'would you two like to take it on?'

'Greatly honoured!' Ceci laughed.

'What about you, Emelda?'

'Darling, I'd be thrilled!'

'Right that's settled then,' Betty said. 'Who's the best man?'

'Stiffy,' said Tito. 'All right, Stiffy?'

Stiffy neighed and parodied himself. 'Like a blessed shot, old boy!'

'Still leaves someone to give the bride away,' Tito said, and put his arm round Anna. 'My little mosca.' He clamped a hand to his mouth. 'Oop! Mustn't call you that!'

'Randy'll do that, won't you?' Betty said, and prodded her husband firmly in the waistcoat. 'And we'll have the children to stay with us while you're away on honeymoon. So there you are, Tito. Everything settled.'

They piled into chauffeur-driven cars and went out to the club. They claimed their table, ordered several bottles of champagne and took to the floor.

'Why is everyone staring?' Anna asked as they danced.

'Because they're green with envy, my darling. You've taken the whole place by storm.'

'I didn't intend to.'

'That's why they're staring. They try. You don't.'

She looked up at him. 'You're not all that bad yourself,' she said, with the result that he held her much closer than before and sent her physical messages that left her in no doubt about the extent of his feelings for her.

Later that evening something happened that slightly tarnished her enjoyment of her first Hurlingham Ball. When she was behind a locked door in the ladies' room two people came in and she overheard part of their conversation.

'. . . what *I* heard was that she was out to get him from the moment she set eyes on him.'

'Well I hope she knows what she's in for.'

'Why? Do you?'

'My dear I wouldn't tell you if I did!'

'You mean –'

'Well. Everyone knows Tito has the sexual appetite of a buck rabbit.'

There was a giggle.

'Someone really ought to tip her the wink.'

'You mean . . . if she doesn't deliver the goods . . .'

'Well. Could end up like the last one, couldn't she?'

'Shhh! There's someone –'

'Oh my God!'

Anna heard another suppressed giggle. A moment later the door banged and the voices were gone.

On the Sunday after the ball, Anna accompanied Tito to Mass for the first time and afterwards they lunched with Annelise and Hugo de Rosslare at the English Club.

'So will she convert to the Catholic faith?' de Rosslare asked.

'Bit early to start thinking about that, Hugo,' Tito said.

'I'd have said it was a bit late.'

'Is she taking instruction?' Annelise asked.

'We're seeing Monsignor Viamonte on Wednesday, mother.'

'I hope she realizes that any children of the marriage will have to be brought up as Catholics?'

'Yes I do realize that, Mrs Cadoret.'

Annelise looked at Anna as if she had only just noticed her presence. 'No going back once the deed's done, you know. Always better to thrash things out first, isn't that right, Hugo?'

The week passed rapidly. Though Marga was a great help with the children, Anna still had to give a lot of her time to Blanca and Luis while trying to fit in visits to the hairdresser, the dressmaker, the dentist and the British Embassy, attend a short course of instruction in the Catholic faith, as well as all the lunches, tea dances, dinners and visits to the theatre to which she and Tito were invited.

Tito played polo at Hurlingham the following Sunday and they were having coffee with Stiffy and Emelda after lunch when the club secretary came into the dining room and clapped his hands for silence.

'Ladies and gentlemen, I have an announcement to make. It has just been confirmed from London that as of five p.m. GMT today, Britain and France will be at war with Germany.'

Somebody said, 'Oh my God. Here we go again.'

Stiffy looked at his watch. 'That's two o'clock our time. Reckon they've got about half a minute's peace left.'

Emelda looked at Anna. 'I say – are you all right?'

'Yes – yes, perfectly.'

Tito patted her knee. 'It won't last longer than a month or two, sweetheart. Now that France and Britain have thrown their hats into the ring, Hitler'll be forced to back down.'

'Absolutely right,' said Stiffy, and winked at Cadoret. 'Don't suppose it'll affect the wedding plans a jot. Mind you,' he added, 'I'll be signing on. I was too young for the last lot. Damned if I'm going to miss the fun this time.'

When they returned to the Plaza that evening, the whole place was seething with gossip. Everyone was asking everyone else what their plans were. Veterans of the previous war were compiling lists of volunteers for this one. German-Argentines had formed a group in one corner of the downstairs bar and Anglo-Argentines a larger, looser group in another, while a third cosmopolitan crowd milled about between the two trying to eavesdrop on both camps.

There was a message at the reception desk for Tito. It was from Rui Botta.

'Damn,' he said when he had read it. 'I have to meet with my lawyer at nine tomorrow. Have to cancel our outing, I'm afraid, Anna.'

They went through to the residents' lounge and he ordered coffee.

'You're very quiet,' he said. 'This war business upsetting you, is it?'

'One can't help thinking. Will you join up like Stiffy?'

'No hurry. Let's wait and see.'

She looked down at her engagement ring. The emerald glinted in the electric light. She had been thrilled with it at first, but now it seemed too large and too flashy. She wondered what Angus was doing, whether he was already married, whether this war would change his plans. And what of her school friends, relations – even her sisters? How many of them would be joining up? How many would survive?

'I think I feel guilty more than anything else.'

'Don't see why you should.'

'Not being there. Not being part of it. I feel I ought to go and help fight the fire.' She looked up. 'I suppose . . . there's no question of our both going to Britain as soon as we're married?'

'Would you like that?'

'At least we'd be doing our bit.'

'What about Blanca and Luis? What about Calandria?'

She sighed. 'Yes. I was forgetting.'

He put his hand over hers. 'You'll feel better once we're married, sweetheart. I'll make sure of that.'

'I'm just confused, Tito. Everything's happened so quickly.'

'Quite understand. Do you know, I'd marry you right away this minute if I could. Never been surer of anything in my whole life.' He lowered his voice. 'I – want you, you know. Right now, I want you.' He looked at her intently. 'I expect you're a bit frightened, aren't you? That's understandable. But there's no need. You won't be marrying someone without . . . without experience in these things. I don't want to boast but, well, I'm not a bad lover.' His glance moved down her body, then up again into her eyes. 'You are a virgin, aren't you, Anna?'

She blushed furiously.

He took her hands. 'It'll be wonderful for you. I'll make sure of that.' He stared intently into her eyes. 'Shall we go up?'

She accepted his hand as the lift doors closed. They went along the corridor to her room and he came in with her and shut the door behind him.

He stood with her, his hands on her shoulders.

'This time next week . . .'

'I know.'

'So . . . not long to wait.'

He started kissing her. Suddenly she wanted him. More than that: she wanted to put a seal on her decision to marry him. She wanted to burn her bridges once and for all so that there could be no question of running away back over them. The door was locked. Colinton was a million miles away. She looked up at Tito and knew exactly what he was thinking.

'We don't have to wait,' she whispered.

When Consuela showed him into Botta's office on the dot of nine the following morning, Cadoret was surprised to see Toni Lambretti also present. Lambretti was lolling in a swivel chair with a coffee at his elbow. The end of Botta's cigar smouldered in an ashtray on his desk.

'We have a problem,' Botta said.

'The interest on your loan,' Lambretti added.

Cadoret accepted a coffee from Consuela. 'What about it? I'm up to date on payments.'

Botta cut the end off a new cigar and took his time lighting it. Lambretti said, 'London has doubled the bank rate.'

'I heard –'

'*Claro*. Then you will understand why we have been forced to follow suit.'

'I'm already paying six per cent.'

Lambretti glanced at his fingernails. 'I think we have known each other long enough to do without the formalities, Tito, don't you? I would much prefer it if you called me Toni. Discussions such as these are always easier if they are conducted on friendly terms.' He turned a signet ring round and round his little finger. 'Our assets in London have been frozen. We have no alternative but to increase our interest rate in line with Paris and London.'

'Are you doing this to all your clients or just the ones with connections in Britain?'

Lambretti glanced at Botta and smiled. 'Naturally we can't reveal information of a confidential nature.'

'All right, so how does this affect me?'

'England has doubled her rate. We must double ours.'

'Double it! That'll bring it up to twelve per cent!'

'Twelve and a half per cent, yes.'

'But this is monstrous! What if I can't pay?'

'When a client is unable to pay interest, we reserve the right to ask him to realize capital in order to settle the loan.'

Cadoret felt sweat breaking out. 'I can't do that. I'd have to get my mother to sell land, and land values are plummeting. I've been selling stock underweight as it is.'

Lambretti glanced at Botta. 'Let's talk about it, Tito. Maybe we can help you.'

Botta said, 'We're on your side. We don't want to see you go under. Just listen to what Toni has to say first, okay?'

'*Bueno*,' said Lambretti, 'the situation may not be as bad as you suppose. You tell me you have been selling stock. Have you been replacing it?'

'I haven't been able to. You've put me in a straitjacket.'

'In that case we can certainly help you. It's clear to me that your estancia is being under-farmed. What is required is to release the capital tied up in stock without depleting the herds grazing the land.'

'Which is impossible.'

Lambretti polished his spectacles with a large white handkerchief. 'Have you never heard of capitalization? You must put your land to better use. Sell your herds and put your money to work. Hire out your land to farmers who are foolish enough to tie up capital in livestock. Don't shake your head, Tito. This is the only way out for you. The alternative is to be made bankrupt. Do you want that?'

'There is a further proposal we should like to make,' Botta said. 'We don't want you to default. We have invested in you so we have everything to gain from helping you. So, we propose to place an administrator in charge of your property, to act as our agent on the spot and to oversee the efficient running of your estancia.'

'Administrators have to be paid a salary,' Cadoret said. 'I thought we were trying to economize.'

'Yes, but if the estancia is inefficiently run through the lack of an administrator and if as a result of that inefficiency you default, that would be a false economy, wouldn't you agree?'

'Can I choose my own man?'

Botta shook his head. 'We already have someone in mind. My cousin, Jorge Stefenelli. An excellent tennis player and a first class accountant. We have such a high opinion of him that if you accept him as administrator, we are prepared to make a reduction in interest. One and a half – perhaps two per cent.'

Cadoret put his head in his hands and tried to think clearly.

The light from the desk lamp glinted in the lenses of Toni Lambretti's glasses. 'We're not running a charity, Tito. If you have a complaint I think you must direct it at the British Prime Minister for making his declaration of war.'

They sat back and looked at him. He had the impression they were both enjoying themselves hugely.

'So . . . may we take it that you agree to our proposals?' Lambretti asked.

'I don't have any alternative, do I?'

Botta blew smoke upward into the fan. 'You should be more optimistic, Tito. Things could be much worse. You might still be married to that Salgado woman. Which reminds me, we haven't congratulated you on your forthcoming marriage. You're a very lucky man, you know. Not many people get two bites at a cherry. I think you must' – Botta changed to English – '"pack up your troubles in your kit bag and smile." Yes?'

10

THE BASILICA DE NUESTRA SEÑORA DEL SOCORRO was a fashionable church, and quite a few of the guests gathered in the confiteria across the road for coffee and a gossip before the service.

The wedding ceremony started at seven thirty prompt. The altar was crowded with orange blossom and the church ablaze with candles. The bride wore white. The organ played the anthem from 'Pomp and Circumstance' as she came up the aisle on Randy Jowett's arm. The press was there in force and photographs were allowed during the ceremony.

As it was a mixed marriage, High Mass was not permitted, so the whole thing took little more than twenty minutes. While the flash-guns popped and she made her promise, Anna experienced a sensation of not being really present or of playing a full part in what was happening. After the couple had exchanged their marriage vows, the choir sang the Ave Maria, and while they were signing the register a soloist sang 'Jesu Joy of Man's Desiring'.

The wedding party emerged from the sacristy, Anna's veil now lifted back, her arm in Tito's. Following behind her came the bridesmaids, all in pale blue, with Blanca (who that morning had cut a large chunk out of her fringe with a dressmaker's scissors) held firmly between Ceci and Emelda. Then, to the thunderous joy of the Halleluiah Chorus played fortissimo, the newly wedded Señor and Señora Cadoret went down the aisle, pausing for a minute at the door for more photographs to be taken.

A black limousine was waiting to whisk them away. Once outside the church, an official encouraged them to leave the plaza as quickly as possible, as another wedding was due to start immediately. The next bride drove up before Anna and Tito had been driven off, and seconds later the organ was blasting out 'Land of Hope and Glory' all over again.

'I thought they'd played that one specially for me,' Anna said as the car moved off.

Cadoret patted her knee. 'Oh – they always play that one at

weddings. Just because it's by Purcell doesn't mean the English have the exclusive right to use it.'

'But it isn't by Purcell! It's by Elgar!'

'You're wrong there, my sweet.' Tito took the form of service out of his inside pocket. 'There you are. Proof. "Song from Pomp and Circumstance by Henry Purcell."' He sat back in his seat, pursing his lips and chuckling at her in triumph.

They were driven at breakneck speed to the Hurlingham Club for the reception. Stiffy gave Blanca a new doll to replace the battered Mimi, but Blanca didn't take to it. She demanded Mimi back, but Mimi had been deliberately left behind in the hotel. Blanca threw a tantrum. Nothing anyone could say or do would console her. She kicked and screamed and threw the doll on the floor. She demanded Mimi back, and when she didn't get her, she pulled the new doll's head off. Anna tried to console her but was punched for her efforts. Paddy Dalligan volunteered to drive all the way back into Buenos Aires to collect Mimi, and by the time he returned the speeches were over and the bride and groom about to depart.

Ceci helped Anna change out of her wedding dress.

'Darling, you are a wonderful, wonderful bride,' she whispered. 'And I really did mean it when I said I wanted us to be friends. Let's keep in close touch, can we? I'd like to make up for all those beastly things I said to you. All right?'

Tito's original idea for the honeymoon had been to splash out and make a grand tour. He had envisaged a flight westward in a privately hired aeroplane to Mendoza and a week of bliss in the crisp sunshine of the wine-growing uplands. Then they would cross the Andes and go into Chile. He had imagined dancing under the stars in Valparaiso and midnight-swimming in the Pacific. After that they would take another flight, southward this time to the bleak but beautiful landscape of Tierra del Fuego. They would go to the very lip of the continent, look out from Cape Horn itself. He would let Argentina seduce Anna as only Argentina could, so that she would never again be tempted by thoughts of returning to Scotland.

But the outbreak of war and the interest rate bombshell Lambretti had exploded under him had forced him to alter his plans. They went, instead, to a guesthouse called El Tropezón ('The Blunder') on an island in the Paraná delta. Run by three sisters and patrolled by numerous semi-domesticated cats, El Tropezón catered for large parties of tourists in the summer, but when Tito and Anna arrived by boat from Tigre it was empty apart from a semi-resident poet, who was to be seen sitting outside at a table in a large white hat drinking Pernod during the afternoons and who never once acknowledged their presence.

There were two flagpoles in the front garden by the little wooden landing stage, one of which flew the blue and white Argentine national flag and the other that of the principal guests. Soon after the Cadorets' arrival, in deference to the English bride, the lady of the house had the gardener hoist a tatty Union Jack which in spite of Anna's objections remained flying upside-down throughout their stay.

They had not made love again since Anna's first time in the Plaza Hotel and Tito had high hopes of a repeat performance; but he was to be disappointed.

'I'm sorry,' Anna said on the first night. 'I'm *hors de combat* for a few days.'

He wasn't very pleased. 'Did you know this was going to happen?'

'Well, I couldn't be sure.'

'Might have told me it was on the cards, at least.'

'Are you very cross with me?'

'Does put the kibosh on things rather, doesn't it?'

'I'm afraid it can't be helped.'

'So you said.'

El Tropezón was a large wooden bungalow on stilts, with a dozen or so tables on a boarded verandah, a bar and a sizeable restaurant. The wide, brown Paraná flowed in front of the garden and mosquitoes whined and hovered everywhere. At night the whole island rang with the sound of insects. For entertainment, there was an old upright piano, somewhat out of tune, on which Anna played in the early evenings. There was also a gramophone with an old-fashioned trumpet loudspeaker and a few records, including Harry Lauder's 'I Have Heard the Mavis Singing', and 'Keep Right on to the End of the Road'. These Anna liked so much that Tito bought them for a few pesos from the landlady and made her a present of them. Apart from these diversions and a picnic outing on the river, there was little to do, and Anna's condition meant that the romantic week of lovemaking Tito had planned was out of the question.

On their fourth day a mixed party of eight Germans arrived on the afternoon ferry. They had brought their own records and that evening danced to Bavarian folk music.

The party went on far into the night. One record was played over and over and over again amid squeals of joy from the fräuleins and gusts of mirth from the menfolk.

Some time after three in the morning the noise gradually died down, only to start again before seven when the men went for a swim in the river.

'This is ridiculous,' Tito said at breakfast. 'What would you say to an early return to La Calandria?'

Anna brightened. 'I'd say yes!'

'In that case let's damn well go. There's a boat at ten. All right by you?'

They packed their bags and within half an hour were boarding the ferry from the end of the wooden pier.

As the boat chugged away across the river to enter the narrower waterways which led to the water terminal at Tigre, Anna took a last glance back at El Tropezón.

She touched Tito's arm. 'Look.'

The Union Jack had been hauled down and a clean new Swastika was flying in its place.

They landed at Tigre and lunched by the river on steaks and salad at the Dorado boating club, then motored into Buenos Aires and checked back into the Hotel Plaza, where they met Stiffy and Emelda for dinner. The meal finished after midnight. Afterwards, Stiffy suggested they all go out for a night on the town, a proposal to which Tito readily agreed.

'Wear a hat,' Emelda advised Anna.

'A hat? Why on earth?'

'It'll stop you being mistaken for a call girl.'

They took a taxi and went to a downtown nightclub called El Tabarís. Tito and Stiffy had just ordered orange curaçao for the ladies and whisky for themselves when Teddy Harrison and Paddy Dalligan appeared. Teddy was small and ginger-haired with a moustache and a dirty laugh. 'Hello-hello-hello!' he exclaimed. 'Fancy meeting you here. Back on the old stamping ground already, TC?'

They pulled up chairs and sat on them back-to-front. Paddy, who was built like a jockey and balding prematurely, looked at Anna in the way most Argentine men look at women in public places.

'Heard the latest?' Teddy was saying. 'The Ambassador's drumming up support for a volunteer regiment. Protection of British interests in the South Atlantic, that sort of thing. Thought we'd take the next sailing in the *Darwin* and muster ourselves at Port Stanley. Bloody good wheeze, don't you think? Good sport to be had on the islands so they tell me. Going to call ourselves the "Tabarís Highlanders". Could be quite an outing. What do you say boys? Are you on?'

Stiffy was very taken with the idea, and was persuaded to accompany Teddy and Paddy down to the men-only basement to meet other prospective volunteers. Tito went with them, and within a minute of their departure Anna and Emelda had been joined by two middle-aged Romeos who wouldn't take no for an answer. One of them was very keen to get Anna to dance. He shifted his chair closer and put his hand on her knee. Anna removed it and stood up.

'Let's take a taxi back,' she said to Emelda. 'I'm not staying here any longer.'

'What about the men?' Emelda said when they were outside.

'I expect they'll manage without us just this once, don't you?'

Tito arrived at the hotel an hour later when Anna had just stepped out of the bath. He talked to her through the open door as she towelled herself dry.

'What happened? Why the disappearing act?'

'I could ask the same question of you, couldn't I? I was under the impression that we were on our honeymoon. It's not exactly the done thing to leave your bride and go drinking with the boys, is it?'

'What can I say?'

'Sorry, perhaps?'

'Point taken,' he said.

She came out of the bathroom wrapped in a towel.

'You look wonderful.'

'*You* smell revolting.'

He hung his head.

'Tito –'

'Yes?'

'Was that the place where you met Magdalena?'

'What gave you that idea?'

'I don't know. Something Teddy said. Your old stamping ground.'

'The Tabarís is one of the old haunts, certainly.'

'But did you meet her there?'

'Is it important?'

'You've hardly told me anything about her. Did you love her?'

He thought a minute. 'I lusted after her.'

'Do you lust after me?'

'Yes, but I love you as well. I didn't love Magdalena the way I love you.'

'*Did* you meet her there?'

He nodded.

'Don't let's go there again.'

'We won't.'

'And you won't go there on your own?'

'No.'

He offered her his arms, and she went to him. 'I want us to be close,' she whispered. 'Everything shared, no secrets. Close, close, close.'

'I want that, too.'

'Will you volunteer for this thing Teddy was talking about?'

'Don't suppose so.'

'What does that mean?'

He sighed and laughed. 'It means no.'

She went into the bedroom and he followed. She turned. 'Have a bath, clean your teeth and come to bed with me.'

His mouth fell open. 'You mean – am I in luck?'

She shook her head in mock amazement. 'Honestly, Tito! Do you think of nothing else? You'll just have to wait and see, won't you?'

They could have prolonged the honeymoon but each had reasons for wanting to get back to La Calandria. Tito wanted to be on hand for the arrival of his new administrator and Anna was concerned that with every extra day of her absence Blanca might regress further; so both were happy to make an early start the following morning and arrived at La Calandria in the evening when the gathering clouds were purple and gold and the pampa was a cobalt green in the evening light.

'You have to see it to believe it, don't you?' Anna said. 'It's almost frightening, it's so beautiful.'

Tito grunted. 'We'll have a storm tonight.'

On Anna's prompting, he had telephoned from the hotel to warn Catarina of their early return, and the housekeeper was waiting for them in a clean apron when the Buick came up the avenue and parked in front of the house. The dogs came bounding round from the kitchens, barking and wagging and going into paroxysms of joy at the return of their master.

'What a surprise!' Catarina exclaimed. 'We didn't expect you back for another week.' She kissed Anna on both cheeks. 'Now look, niña Anna, here's bread and salt. Is a special Russian welcome we give you.'

Marga and the children were still at La Ventolera with Betty and Randy. 'We'll collect them first thing in the morning,' Tito said.

He led the way upstairs and they went into the main bedroom.

'Come here, Mrs Cadoret. Welcome to La Calandria.' He kissed her again, then said, 'Damn.'

'What's the matter?'

'Never carried you over the threshold, did I? All that bloody nonsense about bread and salt distracted me. Now then. What do you say? Bath, drink, dinner, bed, sex. How does that appeal?'

'Not sex, Tito. Love.'

He grinned. 'Well . . . same difference.'

She glanced round at the room.

'Needs a lick of paint, doesn't it? Whole house does. Tell you what, you can choose the colour scheme. That can be your department.'

Piotr came up with their cases. While Tito bathed, Anna unpacked a few things and hung up a dress in the wardrobe, at the back of which she discovered a framed portrait of a glamorous young woman in a low-cut red dress.

'I found this,' she said when Tito emerged from the bathroom.

He was using the corner of the towel to get water out of his ear. He swore under his breath. 'Thought that'd been chucked out long ago.'

'Is it Magdalena?'

'Yes, it's Magdalena.'

'She was very beautiful.'

'Not a patch on you, mosca. Let's chuck it out.'

'What about Blanca?'

'How does she come into it?'

'Shouldn't we keep it for her?'

'I wouldn't bother.'

Anna looked again at the portrait. 'I think if I were Blanca, I would treasure it. Perhaps we should hang it in her room.'

'Oh no. I'm not having that. It gives me the willies everytime I see it. I'll have Piotr stick it in the loft.'

She thought about Magdalena in the bath. Somewhere in the recesses of her mind, a little misgiving lurked. What exactly had been the meaning of those remarks she had overheard in the ladies' room at the Hurlingham Ball? What really lay at the root of all Blanca's hurt and anger?

She got out of the bath, dressed, and went downstairs. Tito was reading his mail in the sitting room. He had poured a glass of sherry for her.

'Good news,' he said. 'Father's probate's come through. There's a telegram there for you. Arrived just after we left. What all the waving from Victorio was about, apparently.'

'It's probably another wedding telegram that went to the wrong address,' she said, slitting it open. But it was not, and as she read it she felt a dull sense of shock.

UNDERSTAND YOU NEVER READ MY LETTER STOP IT EXPLAINED THAT
ANNOUNCEMENT OF MY ENGAGEMENT WAS RESULT OF PRACTICAL
JOKE PLAYED ON ME BY MY FELLOW OFFICERS STOP HAVE REMAINED
AND WILL ALWAYS REMAIN TOTALLY FAITHFUL TO YOU STOP I
BESEECH YOU IF IT IS NOT TOO LATE TO THINK AGAIN STOP I SHALL
NEVER LOVE ANYONE BUT YOU STOP ALL MY LOVE STOP FOR EVER
STOP ANGUS

Tito was still engrossed in his letters. She stood up. 'I'm just popping
out for a breath of fresh air, Tito. Won't be long.'

He didn't look up. 'Help yourself, mosca. It's a free country.'

She walked into the garden and stood on the lawn and looked up at
the stars and the gathering clouds. She could hear the clatter of pans in
the kitchen behind her and the call of an owl somewhere over to her left
in the privet wood. Without taking any conscious decision she began
walking. She went across the park and down the earth ride between
the bending eucalyptus trees. She crossed the polo field, climbed over
a gate, scattered a flock of sheep, and kept on walking. She came to
another fence and beyond it a mill square with the windpump vanes
whirring in the night wind. She skirted a herd of steers, startled a flock
of Ibis and sent them flapping upward on ragged wings. She felt that
if she had come to a cliff edge she would happily have walked straight
over it.

But there was no cliff edge – only the endless, flat pampa, the long
straight tracks, the rectangular fields broken only here and there by
a mill or a trough or an earth road.

She lost sense of time. When she came to gates she climbed them
automatically and went on walking. The thunder, which had been
muttering in the distance for some time, grew louder. Lightning
split the black marble vault of the sky. She went on walking. A
wind sprang up and howled round her and then, as suddenly as
it had come, subsided. And still she walked. A few hailstones fell,
heralding the downpour. There was a sound of tearing calico and an
earsplitting crash. The lightning stabbed vertically downward into the
pampa and for a moment a stampeding herd of steers was brilliantly
illuminated.

The hailstones were the size of marbles and there was no shelter
from them. She cowered, her arms over her head for protection. Within
minutes the pampa was white with melting hail and she was soaked
through and shivering.

Later, the hail turned to rain.

She walked on, not knowing or caring where she was going or how much time had passed since leaving La Calandria. She would have liked to give way to tears, but was unable. All she could feel was an icy numbness of spirit.

The storm moved on. The rain eased, and stopped altogether. How many gates had she climbed? Was she heading north, south, east or west?

She sat down on a patch of tufted grass and leant against a fencepost. Apart from the wind moaning in the fencewires, there was silence. As the storm moved away, a patch of cloudless sky appeared and stars, looking freshly polished, shone out.

She was still clutching the telegram in her hand. She uncrumpled it and stared at it, just able to make out the words. Then she dug into the soft, wet soil with her fingers and buried it.

A dog barked from quite nearby. She realized that she must try to get back to La Calandria, but had no idea which direction to take, so she continued along the path in the direction of the barking and came to an area of rough ground where the path forked. The dog was somewhere ahead among the dark mounds to her left. She wondered if it was a contractor's encampment, or perhaps a mill square with the mill removed. The dog was barking at her, stopping, and barking again. She lifted her head and sniffed: there was a strange, acrid smell in the air. She went along the track a little further, and the smell grew stronger. The dog snarled and barked at her from the darkness. She took a few more steps forward and realized too late that she was off the track. The dog's barking seemed to come from a different direction. She went forward a little further and stumbled suddenly against something not quite soft and not quite hard. At first she thought that it was an upholstered sofa that had been dumped. But it was not a sofa. It was a carcass.

She drew back, turned to the right, and came upon another carcass. Wherever she turned, there were bones, rib cages, skulls, stinking carcasses. The stench of them filled her nostrils. Somewhere close, the dog was snarling and barking. She scrambled and stumbled among bones and skeletons, shrinking away as her hand touched a rib or her foot struck against a gaping mouth.

Having no idea which way to turn, she stood still and recited the twenty-third psalm.

'The Lord is my shepherd,' she said aloud. 'I shall not want. He maketh me to lie down in green pastures: he leadeth me beside the still waters. He restoreth my soul: he leadeth me in the paths of righteousness for his name's sake. Yea, though I walk through the valley of the shadow of death, I will fear no evil: for thou art with me; thy rod and thy staff they comfort me . . .'

A torch beam snapped on some way off and a voice came out of the darkness.

'Hullo? Anyone there?'

When she awoke, the sun was streaming into the room and a calandria was laughing in the trees outside the window.

It had been Randy Jowett's cadet manager who had found her. There had been a long, uncomfortable ride in the saddle behind him and on arrival at La Ventolera – on Betty's insistence – a hot bath and bed. Now all emotion seemed to have been drained from her. She had no more tears left.

She heard voices outside the room and a moment later there was a tap on the door and Tito looked in. When he saw that she was awake he came quickly to her bedside.

'Sweetheart! What happened?'

She shook her head.

'What on earth was in that telegram?'

He was looking down at her, his eyes intense. From this angle he looked like a falcon about to stoop.

'Who was it from?'

'Angus,' she said. 'He was trying to change my mind.'

'Have you still got it?'

'No. I – I buried it.'

He frowned. 'You *buried* it?'

'I – just wanted to put it out of my mind, Tito.'

'What did it say?'

'Oh – that he thought I was making a mistake –'

'What a nerve! After what he did to you! And you ran off into the pampa and got lost.' He patted her hand. 'Poor mosca.'

'I'm so sorry, Tito –'

'Never mind. You're by no means the first person to get lost in the pampa. Right. Well. Have a nice long day in bed and we'll make a fresh start in the morning, all right?'

After he was gone she lay and stared up at the ceiling and thought about Angus. The calandria squawked in the tree outside her window. 'No going back,' it seemed to say. 'No going back, no going back.'

I I

THE NEW ADMINISTRATOR, Jorge Stefenelli, drove up in a Mercedes four
days later.

'I can make you or I can break you,' he said that first day when he
and Cadoret went out on horseback to view the estancia. 'I have the
Banco Pergamino behind me and contacts in every part of the business
world. I can do great things for you, Señor Cadoret, but only if you
will trust me. If not' – he shrugged – 'it will be you who are the loser,
not me.'

They made a tour of the property. They paused to watch the
blacksmith at work; looked in on the peons' kitchen, inspected
the carniceria where three red-handed butchers wielded razor-sharp
knives. Stefenelli was introduced to the foreman and the pony boy. He
was taken to see the stud bulls, the dairy and the polo ponies. They
went down the eucalyptus ride and across the polo pitch.

'Who lives here?' Stefenelli asked, pointing at a small dwelling and
a few outhouses.

'My capataz and his family. My father built it for them ten
years ago.'

'It's in a good position.'

'Yes, but Navarro's a first-class capataz. He's earned it.'

Stefenelli nodded. 'I shall need a house, of course. I can't do a
proper job as administrator if I'm not on the spot. Perhaps you can
come up with a few proposals for a site, Señor Cadoret? If we start
now, I could be in by the end of the summer.' He looked again at the
foreman's house. 'That's certainly a very attractive site. Perhaps we
could move your capataz out and rebuild. At the moment, that site
is wasted.'

'Couldn't agree to that,' Cadoret said. 'I rely heavily on my
capataz –'

'Yes, but from now on you must rely on me. I shall require
power of attorney, you understand that? I think Toni Lambretti
made that clear?'

'Yes, he did mention it.'

99

'Excellent. The sooner we fix that up the better. There's also the matter of my salary. That will be paid out of interest on the loan, and I shall take an additional fifteen per cent of profits as an efficiency incentive.'

Cadoret's face looked like thunder. 'And what do I get in return?'

Stefenelli launched into a string of promises. In return, he said, Cadoret would receive excellent service. He had already noted several areas where improvements could be made. He would re-invest on the patron's behalf. He would modernize and streamline. He would cut away dead wood and start new projects as and when he saw fit.

'But first, there must be trust. Trust, and friendship also. With your trust – and I hope with your friendship as well, Señor Cadoret – I will build you an empire. You will be the emperor, and I will be your prime minister.' The administrator placed a forefinger confidentially against the side of his nose. 'And if ever there is any service of a confidential nature I can render, any private information you wish to obtain, any delicate arrangement that you might wish to be made, then I shall be only too happy to act on your behalf.'

The yerra was the time of earmarking, de-horning, vaccinating and castrating. It took place in October every year and marked the beginning of spring. It was a busy time, with the peons parting and corralling all day, manhandling the animals with brutal efficiency, knocking them over, clipping, marking, injecting, severing.

That year at La Calandria Cadoret decided to revive his father's practice of giving the men an 'asado con cuero' to celebrate the completion of the yerra. It was also a good excuse for a party, and a way of showing off his new wife to the workforce.

A huge log fire was built and a harrow used upon which to place the whole ox that was roasted in its hide for three days. The people sat down to the evening feast at trestle tables under the eucalyptus trees. Every man employed at La Calandria was invited with his woman and his family. Cadoret and Anna shared a table with Stefenelli and Father Michael Tuite, the Irish priest from Cadoret village.

Father Michael was a benevolent, bald-headed soul who liked wine and children. Like every other man on the estancia, he was very taken with Anna.

'Sure, you've a lovely wife here, Tito,' he remarked for at least the third time that day.

'That's why I married her, Father.'

The priest winked at Anna. 'So when will we be having the pleasure of converting her to the one true faith?'

100

'Think you'll have to ask her that yourself, won't you?'

'Well?' said Father Michael, turning to her. 'When are we going to convert you?'

'Oh – I'm very happy with what I believe already, thank you, Father.'

'But you'll be missing your church attendance, isn't that so? Why not come to Mass on a Sunday? That would be a fine example to the little girl, would it not?'

'I'd have to think about that, Father.'

'Well don't think too long, child.'

A guitarist and bandoneonista who had been hired from the village for the occasion started playing and the peons and their womenfolk were glancing across towards the top table.

'We're expected to start off the dancing,' Tito said to Anna, and as they rose from the table and she accepted Tito's hand there was a burst of applause.

'*¡Viva!*' shouted one of the cattlemen in a hoarse voice. '*¡Viva la patrona!*'

Anna loved dancing with Tito. He knew how to hold her and guide her and transmit his intentions to her with his body. On the dance floor, he made her feel like the most important person in the world. They had danced at La Ventolera, at Hurlingham and on the creaking boards of El Tropezón. There had been tea dances in Buenos Aires and dances at the Laguna Blanca club, and since returning from their honeymoon they had sometimes danced to records after dinner. One mad evening when the nightjars and insects were gurgling and buzzing they had danced outside on the patio in the night wind and afterwards Tito had carried her to the swimming-pool changing room where they had made glorious, unforgettable love.

Now, taking the floor alone with him, moving her body to match his, staring eye to eye with him, turning her head dramatically aside for the chassé, Anna left the last worries about war and regrets about Angus behind. She was Tito's wife, she was the patrona and – yes – she enjoyed showing herself off to these hot-faced working men and women with their bad teeth and their lascivious eyes and their coarse, work-hardened hands. What had happened had happened. There was no point in dwelling over what might have been. The only way forward was to put it all behind her and make the best possible success of what she had. And she was already making a go of things. She had established herself as the mistress of the household and commanded the respect of Catarina and Marga and the other servants. Though being a mother to the children made tremendous demands

101

on her, she was making progress with Blanca and was becoming fond of Luis.

There was enthusiastic applause as they returned to their table, and Jorge Stefenelli went on clapping long after everyone else had stopped. He turned to Tito. 'I would not have believed it possible for a woman not born in Argentina to be able to tango so well. So might I have the pleasure of the next dance with your wife?'

Tito handed her over with a glance that told her that it would be diplomatic to accept, so she did so with a good grace.

Before taking her arm Stefenelli took an envelope from his inside pocket. 'By the way, I have something for you, Don Tito. My apologies. It took a little longer to obtain than I expected.' He handed over an envelope then turned to Anna. 'May I have the pleasure, señora?'

He was a few years younger than Tito, good-looking in a Latin way and, like every other Argentine she had encountered, he suffered from an obsessive need to prove his masculinity. He took it for granted that she wanted to be held close and would be flattered by the fact that he was sexually aroused. It was as if he presumed that this first dance must necessarily lead, one day, to a greater intimacy.

They spoke a mixture of Spanish and English.

'I think I will enjoy myself here,' he said. 'La Calandria has great potential, you know that? It will be good for me and it will be good for your husband. And good for you too, Anna – can I call you that? But for it to be good, we have to work together. There has to be trust, you know? Trust and also friendship.' She caught a gust of garlic on his breath. 'It's like a marriage, I think. You agree?'

Sitting at the trestle table, Tito watched them dancing for a few minutes before opening the envelope. Since his first talk with Stefenelli, the administrator had repeatedly asked him if there was any service of a confidential nature which he could render; and Tito, more to give him something to do than anything else, had finally asked him to obtain a copy of the telegram Anna had buried. This was what the envelope contained.

Reading those few stark lines caused a sense of shock and disappointment and jealousy.

So she had misled him. She had told less than the truth. Anna, the one person in the world he had believed would never lie. He wondered what he should do. Confront her? Bring it all out, accuse her, have a showdown?

No, that was not the way. It would kill the marriage stone dead, and he didn't want that. Women, like polo ponies, could be cured of

102

bad habits if you caught them early enough. This telegram proved that Anna was no exception. She was no angel, after all, but a mere mortal like anyone else. The most important attribute of a polo pony was that it should enjoy the game. If a pony didn't enjoy polo it was pointless persevering with it. You might as well sell it or shoot it or use it as a hack. But Anna obviously did enjoy the game. In his thoughts, he privately regarded her as a good ride.

He spent several days thinking about the telegram. Inevitably, his attitude towards Anna changed as a result of it. After a while he realized that so long as she did not know that he had discovered her secret, he had a useful hold on her. He had always been slightly in awe of her, but now he saw that there was no need. She was not the innocent he had always thought. He wanted to forgive her, but at the same time felt that she was now in debt to him. The question was, should he force her to repay that debt? No, there was no need, was there? Because while she was in debt to him, he had power over her. This telegram was bound to be on her conscience. By not revealing that he knew about it, he could keep her in debt. Secrecy, he discovered, was a source of power.

A day or two later when he was out on horseback revising the plantel heifers, it dawned on him that he was in a very strong position. Now that he knew what he knew, he could demand anything he liked of her. If she made any objection, there was always this lever ready to hand.

He turned his horse and headed back towards the house. Why not put it into practice straight away? After all, what was a wife for if a man couldn't make use of her when he felt like it?

Anna was in the schoolroom. She was leaning over Blanca's shoulder helping her to make her letters. She heard Tito coming along the passage and when she looked round he was standing at the door in his boots and bombachas looking fiery and hot.

He beckoned with his finger. She frowned and glanced down at Blanca to show him that she was busy, but he beckoned again.

'What is it?' she asked when they were out of the room.

He kissed her on the lips. 'I want you.'

'What do you mean?'

'What do you think I mean?'

'Tito, darling – I'm in the middle of lessons.'

'They can wait. I can't. I want you now.'

'Honestly Tito – this isn't the time –'

'Go upstairs and get ready,' he said. 'I'll wait down here for a couple of minutes. Go on. It won't take long. I just feel like it.'

'Darling, you're impossible!'

'Don't argue, mosca. You know you'll enjoy it every bit as much as I will.'

She flushed. 'Go and talk to Blanca, then. And – and take the ink away from her, will you?'

After that he made love to her whenever he felt like it. They reached a stage when all he had to do was appear at the schoolroom door or look at her in a certain way in order to inform her that he wanted her.

But a month or so later she asked if he could be less rough with her when they made love.

'What's the trouble? I thought you enjoyed it.'

She shook her head. 'It's not that,' she said in her quiet Scottish way. 'I think I'm pregnant.'

December brought the hot weather. The nightjars gargled and the cicadas rang all night, and by day the woodpeckers and mocking birds flitted about among the trees, laughing and chattering incessantly.

The polo season was over for another year and with it the ritual of lunch at Laguna Blanca every Sunday. Instead, those of the landowning community at Cadoret who had not departed for the beaches of Uruguay or Mar del Plata for their summer holiday took it in turns to play host for the Sunday asado, with tennis or swimming for those who felt like it afterwards.

On the third Sunday of December, it was the turn of the Cadorets. Catarina and Marga and the two extra maids Anna had found it necessary to employ spent the morning preparing the salads and the steaks and Piotr lit the log fire in the garden in time to provide a large heap of glowing embers over which to cook the steaks.

The cars arrived some time after twelve and the landowners, their children, their governesses and their nurses came strolling over the lawn to join the party under the trees.

Randolph and Betty (who was now five months pregnant) arrived with their two-year-old daughter; Tom and Amy Dalligan drove up in a station wagon with their rodeo of five children – all under eight; comfortable chairs were found for George and Bunny Rathbone; Auntie Dot, Annelise's sister, appeared fresh from High Mass in Laboulaye in gloves, high-heeled shoes and carrying a large crocodile handbag; and finally Barty and Avril Harrison, Teddy's father and step-mother, arrived with their two reluctant teenage daughters, Penny and Rita, in tow.

Conspicuous by their absence were Stiffy Rathbone and Teddy Harrison, who had sailed aboard the *Darwin* with the Tabarís Highlanders to join the Falklands garrison, and Hugo de Rosslare and Annelise, who were supposed to be driving down from San Luis but had not yet shown up.

The children dashed off with Blanca to look at pets and ponies; the wives settled down in deck chairs for a good natter, and the husbands fixed drinks, poked at sizzling steaks and discussed the probable fate of the German battleship that had been undergoing repairs in Montevideo for the past four days following the battle with British cruisers off the estuary of the River Plate.

There was much talk about who was joining up and who wasn't and whether they ought to or not. In spite of his wife's pregnancy, Randy Jowett had volunteered to join the Royal Air Force Volunteer Reserve and was due to sail from Buenos Aires in the new year. 'Not a dangerous job, but he says he will never forgive himself if he doesn't do his bit,' Betty explained.

'You poor thing!' Amy said. 'Are you dreading it?'

'I try not to think about it. I mean – one can't even guarantee he'll get there with all these battleships and submarines prowling about.'

'Who'll look after La Ventolera?'

'Oh – I gather Tito's new major domo has agreed to keep an eye on it for us.'

Anna looked up. 'You mean Jorge Stefenelli?'

'Yes. Anything wrong with that?'

Stefenelli had moved into La Calandria so that he could be on the spot to oversee the building of his house and the running of the estancia, and Anna had taken a dislike to him. He was like a cuckoo in her nest. He ate with them in the evenings and accompanied them when they went to neighbouring estancias for lunch. He bought Blanca's affection by giving her sweets and secured Tito's comradeship by having the tennis court repaired and playing tennis with him every evening. Anna had the impression that the two men shared some sort of secret. She could not understand why Tito agreed with whatever Stefenelli suggested.

'I suppose not. Though I'm hardly allowed to tell Catarina to boil an egg without consulting Stefenelli.'

'Tito is having to be pretty careful these days, isn't he?' Emelda said. 'I mean – financially.'

'Yes, but that's no reason for Stefenelli to listen in to other people's telephone conversations, is it?'

The Jowetts, Cadorets, Dalligans, Rathbones and Harrisons shared a party line which all members agreed not to eavesdrop; but when you were alone in the house on a boring empty day the temptation to pick up the phone when it rang twice for Cadoret instead of three times for Dalligan could be irresistible.

'But Anna, darling – everybody does it,' Emelda said. 'It's impossible to keep any sort of secret in the camp.'

'I don't want to keep any secrets. I just don't like the idea of Jorge Stefenelli listening in on the office extension whenever I make a call, that's all.' Anna glanced across at the men. 'So is Stefenelli really going to manage La Ventolera as well as La Calandria?'

'Well, he made Randy a very reasonable offer.'

'I bet he did.'

'Everyone thinks highly of him, Anna. Particularly Tito.'

'That's because Stefenelli lets him beat him at tennis.'

'Oh – I think you're being a bit unfair now!'

'But he's such a greasy little man. He's always slipping off to Laboulaye after supper and coming back with a dirty grin on his face the next morning. I don't trust him an inch.'

'My dear Anna, it's because he's a native Argentine and all natives are exactly the same. You're not in Scotland now, you know. If you're hoping to find some faithful old highland gillie for a major domo, you're going to be looking for a very long time.'

Lunch went on until after four and merged with tea which later merged with evening drinks and a light supper of eggs or steak or salad or all three.

Tito brought a wireless out on a long extension lead and they were listening to the news about the *Graf Spee*, which had been scuttled that day off the entrance to Montevideo, when Hugo and Annelise drove up in de Rosslare's Chevrolet. Annelise was at the wheel and Hugo was fast asleep in the seat beside her. They parked on the grass twenty yards away from where the Cadorets and their guests were sitting.

'Looks as though Hugo had a good lunch,' somebody remarked.

Cadoret walked across the grass to greet them.

'At long last!' he chortled. 'What kept you?'

He opened the driver's door and Annelise stepped out looking hot and flustered.

'Silly bloody fool,' she said, advancing in the direction of the whisky decanter. 'Insisted on eating a steak the size of Dot's handbag and drinking two bottles of wine and then he wonders why he feels queer on the journey. Had to stop three times for him to be sick.'

Cadoret went round the other side of the car and opened the passenger door.

'Come on, Hugo. You've arrived!'

Hugo de Rosslare had indeed arrived. He slumped sideways and fell in a heap on the grass at Cadoret's feet.

'Mother! I think you'd better come here.'

Annelise gripped a tumbler to stop her hand shaking. 'Not until I've had a whisky. Think I deserve one after that bloody journey.'

Cadoret came back to the tables. 'He isn't asleep, Mother. He's dead.'

Stefenelli arranged everything. The police enquiry, the death certificate, the announcements, the flowers, the laying out, the hearse, the priest, the funeral, the burial, the headstone, the reception, the replies to the letters of condolence, the payment of debts outstanding – everything.

At the same time, he stood by Annelise like a son. Wherever she went in those first days after Hugo's death, Stefenelli was never far away. He helped her in and out of cars, he talked to her in the afternoons when Tito was out in the fields and Anna was resting. He listened to her worries about the future – he even gave her a Christmas present. And when the time came to decide who should take over the management of her estate now that her lawyer was dead, he put her in touch with the man he said was the best lawyer in Buenos Aires – his uncle, Rui Botta.

Botta lost no time in returning the favour by recommending that his nephew be appointed as temporary manager of Annelise's estate, which included a floor-polish factory in La Plata and a part-share in a sugar plantation up at Tabacal.

'This is of the greatest possible advantage to yourself,' Stefenelli told Cadoret one evening when Anna had gone up to bed and the two men were having a nightcap. 'Now that your mother has agreed to grant me power of attorney, I shall be able to coordinate the management of the two estates to their mutual benefit.' His eyes flashed. 'And I see no reason why your mother's estate should not contribute towards the interest payments on your loan. That will ease your cash-flow problem and reduce the requirement for further capitalization. It will mean that we can start taking advantage of the increase in demand for beef and cereals in Europe. It means, Señor Cadoret, that this war could make you into a very rich man.'

*　　*　　*

After Hugo's funeral Annelise stayed on at La Calandria and proceeded to flirt unashamedly with Stefenelli, who was thirty years younger than herself; but this did not prevent Stefenelli from taking a trip into Laboulaye for a night out once or twice a week.

They were now four to dinner most evenings, with Jorge and Annelise dominating the conversation and Tito, who had never got on with his mother, behaving like a sulky schoolboy at the end of the table.

It was Anna's first Argentine summer, and she found the heat and the humidity oppressive. A plague of blowfly was followed by another of frogs and a third of ladybirds that got into the fresh-water cistern so that if you wanted a bath you had to strain the tap water through a colander. One stifling afternoon a herd of steers got bunched together and through some freak of nature ran out of air. They collapsed in heaps, and nearly a hundred of them suffocated and died in the middle of a field.

Aware that her pregnancy should be a time of happiness and serenity, Anna took up sketching as a way of escaping from the house and the company of her mother-in-law. There was essentially only one landscape in the camp, and that was a horizontal line broken only by copses, cattle, windmills and wire fences; but the monotony of the land was compensated by an abundance of birds, and she became absorbed in the art of watching and sketching them. With the assistance of books borrowed from the library at La Ventolera, she began identifying the hawks, oven birds, whistling herons, lapwings, kiskadees and little owls that were everywhere.

'The owl is far and away my favourite,' she wrote in a letter to her mother. 'He sits on top of a post and follows you with his eyes as you walk past until he can turn his head no further, and then – quick as lightning – he'll swivel his head round and stare at you over the other shoulder.'

She did not hear very frequently from her parents. Her father had disowned her for marrying a Catholic and Mrs McGeoch was still mourning the loss of her only son. Ursula had had her baby (a daughter) and had emigrated to Canada. Angus was with the British Expeditionary Force in France.

Anna found that the only way to prevent herself dwelling on what had happened was to keep busy throughout the day – whether discussing menus with Catarina, teaching Blanca to read and write, playing with Luis, talking to the ponies, sketching, gardening or playing the piano in the evenings. But however well she filled her days, there were still nights when she would lie listening to the mosquitoes whining and the dormilóns gurgling, and reflect upon what might have been.

Stefenelli decided not to evict Cruz Navarro and instead chose a site for his house on the far side of the privet wood, near the pony paddock. As with everything the administrator tackled, the building went ahead with impressive speed, and it wasn't long before a large, ranch-style building began to rise from the foundations.

Early in the new year Anna noticed that the workforce on the building site included six blond young men who had set up a camp and were living under canvas at the edge of the wood.

'Do you realize that some of the labourers Stefenelli's employing are Germans?' she said to Tito that evening when they met for drinks on the verandah.

'That's nothing unusual. You get all sorts in Argentina.'

'But where did Stefenelli get them from?'

Tito looked past Anna, along the verandah. 'Here he is. Why don't you ask him yourself?'

The administrator was fresh from his shower in a crisp white shirt and well-pressed white flannel trousers. He poured a gin Martini for himself and settled in a cane chair.

'So you've met my German sailors, Señora Anna?'

'Is that what they are? Sailors? What on earth are they doing in Argentina?'

'They're off the *Graf Spee*. Excellent workers, too. If they continue at their present rate I shall have the roof on by the end of March.'

Anna appealed to Tito. 'Surely we can't employ Germans, however efficient they are. We're at war with them!'

'Oh – not at all!' said Stefenelli dismissively. 'Argentina is strictly neutral. The President has given permission for these shipwrecked mariners to be given employment.'

'Did you know they had been taken on?' Anna asked Tito that evening when they were getting ready for bed.

'Leave all the hiring and firing to Jorge these days,' he said. 'That's what he's paid for.'

'But don't you think it's wrong?'

'Why should it be? They're doing honest work for an honest wage.'

'But they're Nazis!'

'What if they are? We can probably learn from them.'

'I can't believe that you mean that, Tito! They're part of a system that's bent on world domination. I don't know about you, but having them on our doorstep like this makes me feel like a traitor.'

109

'Doesn't alter the fact that they're damn good workers.'

She got into bed. 'Couldn't you get Stefenelli to find his bricklayers somewhere else?'

'Could do, I suppose. But I'm not going to.'

'Why not?'

'It's his house. He can build it any way he likes. And anyway, I don't want to fall out with him. He's a damn good administrator.'

'Why do you always say that? Why do you think he's so marvellous? Wouldn't it be a very good thing to override him once in a while? If you ask me he's badly in need of being taken down a peg or two.'

Cadoret paused on his way into the bathroom. 'Look, mosca. Don't start trying to interfere in the running of my estancia, right? Other camp wives have tried the same thing in the past, and they've all come to grief. It just isn't worth it.'

Easter came, and polo started again. Every Saturday afternoon Victorio trooped a dozen ponies to Laguna Blanca and every Sunday morning after an early Mass in Cadoret village Tito rode over to the club for his weekly hour of dust and bad language, followed by a heavy lunch and a drunken ride back to La Calandria before dark.

With the coming of another winter, Annelise started having thoughts about a return to Hurlingham, but every time Anna believed that she would actually go, she postponed the departure.

Stefenelli's villa – which was very modern-looking with a jagged roof line and bright orange tiles – came to be known as 'Casa Nova'. When it was complete, all but one of the Germans moved away to find work elsewhere, but the one who remained, a young shipwright called Karl Hoffmann, proved to be not only a courteous man who was anything but a Nazi, but also a fine carpenter. He presented Anna with a beautifully made redwood garden seat as a token of the friendship which had existed and would one day exist again between Britain and Germany.

At the end of May, Annelise returned to Hurlingham and a week later Stefenelli moved into Casa Nova and threw a large housewarming party. All the landowners from the estancias round Cadoret as well as most of the business people with whom Stefenelli had dealings were invited. The guest of honour was Rui Botta, who came out by train with Consuela.

While Tito mingled with his friends and had useful conversations with business associates, Anna found herself cornered by Rui Botta, who kissed her hand and oozed charm.

'Señora Cadoret – or should I say Mrs Cadoret? We've heard so

110

much about you. Your reputation goes before you. And I must say, you are everything I had been led to expect and more.'

Anna didn't take at all well to flattery.

'Yes,' continued Botta, 'I think your husband made a wise decision when he married you. And I think you made a wise decision to marry him, too. Tito has a great future ahead of him, Señora Cadoret. And so has this country.'

'I hope you're right, Dr Botta, but I think this war has to end before any of us can think about the future, don't you?'

'It's as good as over already! Didn't you hear the news? The German Army has entered Paris. It'll only be a matter of days now before Britain sues for peace.'

'Oh – I hardly think so!'

Botta laughed and looked at the glowing end of his cigar. 'That's because you are new to Argentina and haven't had time to view the world situation from an Argentine point of view. This war will be quickly over. As soon as it is, Germany will lead Europe into a new age. The European nations – Germany, Italy, France – will start investing again in Argentina. Within ten years this country will be competing with the United States of America for world leadership. The world will be stood on its head. The South will rule the North. South America, South Africa, Southern Asia, Australia, Japan – the new countries will overshadow the old, and Argentina will be at their head.'

They had been joined by Tito, Consuela and Stefenelli.

'What's this,' Tito said, 'politics?'

Anna sipped an orange juice. 'You paint a very rosy picture, Dr Botta. But the Nazis still have to win for it to come true, don't they?'

Botta patted her condescendingly on the shoulder. 'Do you seriously think they can be beaten?'

'I don't *think* they can be beaten, I know they will be.'

Tito gave her a ticking-off in the car as they drove back through the privet wood to La Calandria. 'Really must watch your tongue, Anna. We can't afford to fall out with Rui Botta.'

She turned her head to look at him. 'Are you afraid of them, Tito? Is that what it is?'

'Why should I be afraid of them?'

'I don't know. You tell me.'

He kept his eyes on the road ahead. 'No,' he said very condescendingly, 'I am not afraid of them.'

They drove the rest of the way in silence and when they arrived he went into the house ahead of her.

He sat down at the desk in the sitting room to write up the estancia diary. Another day over. He felt depressed. Something seemed to have gone wrong between him and Anna but he didn't know what it was. He helped himself to whisky from the decanter and paced about the room. He didn't want to have a tiff with her, on the other hand he didn't want to appear as if he was apologizing. He knew she would expect him to come to her soon, so he took his time finishing his whisky to make a point.

When he entered their room she was sitting at the dressing table in her nightdress. The sight of her, pregnant with his child, touched him. He searched his mind for something to say that would bring them closer, something to show her that he loved her.

But he was just too late.

'Why do you have to be so cross with me, Tito?' she asked. 'Can't I be allowed to have *any* opinions of my own?'

'It's not a question of that.'

'What is it a question of?'

He breathed out impatiently, looked as if he were about to speak, shut his mouth, then changed his mind.

'Look. I've told you before and I'll tell you again. Don't interfere, Anna. Just keep your nose out of my business. Right?'

She drew herself up a little and he saw her face in the dressing-table mirror. There was something almost regal about Anna at times. She had a calmness and a composure which could be quite unnerving.

'All right, I will,' she said quietly. 'But please don't forget that I am your wife, Tito, so if ever you want to talk about anything –'

She stopped and turned towards him and for a moment he was greatly tempted to go to her and confide the whole story about Magdalena and the bank loan he had raised to buy the annulment and the gift of his polo pony to keep the police quiet; but something – perhaps it was the knowledge that opening his heart to her would in some way be unmanly – stopped him.

'Right,' he said crisply. 'If you will excuse me, I shall now have a bath. I presume there's nothing else you have to say to me?'

'No, nothing else,' she whispered to her reflection after he had left the room.

12

BLANCA WAS ALLOWED TO RIDE alone provided she stayed within the bounds of the park, and when she wasn't eating, sleeping or in the schoolroom she spent most of her time on horseback. The sight of Blanca trotting Chocolata down the eucalyptus ride became a familiar one, and in the evenings when Anna supervized her bath or read her a story before putting the light out, Blanca would sometimes divulge snippets of information about what she had done or seen while out on Chocolata that day.

Her reports were usually terse. 'The capataz caught a comadreja,' she would say, or, 'Victorio took me to the paddock and I saw Mimosa's new foal.'

After Jorge Stefenelli moved into his new house Blanca began to bring back reports of what was going on there too, and Anna was unsurprised to learn that the administrator entertained lady guests from time to time.

'Jorge gave me some dulce de leche,' she said one evening when she was in the bath.

'Oh yes? That was very kind of him.'

Blanca squeezed her hippopotamus under water to make bubbles.

'Do get a move on, Blanca. Wash!'

'He gave me a piggy-back,' she said, and looked covertly at Anna to see if she approved or not.

'Oh yes? I'm surprised he has time to give you piggy-backs.'

'And he tickled me.'

'Did he?'

'Yes. He tickled me here.'

'I'm sure he didn't do that.'

'Yes he did. He gave me a piggy-back and he tickled me at the same time.'

'In that case I don't think you'd better go to Stefenelli's on your own again.'

'Why not?'

'Because I say you're not to, that's why.'

'Daddy said I could.'

'Out you get. Quickly, or there won't be time for a story.'

'I don't want a story if I can't go to see Jorge.'

'That's just silly. Now stand up and let me dry you.'

Blanca made no move. She lay in the bath squeezing the hippo-potamus and gazed insolently upward.

Anna straightened her aching back. 'Do you want to go straight to bed with the light out and no story, Blanca? Is that what you want?'

Blanca stood up. 'Is that what you want?' she mimicked, and punched Anna's swollen belly as hard as she could.

'Blanca! That hurt!'

'I don't care,' shouted Blanca and ran sobbing from the bathroom, down the stairs and into the sitting room, where her father was reading a newspaper.

'Anna says I can't go and see Jorge any more!' she bawled. 'It's not fair! It's not fair!'

Wet and naked, she sobbed and fought and screamed and said she hated Anna and Catarina and Marga and Chocolata. Anna said she mustn't go to see Jorge any more and it wasn't fair. Anna wasn't her mother and she hoped the silly baby she had in her silly tummy would be dead.

For the first time, Anna was afraid of her. She stood back while Tito restrained her and left it to Catarina and Marga to take her upstairs and put her to bed.

'What was that about not being allowed to see Jorge?' Tito asked when it was all over and they were sitting down to dinner.

'Yes, I was going to tell you about that. According to Blanca, Stefenelli has been interfering with her.'

'I beg your pardon?'

'She said Stefenelli had tickled her bottom.'

'Is that all?'

'Isn't it enough?'

'And is that why you told her she wasn't to go to Stefenelli's?'

'Yes. Then she punched me – here – and we had the tantrum.'

'All sounds pretty unnecessary to me. Little fiend probably made it up to see what sort of a reaction she could get out of you.'

'I don't think so, Tito. I can tell when she's lying.'

'Well. She won't be the first little girl who's had her bottom tickled. Probably liked it.' Cadoret looked up from his plate. 'After all, you do, don't you, mosca?'

Anna stared at him. 'I think that's the most despicable thing to say, Tito. I can't believe you meant it.'

114

'Oh, come off it. Stop playing holier-than-thou!'

'I'm not doing any such thing.'

'Well stop over-reacting then.'

'Is that what you think? That I'm over-reacting?'

'She hasn't been raped, has she?'

'You think I'm just making a fuss, don't you? Well I'll tell you one thing, Tito. That child is not to be left alone with Stefenelli again. And what's more, I think you ought to tell Stefenelli the reason why.'

'So here we go again.'

'What's that supposed to mean?'

'You know damn well: putting your oar in, telling me how to do my job.'

They were silent while Marga served the second course. When she had gone, Anna said, 'I am not interfering. Blanca is every bit as much my responsibility as yours. She's already had the worst possible start in life. Surely you of all people can see that. Surely you can see that we have to be doubly careful with her. And if Stefenelli has been interfering with her –'

'There you go again! Condemning the fellow without trial.'

'Why do you always have to defend him? Why do we always have to fall in with whatever he says? Why don't you admit it? You are afraid of him, aren't you?'

'Stefenelli is a bloody good administrator.'

'So you've told me at least a dozen times. I don't care if he's the best administrator that's ever walked this earth. If he's interfering with Blanca, I want him off this property. Why can't you see it my way for once? Look at the way he behaved with your mother. Like some sort of gigolo. And what about all those trips he takes to Laboulaye? What about all the lady friends he has to stay?'

Cadoret put his knife and fork together and leant back in his chair. 'He's a single man. Any man would do the same, given the opportunity.'

'Including you, I suppose.'

'No, because I'm married to you. Don't look like that, Anna. This is the way the world works.'

'Not where I come from it doesn't.'

'Yes, but this isn't Edinburgh. If you think I'm going to get rid of Stefenelli because he has an eye for the ladies, you're going to have to think again.'

'All right, I won't ask you to get rid of him. What I am asking is that you back me up for a change. Either that or –'

'Or what?'

She shook her head. 'Nothing. Forget it.'

'I can't very well forget something I don't know about.'

There was a silence.

'Or what?' he repeated.

She was tired and heavy and impatient with carrying this baby for so long. Her stomach hurt where Blanca had punched her and she was worried because Tito had promised to arrange for her to go to Buenos Aires in a fortnight's time to have the baby but he still hadn't booked her in at the British Hospital.

'Explain why,' she said. 'Why you always have to defer to him, why you defended him over those German sailors, why you're defending him now. Explain why I wasn't allowed to stand up for my country against that reptile of a lawyer of yours.'

'Rui Botta's no reptile. He just happens to have Italian roots, that's all. That's why you're so prejudiced against him, isn't it?'

'I'm not prejudiced –'

'It's because he's a hot-blooded Latin. A Latin not a Celt, a Roman Catholic and not a Wee Free.'

'I am not at all prejudiced. It isn't what Stefenelli is, Tito, it's the way he behaves. Whenever he's present I have the feeling that he knows something that I don't know. That he's using you and laughing at me.'

'In other words, you don't trust him.'

'No. I do not.'

'But I do trust him, Anna. So if you don't trust him, you don't trust me.'

'I do trust you, Tito –'

He laughed. 'Oh yes? Pull the other one!'

'I do trust you. I just feel that I'm being kept in the dark the whole time. I don't feel that I really know you. I feel – insecure, I suppose. It's probably the baby, I know that. I need your reassurance –'

'Oh my God! Not that again.'

'I need to know that you're on my side, that's all. I feel as though there's a part of you that you keep locked away from me the whole time. I still don't really know what happened about Magdalena. I've heard things –'

He bristled. 'Oh yes? What things?'

'I'm not going to repeat it. It was malicious gossip. I never believed it. But you've told me so little and I can't help wondering –'

He was at work with a toothpick, concealing his activities with a cupped hand. He stopped suddenly.

'Of course I could say the same about you, Anna.'

She blinked in surprise. 'What do you mean?'

'Well – can you put your hand on your heart and swear that you have never kept a single secret from me? Can you do that?'

He looked at her in that predatorial way of his: the eagle stare, the piercing blue eyes, the military moustache.

'Well? Can you?'

He saw her falter and seized the advantage. It was like breaking through the opposing team's defences and galloping after the ball towards an open goal. The opportunity to score was irresistible. He had never meant to mention it, had always intended to use what he knew as a source of power over her. But this was such an easy shot that he couldn't stop himself taking it.

'What about the telegram?'

She flushed immediately. 'What telegram?'

'The only telegram you never showed me. The telegram that sent you running off into the pampa in the middle of the night.'

The colour drained from her face as quickly as it had arrived.

'Did you really expect me to believe that cock-and-bull story you dreamed up? That it was just your soldier-boy trying to change your mind again? Well did you?'

'That's not fair,' she whispered.

'Why isn't it fair, Anna? You accuse me of keeping you in the dark. You say you feel I'm not on your side. But when I suggest that you may have concealed something from me then that's not fair. Well? What did that telegram say? There was more to it than you said there was. I'm right, aren't I?'

She nodded.

He threw his hands up in triumph. 'So you *did* lie to me. On the first day back from our honeymoon. You told me a direct, blatant lie, Anna. Did you or did you not?'

He sat and watched her, and for some time the only sound in the room, apart from the tick of the bracket clock on the mantel, was the catch of her breath.

Part of him knew that he was being unfair and that he should not bully her in this way. But she had started it. She had asked for it.

'May as well have the whole story, Anna. What did the telegram say?'

She avoided his eyes. 'He was never engaged. The announcement was a mistake.'

'Never engaged?'

117

'Never engaged to someone else. It was a joke. Someone put the announcement in the paper for a joke.'

'So . . . if you'd known, you could have married him after all.'

'Yes.'

'And when he sent that telegram, the one Victorio waved at us when we left for BA, he was trying to get you to call off the wedding.'

'Yes.'

'And you wished you had.'

'No –'

'Of course you did! Why else would you have lied to me – you of all people, Anna? Why else would we be having all these tears? It's because you loved him, isn't that right? You loved him and you still love him. You love him even now at this very minute.'

'No! No, Tito. Oh –' She pushed her chair back suddenly, clasping her stomach.

'Anna – love – what is it?'

'The baby. I think the baby's started.'

13

WHEN ANNA BROUGHT Baby John back she said everything would stay exactly the same as it was before she went to have him. She said, You're every bit as important to Daddy and me as Luis and Baby John, Blanca. She said that nothing had changed and that she loved you every bit as much as she always had done. She said that with every little baby God sent into the world he sent a great big parcel of love that was far more than enough for the baby and that was why you should never feel jealous or afraid that Luis or Baby John was loved more than you. Of course, because tiny babies need lots of care and attention, you would have to be more grown up about things. You couldn't always have a story read to you because sometimes Anna took longer to feed Baby John. Sometimes Anna didn't want to come riding because she was tired out from being up in the night with Baby John. Here you are, Blanca, Anna said when she came home and Jorge brought her from the station. Here you are, say hello to your new brother, Baby John. Baby John had a face like a squashed orange and when he cried it made you want to pick him up by his red feet and twist his head and jerk it the way Piotr throttled a hen. He didn't look like a brother and he didn't feel like a brother because Anna wasn't your mother and Daddy wasn't your father. Even Luis was only half a brother. Nothing was real, nothing was the same, nothing was what it was supposed to be, nothing was really yours except Mimi and she was only a doll and her arms had come off and Catarina had thrown them away.

Miss Tucker was the new governess. She had baggy stockings and horny hands and she smelt sweaty on hot days. She called you a little devil when no one was listening and secretly pinched the back of your hand when she wanted to make you behave. She made you start learning to read and write all over again because she said you had been taught wrong and she had a Method. She was afraid of horses and tried to stop you looking at Samson because he was a stallion and she said it was disgusting. She slept in the room next door and said ten beads out loud every night when she went to bed. She always said it the same way so that you could hear her through the wall. Hell merry full of gobble, she went, because you could only hear the first bit of each one. Hell merry full of gobble. Hell merry full of gobble gobble gobble. She always said the last one loudest and then she made little crosses on her head and her lips and her bosom which she kept up with pink braces that did up with rubber buttons that fitted into metal clips, which you could sometimes see her doing up because she left her bedroom door open a crack to prove she had a clean conscience. Daddy called her Vinegar-Drawers and Anna said Shhh, Tito.

Miss Tucker was Irish and so was Father Michael and so were the Dalligans. Uncle Tom Dalligan, who wasn't an uncle, was huge with rough red hands and Mrs Dalligan, who was called Amy, was small and neat like a hummingbird. They had seven children, Sean, Thomas, Liam, Maeve, Eileen, Phillip and Aidan. Sometimes you went to their estancia, La Playosa, to join in with their school because Anna said it was good for you and after lunch you had to lie down on a rug for quarter of an hour while Madame had coffee. You shared a rug with Phillip Dalligan and made it into a tent and he let you play with his poronga but one day you went to La Playosa he said he wasn't going to play under the rug again because his governess had told him that if he played with his poronga it might fall off.

Why are you crying? you asked and Anna who was Mummy but not your mother said, Because I'm sad. There was a letter beside her chair where she sat in the afternoons because she was going to have another baby. Is that a letter from Scotland? you asked and she said Yes, yes, in a sort of sad whisper, Yes, it's from Scotland. Has it made you sad? Why? Why are you sad? Because of the war, Blanca. Because someone I love has died in the war. Was it your mummy? you asked, but Anna shook her head and said no. Who is dead then? you asked and your mother, who was not your mother but Anna, took you in her arms and cried and whispered If only you knew, if only you knew and patted you on the back and put her fingers through your hair like a comb, which she sometimes did. Knew what? you asked and she looked at you in her funny sad way and shook her head and then your father came in in his bombachas and stared at you both and said La gran puta, and later you heard him shouting and Anna was saying Well anyway now he's dead, do you hear me Tito, he's dead.

*   *   *

120

You weren't allowed to go and see Jorge because he tickled your bum and you weren't allowed to play under the rug with Phillip because his poronga might fall off. Boys were fun but they were dirty and men were always trying to get at your bum. You were growing into a big girl and you had to go to catechism and learn about God. You were seven years old and that was the age of reason when you ought to know the difference between right and wrong. You had to wear a white dress and kiss the bishop's ring. You were a Child of Mary and you put your hands together under your nose when you prayed. You had to learn how to search your conscience before confession and bang your chest with your fist and say mea culpa, mea culpa, mea maxima culpa, which meant your fault, your fault, all your fault. You had to make the sign of the cross and go up to the altar and put your tongue out and the holy sacrament tasted more like a bit of ice-cream wafer than anybody's body and blood, let alone the blessed Lord's.

Anna was always having babies. First she had John and then she had Marc and then she had Larry and then one that was dead. Father called them his rodeo and was pleased because they were boys and he was going to teach them to play polo so that one day they would be a team. Anna wanted to go to Scotland and see her mountains but she couldn't because of the war and anyway she was expecting another so they all went to Mar del Plata with the Dalligans instead and stayed in a hotel and played by the sea. It was 1944 and you were ten. The war was over but it wasn't over. You sat on the beach and the wind blew the deck chairs inside out and you watched boys in their swimming trunks playing football and when you went for a walk along the beach with Miss Tucker there was an old man lying up under the dunes and Miss Tucker put her hand over your eyes because it was a filthy abomination. Luis was six and Johnny was four and Marc was two and Larry was one. They had a new nurse called Linda who was a porteña which meant she came from Buenos Aires. You said, I'm a porteña too, but Linda said, No you aren't, Blanca. Yes I am because my mother came from Buenos Aires. No Blanca, she didn't. She did, she did, she did. Then something went wrong, which it sometimes did. Things went fuzzy and grey. The man in the car was holding onto your wrist and Mama's shoes were coming off. The one who had tickled you was undoing his trousers and the man who had been driving was holding his hand over Mama's mouth and dragging her backwards and another one was on top of Mama and there were black hairs on his bottom and blood on Mama's leg and you could see her legs kicking and kicking and kicking. She did, she did, she did.

No, Blanca, your mother did not come from Buenos Aires, she isn't a
porteña, she is from Scotland. *That isn't my mother!* you screamed, and
you scratched Linda down her face and it served her right because
she didn't know anything. Mama was a porteña. There was blood on
her leg and Mimi had no arms and Anna wasn't her mother because
she came from Scotland.

When you were eleven they took you to see the new school you would
be going to. It was called Michael Hamm and was in a place called
Vicente Lopez. It looked more like a church than a school and there
was a high wall round it and Daddy said they had built it specially
when they heard Blanca Cadoret was coming. So you can't escape,
Blanca, he said and laughed his stupid laugh. What is your name?
Mother Lickfold asked, and you said Blanca Salgado and Mother
Lickfold looked at your father and he shook his head and he said, Not
Salgado, Cadoret, because it had been changed. Michael Hamm was
full of girls and postulants and sisters and mothers superior and nearly
all of them were Irish. You didn't want to go there but you had to.
There was early Mass and silence at meals and beads and benediction
and when you had a bath you weren't supposed to look because the
devil was waiting to tempt you. The postulants gave you holy pictures
and said glorybetotheholyghost when they were surprised. You danced
to gramophone records on Saturday afternoons and Cousin Ceci, who
wasn't a cousin but a Universal Aunt, came in her car and took you
out to tea. Cousin Ceci was a lapsed Catholic and she always jumped
when you came into the room because she had nerves. Her house was
in Belgrano which was the name of a famous general. All the streets
were named after famous people or places, and wherever you went
you found the same names: Lavalle and Maipú and San Martín and
Yrigoyen and Moreno and Alsina and Sarmiento. It was because
Argentina had a glorious history fighting wars with the indios, who
had lances fifteen feet long with feathers on them and whirled bolases
called the Three Marias. Argentina was one of the biggest countries
in the world and it was certainly the best because of all the great
generals and leaders who had saved the Republic from colonial rule
and driven the British out of Buenos Aires in eighteen-o-something.
The British always boasted about what they had done for Argentina
but really they had done nothing at all except build silly railways to
make money out of the land and steal the meat out of other people's
mouths to feed their soldiers every time they started another war. Jorge
said the British were as bad as the Jews. It was the Jews and the
British who had bled Argentina white and the Jews and the British

122

who had started the silly war everyone always talked about, the war the British had only won because Mr Churchill's mother had been American and he had persuaded the Americans to join in. But now, Jorge said, everything was getting better because of a new colonel. He had a big smile and white teeth and shiny black hair and he wore boots and riding breeches and he was always laughing and joking. Wherever he went, people followed him. He was called Juan Perón and he was going to get rid of the Jews and the British and make Argentina a better country. His wife said that she was going to make everyone richer and happier. All the poor people without shirts who didn't have enough to eat would be fed and clothed and the children would be sent to schools that had numbers instead of names. Children who went to state schools had to wear white overalls to make them look the same and just so that everyone would recognize Colonel Perón if they saw him or he came into their shop to buy a present for his Evita, there were big pictures of him put up in the school and on the railway stations and there he was in his shining boots and his shining hair with his big white smile and the people were crowding round and cheering and laughing and shouting Perón, Perón, because he was changing everything.

There was a summer holiday when the Clydesdales were sold and tractors took their place. That was the summer the locusts came. They were like an inky scribble at first and Anna said it looked as if someone had tried to write their name in the sky. Everybody had to run out and bang tins to stop them landing. The capataz and his family and all the peons and maids came out to bang tins and so did Catarina and Piotr and Marga, who was going to marry Hoffmann because he had managed to get his poronga through the iron bars of her bedroom window and she was going to have a baby. The black scribble in the sky turned into a smudge and then a blot and then a filthy clicking and whirring cloud and however hard you banged the tins they still settled until every tree and post and plant was black with them. The peons made fires with paraffin to burn them but it didn't work because there were so many. They stripped the maize and ate the leaves off the trees and ate holes in the bed sheets Catarina put over the vegetable patch to protect the tomatoes and lettuces. At the end of the day Father came in and shook his head. After the locusts left even the hens' eggs were smelly and tasted filthy because the hens had eaten the locust eggs and Father Michael said in his homily at Mass in Cadoret that just as the eggs were defiled by the foul spawn of the locusts so your soul was defiled when you committed a mortal sin.

*   *   *

When the baby locusts hatched the hoppers came. The hoppers were worse than the locusts. They were small and green and came out of holes in the ground and started hopping because they couldn't fly. The peons worked all day unrolling long rolls of zinc and digging pits and sweeping the hoppers and burning them and the smell of them hung about all day and made you want to throw up. Anna would have gone to Scotland after that summer but the locusts changed everything and she didn't.

There was a hot Christmas when you were thirteen and there was a big party because the new swimming pool was finished and Father wanted to show it off. The Dalligans came and the Jowetts with Jane and Belinda and Alexandra, and Cousin Ceci and Gangan from Hurlingham and old Mr Rathbone who stuttered and Uncle Stiffy who wasn't an uncle and who limped because of the war and Teddy Harrison who didn't and Emelda who was so pretty and should have been a film star and Jorge Stefenelli and Isadora, who was his fancy woman. You went to midnight Mass so you didn't have to go again. You had a stocking in the morning and after breakfast you all sat in the shade on the verandah and opened your presents and Gangan gave you a red and white striped bathing suit. You put a red velvet ribbon in your hair and a towel round your shoulders and white open-toed sandals on your feet and you went downstairs and out into the sunlight and everyone was there by the pool waiting for you because Father had promised that you could be the first person to swim in the new pool because you were the eldest. Uncle Stiffy whistled when he saw you and Father said, Wow. All the men were looking at you because your breasts were bigger than they expected. Father said, Let's see you dive, Blanca, and the water was bright in the sunlight and calm because no one had been in it. You dived in with your toes pointed and your feet together the way they taught you at Michael Hamm and swam a length under water and when you reached the end Anna was there to meet you with a towel saying, Out you get. I've only just got in, you said, and Anna sighed and whispered, Don't argue, Blanca, get out of the pool. Why should I? you said and Anna said, Just do as you're told for once, will you? But I've only just got in. Blanca, said Anna. Look. So you looked. Father said, La gran puta. Luis was standing with a silly smile on his face and Gangan was saying Ay-ay-ay, señórita. So you got out of the pool and walked without hurrying over the grass, past the tables under the trees that had been laid with silver and cut-glass and flowers and Christmas crackers, along the verandah where the glasses were and the champagne was standing in silver ice-buckets and into the house. Anna came upstairs after you and started fussing, taking you into the bathroom and making you stand in the bath and you knew that you had Started.

Luis was nine and noisy and he always got the best presents. First he liked hats and balloons, then he liked swords and tractors and finally he liked cars and guns and aeroplanes. Every time Father came back from Buenos Aires he brought back another gun or another car or another aeroplane for Luis, but he never brought anything for you because you were only a girl. Johnny was seven and he was holy because he had just been confirmed and was allowed to serve Mass for Padre Michael and when you went up to the rail there he was, tinkling bells and looking important. Marc was nearly five and was always in the way because he followed you round everywhere and wanted to get into your bed, but he was also dangerous because if you teased him or made him cry he went and told Miss Tucker and Miss Tucker told Anna and Anna looked tired and said, Was it really necessary, Blanca? Larry was pale and small and poorly and Anna was expecting again. She called you darling when she told you off and sometimes at the beginning of the holidays she would say, Let's take the dogs for a walk, Blanca, just you and me, and she wouldn't say very much but she would hold your hand which she said was a small comfort in a wicked world. Her hair had threads of silver in it. You walked together out along the ride and across the wide, wire-fenced fields and the ibis would flap overhead and the curlews would cry and swoop in the wind and she would stop suddenly and say, Oh – look! and far up in the sky a V of geese would fly, and she would say, I don't know why, but I always think that they're going home; and on the way back you walked through a dark wood in the middle of which was a single silver eucalyptus that shone in the evening light, like a ghost. This tree always makes me shiver, she said. And when they got back into the house Father was in the hall talking to Jorge about blowfly and Miss Tucker was cross because Luis and John were still in their riding gear and Catarina was panicking because the Jowetts and the Rathbones were coming to dinner and Anna would be extra polite to Jorge Stefenelli because she hated him.

Twice a week you had to have history and geography classes in Spanish so that you could learn about the great Argentine heritage and the injustice of the British. Now Colonel Perón was making Argentina strong again, it wouldn't be long before all the British would be sent home and the Islas Malvinas would be restored to the Fatherland.

125

One day you were taken by bus to Palermo Park to see Perón. He swept up in a black car with Evita beside him. It was a hot spring day. The crowd broke down a barrier and ran across a road and up to a line of policemen. You got separated from the class. Everyone was jostling and trying to get a better view and a policeman asked your name and promised to take you back to your class. Colonel Perón said that everything was changing and getting better. His voice barked and echoed across the park. He said that Justicialism would give the shirtless-ones liberty, democracy and justice. You shouted Perón, Perón and waved your blue-and-white flag and the policeman stood behind you and pressed up against your bottom and put a card into the top of your bra which said 'Tango Every Night at the Zig-Zag, Admittance Free for Young Ladies'.

There was a new nun called Sister Meganitty who took you for English Language and English Literature. Sister Meganitty said that the aim of art was the creation of beauty. She made you write compositions about 'A Day at the Seaside' or 'My Hobby' or 'My Favourite Saint' or 'Christmas'. To gain Sister Meganitty's approval, you had to write what she wanted you to write. You got a merit star for a composition called 'My Most Memorable Birthday', in which you wrote about your fifth, when you had been given a doll called Rita and your three uncles took you and your Mama for a drive and you had a lovely picnic in the woods and Mama scratched her leg climbing over a fence. Sister Meganitty said that it was an excellent composition. Blanca has created something that is beautiful, she said. Beauty is truth, truth beauty. Who wrote that? Can anyone tell me?

You had to read the Father Brown stories in class and because there weren't enough books to go round you had to share. You pulled your desks together and sat next to Libby MacNamara who had a squint and whose mother had jumped under a train. She went red in the face but never tried to stop you. She made it easy for it to happen every time you pulled your desks together and read the Father Brown stories. In Biology when Sister Latour was dissecting a rabbit Libby stood close behind you and when you were waiting for the tennis court, lying in the shade on the sloping grass by the oleanders, she edged closer so you could get at her. Things went grey. You didn't know why you did it and when you did it it didn't feel as if it was you that was doing it.

When Lent came you had a special retreat. You had to search your conscience and listen to a talk by Brother Patrick. My dear little sisters in Christ, said Brother Patrick, What a wonderful thing is the sacrament of confession. He smiled at you and said, Is it not? Well, is it not? and you were expected to nod and say Yes Brother Patrick to show you were listening and entering into the spirit of the retreat. But I wonder how many of us have stopped to consider whether we use it in the way it should be used. We haven't, have we? And at this, you had to look contrite and shake your heads. Little sisters, said Brother Patrick, It has been said that to err is human but to forgive divine, but our Lord has urged us to forgive as well as to ask forgiveness. We say, do we not, dimitte nobis debita nostra, sicut et nos dimittimus debitoribus nostris, but the act of forgiveness on our part is all too often overlooked. We are urged, are we not, to bless those who curse us and do good to those who wrongfully use us, but how often do we obey our Lord's command in this respect? Not very often, do we? And are not feelings of bitterness, of spite, of revenge, of envy every bit as bad as the everyday sins that we recite so easily every time we come to confession? It's true, isn't it? And yet we all have these feelings, don't we? Perhaps against our parents. Perhaps against our brothers and sisters. Perhaps against our friends – perhaps even against the Sisters of Mercy here at Michael Hamm. We have, haven't we? And what a wretched sin it is to have on our conscience! This sin of wishing evil to another. This desire of an eye for an eye, a tooth for a tooth. But, little sisters in Christ, this wish for revenge destroys those whom it possesses. Vengeance is mine, saith the Lord, I will repay. So let us now, as a preparation for confession, search our minds for the grudges we may bear against others. Let us kneel together and contemplate our past lives. Is there, lurking deep within us, a smouldering bitterness, a hatred even, for some person or persons? Let us meditate on that. And remember: our hatred, our bitterness, our need for revenge may be justified. It may be that we have indeed been wronged. But that does not lessen our sin in refusing to forgive our malefactors. If we truly wish to receive God's forgiveness through the sacrament of confession then it behoves us first to forgive those who have trespassed against us. We must forgive them in our hearts and having done so we should forgive them personally just as our blessed Lord forgave those who nailed him to the cross. So let us now, each and every one, forgive in our hearts those who have trespassed against us; let us confess our sin and seek absolution of it, and let us approach those from whom we have withheld our forgiveness and make it known to them that we no longer hold ill feelings towards them and that, if we have hurt or abused them in any way, we seek their forgiveness in return.

*　　*　　*

127

You didn't try to forgive anyone because if you did you would have to forgive the men who killed your mother. It was a truth that was not beautiful. It was an event that was burnt into your memory. You were branded with it as surely as the steers at La Calandria were branded with the image of an encircled mocking bird. One day, one day, you would find out why they did what they did to your mother and who had ordered them to do it. You would find out who was to blame and you would punish them. Michael Hamm, the Blessed Virgin, Sister Meganitty and Brother Patrick were all part of the same joke, a joke that turned everything they said upside-down and inside-out, so that right was wrong and wrong was right and it didn't matter what Jorge or the policeman did to you or what you did to Libby MacNamara.

When Libby came out of the confessional her eyes went sideways and they met yours as she walked past. You entered the confessional and knelt and made the sign of the cross and said, I have neglected my morning prayers and have had impure thoughts. I have withheld my forgiveness from my brother because he hit me with a rebenque. I have neglected my morning prayers and told lies of excuse. Well done for making a good confession, said the priest, now for your penance say ten Hail Marys and make a good act of contrition. O my God, you said, I am truly sorry that I have offended against you and by the help of your grace I will not sin again and when you came out Sister Meganitty gave you a look. You knelt and said some Hail Marys then made the sign of the cross and went out of the chapel and straight up to the dormitory. Everyone else had gone down to the refectory for supper so it was safe, and anyway you always had plenty of warning if a nun was coming because the dormitory was at the end of the corridor and the nuns wore shoes with crêpe soles that squeaked on the parquet. Libby was putting away her missal. Things went grey. You didn't feel as if you were you. Libby said, I've only just confessed it. So what? you said. But it's Lent, Libby said. What difference does that make? you said and Libby said nothing but squirmed and stood like Jemima did for Samson and Sister Meganitty had taken her shoes off. She came in like a penguin in a whirlwind and stopped dead. Blanca Cadoret, she said. I knew it. I always knew it.

14

CADORET WIVES HAD BEEN FORMED in 1941 with the aim of raising funds for the war effort, and had continued after the war with the new aims of regenerating a community spirit and raising money for various charities; but its main, unstated function had been that of helping to relieve the boredom of estancia life by providing a forum for the exchange of novels, children's clothes and hot gossip. Meetings were held three or four times a year and occasionally guest speakers were brought in to give talks with titles like 'Spare The Rod', 'First Aid at the Roadside' or 'I Left My Heart in Tierra del Fuego' (with slides).

This afternoon the meeting was being held at La Calandria and the talk was 'Look Young, Look Beautiful' (with demonstration) given by Mrs Emelda Rathbone.

Emelda had married Stiffy when he came back from the war but had since discovered that Stiffy could not give her children. They were still together and Emelda still managed to look young and beautiful, but all the Cadoret Wives knew that her marriage was decidedly shaky.

Anna had been volunteered to act as a guinea-pig. Wrapped in a bedsheet, she sat on an upright chair that had been placed on wooden blocks in the schoolroom so that all nine members of the audience could see. Emelda demonstrated the use of a mudpack, cleansing milk, skin toner, foundation, blushers, lip pencil, eye shadower, lash brush and mascara, with the result that when she had finished, Anna looked more like a Cadoret Tart than a Cadoret Wife.

'Of course this is only a demonstration,' Emelda laughed nervously, 'so obviously I've had to overdo it a bit in order to show you the various techniques.'

Betty Jowett, who was Madame President, came to her rescue. 'If there are no other questions, I suggest we break now for the excellent tea that awaits us in the dining room.'

Just then, the telephone in the hall gave two long rings – the code for La Calandria – and a moment later the maid came in and said it was for Anna.

Anna went along the corridor to take the call. There was a mirror beside the wall telephone. The line was not very good, and she was so horrified at her own reflection that she did not at first take in the name of the caller.

'Who?'

'Mother Lickfold. From Michael Hamm School.'

'Oh, yes –'

'It's about Blanca, Mrs Cadoret. I'm afraid I must ask you to remove her from the school.'

'I don't understand. Has she had an accident?'

'She's to be expelled, Mrs Cadoret. She has misbehaved in a way that cannot be tolerated. We have no choice but to ask you to remove her immediately.'

'Immediately?'

'At once, yes. She has a guardian in Buenos Aires, doesn't she?'

'What has she done?'

There was a pause at the other end. Then: 'Indecency.'

'I don't understand –'

'With another girl, Mrs Cadoret. I'm not prepared to say more than that over the telephone. I shall write a letter to you and your husband to give you a full account. In the meantime I must insist that Blanca is removed from Michael Hamm without delay.'

Anna stared at herself in the mirror. 'My husband's in BA at the moment. I'll get him to contact you as soon as possible.'

'That would be appreciated, Mrs Cadoret. Thank you.'

They rang off. When she went back into the schoolroom, curious faces turned in her direction.

'Trouble?' Betty asked quietly.

She felt a stab of anger. It was impossible to have any privacy in the camp. Though your neighbours might live five leagues away, they knew more about you and yours than if you shared garden fences. It was written all over their faces: they couldn't wait to get out of the house and start speculating on who 'she' was and what 'she' had done. The chances were high that one of the husbands or managers on the party line had listened into the conversation. The drums would beat all night.

'You may as well all know,' she said. 'You're bound to hear about it sooner or later. Blanca's been expelled from Michael Hamm.'

'Oh, my dear!' somebody said, and there was a buzz of conversation.

'But why?' whispered Emelda, as if she had a special right to know. 'What on earth can she have done?'

'I don't have the details, Emelda. Now can I please have this stuff removed from my face?'

Tito was also looking at himself in the mirror when the telephone rang, but for a very different reason: he had recently been initiated into Rui Botta's Lodge, and was admiring himself in his apron for the first time. He was in an excellent mood: over a three-hour lunch with Rui Botta and Toni Lambretti it had been made clear to him that a bright future lay ahead. Botta had promised a much closer business association with him and had hinted that it would not be long before many other benefits began rolling in.

The call was from reception, to say that there was an urgent message for him to ring his wife.

'What's the problem?' he asked when he finally got through to Anna.

'Blanca's been expelled.'

He was still looking at himself in the mirror. The apron was of embroidered silk with emblems of sun, moon, serpent and cross worked in gold, silver, green and scarlet.

'Oh yes? What's she been up to?'

'I can't explain over the telephone, Tito. Mother Lickfold rang an hour ago and I've been trying to reach you ever since. They want her to be collected straight away. I said I'd contact you and ask you to make arrangements with them direct.'

'Why didn't you ring Ceci for God's sake?'

'Tito, I can't explain over the telephone. All I'm asking you to do is collect her and bring her back with you.'

'I'm not a nursemaid, Anna. This is a business trip, not a school outing.' He took a card from his inside pocket which Botta had given him. It bore the address of an exclusive Buenos Aires night club at which he had been pressingly invited by Botta to spend the evening. Consuela would be there and Botta had promised to fix Cadoret up with an escort. 'Besides, I shall be in a meeting this evening. I shan't be back until tomorrow, possibly the day after.'

'Well, will you please ring the school, then? They were insistent that Blanca should be collected right away.'

'Did they give you a reason?'

'Yes, but –'

'Why can't you tell me?'

'Tito I really would rather not. I'm sure you know why.'

He grunted. 'All right. Tell you what I'll do. I'll collect Blanca now

131

and put her on the night train. Gets in at seven. You can meet her at the station. Happy?'

He heard her sigh. 'I don't think she should travel on her own.'

'Why not?'

'She's only fourteen, Tito –'

He laughed. 'You worry too much! It's only an overnight trip. I'll talk to the guard. He can keep an eye on her.'

'I really don't think –'

'That's my decision,' he said crisply, and hung up before she had time to reply.

Anna was sitting in the car alongside the wooden platform of Cadoret station the following morning when the Buenos Aires train appeared on the horizon. For a long time it seemed to be stationary, but then the rails shivered and a minute later it arrived, panting and belching steam.

There was only one familiar face among the half-dozen passengers who stepped down onto the wooden planks, and that was Stiffy Rathbone's. Stiffy had always had a soft spot for Anna and never let an opportunity to kiss her on both cheeks go by. 'Anna, girl! What are you doing here?'

'I'm meeting Blanca.'

'End of term already?'

'No, but she – oh, you may as well know, Stiffy. Everyone else does. She's been expelled from Michael Hamm.'

'Well that's not the end of the world, is it? Ah. Here's my manager. Must dash, Anna. See you soon, I hope.'

Anna turned back to watch for Blanca, but she did not appear. While the goods van was being unloaded, she boarded the train and went along to the night steward's compartment to ask him if he had seen her.

The steward was one of the old school: smart, efficient, respectful. 'About fourteen, was she? *Sí, señora.* There was a girl who got onto the train at Once. I examined her ticket myself.'

'Then perhaps she overslept –'

'I don't think so. I took early tea to all the sleeping compartments, and hers was empty.'

'She was fourteen but might have looked older. Quite tall for her age, with long dark hair down to her shoulders and a fringe –'

'Yes – that's the one. I examined her ticket –'

'Then why isn't she on the train now?'

The steward shrugged. 'Perhaps she got off. Who knows?'

132

'Can you show me the compartment she was in?'

'Of course.'

She followed him along the corridor and he opened the door to a sleeping compartment.

'But the bed hasn't been slept in!'

The steward said quietly, 'I think she must have got off at Junín, señora.'

'Did you see her leave the train?'

'No.'

'But –'

A whistle blew. There was a shout and the train jerked forward. She stepped down onto the platform. A smell of fried bacon came from the dining car as it slid past, and then she was alone on the platform and the rails were trembling at her feet.

They searched and they made enquiries, but Anna never felt that they searched hard enough or long enough. Stefenelli went to Laboulaye to report Blanca as a missing person and the name Blanca Cadoret was duly noted in the police files.

'But she won't use that name,' Anna said. 'She hated having her name changed. She'll call herself Salgado, I know it.'

'Academic,' said Tito. 'The police have better things to do than round up runaway teenagers.'

'You realize that she's almost certainly in moral danger? If only you'd come with her on the train, Tito.'

'Oh – I see. I'm to blame now, am I?'

'Well you must admit she wouldn't have run off if you had.'

'Not this time, no. But she would have gone sooner or later. And if it comes to that, you could have gone and collected her, couldn't you? Or you could have got Jorge to do it. But you wouldn't do that, would you? You don't trust him, do you? Perhaps things might have been different if you hadn't kept her on such a tight rein.'

'I'm not trying to blame anyone, Tito. I'm just saddened that we've failed her.'

'Speak for yourself,' he said. 'I haven't failed her. If anyone's failed her it's been you. You were the one who always gave in to her. You were the one who always said we had to treat her with kid gloves. And you were the one, I seem to remember, who put your puritan foot down whenever she engaged in the mildest experiment with sex – as every other child does at some time or other.'

She rounded on him. 'All right, yes, of course I have to take most of the responsibility – don't you think I'm aware of that? Don't you think I lie awake wondering where she is, what's happening to her? I'm worried sick about her. She may be on the streets by now, for all we know.'

'What if she is? She had her chance. In fact she had any number of chances. Blood will out, Anna. Her mother was no good and nor was she.'

It was pointless to continue the argument. She had discovered a terrifying streak of ruthlessness in Tito. The accumulation of money and power seemed to be taking an ever-increasing priority with him. He loved his children because they were boys and would become members of his empire. He kept on the right side of his mother, though he hated her, because he stood to gain hugely from her death. Blanca had been an encumbrance, a legacy from his past. His relief at being finally rid of her was all too obvious.

In the weeks following Blanca's disappearance, however, Tito seemed to undergo a subtle change. He made more frequent visits to Buenos Aires and from time to time Anna was called upon to help him entertain his business acquaintances, many of whom were Italian or Italian-Argentine. The visitors would be met at the station by Stefenelli and Renaldo, the new cadet manager, and the party would arrive in the Chevrolet and the Ford. Stefenelli always ensured that the visitors from abroad were provided with ladies from a Buenos Aires escort agency, who were usually introduced as 'friends'. The visitors would be taken on a tour of the estancia and sometimes Stefenelli would organize the peons to put on a display of cattle-herding or lassoing for their benefit. In the summer there would be swimming and tennis and polo – which was now played all the year round – and in the evening there would be an asado and the local payador would be brought to the verandah to entertain the visitors on the guitar.

Stefenelli would display his prowess at the tango. He would cast about for a willing woman and the bandoneón would strike up 'El Día que me Quieras' or 'Tomo y Obligo' or 'Nove de Julio'.

A more perplexing side to Tito began to emerge. He seemed suddenly bent upon proving himself beyond reproach in all things. He even began a drive to convert her to Catholicism, and insisted on the whole family attending Mass on Sundays. But as far as Anna could understand, this new piety was not based upon a love of God so much as a need to keep in with the Bishop, which was in some complicated way also a way of improving his standing in the eyes of the business community. That there must be an ulterior motive, she was sure: she could not believe that Tito would go to so much trouble to curry favour with the Church without any expectation of

134

getting something back. It was, she decided, one more facet of an unstated philosophy. Whatever he did, whatever he touched, had to succeed. Every time he hit, he had to score. Every party had to be a success, every deal had to show a profit, every game of polo had to be a triumph.

She was sent to Uruguay for the birth of her fourth child. This was so that the boy (Tito always presumed it would be a boy, and so far he had always been right) would be able to sidestep Perón's latest legislation and retain dual nationality.

The birth of Santiago, who was known as Jimmy from the start, was not an easy one and a month later, on her tenth wedding anniversary, Anna went to see a specialist at the British Hospital who told her that if she wanted to preserve her health she should take steps to ensure that she did not have any more children.

Tito was not at all pleased. The Church's ruling against contraception was crystal clear, he said, and he had no intention of placing himself in a state of mortal sin by contravening it.

It became a subject for increasingly bitter argument. Anna could not accept that contraception destroyed life and argued the point forcefully. She said that the male seed was not a seed at all, but like pollen.

'Couldn't we at least practise the rhythm method, Tito? The Church allows that, doesn't it? You'd only have to do without me for four or five days a month.'

'Four or five *more* days a month, more like. You seem to be out of action half the time as it is. I didn't marry you to do without you. If I'd wanted that, I would have married a nun.'

'And I suppose Jorge would have squared *that* for you with the Pope.'

'Sarcasm ill becomes you, Anna.'

They were preparing for bed. He was plucking hairs from his nostrils with a pair of tweezers.

'I can get a calculator,' she persisted. 'I saw them advertised in the BA *Herald*. They're made in Switzerland. It tells us when I'm safe. I'd like to try it, Tito. It seems absurd to pay a doctor and then not take his advice, doesn't it?'

He gave way, but very reluctantly, and punished her by turning off his affection and becoming silent and surly towards her. Having made constant demands on her in bed throughout the ten years of their marriage, he now ceased to make any demands on her at all.

She decided that the only way to react was to remain her normal, cheerful, capable self and above all, to *keep busy*. That was what every woman had to do in the camp in order to avoid alcoholism, adultery or nervous breakdown. The advantage of having plenty of children was that keeping busy was not difficult. She spent time with her baby and her boys. She breast-fed Jimmy and welcomed Luis and John when they came back from boarding school. She ferried Marc and Larry to La Ventolera for the birthday parties which Betty organized for her children, and organized teas and asados by the pool in return. She made sure that the servants washed the curtains and covers regularly, that the bedrooms were distempered in turn and that the new servants' wing was properly furnished and decorated. Every Sunday she took the children to early Mass in Cadoret and afterwards took them to Laguna Blanca to watch their father play polo or play polo themselves.

There was gardening to do, too: against Piotr's advice she introduced several new varieties and replaced the shrubs and trees that had been destroyed by the locusts in '46. She filled her life to the brim in order to allow herself no time to think. She rose at six in the morning and went to bed at nine thirty at night, falling asleep as her head touched the pillow; but very occasionally, usually when she was out alone on Jemima, she would wonder what she was doing, where her life was going. It dawned on her one day that in spite of her children and her friends and acquaintances, in spite of the house parties, the dashes into Buenos Aires to have her hair done or buy summer clothes or see the dentist, she was desperately, unutterably lonely.

Riding along beside the eternal wire fence, upon whose posts the horneros built their miniature mud ovens and the little white owls perched, watching her go by, she was overcome by a terrible sense of the sheer waste of this life of hers. She was already thirty. With Blanca gone, she felt unimportant and useless. She had dozens of acquaintances but no close friends. There was no one in the world — not even Jimmy now he was weaned – for whom she was indispensable. Since Blanca's disappearance, Tito had in some extraordinary way managed to relegate her to the status of an employee. Her opinion no longer counted with him. If her wishes conflicted with his own, they were ignored. He had started recently to make fun of her to his friends in her presence. She was 'only Anna', who didn't have to be taken seriously because she was just a wee Scots lassie and didnae have a clue about business or the ways of the worrrld, ha-ha-ha.

Yes, it was true that she loved her children, but Tito managed to make her feel that they were more his than hers. They were Roman Catholic, they were Argentine, but above all they were *boys*. If only she had had a daughter. Just one daughter. A Scottish daughter, a Protestant daughter, a daughter she could teach Bible stories from the King

James Version instead of the Douai translation which seemed to take all the edge off the good old English prose. Yes, if she had had a daughter, she would have gone to school in Scotland, away from the Ruis and Jorges and Lucianis and Victorios of this brash and brittle land.

Where would she be ten years from now? Still here at La Calandria being laughed at by the calandrias? Still on her knees weeding the herbaceous borders, still discussing menus with Catarina, still talking to the ponies or washing the cushion covers or sketching the scissors birds?

She sat on Jemima's back and felt a sense of panic. 'What am I doing here?' she asked aloud. 'What's my life for?' – but the only answer she received came from a sudden gust of wind that shrieked in the fence wires and sent a flock of curlews flapping upward into a cerulean sky.

'Backhand under the neck!' Tito shouted, and as Luis wheeled left and cantered across the pitch, whacked the ball for him.

Luis dug his heels into Trumpeter's flanks to intercept.

'Too late, too late! Try again.'

Another whack, another thunder of hooves. This time Luis made contact.

'Well played, sir. Keep after it now – keep after it!'

The two ponies galloped down the pitch after the ball.

'Ride me off. Come on, boy, ride me off!'

But Luis was unable to do so, and Tito played a backhand behind the legs, reversing the direction of the ball and wheeling his pony round to chase after it.

'Off-side forehand!' bellowed Tito. 'After it, boy!'

Back and forth they went, Tito driving himself as hard as he drove his son. Luis was promising well: he was twelve years old, built like an Indian and fearless on a horse. He wanted to join the Army but his colouring and features were against him. Tito would have to pull strings with his old friend José Ocampo if he was to have any hope of getting him into a decent cavalry regiment.

He hit the ball ahead for Luis and chased after him, confident that he could out-ride him.

'Give way, give way!' he shouted as the ponies converged.

But Luis did not give way. Out of the corner of his eye, Tito saw his son's stick whirl, then there was an explosion in his head.

When he came round Anna was beside him. He gazed up at her, unsure of why he should be lying on his back in a field.

'How long have I been out for?'

'Not very long.'

'Where's Luis?'

'Gone to get help.'

He tried to raise his head. 'Don't need any help. Be all right in a sec. Just a bit of a bonk, wasn't it?'

'Lie still, Tito.'

'Perfectly all right –'

'I said lie still.'

The sky was the colour of an old bruise. He didn't know why but he was glad Anna was there with him.

'What are we waiting for? Where's Luis?'

'He's gone to get help.'

'Don't need help. Be all right in a jiff.'

She took his hand, and he was glad to have the comfort of it. He was about to ask where Luis was again, but then he remembered that he had gone to get help. There was strength and comfort in Anna's hand and he was glad she was there with him. She looked at him lovingly in a way she hadn't for a long time. He felt weak, and suddenly emotional.

'How long was I out for?'

'Just lie still, Tito.'

Luis arrived with Stefenelli, Victorio and a couple of peons. He was lifted onto a stretcher and carried across the polo pitch and down the eucalyptus ride to the house. On the way up the stairs to the bedroom, he heard Anna say to Stefenelli, 'No you are *not* to give him brandy.'

The doctor arrived from Laboulaye that evening. He could not say for sure whether the skull had been fractured. When he had gone, Anna came in.

'You've been quite badly concussed, Tito. You're to stay in bed for three days and you're to be kept quiet.'

He had no objection to that. He had a splitting headache and felt sweaty and weak as a child.

She sat on the bed. He reached for her hand. His eyes filled suddenly with tears. 'My little Anna,' he whispered. 'I don't deserve you, do I?'

'Don't be silly, Tito.'

'No I don't. I've been rotten to you these last few months. Rotten. Will you forgive me?'

'There's nothing to forgive.'

'Yes there is . . . know I've had a bang on the head, but –'

'But what?'

The mists in his mind seemed to clear. 'How about a trip to England? Just you and me? What would you say to that?'

138

15

THEY SAILED IN MID-APRIL. For three weeks they forgot what was happening in the outside world. They played deck tennis and deck golf; they watched films in the radio officer's cabin; they did their boat drills, dined with the captain, guessed the distance run and went up to the bridge to look at the radar.

The ship arrived at Dublin on the first day of May and four days later anchored off Dungeness because of fog. The following afternoon, when they were going up the Thames, Tito found Anna standing by herself on the boat deck.

'What are you thinking?'

'That there were times when I thought I'd never come back.'

'Well you did, didn't you?'

'Will you come up to Scotland with me?'

'Have to see how we get on. There's a lot to do. Only got four months.'

They stayed at the Savoy for two nights before going down to Sussex to stay with Roger and Penelope Smythe, who were relations of Tito's. The Smythes farmed and owned a racing stud. Roger was heir to a baronetcy. He had served in the Navy and had played polo with Mountbatten in Malta before the war.

The Smythes lived in a large Georgian house near Petworth. Their daughter was at Cheltenham and their two sons were at Eton. Penelope's life was entirely taken up with her horses, her tennis and her labradors. Her conversation was like her tennis: you didn't have a hope against her unless you could return every shot on the volley.

There was a tremendous amount of shopping to be done. They made repeated forays up to London and bought clothes for the children and themselves, a whole host of medical supplies, a washing machine, a vacuum cleaner, a deep-freeze refrigerator and a spanking new Humber Hawk, all of which were to be shipped out by sea to Buenos Aires.

When the six polo ponies they had brought with them had recovered sufficiently from the voyage, Tito ignored medical advice and began playing polo at Cowdray. Anna was a loyal wife and went along with

Penelope to watch him and on one occasion had the honour of sitting next to Princess Elizabeth while their respective husbands battled it out on the pitch.

They went to the theatre and the opera and the ballet and the Chelsea Flower Show and the Festival of Britain, whose strange, ultra-modern mushroom building had pushed up from the rubble of bomb sites on the South Bank.

May and June fled by. They did Ascot and Henley and Wimbledon and the polo championships. Then they spent a week in Paris.

Away from Argentina, Tito was a changed man: gentler and less domineering. He seemed to have left his cares behind him.

'Things have been so much better, haven't they?' Anna said on their first night in Paris. 'Let's try and keep it that way, shall we?'

'That reminds me,' he said. 'Got something for you.' He produced a narrow oblong box. 'Go on, open it.'

It was an eighteen-carat gold chain. She loved him for giving it to her but did not entirely admire his taste. It was so heavy, so expensive – so much the sort of thing an Argentine man would put round his wife's neck to prove to the world what a wealthy man he was.

'Do you like it?'

'It must have cost the earth!'

He looked pleased. 'Well. Didn't get it at Woolworth's. Aren't you going to put it on?'

'Help me with the clasp.'

He obliged, and then proceeded to undo her dress.

'Tito –'

'What?'

'I don't want to get pregnant. According to that calculator, we shouldn't make love for another two days.'

He slipped the dress off her shoulders. 'Bugger the calculator,' he muttered in her ear. 'I want you now, not the day after tomorrow.'

Tito had business to do with his banker in Geneva, so at the end of their week in Paris they agreed to go their separate ways for a fortnight so that Anna could visit her parents.

She took the day express to Edinburgh. It was harvest time: a perfect summer's day, with stooks dotting the fields and the combine harvesters and balers at work. They went through York and Newcastle and Berwick-upon-Tweed. She caught a glimpse of Bass Rock before the train turned westwards along the Firth of Forth. Then a little while later the train entered the slums of Edinburgh, went through a tunnel and arrived in Waverley station.

The taxi driver was cheerful and talkative. It was wonderful to hear the Scots accent again. They drove out of the station, up the short hill to Princes Street and turned left past Jenners and the Scott memorial. And there were the castle and gardens, more crowded with trippers and tourists than she had ever seen them.

'Know Edinburgh, do you, miss?'

'I was brought up here. At least – in Colinton. It's my first time back for twelve years.'

'That's a long time to be away. Were you abroad?'

They reached the end of Princes Street and turned left into Lothian Road.

'Argentina.'

'Is that right?' he said. 'Where the corned beef comes from?'

As they went through Morningside she saw the house where she used to have music lessons, and as they left the city behind the Pentland Hills came into view. They went down the hill into the valley at the bottom of Colinton village, up again, and right into Pentland Neuk.

The driver unloaded her case. 'I'm thinking you'll no stay away so long next time, miss, eh?' he said, and drove off with a wave.

The front door opened as she approached it and there, so old, so small, so frail, was her mother. They stood a moment, looking at each other. Then they fell into each other's arms and hugged.

It was not an easy fortnight. Her father's memory had gone and he was frail and confused. It was difficult to believe that this dribbling old man in his tartan slippers who warmed his liver-spotted hands at an empty grate and kept asking whether it was time for tea could be the strict father she had once known.

Her sisters came to supper on her second evening and they sat down to a small joint of roast beef with Yorkshire pudding and roast potatoes and horseradish sauce, and Mrs McGeoch said grace because her husband could no longer remember the words.

Evelyn and Harriet were sharing a flat in Corstorphine. Neither had married. Evelyn was teaching at Oxgangs Grammar, and Harriet was a clerk with the Coal Board. They eyed Anna's clothes, her permanent wave, her sheer nylons and the gold chain she wore about her neck, and drew silent conclusions.

She went to church with them on Sunday, and saw the little memorial plaque to her brother – 'called away while on the Lord's service in The Argentine'. After the service, the minister, whom she had known as a child, held her hands and shook his head, looking at her with sad eyes. 'So this is my wee Anna. Well, well, well.'

His housekeeper was not so gentle. 'Look at her, then,' she said through her nose. 'Half a crown to talk to your daughter now, is that not right, Mrs McGeoch?'

She had brought her photograph albums with her. One evening while her father dozed in his chair and occasionally broke wind or made nonsensical interruptions, she showed them to her mother and tried to explain what it was like to live on an estancia. But she had not appreciated how the years had separated her from her family and how wealth could turn you into a stranger to your own kin. She knew that she must look as brash and worldly to her mother as Ceci had looked to her on the day she first stepped ashore at Buenos Aires.

'But are you happy, Anna?' her mother asked more than once, and each time she did so it was more difficult to assure her that she was.

'One day you must come out and meet all your grandchildren, mother.'

But Mrs McGeoch, who had never ventured further south than Bowness-on-Windermere, said that her days for making sea voyages were long past. Then out of the blue she said, 'You should have married the McNairne boy, Anna. That was a great mistake. A great mistake.'

'It was my decision,' Anna said quietly. 'And I doubt if having me for a wife would have prevented poor Angus being killed.'

Mr McGeoch heaved a deep, rumbling sigh and muttered, 'Tatties and mince. Tatties and mince, and that's a fact . . .'

'Did you have any contact with his family, mother?' Anna asked. 'I mean – after he was killed?'

Mrs McGeoch stared into the little lamp-blacked grate for a long time. Then she said very quietly, 'He wasnae killed, Anna.'

She felt as if she had been punched in the stomach.

'What do you mean? You wrote. You told me –'

'Aye, I told you what I thought best to tell you. He was reported missing presumed dead. Now hold your tongue a minute, let me explain. You don't remember the Great War. You never saw the heartbreak and grief of women waiting and wondering about the men they said were missing presumed dead.' There was a little lift of the sparse eyebrows, and Mrs McGeoch proceeded to go off at a tangent. 'That was a bad business. Him having his name put in the paper to be married to a barmaid. That's what she was, you know. And all for a joke. Some joke, I don't think. Then we had the telegram saying you were to be wed in some Papist basilica and we both knew straight off that you couldnae be in love with the man. It broke your father's heart, you know that? He was never the same after that. Never the same after hearing that you would be married to a Papist. Never the same.'

Anna glanced at her father. 'Wasn't it father who stopped me marrying Angus in the first place? Wasn't it you who backed him up?'

Mr McGeoch seemed to catch an echo of what was being said. He pointed a finger at Anna and said in a loud, accusatory voice, 'Did you not say it was Tuesday?'

Mrs McGeoch reached out and patted her husband's hand, and he subsided into a muttering silence.

Anna said, 'When did you hear he was alive?'

'Oh . . . forty-one I think it was. It was in the paper. He escaped into Spain, seemingly. He was a two-day hero, you know.'

'But *why* didn't you tell me he was alive, mother?'

Mrs McGeoch looked back at her sharply. 'Is that what you would have wanted?'

'Did what I wanted matter when he came here and asked if we could be married?'

Her mother sighed again and sat back in her chair. 'No good raking over the past, Anna. It's all over and done with now. We did what we thought best. That's the beginning and end of it.'

'In that case, why did you have to tell me that he's alive? Don't you realize? This makes everything much, much worse.'

'You can't have it both ways, Anna. That was always your trouble. Always wanted to have your cake and eat it.'

Mr McGeoch looked up, his wet chin moving up and down like a puppet's. 'Is it not teatime?' he asked, as if posing a tricky question.

'Och, look at you, man,' muttered Mrs McGeoch tiredly. 'You've gone and wet yourself.'

Anna went shopping in Edinburgh towards the end of the fortnight and, while choosing a length of the McGeoch plaid to make up into an evening skirt, bumped into an old school friend. It was Ailsa Tulloch – somebody she hadn't even thought about in fifteen years. Ailsa had been captain of the school hockey team when Anna had played centre half. She was rosy-cheeked and generous-hearted – the sort of person people talked to. She had married a psychiatrist and looked prosperous and happy. Anna had not been close friends with her at school but now, for some reason, they clicked.

'I tell you what,' Ailsa said, 'my car's parked in George Street outside Blackwoods, you know it? Why don't we rendezvous at the car in half an hour, and I'll drive you out to Howgate for some lunch?'

The house was warm and welcoming. They lunched in the kitchen on field mushrooms garnished with chives and French wine and home-baked brown bread and butter. Ailsa wanted to hear all about Argentina and Anna's life on an estancia. She made coffee and they sat in the sun on a paved patio overlooking a granite-walled garden. Anna needed to talk. She told Ailsa about the problems of bringing up children in Argentina, Blanca's disappearance, Tito's accident, the locusts, trips into Buenos Aires, riding, entertaining, tennis, swimming.

'It sounds a wonderful life,' Ailsa said eventually. 'I bet you love it, don't you?'

'Oh – yes. Yes, it's wonderful.'

Ailsa said nothing, and the conversation halted for the first time since they had sat down to eat.

Suddenly Ailsa said, 'You don't have to pretend, you know.'

'Pretend?'

'About loving Argentina.'

'What makes you think I am?'

'Anna – I first met Doug when he was an Army medic doing psychiatric work during the war. I worked as his assistant. One learnt to spot certain signals people make.'

'I wasn't aware I was making any signals.'

'Well you are. Very clear ones. I don't suppose you've said a thing to your mother about the bad parts, have you?'

Anna shook her head. The situation at home had been such that she had felt obliged, all the time, to reassure her mother that she had no regrets and that all was for the best in the best of all possible worlds.

'What's it really like?' Ailsa said gently. 'Go on. You can say anything you like about it to me. I won't tell a soul. Not even Doug. No one.'

'I – don't know if I can tell you,' Anna said.

'All right, I'll help you. Do you love it, do you like it, do you grin and bear it – or do you secretly hate it?'

'Can I answer truthfully?'

'That was the general idea.'

'I – I think I hate it.'

Ailsa looked quite unsurprised. 'Why do you hate it? Tell me. Come on, Anna. It's important.'

Anna's eyes filled with tears. 'Tito and I were very happy when we were first married. An ideal couple, really. But . . . in a superficial way. That's the trouble with Argentina. Everything's superficial. And . . . I loved the country, too. The camp can be astoundingly beautiful. For a man, its heaven on earth. Beautiful ponies. Beautiful women.

144

Every sort of sport. They can even dress up and play cowboys and Indians.'

'And for a woman? For you?'

Anna looked away across the garden at the sweep of the Pentland Hills that were mauve with heather.

'It's become the biggest open prison in the world. A prison and a breeding ground. Spiritual and cultural starvation. The only useful thing I've done since I went to Argentina is breed children for my husband.'

Ailsa reached out to her. The dam burst. 'Oh Ailsa,' she sobbed. 'You're the first person I've ever told.' She sniffed and smiled. 'Silly, isn't it?'

'It's not silly at all. It makes me very, very angry.'

'The worst of it is that I've never made a close friend out there. Not one. We have our social circle and the Cadoret Wives Club but they're all Tito's friends or relations and most of them are older than I am. I'm still the wee lassie from bonnie Scotland even now, twelve years on.'

'It was your brother who was killed out there, wasn't it? I remember something in the school mag about it.' Ailsa offered a handkerchief. 'Here. Have mine.'

'Yes, he was attacked by an animal in the monte. His body was never found.'

'And you'd volunteered to go out and work with him, hadn't you?'

'Well – I was volunteered. I wanted to marry somebody else, I don't think you would know him. Angus McNairne. He was in the Army. My father said we were both too young and insisted that we wait a year, and I was packed off to South America to cool my ardour – what's the matter? What have I said?'

'What was that name again?'

'Who?'

'The young man you were going to marry.'

'Angus McNairne.'

'I don't believe it!'

'Why – do you know him?'

'My dear – of course I know him! He lives only half a mile up the road. Doug and I are going to drinks with them tomorrow evening. He's celebrating because he's just been given his own battalion. Angus is such a dear. He's one of my favourite people. Look – I could pick up the phone now and ask Wendy if we could bring you along tomorrow. I'm sure they'd love to meet you. Why don't we do that?'

The thought of it terrified her. 'I'm not sure, Ailsa. I don't know if that would be such a good idea.'

But Ailsa was insistent. She said that they were both grown-up people, both married with children and that it would be ridiculous to come halfway across the world and not make contact. Angus would never forgive her for not doing so, she was sure of it.

'What about getting here?'

'I'll be in town tomorrow. I can come via Colinton and pick you up. And I'm giving a supper party after Angus's do, so you can come to that afterwards. We'll put you up for the night and I'll run you back in the morning. It all fits in perfectly.'

Anna hesitated. 'I'm still not sure about it.'

'It's only a drinks party, Anna. Not a dirty weekend!'

'All right.'

'Marvellous. I'll go and phone Wendy now.'

Anna sat on the patio and panicked. She had already made up her mind not to tell Tito that Angus was alive. She didn't want to open up that old wound again. But did this change things? Was going to a drinks party and not telling your husband an act of infidelity? What would Tito say if she told him? Would she tell him? Should she tell him? And what would it be like to meet Angus again? The very thought of it terrified her. She would know – they would both know – if the love was still there. It would be instantaneous. He would be different, of course. She was different, wasn't she? Or was she? What would he think of her? What would she wear? What was his wife like? Wouldn't she be fiendishly jealous?

She rushed into the house. 'I've changed my mind, Ailsa. I can't possibly –'

Ailsa came in from the hall. 'All fixed,' she announced.

There was a crowd of Army people and their well-to-do civilian friends. There were his children: Rob, a straight-backed, smiling eight-year-old in a kilt who showed them the way through the house to the long, sloping lawn where the party was being held, and his younger sister Kate, a freckly little girl with a mischievous smile who was handing round the cheese-and-pineapple sticks. There was the house: big and old, with huge fireplaces, flagstones, ancestral portraits. There was his wife, Wendy: tall, willowy and English, with long fair hair and a languid, upper-class drawl.

'Ah,' she said. 'Now you must be Anna. I've heard so much about you!'

There was Angus. A decorated lieutenant colonel now, in command of his own battalion.

He was taller and more heavily built than she remembered him, but essentially the same in his kilt and sporran and his brogues. Overweight? Well fed, more like. Well fed and well cared for by a wife who was, no doubt, as loving as she was lovely.

Though she stood and talked with him for some minutes she was later unable to remember what either of them said. All she was aware of was a sad, yearning look in his eyes, a look that made anything but banal exchanges on the lines of 'how lovely to see you after all these years' out of the question, because the only alternative would have been to fling herself into his arms and sob her heart out for the love and happiness that had been so nearly theirs.

Yes: the love was still there, still intact. She knew, without any doubt, that if they had been free to do so they could have taken up exactly where they had left off twelve years before. Wendy seemed to sense it, too. She took Anna by the arm and led her away. 'Now there are all sorts of people who I know would like to meet you,' she said, and interrupted a circle of upper-class Edinburgh worthies who obviously knew each other extremely well and were quite happy with their own conversation.

'This is Anna Cadoret – or do we pronounce it the French way? No? Anna Cadoret, who lives in the Argentine – or is it Argentina?'

After that it was the usual sort of cocktail party with the usual sort of chit-chat, and it wasn't until she was about to depart with Doug and Ailsa that Anna spoke to Angus again. They were among the last to leave and Wendy was being effusively thanked by a brigadier and his wife. Anna found herself standing beside Angus and he turned to her suddenly and said very quietly, 'Nothing changed, you know.' Then Wendy turned back; she said her goodbyes and the moment was gone.

On arriving back at the Tullochs she discovered that she had left her bag behind.

'I'll run you straight back,' Doug said. He was an amiable, gentle man with a Shetlandic lilt in his voice. On the way he remarked, 'If you're anything like Ailsa, your handbag is part of yourself.'

He waited in the car while she went into the house. The front door was open but the party was over and the hall empty. She looked round for her bag and found it, to her amazement, hanging on a hook underneath an army uniform cap which could only belong to Angus. At the same moment she heard Wendy's voice coming from the direction of the kitchen: 'I must say I thought your little Argentine heart-throb was a bit of a come-down!'

Anna took her bag down from the hook, and fled.

16

THE SHIP PLUNGED gently along over a calm Atlantic. On the sundeck, the passengers reclined in deck chairs and waited for tea. Tito had tipped his sunhat over his eyes and appeared to be asleep. The newly-weds, Miles and Monica Gordon-Thomson, were holding hands and gazing into one another's eyes. Mrs Secker was knitting. Mr Secker, managing director of a wax factory in Rosario, was snoring lightly.

Reclining in a deck chair with a book open on her lap, Anna was gazing thoughtfully at the sky.

She was Late. Not just a few days late, not even a mere three weeks. But Late with a capital L. Five weeks and four days Late to be precise, which meant that she was not Late at all, but Pregnant.

And I did not want to be pregnant, she thought. I'm not ready to be pregnant. My body isn't ready. It doesn't feel right. It is simply not fair.

She knew when it had happened. It had been their first night in Paris, the night he had bought her favours with this gold chain which hung about her neck. She picked up the book again, read the same sentence four times without taking in a word of it, gave up and closed her eyes.

Another week to go, and they'd be there. Early October. Spring in Buenos Aires. The Jacarandas coming into blossom. A few days at the Hurlingham so that Tito could play some polo. The obligatory afternoon tea with her ageing mother-in-law, who seldom ventured from her house now but sat with her lap dogs surrounded by silver-framed family photographs in a cluttered drawing room.

Then the drive in the new car to Cadoret. A return to her other self, a return to the act she had to perform, the façade she would have to re-erect. The transformation back into her role as Tito's wife, the heart-throb from Argentina. One step-daughter, whereabouts unknown. One step-son, mother abducted and murdered. Four sons, a fifth on the way. A handsome husband and ten thousand a year.

'Tito?'

He grunted.

'There's something I think you ought to know.'

He grunted again. She felt her heartbeat gathering pace. She didn't want to tell him, but she had learnt her lesson, long ago. Ailsa had promised to write. He would see the envelopes from Scotland. Questions would be asked in the house. It was safer to come clean than to risk an unholy row later. She should have told him before, but better late than never. She took a deep breath.

'Angus wasn't killed after all.'

He opened his eyes. 'Oh?'

'No. He was reported missing presumed dead, but my mother told me he was dead to stop me wondering. He was taken prisoner but he escaped.' She rushed on, anxious to say it all. 'And the funny thing was, that school friend I bumped into, Ailsa, the one I told you about, lived only a mile or so from him and his wife.' She gave a short laugh that sounded to herself as if it had been produced by a ventriloquist. 'I – I went to a cocktail party at their house. He's married with two children. Still in the Army. I'm sorry I haven't told you this before, Tito, but somehow the moment has never seemed right –'

She stopped. Why on earth should she be apologizing? What had she done wrong?

He grunted and closed his eyes. While the ship rolled on over a tropical sea, Anna recognized the tactic. At some time or other she would pay for this. Either they would have a long silence or there would be a row about something quite different or he would belittle her in front of his friends. But she would pay. She would pay in full, with interest.

She returned to her book but was interrupted almost immediately.

'Mr Cadoret, sir?'

A steward had brought a message.

'Radio telegram, sir.'

He accepted the telegram, read it and muttered, 'Bloody hell!'

'What is it, Tito?'

He glanced at her and gave her the telegram. 'See for yourself.'

HAVE TO ADVISE YOU THAT PRESIDENT HAS EXPRESSED A WISH TO
PURCHASE LA VENTOLERA. WE ARE TAKING THE MATTER UP WITH
THE BRITISH CONSULATE IN BA. REQUEST EARLY CONFIRMATION
YOU ARE PREPARED TO JOIN FORCES TO CONTEST THIS. REGARDS.
RANDOLPH.

'The President? Does he mean Perón?'

'I don't think he means Harry Truman, do you?'

149

Anna handed the telegram back. 'He can't just walk in and buy a place that's not for sale, can he?'

Tito snorted. 'Where have you been for the past five years?'

'What will happen if he succeeds? I mean – if he gets his hands on La Ventolera –'

'He'll effectively be able to control La Calandria. He'll own the approach road and surround us on three sides. Just be a matter of time before we're eased out. Probably why he chose La Ventolera in the first place.'

'What about La Tijerita?'

'All part of the deal, I shouldn't wonder. Three for the price of one. Make a nice little birthday present for Evita.'

'Will you fight it?'

'Don't see I can do much else.'

'What if you lose?'

'Got a few tricks up my sleeve, yet, mosca. I've never been a loser and I don't intend to start losing now.'

'But what if you *do* lose?'

He laughed under his breath. 'I suppose you want me to say we'd have to leave Argentina and live in England, is that it? Well you can forget that idea. Argentina's where I belong and Argentina's where I intend to stay.'

He contacted Botta at the first possible opportunity on arriving at Buenos Aires and called personally on the lawyer that evening at his luxury home in Olivos, not far from the presidential palace.

'If the General gets control of La Ventolera, he'll have La Calandria within a couple of years, and if that happens, you can kiss goodbye to your loan, Rui, because I shall be bankrupt.'

Botta nodded suavely. 'I see what you mean.'

'What do you think – will a face-to-face meeting achieve anything?'

Botta gave a gravelly chuckle. 'You English. This is no big problem. Yes, you can go to your friend's meeting. It will make the British Consul feel important and it will give the Generalissimo a reason for changing his mind.'

'But his mind has to be changed first, doesn't it?'

Botta leaned back and blew a perfect smoke ring. Then he smiled his crooked smile and said, 'Leave that to us, Tito, okay?'

He met Randolph at the British Embassy two mornings later and they went with the Consul General in an embassy car to the Casa

Rosada. They were escorted by a cavalry officer into an ante-room where they waited for nearly an hour before being called to meet the President.

He was standing with his back to an ornate fireplace and wore riding breeches tucked into highly polished boots. Jowett and Cadoret were presented and they all sat down at a conference table and coffee was served. A large-scale map was unfolded on the table and the Consul General began to outline the history of the Cadoret district. He pointed out that the Jowetts and the Cadorets were old established families in the Argentine with impeccable reputations for loyalty to the Republic. Sr Cadoret had only just returned from a successful business tour in Europe during which he had represented Sr Jowett's interests as well as his own, and had won valuable orders for Argentine beef, grain and polo ponies. This Anglo–Argentine link was one of many such that made a valuable contribution to the Argentine economy. If La Ventolera were to pass out of the hands of the Jowetts, it was likely that Sr Cadoret would feel obliged, because of the inter-dependability of the two estancias and the long-standing friendship between the two families, to relinquish his own property. This would undoubtedly have a de-stabilising effect in that part of the province, especially among the several neighbouring families with connections in England. It was even possible that a wider effect might be felt and that European confidence in Argentina and international trade could be adversely affected.

'So, Generalissimo,' he concluded, 'we have not come here to plead a foreign cause so much as the cause of Argentina itself.'

Perón sat silent for a while after the Consul General had finished speaking. And then, without even consulting the grey-suited ministers who were there to advise him, he abruptly smacked his hands down on the table and agreed, there and then, to look for a property elsewhere. After that there was a lot of handshaking and baring of teeth, and the visitors were ushered out.

'Wasn't that absolutely amazing?' Randolph said in the car on the way back to the embassy. 'What a man! What an extraordinary man!'

Tito pretended to a similar amazement, but it was one that he did not feel because he had known from the moment he shook one of Perón's senior advisers by the hand that the Brotherhood was on his side.

The Humber Hawk was coffee-cream, with soft leather upholstery and a walnut dashboard. Its speedometer went up to a hundred and ten

151

miles an hour, which was a little optimistic as far as Argentine roads were concerned, but it gave one a sense of power all the same. The engine purred like a contented cat. It even had a radio.

The first trip they made in it was to Quilmes school to see Luis and John, and early the following morning they left Buenos Aires to drive out to the camp. They stopped for breakfast in Luján, lunched at Junín and arrived at La Calandria in the afternoon in time for tea.

As they turned into the long, straight avenue of paraisos, they caught sight of a huge banner, draped across the front of the house: WELCOME BACK MUMMY AND DADDY.

They parked in front of the house and got out of the car. Nobody seemed to be about. Tito was just observing that Stefenelli had had the house whitewashed as promised when there was a shout and Betty Jowett accompanied by Marc, Larry and Jimmy and followed by the entire household staff, plus dogs, appeared round the side of the house.

There was a pandemonium of welcomes and hugs and kisses and exclamations at how much the children had grown; and Anna, with her children round her again, realized that she was very glad to be back.

Betty took Anna's arm and they went into the house with Jimmy and Paula his nurse, leaving Tito with Piotr and the boys, who wanted to admire the new car.

Betty was very welcoming. 'It's *so* good to have you back, my dear. Cadoret hasn't been the same without you. Randy arrived this morning, so I've heard the good news. What a relief that was! We thought we'd have to pack our bags at one stage, you know. We've had fleets of limousines crawling all over the place for the past month. We even had to entertain them – Perón and Evita and all their lackeys and hangers-on, the whole caboodle. Honestly – what a team of spivs. You would hardly credit it!'

They sat down in the big drawing room, whose French windows overlooked lawns and flower beds. Anna took Jimmy on her knee, but he obviously preferred his nurse, so she surrendered him back to Paula.

'Good to be back?' Betty asked.

'Wonderful!' Anna said, and nearly meant it.

They were still exchanging news when Marc and Larry came rushing in from outside. 'Mummy! Mummy, come and look! There's a comadreja in the tree by the tennis court!'

She allowed the two boys to drag her outside and along to the tennis court. The possum was lying in the fork of a conifer, at about shoulder height. It was hissing and snarling every time Tito's boxers jumped up at the tree to get at it.

'Daddy's gone to get his gun,' Marc said, and his eyes shone with anticipation.

'In that case I really don't want to see any more.'

'Oh – *Mummy*!'

Tango and Zamba leapt and barked, and the possum hissed its defiance. Tito appeared from the garage carrying not a gun but a pair of long-handled pliers.

At first Anna thought he had come to rescue the possum. Quite why she thought that she didn't know, because she knew that Tito hated possums. They ate the vegetables, stole eggs from the hen run and stank to high heaven. They were also extremely difficult to kill. You could leave a possum for dead and it would crawl away four hours later.

'What on earth are you going to do?' she asked.

He winked. 'Just wait and see.'

And then – before she could stop him – she did see, and what she saw made her cry out at the bestial cruelty of it.

'Oh – no, Tito – no! *No!*'

'Oh – *Mummy*!' Marc shouted again, and danced about in excitement, because his father had closed the long-handled pliers about the lower jaw of the possum and had dragged it out of the tree. He held it up so that Tango and Zamba could get a good hold on it before he released the pliers. The dogs locked their jaws into its flesh and played tug of war with it, tearing it apart, ripping out its entrails. It was a female, with unborn babies in its womb.

Anna stayed in the bedroom for the rest of the afternoon and didn't come down when Catarina sounded the dinner gong.

When Tito came up to see her she was sitting on the window seat staring vacantly out over the park. She glanced at him then looked away.

'Come on, Anna,' he said. 'Betty's fixed up a family supper for us. Randy's here and the boys are wondering what the hell's going on. Larry says he won't eat any supper unless you come down.'

He stood and waited. She remained sitting in the window, staring out.

'Well? Are you coming down or aren't you?'

She said suddenly, 'No question of an apology or anything like that, I suppose?'

'What is there to apologize for?'

She turned. 'That was the most bestial thing I have ever seen in my life. It was unnecessary and it was vicious.'

'For God's sake! That sort of thing happens every day in the camp, as you well know.'

'In front of impressionable little boys? What sort of people do you want them to be, Tito?'

'It was only a possum, for God's sake.'

'If you had to kill it, you could have shot it.'

'I wouldn't waste a bullet on a comadreja. Besides, I wanted to give the dogs a treat.'

She turned away again and gazed out of the window. Yes, she thought. Give the dogs a treat and punish the little woman.

'So you're going to wreck our first evening back, are you?' he said. 'What do you expect me to tell Marc and Larry?'

She whipped round, her eyes red and blazing. 'Why don't you tell them the truth, Tito? Why don't you tell them about their uncle who was torn apart by wild animals in the monte? Or about Magdalena being raped and murdered? Why don't you tell them that the things that they saw in the possum's tummy were baby possums, and that Mummy has a baby inside her tummy too? Yes, she does for your information. I'm pregnant, Tito, do you hear me? I'm pregnant and I wasn't supposed to get pregnant again, remember? I thought it might be possible to make a new start. I – I told you about Angus deliberately so that we could have a clean sheet. And within half an hour of our arrival you –'

She broke off, then after a moment continued much more quietly. 'Please go and tell Marc and Larry that Mummy has just come back from a civilized country where people do not give animals to their pet dogs to be eaten alive. Tell them that, Tito. Just go and tell them that.'

Nicola Cadoret was born at a private nursing home in Colonia, Uruguay, on 21 April 1952, two months after the death of King George VI and a few weeks before the death of Eva Perón. On Anna's insistence, she was registered as a British subject.

Tito doted on her. 'No one's ever going to hurt you,' he said when he first took her in his arms.

The baby's arrival marked the beginning of a new era at La Calandria. The advent of this delicately coloured child, with her sandy hair and cheeky, dimpled smile brought a new atmosphere of happiness to the household. The boys – with the exception of Larry, who was the loner of the family – were captivated by her. Jimmy was nearly three when she was born and became very fond of his little sister; and Nikki responded to him, gurgling and laughing when he came to her cot and later, as they grew up together, sharing secrets with him during the school holidays when they played in their den in the privet wood.

For Anna, Nikki was a life-saver. Here was the daughter she had longed for and dreamt about so often. Here was the child that was to be really hers.

'Sometimes I wonder if I love her too much,' she confided to Tito.

He grunted. 'Wouldn't have had her at all if I'd done what you asked that night in Paris.'

'I suppose not.'

'No suppose about it. You wanted me to practise contraception and I said no. Why don't you admit it? You've got a lot of things to thank the Catholic Church for, and Nikki's one of them.'

But she would not admit it. Though Tito and the older boys were always getting at her to join the Church, she was determined never to do so. She was equally determined not to turn Tito's battle for her soul into a family issue. She had discovered that it was better not to argue. Life was so much easier when one stopped fighting, and after Nikki's birth she didn't have the energy for verbal skirmishes any more. Besides, she didn't want Nikki to grow up in an atmosphere of bitterness and backbiting. There were far too many estranged marriages among her acquaintances in the camp already. Over the years she had seen too many lonely little Meryls and Yvonnes being pushed to one side to make room for their parents' selfish pursuit of wealth and happiness. She was determined never to join that throng of estranged wives and mistresses who lived out their embittered lives in the suburbs of Buenos Aires.

When Nikki was four, Luis left school and entered the Argentine Air Force to train as a pilot. Three years later, after completing a year's compulsory national service, Johnny started at university in Cordoba. Marc won every sports trophy that Quilmes school had to offer and by the time he was eighteen had a polo handicap of seven. Larry filled his room with posters of rock stars and Che Guevara and spent hours up in his bedroom twanging a guitar.

Anna's fortieth birthday came and went. A year later Tito's fiftieth was marked by a big party. George Rathbone took his wife back to Ireland and left Stiffy, whose marriage to Emelda had turned sour, in charge of the estancia. Tom Dalligan gave up riding when he was fifty and died of a heart attack two years later. His widow, Amy, sold the estancia to Rui Botta's cartel in order to clear her husband's debts, and moved into the suburbs of Buenos Aires. Randy and Betty lived on at La Ventolera, and their children grew up, went to schools and universities in England and came back only for holidays.

In the space of ten years, the political and social scene in Argentina changed radically. The nation's love affair with Evita had turned her into an idealized image for Argentine women to look up to. After her death, nothing could ever be the same again. In some of the poorer communities, Eva Perón became as important in the people's mind as the Virgin Mary. Inscribed on the black marble of her grave in Recoleta was the promise 'I will return and I will be millions', and it seemed that the prophecy came true, for millions of Argentine women modelled themselves on Evita and every Argentine citizen seemed to have been infected by the false expectations she had raised.

Intoxicated by Peronist promises of fortune and illusions of national grandeur, Argentina began lurching from crisis to crisis. While politicians sought to control the unions and stabilize the economy, the Church, the Army and the unions themselves brawled with each other for power. Strikes, riots and attempted coups became commonplace. Machine-gun fire stuttered behind the walls of the army barracks of Campo de Mayo, and the following morning porteñas read of yet another unsuccessful attempt to overthrow the government.

Within two years of being elected, the left-wing President Frondizi was defeated in the Congressional elections of 1960 and for the remainder of his term in office was kept in power by the backing of right-wing elements in the Army and the Church. At the same time, the Peronists split into two main factions, one backed by the military fascism of the armed forces, the other finding support from militant Marxists in the trade unions. Each side was convinced that their brand of Peronism was the one true faith.

Something terrible had happened to Argentina, the land that had once been so full of promise. The dogs of the left and the dogs of the right, kept loosely in check for so long, had been unleashed. It seemed that no one could bring them to heel.

17

HMS PANTHER BERTHED at Buenos Aires naval base five days before Christmas, and as soon as the gangway was in place the British Naval Attaché came aboard and the officers assembled in the wardroom for a briefing on what to expect and how to comport themselves ashore during the ship's visit. In Argentina, they were told, appearances could be extremely deceptive. The most anglicized Argentines could turn out to be the most anti-British. Certain subjects were taboo: the future of the Falkland Island dependencies should not be discussed, nor should the problem of the conflicting Chilean, Argentine and British territorial claims in Antarctica. The subject of possible defence cuts should be avoided and if the question of a withdrawal of the South Atlantic Squadron were raised, any knowledge of it should be denied.

The attaché then went through the various invitations that had been extended to the wardroom and ship's company. There were days out on the Paraná at Tigre, weekends at Mar del Plata, visits to estancias, tennis matches, barbecues, coach tours, day trips to Luján and tours of the city.

Commander Sears took a sip of coffee which had gone tepid in a wide, crested cup. 'Inevitably, you will be seen as ambassadors for Britain, so make sure you do a good job.' He looked round at the officers in their tropical whites. 'Now which of you is Midshipman McNairne?'

The larger of the two midshipmen raised a finger. 'That's me, sir.'

'Does the name Cadoret ring any bells?'

'No, sir.'

'I've got a personal invitation for you to spend Christmas with them on their estancia.' Sears turned to Dwyer, the first lieutenant. 'Can he be spared?'

Dwyer, like most first lieutenants on the first day in a foreign port, was feeling overworked and underpaid. 'Hardly, sir. He'd have to do a lot of extra duties to make up.'

Rob McNairne had seen the guest list for the official cocktail party

157

to be held on board that evening and had mentally reserved one of the embassy secretaries for himself. 'I really don't mind at all if I can't go, sir,' he offered.

'Your wishes aren't part of the equation,' said the first lieutenant.

'It'd be three days,' Sears said. 'I wouldn't press it, but Cadoret's a bit of a wheel. It might cause offence to turn him down.'

So it was decided. Midshipman McNairne would stand duty on the gangway during the cocktail party on the day the ship was open to visitors. He would not be able to attend the embassy reception, nor would he go on the banyan up the Paraná with the fo'c'sle division, nor would he take part in the officers' sports afternoon at the Hurlingham Club.

'Dipped out again,' McNairne muttered.

'You won't regret it,' Sears said. 'The Cadorets are well known in the camp. They're as rich as Croesus. You'll have a super time.'

'Have they got any daughters, sir?'

'One.'

McNairne looked suddenly hopeful. 'How old, sir?'

'Ten, I believe.'

The officers rocked with laughter. Midshipman McNairne was not amused.

He travelled out by overnight train and arrived at Cadoret station at seven in the morning, two days before Christmas. He was met by a bronzed, athletic and monosyllabic young man in bombachas and open-necked shirt.

'Marc Cadoret,' he said, as they shook hands. 'You're lucky. We've had no rain for a week so the road's in good shape.'

They drove fast along a straight earth road until they came to a herd of cattle moving towards them. Marc stopped the Ford truck and the animals lurched slowly past.

'What breed are they?'

'Cross between Brahmins and Angus. We call them Brangus.'

'Are they yours?'

'My father's, yes. Do you ride?'

''Fraid not.'

Marc shot him a look of withering scorn and made no further comment until they arrived at the estancia.

McNairne was introduced to Mrs Cadoret, a small but very upright lady with greying hair and gentle, searching eyes.

'Welcome to Calandria, Robert. Come along in. Breakfast's on the table. I expect you're ravenous, aren't you?'

158

There was porridge with cream, scrambled eggs and bacon, fresh rolls with yellow butter from the dairy and the best coffee he had ever tasted. A dusky housemaid eyed him furtively, leaning closely over him when she removed his empty plate. One by one, the other boys came in, introduced themselves and sat down: Johnny, who was quiet and wore glasses, Larry, who wore denims and cowboy boots and whose hair needed cutting, and the youngest, Jimmy, a cheerful thirteen-year-old with intelligent eyes.

'My eldest is driving out from El Palomar today,' Anna said. 'He's in the Air Force. Do you ride, Robert?'

'No, he doesn't,' said Marc.

'We'll have to get you on the back of a horse,' Anna said. 'You can't possibly stay on an estancia and not ride.'

The daughter appeared.

'This is Nikki. Nikki this is Robert McNairne who I told you about.'

She had sandy hair done in two tight pigtails and a slightly oversize nose. When she smiled, her gums showed as well as her teeth. She said hello and, with considerable poise for a ten-year-old, sat down opposite him and helped herself to cornflakes.

'Robert's in the Royal Navy, Nikki,' Anna said. 'You remember we went on board a naval ship last year.' She turned to McNairne. 'I think it was HMS *Puma*.'

'That's right. She's in the same squadron as we are.'

Nikki looked up. 'Are you the captain or something?'

'No, I'm just a midshipman.'

'What comes after midshipman?'

'Sub lieutenant. Then lieutenant, then lieutenant commander, then commander, then captain. So I've got quite a long way to go.'

She studied him for a moment. Then she asked, 'Can you ride?'

After breakfast Anna and Nikki took Robert to the paddock and introduced him to the ponies.

'They nearly all have one personal friend, you know,' Anna said. 'They pair off and stay friends for life. This one's Canasta. She used to have a friend called Victorica but she was struck by lightning, since when Canasta has been on her own. She's *such* a dear, but I do wish she could make friends with someone of her own age.'

'And this one's Violeta,' said Nikki, stroking the nose of a chestnut mare. 'She's going to be mine next year, isn't she, Mummy?' Nikki embraced the pony and murmured 'Hello, darling, have you been missing me?'

'I expect you think we're quite crackers, Robert,' Anna said. 'But they really do become like people after a while.'

Standing a little way off from the other ponies, a very old mare stood alone. Anna saw Robert looking at it and said, 'Now that's my darling Jemima. She must be twenty-five if she's a day. My husband says she ought to be shot, but I haven't the heart. She's lived all her life here in this paddock and I think she ought to be allowed to die here too, don't you? See the mark on her forehead? It was a perfect heart when Tito gave her to me. I've never ever seen a prettier pony.'

They walked back past the administrator's villa and along a track that led through a wood.

'Would you do us all a great favour, Robert?' Anna asked when Nikki had gone on ahead with the dogs. 'Would you dress up as Father Christmas for us? We're having a couple of other families here for Christmas lunch, and there'll be quite a few young children. My husband usually does it but they always guess who it is. They won't have a clue who you are. Will you do it for us? It'd be such a thrill for them!'

He met Mr Cadoret that afternoon when the family was having tea by the pool. He strode over the grass in his boots and bombachas and silver-studded belt looking like the last of the great caudillos: a fiery, intimidating man with an uncomfortable handshake and a complexion like a furnace.

'Midshipman McNairne, I presume?'

'That's right, sir.'

Cadoret looked at his wife and smiled in a way that was not entirely affectionate. Then he turned to Marc. 'How's Serenade?'

'Not too bad.'

'All right for Boxing Day?'

Marc grinned. 'Providing you ride him, Dad.'

'Cheeky bugger.' Cadoret turned abruptly back to McNairne. 'You naval officers know all about rigging, don't you? Right, well, you can make yourself useful. See that flagpole? I want to fly the Union Jack from it on Christmas Day. We've got the flag and the string but it needs to be threaded through the pulley. Have to go onto the roof and climb out along the what-you-call-it. Just the job for a sailor, eh?'

'I'll certainly see what I can do, sir.'

'Right,' said Cadoret, and stumped off to have a shower and change before joining them at the pool.

'Do be careful, Robert,' Anna said when her husband was out of earshot. 'We haven't had a flag up there for years, and I'm convinced the staple in the wall must be badly rusted.'

He borrowed a coil of rope from the tack room and rigged an extra stay to make sure the staple would not pull out of the wall when his weight was on it. Then, with Nikki and Anna watching him, he climbed out along the gaff with the halyard in his teeth and rove it through the block. By the time Mr Cadoret emerged from the house after his shower, the flag was flying and the length of rope had been coiled up and returned to the tack room.

Cadoret glanced at the flag. 'Is it the right way up?'

'Yes, sir.'

'Sure?'

'Quite sure, sir.'

'Hmmph,' said Cadoret, then: 'Do you ride?'

'No, but I'm very willing to try, sir.'

Cadoret turned to Marc. 'Get Renaldo to fix him up. Give him Cornet or Trombone.'

Trombone was a palomino gelding that was used as a hack for visitors. He was willing to trot but reluctant to canter. McNairne felt he was doing rather well until Trombone seemed to make up his mind that he had had enough of this tomfoolery and cantered back to the house, stopping so suddenly that the midshipman was deposited unceremoniously on the lawn, to the delight of Mr Cadoret and his sons.

'Bring a lanthorn!' Cadoret roared. 'Make way for a naval officer!'

'That wasn't fair, Tito,' Mrs Cadoret said. Then she turned to Rob and said, 'Are you all right, Angus – I mean Robert?' – and promptly went bright red.

Mr Cadoret laughed all the louder. He seemed to put on a great act of laughing uncontrollably. He doubled up, hugging himself and rocking from side to side until the tears streamed down his cheeks. McNairne had the uncomfortable feeling that his host's amusement had nothing to do with sailors or horses but that it was entirely at Mrs Cadoret's expense. He glanced at her. She was no longer blushing, but had a fixed smile on her face.

Luis drove up in a sports car when Marc was beating Rob at tennis. Luis looked much more Argentine than his half-brothers, with a low brow, flared nostrils and thick, sensual lips that turned outwards when he laughed. He brought with him a girl called Juanita who wore a short, tight skirt and a pink chiffon scarf with the knot to one side. She made eyes at Rob and laughed a great deal. Her bust strained against a white blouse that was knotted at the waist to reveal a neat umbilical and an extraordinary pair of hips.

Cadoret volunteered Rob to light the fire and barbecue the steaks and when the fire was alight Nikki, who belonged to the Brownies, took him to the kitchen to show him how steaks should be prepared. He was introduced to the cook. Catarina chattered in Spanish to Nikki and then went to the larder and took out two dozen T-bone steaks.

'How many are there of us?' Robert asked.

'About ten or twelve. But the boys always have two and the dogs eat anything that's left over.'

'They look a bit fatty.'

'Brown Owl calls that "well marbled". It's a good thing because they taste better.' She took some kitchen scissors from a drawer. 'We have to make snips in the fatty bit along the edges like this, so they won't go curly when you cook them.'

'Who's Brown Owl?'

'Mrs Jowett. She lives at the big house.'

He set to work with the kitchen scissors and while he did so Catarina said something to Nikki and laughed.

'What did she say?'

'She was just being silly, weren't you, Catarina?'

Catarina, it turned out, spoke English.

'I say that you will make good husband for niña Nikki, señor.'

'I said she was only being silly,' said Nikki. 'What you have to do next is sprinkle salt on them. But not like that. Sprinkle it from high up so it goes on evenly.'

He carried the steaks outside on a huge platter, and when the fire was hot enough the steaks were thrown down on the grid and left just where they were until they began to sweat, which, Nikki said, meant they were ready for turning.

They ate at a long table on the verandah. The steaks were delicious.

'So who's going to midnight Mass tomorrow?' Cadoret enquired.

'We all are, aren't we?' Johnny said. 'I am, anyway: I'm serving.'

Larry said, 'Well I'm not going inside that sweaty little church again. It's all spit and smelly armpits.'

'If you go to midnight Mass, you don't have to go on Christmas Day,' Mr Cadoret said, and turned to McNairne. 'What about our guest?'

'I'm not a Catholic –'

'Nor am I, Robert,' Mrs Cadoret said. 'But I go all the same.'

Johnny put his arm round his mother's shoulders. 'Mummy's a born-again heretic, aren't you, Mummy?'

Larry said, 'It's worth going once, just for a laugh.'

'So who is going?' Marc asked.

'Every year,' said Larry, turning to Rob, 'we have the same conversation. It's one of our traditions. Christmas wouldn't be Christmas if the entire family didn't bicker about who was going to which Mass.'

'That's enough from you,' his father said.

Luis changed the subject. 'So you're in the Navy, are you? What sort of ship?'

'Anti-aircraft frigate.'

'Have you shot down many aeroplanes?'

McNairne laughed. 'There hasn't been any call to.'

'What sort of guns have you got?'

'Four point fives. Bofors. Oerlikons.'

'Guns are useless against modern aircraft.'

'I'm not so sure about that. What sort of aeroplanes do you fly?'

'Fighters,' said Luis.

'They're the most frightening things I've ever seen in my life,' Anna said. 'They come screaming overhead about six feet off the ground and by the time you hear them they've disappeared over the horizon.'

It didn't get dark until late. They sat on the verandah and Larry fetched his guitar and played flamenco dances as the sky turned from blue to azure to a startling crimson.

'Bed, Nikki,' Anna said, and Nikki obediently kissed her parents and brothers in turn.

Luis and Juanita went off for a starlit stroll in the park and the other boys drifted away. Cadoret announced that he had to write up the diary and went inside. McNairne found himself alone on the verandah with Anna.

'It's so good of you to come and share our Christmas,' she said. 'It makes such a difference having a visitor. We don't fight nearly so much.'

'It was very kind of you to ask me, Mrs Cadoret.'

'You know why you were asked, I suppose?'

'No?'

She looked at him for a moment. 'You have no idea of the connection?'

'Well – I remember a long time ago when I was about Nikki's age, there was a party of some sort, and there was a lady guest who was from Argentina. 'Would that have been you?'

'Yes,' she said, and looked away across the park to the horizon. 'That would have been me.'

'So . . . you know my parents.'

'I knew your father, Robert. I – oh, you may as well know, everyone else does in this house. I nearly married him.'

'I see . . .'

She glanced back and smiled a sad smile. 'Do you?'

There was a silence. A cicada started up, close by. They sat in the candlelight for a minute or so. The cicada rang out insistently and further off a dormilón made its oily, chuckling call. He heard a catch in her breath and realized with horror that she was crying. He was greatly relieved when Mr Cadoret came out again and his wife went up to bed.

'You'll take a nightcap?'

'Thank you, sir.'

'This is Argentine cognac,' Cadoret said. 'Comes from our vineyard in Mendoza. What do you think of the camp?'

'Wonderful, sir. It was extremely kind of you to invite me.'

'Don't thank me, thank my wife. She was the one who spotted your name on the list of officers and insisted on asking you.' Cadoret lit a cigar. 'Has she explained how she knew the name?'

'She did mention that – that you know my parents.'

'Not me, skipper. I've never laid eyes on 'em.' Cadoret's cigar glowed red. He lowered his voice. 'For your information my wife's . . . a bit neurotic. Nerves, you know. The camp does that to some women.' He raised his glass. 'Well. Here's to the Royal Navy. Hope you enjoy your stay with us.'

Christmas Day was boiling hot, but they sat down to roast turkey with all the trimmings nevertheless – twenty-six of them in all, because friends or relations or both (McNairne was unable to distinguish one from the other) came over from neighbouring estancias and brought their children with them.

After lunch Rob was required to sweat it out in a Santa Claus outfit for half an hour and dole out presents while the Cadoret grandmother and great-aunt sat side by side in wicker chairs yelling into each other's ears and getting steadily drunk.

There was a polo match at the local country club on Boxing Day which was marred when Serenade, Mr Cadoret's favourite gelding, collapsed in the third chukka and had to be destroyed; but the Cadoret team – Mr Cadoret, Luis, Marc and Larry – won the match all the same. Afterwards, there was a champagne lunch party in the clubhouse. Betty Jowett had arranged the seating and Rob was placed between Ceci Jowett on one side, who owned the estancia La Tijerita, and Mr Cadoret's mother, Annelise, who was known to the family as Gangan.

'When's your birthday?' asked Annelise when Rob held the chair for her to sit down.

'I'll be twenty in March.'

'What date in March?'

'The twentieth.'

'O my God! You're a Taurus. I can't possibly talk to a Taurus!' She turned away. 'Betty! I can't sit next to this young man. He's a Taurus and you know what Tauruses do to me.'

Betty Jowett appealed to McNairne. 'Do you mind moving? I'm so sorry about this.'

He was moved to the bottom of the table among the children and found himself sitting next to Nikki.

'What are you going to do when you grow up?' he asked.

The answer came straight back: 'I'm going to be a vet.'

'What – here in Argentina?'

She nodded her head. 'Probably. I'd like to live in the north with the indios like my uncle.'

'Is he a vet?'

'No, he was a doctor. A missionary doctor. But he's dead. He died before I was born.' She had grey-green eyes like her mother's. 'He was eaten by wild animals.'

'How terrible!'

She smiled faintly.

'Where do you go to school?'

'I used to do my lessons at home with Mummy and Miss Bannister, who was my governess. But she's left. I'm starting school in BA next term.'

'Looking forward to it?'

'Not much. It's a convent. The Michael Hamm. Are you leaving today?'

'Afraid so. Midnight train.'

'Don't you want to stay any longer?'

'I'd love to, but my ship sails the day after tomorrow.'

There was a commotion from the far end of the table. Annelise had choked and was struggling for air. Unable to get round the table, Betty Jowett screamed, 'Help her someone! For God's sake help her!'

The old lady's head had gone back and her eyes were rolling. Her false teeth had come loose and her lips were turning blue.

It was Anna who forced her way through the crush, Anna who put her fingers into Annelise's mouth, got her false teeth out, turned her

165

onto her side and set about trying to clear her air passage; and while she did so Ceci came down to Rob's end of the table. 'Would you be a great help and take all the children outside?' she asked.

He ushered them out into the blistering December sunlight and organized a game of tip and run on the cricket pitch.

Cars came and went. Eventually, Marc Cadoret walked over. 'My grandmother's dead,' he said. 'You've a train to catch, haven't you? I'm going back to La Calandria now. I'll give you a lift to collect your things and then take you straight to the station.'

The following morning Rob reported for duty on board HMS *Panther*.

'So how was your foray into the hinterland?' the first lieutenant asked over the coffee at stand-easy in the wardroom.

Rob thought for a moment. 'Different,' he said.

18

A FEW DAYS AFTER THE FUNERAL, Botta came out to La Calandria to read the will to the family. Anna told Tito that she had no wish to attend this ceremony, but Tito insisted that she must, along with all the children, so at eleven o'clock in the morning they filed into the dining room and sat down at the big oak table. Botta presided, with Jorge Stefenelli on his right and Tito on his left. Anna sat between Nikki and Jimmy; Johnny put on a dark suit; Marc hadn't bothered to change out of bombachas and Larry had to be fetched from his room and turned up in denims and a Che Guevara sweatshirt.

'It's like dinner without any food!' Jimmy whispered to his mother.

Botta lit a fresh cigar and in a tarry voice explained that under Argentine law four-fifths of the estate had to be divided equally between the children, but that the deceased had been at liberty to dispose of the remainder of the estate as she pleased. What he did not explain was that he had been in a position to arrange matters so that those parts of the estate which were left to the offspring had been considerably overvalued while the remaining fifth had been vastly written down.

Since taking over Annelise's affairs Botta had managed to persuade his client to make significant changes in her will, and it came as a shock to Tito to hear that the undervalued fifth of the estate had been divided according to age among Stefenelli and the grandchildren so that while Stefenelli received the lion's share of something in excess of fifty thousand US dollars, Nikki stood to inherit about two thousand.

Cadoret's two sisters still lived in Ireland and Australia, and as they were not prepared or able to come to Argentina to claim the land that had been left to them, they forfeited the title in accordance with the law.

'This is very good news for you, Tito,' Botta told him when they were sitting on the verandah after lunch. 'We invested a good proportion of your mother's capital on Wall Street – oil and blue-chip corporations mainly – and the investments have done well.' Botta winked. 'I always said you'd do well to stay with me, and now here's the proof.'

'So I can pay off my Banco Pergamino loan at long last. That'll be marvellous!'

Botta shook his head. 'You'd be a foolish man if you did.'

'Why?'

'Isn't it obvious? We wouldn't be able to get round the importation tax on the currency from the States, and even if we could you might draw attention to yourself. That's the last thing you want to do. If the tax people found out about your fiduciary account in Geneva you could end up having your land confiscated in lieu of tax debts. You could finish up with no money in the bank and no land on which to fatten steers.'

'So will I ever be able to pay it off?'

Botta stubbed out his cigar and proceeded to give Cadoret a lecture in economics. He explained that the freezing of Britain's overseas debt after the war had left Argentina in the situation of being unable to invest at home, and that the nationalization of the railways by Perón had incurred expense instead of generating profit. What this meant for landowners was that it was important to appear as poor as possible, which in turn meant keeping himself in debt to the Banco Pergamino. 'Why are you so afraid of this loan? You must borrow as much as you can. Think about it. It's obvious isn't it? Why use your own money when you can use someone else's?'

'But wouldn't it be a good idea to –'

'To what?'

Cadoret sighed. 'Oh – nothing. I suppose you're right.'

Botta showed a glint of gold when he chuckled. 'Of course I'm right, Tito. Of course I'm right.'

In the second week of January, Tito and Anna took Nikki to Buenos Aires to put her into the Michael Hamm school for her first term as a boarder, and after depositing her with the nuns (Anna would far rather she had gone to Northfields) they stayed on at the Plaza for a few days in order to shop, see the dentist and have their annual medical check-ups. On Sunday evening she went to evensong with Ceci in the Anglican cathedral and Tito went to a Lodge meeting. Afterwards, Botta, Cadoret and José Ocampo, who was now a colonel, went to The Rhinoceros, a nightclub recently opened by Botta. Dancing partners were provided and after the last floor show Tito took a girl to an amueblado for sex.

He arrived back at the Plaza in time for breakfast. When he entered the hotel suite, Anna was just out of the shower. There was no need

168

for explanations: he had told her that he would dine with Botta and might spend the night at his flat.

'Did you have a good evening?' she asked.

'Excellent. What about yourself?'

'Very quiet. We came back and had dinner together here. Ceci gave me that magazine on the dresser. I think you ought to have a look at it.'

He grunted. 'Since when have I been interested in women's magazines?'

'Just have a look at the model on the cover, Tito. I think you may recognize her.'

He felt a little flutter of fear. Had Anna found something out about his private life? He picked up the magazine. The model was wearing a slinky black dress, long black gloves and a sombrero hat tipped seductively over one eye.

'See what you mean,' he said. 'There's a resemblance, certainly.'

'It's more than a resemblance, Tito. It's Blanca. I'm sure of it.'

'Could be, I suppose.'

Anna tried to contain her impatience. 'It couldn't possibly be anybody but Blanca!'

'Yes. You're probably right.'

'So . . . what shall we do?'

'Do? Why should we do anything?'

'Tito, we must! We should contact the magazine for a start.'

His night had not been very satisfactory. He felt tired, hung-over and tainted by self-dislike. Getting old, probably. 'What is it – thirteen, fourteen years since she ran off? If she'd wanted to contact us she could have done so years ago.'

'Could she? How do we know that? We know nothing at all about her circumstances. And there's another thing. What about your mother's will?'

'What about it?'

'Won't Blanca be a beneficiary?'

'Not if I can help it.'

'You changed her name. You made her into a Cadoret.'

'I had no obligation to do anything for her at all, Anna. She wasn't my daughter. I only agreed to take her in because –' He stopped, and started again. 'All right. So it's Blanca. But she's obviously in clover, so let's be thankful for that and leave her to get on with her life. Agree?'

'No I don't agree. We owe that child a huge debt –'

'She's not a child. She must be pushing thirty by now.'

'She could be pushing sixty, and we would still owe her a debt. The very least we can do is see that she gets what she's legally entitled to.'

'Yes, but we don't know if she is entitled, do we?'

'So we must find out.'

'How do you propose to do that?'

'For goodness sake, Tito! Ask Botta. Get him to contact her through the magazine. We don't have to meet her if she doesn't want to see us. I don't suppose you would have to meet her at all if you don't want to. But if we dodge our responsibility over this, I'll have it on my conscience for the rest of my life.'

He snorted. 'Yes, well. Your conscience has always been on the tender side, hasn't it?'

She had talked to Ceci about it at length the night before and had had plenty of time to think. This time she was determined that Tito would not override her. 'Of course, there is another aspect you may not have thought of.'

'What's that?'

'If she's entitled to part of your mother's estate and she finds out that you made no attempt to trace her, she might have a very strong case in law. It's a big estate, isn't it? It's bound to be reported in the papers. And knowing Blanca, I think she would fight very hard to get what was rightfully hers. Don't you?'

At the southern end of Buenos Aires, beyond the bleak wilderness of docks, cattle markets and refrigeration plants, is an area known as the 'Boca', where the first Italian immigrants built their tin houses and painted them in brilliant blues and yellows and reds.

The main street of the Boca – Calle Caminito – emerged, over the years, as a centre for the folk art of these Italian immigrants. Gradually, the slum became favoured by painters and musicians. On sunny mornings the bandoneón and guitar were played and tango was danced by young men in black trilbys and young women in tight skirts; and at night, the people sat over their evening meals in the street and chattered to each other under the stars in Lunfardo, the patois of the Buenos Aires docklands.

Blanca first walked down Caminito soon after being expelled from Michael Hamm. She had run away from the Zig-Zag Bar and had walked from the city centre until she reached the Boca.

She had been taken in by Pepito Battisti and his wife, who owned a waterfront bar called La Ribera. They gave her a bed and fed her on soup and pasta in return for working all hours. Blanca met people – men, principally – and she did what she had to. The excitement of Evita's new era was still in the air, and it was probably more intense in this part of Buenos Aires than anywhere else in Argentina. By the time she was sixteen, Blanca had a permanent lover, a married police sergeant called Emilio.

When Emilio came into La Ribera in his uniform, the conversation would die momentarily. Blanca stayed with him for nearly two years until the night he was beaten up so badly that he could remain neither a policeman nor a lover and returned as an invalid to live with his wife in a tenement block at the back of Constitución railway station.

After Emilio there were more lovers, some less satisfactory than others. Blanca moved, very slowly, up market. She despised men, but men wielded power and it was only through men that she could hope to have a share of it.

She was driven by anger. It lay deep inside her, a dangerous anger, anger that smouldered like a sleeping volcano. Even now, hardly a day went by when she did not experience a sudden stirring of anger. With it came the brief vision of her mother being murdered. That single event had turned Blanca into an outsider, a person who owed allegiance to no creed, no morality; a woman who thought only of herself.

The Boca began to attract tourists. Blanca was part of that attraction because she danced in the street for money. People took photographs and asked her to pose for them. She learnt how to use her body: how to pout, how to tilt her hips, how to flaunt her breasts and look haughtily over one shoulder.

It was her success in front of a camera that brought about her acquaintance with Raul Girondo, a stuttering, neurotic freelance photographer. Raul never wanted Blanca for a mistress but he did want to take her picture and was prepared to pay her for the privilege. He used her legs for an advertisement for ladies' stockings; he used her bosom for a feature on ladies' underwear, her lips – in stunning close-up – for the jacket design of a popular novel. Later, he moved her into the fashion market. She modelled swimwear at Mar del Plata, a riding outfit at Palermo, casual wear on a boat at Tigre. Now, it seemed, she had arrived: her face had appeared on the front cover of a fashion magazine.

Two years after meeting Raul she had been able to afford the rent of a one-room apartment on the Calle Zolezzi, within a few hundred yards of the Calle Caminito. She felt at home in this part of Buenos Aires: she had lived almost half her life in the Boca and had metamorphosed first from a runaway schoolgirl to a street-wise tart and now to a sophisticated fashion model who kept herself very much to herself. But though her circumstances were considerably improved and she could have been said to be doing very well, Blanca Salgado was by no means content with life. She was still dependent on Raul, even if she did not have to oblige him in bed. As far as Blanca was concerned, she could never regard herself as successful until she no longer had to work and was not in any way dependent on a man.

There was a Mercedes convertible parked in the road outside her apartment when she arrived back from a session in Raul's studio. It was a blazing hot February morning and she had spent most of it sweating in furs and boots because Raul wanted to get the winter fashion pictures underway in plenty of time.

As she approached the flight of outside steps that led up to her door, a man in dark glasses got out of the car and intercepted her. He was in his late forties: expensively dressed in a dark, tailor-made suit, with black, pointed shoes and a heavy gold watch.

'Jorge Stefenelli,' she said. 'What are you doing here?'

His gaze wandered over her. She saw the look of approval that this short tour of her body brought about.

'What do you think I'm doing? I've come to see you.'

'How did you find me?'

'It wasn't difficult, darling. You're famous.'

'So what do you want?'

'I have . . . information for you. Information that you may like to hear.'

'What sort of information?'

He glanced up the short flight of steps which led to her apartment. The corrugated iron roof was painted yellow and the walls an electric blue. Brilliant geraniums spilled out of their pots on the balcony. A sleeping cat sprawled in the sunshine, one paw hanging lazily over the arm of a cane chair.

'Aren't you going to invite me up?'

She shook her head. 'Nobody goes in there but me.'

He laughed gently. 'So you're still the same Blanca.'

She said nothing.

'Okay. Have lunch with me. You're a big girl now. Mummy won't be cross any more, will she?'

He took her to a steak house on the Avenida Costanera. They sat outside under a trellis. Traffic hurtled past. The sun glimmered on the estuary of the River Plate. White sails bobbed on the horizon.

'You're looking very good,' he said.

172

She looked straight back at him. 'It's my job to look good.'

'I can see that.'

'So what's brought you out of the woodwork, Jorge?'

He made soothing gestures with his hands. 'Be nice, Blanca. Be nice please.' He gazed at her for a few moments. 'You are a very, very beautiful woman. I can't take my eyes off you, you know that?'

She sighed impatiently, causing a movement that fascinated him even more.

'Just tell me why you're here, Jorge.'

'Okay. Your mother, that is' – he shrugged and raised his shapely eyebrows – 'Miss Anna, saw your picture in a magazine. She wants to meet you.'

'Why?'

'Do I have to tell you why? She was very ill, you know. After you went. She blamed herself. Now she wants a reconciliation. Would you like that?'

Blanca looked at him twice, sighed and shook her head.

He laughed. 'You never wasted words, did you, darling? Listen. Anna had two more children, after you left. A boy and a girl. So now you have five brothers and one sister.'

'My name's Salgado, Jorge. They aren't my brothers. Luis is the only one who's related to me and he's only my half-brother.'

'Luis is a pilot in the Air Force now. Remember Marc? He's a hired assassin. A polo champion.'

She looked bored.

'He put his hand over hers. 'Remember how you used to come to my house and see me in the afternoons? Those were good days, weren't they?'

She did not think that they were good days. She detested the English and all that they represented.

'So . . . you're a Peronista, yes?'

'I'm not anything.'

'But don't you want to kick them out of this country? People like the Cadorets? The British community? Don't you want to get rid of them?'

She had a way of showing no response to what he said. He felt that the real Blanca was watching him unobserved. She was unlike any woman he had ever known, and he prided himself that he had known a few. Other women admired him and seduced him with their eyes. They made it possible for him to love himself more completely. They flattered him, accommodated him, invited him in. Blanca was not like that. She was neither tigress nor kitten – more of a sphinx. There was a coldness in her eyes, a calculating ruthlessness that challenged him in a way he found difficult to resist.

She was smoking a Balkan Sobranie, leaning forward with her elbows on the table. She was an extraordinary mixture of feminine sensuality and mannish aggression.

'You'll come back with me to my apartment?' he asked when the bill was paid.

'What for? If you want to do business that'll cost you a lot of money, Jorge.'

He laughed. 'I want to do business, but not the business you think. I want to do you a favour, Blanca. I want to see you inherit the money that's yours. Cadoret money. What do you think? Do you want to hear more?'

That autumn was a depressing time for Anna. Her health wasn't what it used to be and now that Nikki had started at boarding school she felt bereft and useless. The house was too big and they had too many servants. There was a limit to how much time you could spend walking the dogs, riding a pony or sketching birds, and dissatisfaction with her progress at the piano had caused her to close the lid of the Steinway and leave it closed.

March was the time that the calves were marked, wormed and weaned. Separated from their mothers, they bellowed for days on end. It was also the time of preparation for winter. Old trees were felled and for a week the circular saw beyond the workshops sang every day. The evenings began to draw in and with the coming of the first rain for many weeks the roads turned into canals of mud.

Tito had told Anna that he had placed the problem of contacting Blanca in Rui Botta's hands, and that they must leave it to him to make the first approach. That had been nearly two months ago, but there was no question of asking Tito if any progress had been made. She had learnt that lesson: anything that was in Botta's hands became taboo. If she so much as mentioned Blanca's name she would be ticked off for meddling in matters that did not concern her.

The old schoolroom had been turned into an office, and Tito was spending more and more of his time at the roll-top bureau which had been moved from the sitting room. The number of forms and returns required by the government seemed to increase by the week, and he spent more time answering the telephone, negotiating prices or discussing crop yields or bovine diseases with neighbouring estancieros than he did out in the fields with his foreman. He was playing less polo too and often took the Ford truck to visit the outlying parts of the property instead of going on horseback, with the result that he was putting on weight. The years of good living had given him a jowly look; his hair was receding and going white.

Anna was discussing the coming week's menu with Catarina on a Saturday morning when the telephone gave two rings. She waited for Tito to answer it in the office, but when it rang again she went into the hall and answered it herself.

Cadoret was talking to his pony boy outside the office door when the phone went. He heard Anna answer it and by the time he got back inside she had put the phone down.

'Who was that?'

'Stefenelli.'

'Why didn't you tell him to hold?'

'There was no need. Tito – he's driving out today and bringing Blanca with him. They'll be here this evening. Isn't that wonderful?'

He did not think it was wonderful. He allowed Anna to hug him and sob in his arms but he did not think it was wonderful at all.

Catarina put her face in her apron and wept. 'Ay señora! Who thought we would ever see her again? To think of it! Niña Blanca herself!'

'So we shall be two extra for dinner, Catarina. Lay the table with the fiddle-pattern silver and the Edinburgh crystal, and tell Piotr to put two bottles of champagne on ice, understand?'

Dinner at La Calandria was always at eight on the dot, but when it was time to sit down, Jorge and Blanca had not arrived.

'There's probably been a rainstorm on the way or they've had a puncture,' Anna said. 'I'm sure they'll be here soon. Do let's wait for them, Tito. It would be such a pity if we sat down now and they drove up ten minutes later.'

So they waited – for half an hour, an hour, two hours . . .

'Trust that bloody child!' Tito muttered, gazing out into the darkness. He looked at his watch. 'Right. I've had enough of this. Ring for Catarina and tell her to start on the steaks.'

'Couldn't we just wait another half hour, Tito?'

'No we bloody well could not.'

'If they're keeping Buenos Aires hours, ten thirty won't be a bit late –'

'I don't care what hours they're keeping. We're going to eat now. Will you kindly ring that bell?'

She picked up the little brass bell and did as she was told, and half an hour later when Etelvina was clearing away their plates headlights appeared in the drive.

'I knew it,' Anna said. 'I knew this would happen.'

'Yes, well you always do, don't you?' Tito snarled. 'Go on then. Off you go. Fall on her neck and kiss her.'

He followed her into the hall. At first, seeing Stefenelli help a woman from the car, he thought that Blanca had not come after all. But it was Blanca. A sophisticated, brazen Blanca: black hair bouffant, sheer stockings, impossibly high-heeled shoes, a suit with a flared waist, a pencil skirt and a silk blouse. But her face? Where had he seen that face before? With a shock that made his heart do one of its double beats, he recognized her. She was the image of Magdalena.

Anna was equally nonplussed. 'I'm so sorry – we waited dinner –'

'It's nothing,' Stefenelli said, and his manner was that of a master to a subordinate. He put his arm round Blanca. 'Go on, sweetie. Tell them the news.'

Blanca held out her left hand to show them an enormous ruby ring on her third finger. There was a look of triumph in her eye that sent a shiver down Tito's spine.

'You're . . . engaged?'

'That's right.'

'You mean –'

'Yes. To Jorge. We're going to be married as soon as possible. Don't look so surprised, mother! Jorge was my childhood sweetheart, weren't you?'

When they kissed, Anna turned away. The sight of Blanca's tongue going into Stefenelli's mouth made her feel physically sick.

19

NIKKI HAD A CAKE for her eleventh birthday and Aunt Ceci took her
and Bod Murphy out for the day at the weekend and they had lunch at
the Hurlingham Club. There were cards and presents from her mother
and father and Johnny and Jimmy, but having a birthday at school
and being taken out for the day could never be the same as having
it at Calandria.

Her mother had drawn her an elephant waving its trunk in the
air and had divided it up in coloured squares, one for each day of
term so that she could cross them off one by one. She had also
written her a long birthday letter with drawings of all her pets,
and said that she would have her proper birthday present when she
got home. 'Would you like to know what it is now, so that you have
something to look forward to, or would you like it to be a surprise?'
she asked.

Nikki decided to wait for the surprise, but the following week there
was a completely different sort of surprise, because her mother wrote
and said that her step-sister, the one she had never met who had run
away when she was only fourteen, had come back and was going to
marry Jorge Stefenelli. The wedding was going to be held at Calandria
a few days after the end of term and Blanca had invited her to be a
bridesmaid.

Aunt Ceci took her to Harrods in Buenos Aires to be measured for
a bridesmaid's dress, which was orange and flouncy, and she had to
wear two petticoats with it to make the skirt the right shape. A woman
grovelled about on the floor with a mouthful of pins and Auntie Ceci
said, 'Stand up straight, dear,' while they put the padding in to give
her a bit of a bust.

She didn't want to have a bit of a bust. Bod Murphy's bust had
already grown and she was so embarrassed about it that Nikki hoped
hers would not grow too early or get too big. Her mother had said
that it wasn't a good thing to grow up too quickly because there were
lots of things to enjoy when you were young that you couldn't possibly
enjoy later. She said there was plenty of time and not to be in a hurry

because she had all of life ahead of her, and you should enjoy each part to the full.

At the end of term Aunt Ceci collected her in the car and the next day they travelled out to Cadoret together on the train and had lunch in the dining car with Mr Rathbone, who lived alone on his estancia because his wife had run off with Miles Gordon-Thompson. Aunt Ceci called Mr Rathbone Stiffy and when the coffee came she told Nikki to go back to the compartment by herself because they wanted to talk.

When she got to the compartment there was a man sitting in the corner seat opposite hers and he had a newspaper open on his lap. He smiled at her as she sat down and she smiled back. He was neatly dressed with black, smooth hair and penetrating eyes. She sat opposite him and looked out of the window at the pampa and the telegraph poles going past until the man coughed and when she looked round he had raised the corner of his newspaper that was nearest to the window in order to show her what he had been hiding underneath it.

Her mother had said there was nothing you could do about it when men did that except ignore them, so she went back to the game she always played on long journeys of imagining that she held a long, sharp knife out of the train window and that it sliced through each telegraph pole as easily as if it had been made of soft chocolate. Suddenly the man asked her if she was on her way home for the holidays. His hands were suntanned and he had oily brown eyes, long eyelashes and black hair with a precise parting that was almost in the middle. He was dressed in a blue suit and he had a signet ring with a fox's head on it on the little finger of his right hand. He spoke in English with an Argentine accent. She didn't want to talk to him so she just nodded and looked out of the window again. 'Where are you going?' he asked. 'San Luis?' She nodded again. She wasn't going to San Luis but she didn't want to say anything to him at all. Then he moved across and sat beside her. She did not smile or look at him. The telegraph poles fled by the window but she no longer cut them down with her imaginary knife. The man was sitting close to her and she could feel the heat of his leg. She decided to go back to the dining car. He said, 'Going to spend a penny?' She tried to slide open the compartment door but it was stiff and before she could manage it he got up and did it for her and followed her out. When she had come back from the dining car she had gone past the right compartment and had had to turn back. Now, she realized that she had turned the wrong way and was not going towards the dining car where Aunt Ceci was, but away from it. She went quickly along the corridor but the man kept up with her.

178

When she looked back he smiled and it was then that she began to be terrified. All she wanted to do was get away from him. The lavatory at the end of the carriage was vacant so she went straight in but as she tried to close the door he put his foot against it and before she knew what had happened he was in the lavatory with her and had locked the door behind them. He said, 'Good girl. Now we can have a bit of fun.' He stood between her and the door so she couldn't get past him. He tried to kiss her and fondle her but when she struggled, he got angry and said that if she wanted to be rough he could be rough too, and he crushed her hand to prove it. 'Be a good girl,' he said, 'and I'll be gentle. Be a bad girl, and I'll push you out of the window.' It was a small window but she knew that if he pushed hard enough he would be able to get her through it. It was frosted but she could see the shadowy telegraph poles going past outside. She was shaking with fear. There was nothing she could do to stop him because he was so strong. It was horrible. When he was zipping up his trousers again he said, 'I am an officer in the army. If you say anything about this to anyone, I'll send my soldiers along and they'll do it to you again.' The train slowed down. It was approaching a station. He told her to stay inside the lavatory with the door locked until after the train had left. He said he would stand outside the lavatory door to make sure she did what she was told and that he wouldn't leave the train until the last moment so it wouldn't be any good trying any tricks. He was out of breath and red in the face and he looked frightened. 'Remember what I said,' he said. 'If ever you tell, I'll send my soldiers.' Then he left and she locked the door after him and as soon as the train had left the station she washed herself as well as she could in the handbasin and put her clothes on and when she saw herself in the mirror it was as if a total stranger was staring back.

Marc was at Cadoret station to meet them with the Ford and he dropped Aunt Ceci off at Tijerita before going on to Calandria. It had just stopped raining when they drove up under the dripping paraiso trees and her mother was there waiting for them and the peons were putting up a marquee in the garden with a tunnel that joined on to the verandah, and Catarina was in a fluster and Luis was on leave for the wedding and Jimmy was back from school and Larry was making a din in his room with his drums and Johnny, who had just finished at college and was going to be a schoolteacher, made her pretend to arrive all over again so that he could take a film of her on his new cine camera.

Her mother had told the pony boy to have Violeta saddled and ready, which Nikki had asked her to do in her last letter, and the first thing she did after having a shower and changing into her holiday things was go for a ride by herself. She cantered along the ride and went across the polo pitch and on, past the corral where the peons were planting willow trees and along the long straight earth track, with the wind in her face and the birds flying up ahead and a hare darting out at her approach and the smell of the damp earth clean in her nostrils.

She reined in Violeta and stared up at a carancho that was circling high overhead.

Gradually it dawned on her that until now she had been a child and dependent on grown-ups to make her decisions. But having decided to keep what had happened entirely to herself, she was already less of a child and more of a grown-up. She was eleven years old and she knew something that none of her friends at school knew. Her mother had said that you could use everything that happened to you in life, whether it was good or bad, to make you stronger, and that a time came in everyone's life when you needed to be strong. She needed to be strong now, so as she trotted back along the eucalyptus drive she made up her mind that she would be strong. She would keep her secret, she would tell no one. She would not even think about it herself. She would bury it deep down inside herself where neither she nor anyone else could ever get at it again.

When she got back to the house her father and Stefenelli were there and so was her step-sister. Blanca refused to speak in English and smoked black cigarettes with gold tips. She had a loud voice, and was wearing huge earrings, two necklaces and about twelve bracelets. She called Nikki darling and held her cheek for her to kiss, but it wasn't a proper kiss and although Nikki had always wanted a sister, Blanca wasn't the sort of sister she wanted.

They all sat down to tea and when Larry came down Anna said a prayer to thank God for bringing them all together as a family for the very first time.

'Now for your real birthday present,' Anna said when Nikki had blown out the candles on the birthday cake; and Jimmy, who had slipped out of the room a minute before, opened the door and in rushed a puppy, a golden retriever bitch, so pale she was more cream than golden, with a black nose and melting eyes and furious wags, and Nikki caught her in her arms and hugged her.

'Darling!' she said. 'Oh darling!' and hugged her again, and the puppy licked her face and her father said that she would have to look after it herself, and train it and make sure it didn't go worrying sheep or chasing chickens.

'Have you thought of a name?' Stefenelli asked.

'Pollyanna!' said Nikki, so Pollyanna it was.

Padre Pellegrini, the new priest from Our Lady of Sorrows in Cadoret, came to lunch the next day to conduct the rehearsal. While they waited for the bride and groom and best man to arrive so that he could go through the wedding service with them in the marquee, he had a talk with the family on the verandah. He said that Señor Tito and his wife could use the occasion to renew their marriage vows and that Luis, John, Marc, Laurence, Santiago and Nicola could learn both from the wedding ceremony itself and from the splendid example of fidelity and love their parents had set them. He said that they should give thanks for the fact that they were members of a happy family and had been given a sound Catholic upbringing.

Padre Pellegrini was not a bit like Father Michael, who had died. Father Michael had been poor and there had been stains on his lapels and his hair had always needed washing. Padre Pellegrini was rich and round and neat and pink and very respectful towards Stefenelli and he put his hands on your shoulders when he was talking about you. Johnny, who had always been the holy one of the family, was going to be the server at the nuptial Mass and after Padre Pellegrini had seen the marquee and had made sure that the altar would be in the right place he reminded them all that although this was a very happy occasion it was also a very solemn one.

Then he looked at his gold watch and wondered where the bride, the groom and the best man had got to. Marc was sent to see if they were on their way from Stefenelli's house yet, and when he came back he said they were and Nikki heard him whisper to Larry, 'The lazy sods were still in bed.'

Half an hour later the bridal trio arrived and Jorge Stefenelli introduced his cousin, Colonel Ocampo, who was going to be the best man. Colonel Ocampo was an old friend of Daddy's and they had played polo together before the war. He was smartly dressed in a blue suit and he had dark brown eyes and long eyelashes and black hair with a parting that was nearly in the middle and a signet ring on the little finger of his right hand that had a fox's head on it. He shook hands all round and when he came to Nikki he stared straight into her eyes and said, 'Well, well, well! You're the little girl I had such a nice talk with yesterday on the train, aren't you?'

*　　*　　*

The wedding was at six p.m., and the cars started arriving soon after five. Renaldo, the pony boy, had been put in charge of the car-parking and he took his duties very seriously, arranging the Fords and the Daimlers and the Humbers and the Mercedes in neat, gleaming rows on the grass at the side of the house. Luis wore uniform, Johnny served the Mass and Larry and Jimmy were ushers. The bride, the groom and the best man took the blessed sacrament. There was an abominably behaved six-year-old page-boy called Peppé who was dressed like a miniature cavalryman and wore a shako and who deliberately trod on the bride's train as she went up to the altar. The marquee, which had been made into a temporary church, was packed to capacity with Anglo-Argentines and Italian-Argentines. These two groups were like oil and water. The occasion should have mixed the Jowetts and the Harrisons and the Rathbones with the Stefenellis and the Bottas and the Lambrettis; but the mix was only temporary, and the bonhomie and courtesy shown by each side to the other was forced, and concealed a mutual mistrust.

Rui Botta proposed the toast to the bride and groom and Jorge thanked his uncle for all he had done for him in the past. Then Colonel Ocampo stood up and made a speech about Stefenelli's many affairs of the heart over the past twenty years which was supposed to be funny. He then presented Peppé with a Swiss watch and Nikki with a pearl necklace. After that there was dinner and dancing to a six-piece band and when no one was looking Nikki threw the pearl necklace Colonel Ocampo had given her down among the prickly leaves of a big cactus bush where no one could possibly find it.

Tito enjoyed the party to the full. He danced with Betty, he danced with Emelda, he danced with Ceci and he danced with Blanca. He even danced with his wife. He also danced with the new maid, a sixteen-year-old called Chiquita, who he had recruited from Laboulaye a few weeks before. She blushed furiously when he invited her to join him on the dance floor in the marquee.

All the peons came along in their best clothes and hung about watching until Blanca said she wanted everyone to join in. When the band took a breather, the payador from the village took over and the tangos and foxtrots gave way to the thrumming beat of the zamba. There were no neighbours to annoy, no babies that needed their sleep. A hundred leagues from nowhere, under a starry sky, a little piece of pseudo-Europe frolicked through the night.

Just before dawn, Anna woke suddenly from a nightmare. She had gone into the kitchen and found one of the peons boiling something in a pot. He was bending over it and muttering words she didn't understand, and she knew what was in the pot but didn't dare look; and then all her teeth had turned rotten and she had woken up with every muscle in her body taut.

She got out of bed and went to the window. The party was still going on. A blood-red dawn was streaking the sky, and Larry was playing the mournful glissandos of 'Mi Favorita' on his guitar.

A private aircraft touched down on the polo pitch later that morning, and the newly-weds departed on their honeymoon. A crowd of guests gathered to see them off. Watching Blanca accept the congratulations and kisses of the Bottas and the Lambrettis and the Ocampos, Anna found it impossible to connect this big, loud, extravagantly dressed woman with the troubled little girl who had once crouched, wordless, behind a door.

The Piper aircraft revved, turned and leapt quickly upward into the wind, and the guests turned and made their way back to the house.

Tito walked with Rui Botta and José Ocampo, and Johnny with Padre Pellegrini. Luis and Marc had already left for Buenos Aires because one was due back at his squadron and the other was playing polo the following day at Palermo. Larry was asleep with his guitar in an armchair on the verandah.

Anna linked arms with Jimmy and Nikki, her two babies. Nikki had been very quiet since coming back from school, and Anna wondered if something was wrong. But she knew better than to ask, because Nikki was getting to the stage when she liked to keep some things private.

They came to the gate out of the polo pitch and entered the eucalyptus drive. The trees were swaying and whispering in the wind.

Jimmy said, 'She wasn't at all what I expected.'

'Who's "she"?'

'Mummy! You know. Blanca.'

'Well. People very seldom are.'

'Are you glad, Mummy?'

'Glad about what?'

'That she's married Stefenelli.'

Jimmy was the one who asked the difficult questions. There was an honesty and a gentleness in him that was not present in his brothers. Tito called him wet and scoffed at him openly. Though she knew she should have no favourites, Anna had always regarded Jimmy as special because she could see something of her own brother in him.

'I don't know. Yes, I think I must be. They're both grown-up people, and provided they're happy –'

She stopped, and Jimmy glanced quickly at her. 'It won't be the same though, will it? Something's changed, hasn't it?'

She drew them closer to her. 'Life is always changing,' she said. 'Especially when you're young.'

Nikki heaved a deep sigh. 'I wish it wouldn't,' she said, and leant her head against her mother's shoulder.

After the wedding Larry went to stay with a school friend in Buenos Aires and Johnny went to a retreat in Cordoba. To his father's disgust, Jimmy spent a lot of time reading or writing poetry. He was nearly fourteen now; he and Nikki were still close, but Nikki seemed to have become more at ease in the company of animals than of human beings, and closer to Pollyanna than to her brother.

She devoted nearly all that autumn holiday to her animals. She visited her rabbits every morning and evening; she groomed and rode Violeta daily; before she went to sleep she watched the hamsters which she kept in her bedroom, and she scattered food for the ducks and bantams every morning after breakfast. But most of her time was taken up in training Pollyanna.

Pollyanna was three months old, greedy as only golden retrievers can be and passionately in love with the entire human race. Nikki set about training her to sit, stay and walk to heel, and within a fortnight Pollyanna was retrieving a ball and dropping it on command.

Nikki only had to appear at the paddock fence for Violeta to come whinnying towards her, and after the first tentative nose-to-nose encounter, Violeta and Pollyanna struck up an animal friendship. The three became almost inseparable, so that Nikki came to spend more time in the company of her pony and dog than with her family.

But Pollyanna had bad habits. Though she walked to heel quite well she could not be relied upon to remain at heel if a human being appeared on the horizon. She was also a terrible scavenger. The peons on the estancia were often too far from home during the day to use the proper place to relieve themselves, and one day it came as a rude shock to Nikki to discover exactly what sort of morsel Pollyanna found to eat in the area of rough grass in the mill square at the corner of number twelve field.

'You filthy, filthy, filthy bitch!' she screamed, and chased her off it with her hand raised. The dog dashed off and it took her half an hour to coax Pollyanna back and put her on the lead.

A few days before the beginning of the school term, Jorge and Blanca returned from their honeymoon and held a large house party at Casa Nova, to which neither Tito, Anna nor any other Anglo-Argentines were invited. The following day, Nikki took Pollyanna for a walk.

There was a reedy lake a couple of miles from La Calandria where her father and his friends sometimes shot duck, and here Pollyanna took great pleasure in wallowing in the muddy water and hunting water rats. On the way back, a familiar figure came into sight. Colonel Ocampo, one of the house-party guests, was out for a stroll with a shotgun over his arm.

There was not another soul in sight. Pollyanna had gone ahead and was digging a hole in the middle of a field, burying her nose, snuffling and sending a shower of dirt back between her hind legs. When Nikki called to her she was too engrossed with the scent of vizcachas even to look round.

Ocampo waved. 'Hello there!' he shouted.

Nikki ignored him and went on calling Pollyanna, but the dog only paused for a moment, revealing a nose caked with earth, before returning to her burrowing.

Ocampo strode towards Pollyanna. Nikki screamed, 'Pollyanna! Will you come here!' but the dog continued to burrow. Then Ocampo whistled shrilly, the dog looked up, saw that there was a new face to meet, and bounded over to meet him, wagging round his legs as if he were a long-lost friend.

'It's okay,' Ocampo called. 'I've got hold of him.' Holding Pollyanna by the collar, he continued towards her.

For a few moments she stood and watched Ocampo approaching with Pollyanna, who was now being dragged along. Then she turned and ran.

He shouted after her but she didn't stop. She ran and ran until her windpipe felt as if it had been sandpapered and she had a stitch that was like a knife in her side.

She stopped and looked back. Ocampo was no longer in sight, and nor was Pollyanna. She struck out across field after field, making a long detour to get home.

Her mother was in the drawing room with Betty Jowett.

'What on earth's the matter, darling?'

Nikki broke down in floods of tears. 'Oh Mummy!' she wailed. 'I've lost Pollyanna!'

They went upstairs and sat on Nikki's bed.

'Now when did you last see her?'

'On the way back when we were in forty-four field. She was digging and we met Colonel Ocampo. I called to her but she took no notice and then she ran off.'

'Where, Nikki? What direction was she going in?'

'Well, sort of – to Colonel Ocampo. I called and called to her but she wouldn't come.'

'But didn't Colonel Ocampo help you try and catch her?'

'Well, yes, but –'

'But what, Nikki?'

Nikki shook her head.

'What?'

She began to cry.

Anna took her in her arms and soothed her. 'Now tell me all about it. What's happened? Something's upset you hasn't it? Did Colonel Ocampo tell you off or something?'

'No.'

'What was it then?'

'I – I just didn't want to talk to him, Mummy.'

Anna took her hand. 'Why not, darling?'

Nikki bowed her head and sniffed. Anna said, 'Whatever it is, whatever's happened, you must tell me. I must know, do you understand? If you've done something naughty or – or if Colonel Ocampo has done anything at all to make you frightened of him, you must tell me. See?'

Nikki nodded.

'Now is there something you haven't told me? There is, isn't there?'

Nikki looked into her mother's eyes and shook her head.

'Please darling,' Anna said. 'I won't be cross with you – whatever it is. But you must, must tell me. See?'

She had to say something. It was impossible to say nothing but also impossible to tell the truth.

'Please, Nikki,' said Anna. 'Please tell me what happened.'

The lie came to her as if by magic.

'I lost the necklace Colonel Ocampo gave me at the wedding.'

Anna heaved a sigh of relief. 'Well that's nothing to worry about. I suppose you were afraid he'd be angry, were you?'

Nikki nodded and began to cry again.

Anna put her arm round her. 'Darling! It's not as bad as all that! You never know, we might be able to find it. When did you last see it?'

She lied again. She plunged deeper and deeper into lies. She said she had worn it while out riding and hadn't discovered it was missing until she got home. It could be practically anywhere on the whole estancia.

'In that case I'll tell Daddy and he can ask if any of the peons have picked it up. And don't worry about Pollyanna, either. I'm sure we'll find her. I expect she'll be hungry and come home of her own accord. And next time this sort of thing happens come and tell me straight away, see? Never bottle things up, Nikki. It never works in the long run.'

Anna found Tito in the office with Stefenelli. Tito was never pleased to be interrupted during the working day, but Anna insisted on having a word with him in private. Stefenelli took the hint and paced pointedly up and down outside the office window while they talked.

'Well? What is it this time?'

'Nikki's lost Pollyanna.'

'Is that all?'

'No that is not all, Tito. I don't think it was her fault. She met José Ocampo and ran away from him. She says she was afraid to meet him because she'd lost the necklace he gave her, but I'm convinced there's another reason.'

'Like what?'

'Well, she met José in the train coming back from school didn't she? And as soon as I started asking her about him she looked frightened and shut up like a clam. She also says she went out riding wearing the necklace, which I find very hard to believe. Nikki has more guts than to run away from Ocampo just because she'd lost his necklace. There must be more to it than that. There simply has to be a better reason for her to be frightened of Ocampo than losing a necklace.'

'So what you're saying is, she's lying.'

'No. I think she's bottling something up.'

'Comes to the same thing doesn't it?'

'Not when you're eleven years old and terrified out of your wits, Tito.'

'So what do you expect me to do about it?'

'Have a word with José this evening when they come for drinks.'

He looked heavenward. 'For God's sake, woman!'

'Is that all you have to say, Tito?'

'What do you expect me to say? Not much else a man can say, is there?'

'Well I think there's a great deal you can do. You can organize a search for Pollyanna for a start. And you can ask Ocampo about it this evening.'

'Oh yes? And what do you suggest I ask him?'

'Why Nikki should be so terrified of him that she runs off and leaves

187

Pollyanna with him. Why he let the dog go, for that matter. There is something behind this, Tito – I know there is. I haven't brought up seven children for nothing. I know when a child is genuinely frightened and I know when she's hiding something from me – Nikki especially. Call it a mother's telepathy if you like, but I am convinced something has happened. I am convinced something has gone very, very wrong.'

'Like what?'

'I don't know. She may have been interfered with for all we know.'

'Are you seriously suggesting that Ocampo –'

'You don't know what it's like to be a woman in this country, Tito. You don't know what it's like to be the only woman in a lift, or standing in a bus or walking on a beach or in a park. Nikki's just coming to the age when she's most vulnerable. And she has been hurt. I know it. I can see it in her eyes. She's been hurt and she's saying nothing and I want to find out what's hurt her. She's your only daughter, Tito. Is it so very unreasonable to expect you to want to find out too?'

He turned away. 'Well I'm sorry to disappoint you, but I think you're blowing this up out of all proportion. It's pure conjecture, isn't it? Not a scrap of evidence. Not even hearsay. I don't know if it's your time of life or something, Anna, but if you think I'm going to start quizzing business associates about nursery matters every time the bell strikes you can just think again.'

Pollyanna was still missing when Stefenelli and his house guests came to drinks that evening. Standing on the verandah flagstones with a chunky glass of bourbon in his hand, Ocampo was as urbane as ever. When Anna asked him about his meeting with Nikki, he explained that he had released the puppy when he saw Nikki running off in the opposite direction.

'I think she thought I was going to punish her for not controlling the dog,' he said. 'Of course, nothing was further from my mind.'

He met her eyes with the confidence that military service instils in a man. 'I do hope she gets her puppy back. She was obviously quite upset.'

'Never bottle things up,' Anna told Nikki again that evening when she went up to say good night. 'Will you promise me that?'

Nikki wanted to forget the whole thing. She wished she hadn't said what she had about the necklace and she wished her mother hadn't said anything to her father about her running away from Colonel Ocampo.

She gave her promise, but it was a meaningless one. Everything was

188

meaningless now. It wasn't even any use asking God to help her find Pollyanna because God wasn't friends with little girls who told lies.

The following day was the last one of the holidays. Nikki went out on Violeta immediately after breakfast to look for Pollyanna. She stayed out until lunch time but found no trace of her. She asked the peons and the foreman if they had seen her, but none of them had.

It drizzled most of the day. Nikki went out on another search in the afternoon. Then, when they were having tea, Chiquita came in to say that the estancia foreman was at the back door asking to speak to the patrón. Tito went out to see what he wanted and when he came back he looked at Nikki and said, 'Your dog's turned up.'

'Oh – wonderful!' Anna said. 'I've been praying so hard. Where is she?'

'Scavenging in the cattle cemetery. So she'll have to be shot.'

That was the rule at La Calandria. There was good reason for it: the rotting carcasses were invariably diseased and once a dog ended up among them it was virtually impossible to catch and quickly went wild.

'Tito surely –' Anna started.

But Tito had turned to Chiquita. 'Tell the capataz that I'll come right away.'

Nikki said, 'Can I come too, Daddy?'

Tito glanced at Anna and grunted. 'Better not.'

'I'm *sure* I can catch her.'

Anna said quietly, 'You must let her try, Tito.'

Jimmy added, 'I second that.'

Cadoret looked round at them. 'All right. But I'm going now while there's still some light.'

He took the Ford truck and put a hunting rifle in the back. Nikki sat between him and the foreman and they bumped along over the fields to the far corner of the property.

Pollyanna appeared almost immediately. She was right in among the carcasses at the centre of the dump and as soon as she saw them started barking.

'All right, Nikki,' Tito said. 'I'll break my own rule. If you can catch her you can take her home. But you're not to go off the path, understand?'

The path led a little way into the cemetery and then stopped. The stench of dead cattle, the flies buzzing and the feeling of death on all sides made her want to be sick. But she fought back her nausea and while the men stayed in the truck a couple of hundred yards back she began calling and pleading to Pollyanna to come to her. She had brought some biscuits and threw one. She talked to Pollyanna, called her and threw more biscuits.

Slowly, the dog came nearer. It took a long time but there was no doubt that Nikki was making progress. Pollyanna would advance a few yards, snatch a biscuit from the ground and retreat. Then at last Pollyanna came to within three feet and Nikki lunged to grab her by the collar. But Pollyanna had been on her own for more than twenty-four hours and having tasted freedom did not want to lose it. As Nikki's fingers closed on her collar she took off and returned to the centre of the carcass dump, barking her defiance all over again.

'Nikki!'

She turned. Her father and the foreman were getting out of the truck.

'That's enough. Come back here now.'

'Daddy please let me have one more try!'

'You've had quite enough tries. Come back here.'

In the end he had to collect her. He took her arm and pulled her weeping back to the truck. He said, 'I don't like doing this but it has to be done,' and a little while later when she was in the cab of the truck there was a single echo-less shot and for a short while the sound of Pollyanna yelping until a second shot brought silence.

20

LARRY WAS EXPELLED from Quilmes later that year for 'subversive political activities and theft of a portrait of Eva Perón' and instead of returning home began living in a commune of artists and musicians in San Telmo, the Bohemian district of Buenos Aires.

Cadoret tried to pull strings to have the decision reversed, but was persuaded by Ocampo that intervention was not appropriate. The knowledge that his son had been branded a thief gave him such a jolt that within a week he was experiencing chest pains and an irregular heartbeat. When he visited a heart specialist he was advised to eat less meat, drink less alcohol and cut back on his sex life.

After the appointment he met Stiffy Rathbone and they drove out to Hurlingham for lunch.

It was spring again; the city parks were full of flowers and blossom. But Tito was not in a spring mood. 'So that's that,' he said as they sat down to lunch at the club. 'Another year or two and I'll kick the bloody bucket.'

Stiffy remarked that Cadoret was not the only one with problems. 'Emelda playing up again, is she?'

Rathbone nodded. 'She's taken up with some bloody little chauffeur twenty years younger than herself. That woman's a nympho if ever there was one. Can't think why I married her. At least you've got Anna. That was the best day's work of your life, TC, the day you married Anna. I never thought anyone would keep you on the straight and narrow but my God, she has.'

Tito shook sauce on his fairy toast and inspected the menu. He was still irked by the order to cut back on sex. Screwing, the younger generation called it. Well he liked screwing and always had. He'd taken precautions with Chiquita and they had a nice little arrangement. But Chiquita would have to go now. He'd have to have a word with Stefenelli. It would be easy to arrange. She was illiterate and an orphan and entirely dependent on her employer. He would have her sent up north.

'Stuff it,' he said when the waiter came for the order. 'I'll have

191

a T-bone and a bottle of Perdriel, and to hell with my heart-beat.'

With the exception of Larry the other Cadoret boys were doing well. After working for two years as a teacher Johnny finally decided to enter the priesthood and started his long training at a seminary in Cordoba. Marc was making a lot of money out of playing polo and was well on the way to his first million. Luis had flown for three seasons in the FAA aerobatics display team and had been selected as an aide-de-camp at the Casa Rosada. But though he always seemed to be surrounded by sophisticated women, he remained unmarried. As the years passed, he became an increasingly private and lonely man, devoted always to his flying, fascinated by power and often seen wearing dress uniform and white gloves as he helped the wives or mistresses of public figures in and out of limousines.

As he approached sixty, Tito began to mellow. He used to boast that each of his children would perform a valuable function for him in his old age. Luis would protect him, Johnny would look after his spiritual well-being, Marc would provide for him financially and Jimmy, who was the literary genius of the family, would chisel the name of Cadoret upon the honours boards of Academia. As for Nikki, her ambition was to be a veterinary surgeon, so although he couldn't really see it happening, Tito claimed that she would end up looking after his polo ponies.

Nikki's teenage years were not happy ones. Her school reports spoke of her as a quiet child who seemed reluctant to play a full part in the life of the school. Tito blamed Anna for allowing Nikki to turn the shooting of Pollyanna into a major drama. He offered to give Nikki a replacement dog, but she declined. From being an outgoing, fun-loving, plaits-and-sandals little girl, she became a withdrawn adolescent who was modest to the point of prudishness, reluctant to go to parties and constantly wary of the opposite sex.

Anna saw what was happening to her, but felt powerless to help. Ever since the incident with José Ocampo and Pollyanna, Nikki had managed to keep her at arm's length. Anna was at first bewildered that her daughter should be so independent, so private, but later she realized that she had herself undergone a very similar change as a result of the telegram she had received from Angus after her honeymoon.

She guessed that Nikki had been wounded in much the same way as she had been wounded. Her vivacity, her self-confidence had been damaged – perhaps irreparably. What had been the cause? Surely it could not simply be the shooting of Pollyanna? The only explanation she could think of was that something else had happened – that Nikki had not admitted the whole truth about Ocampo. But whenever she brought up the subject in conversation, Nikki was obviously so hurt by the suggestion that she might have withheld the whole truth from her mother that Anna eventually decided that it would be better not to mention it again.

So the whole problem of Nikki's self-consciousness and shyness was swept under the carpet. Her parents pretended that there was no problem. Anna didn't like doing that but there seemed no other solution short of sending her for psychoanalysis, and she was old-fashioned enough to believe that that might do more harm than good.

In the country at large, unrest became the rule rather than the exception. In March 1962 President Frondizi was ejected from office by a coup led by the military under General Poggi, and José Guido, a former head of the Senate, was sworn in as President in his place. Guido lasted for eighteen months and was kept in office by the anti-Peronist military factions known as the Reds and the Blues. The Reds wanted to outlaw Peronism but the Blues stood for less harsh measures and an early return to what was becoming an increasingly elusive ideal: a constitutionally elected government. The moderate Blues won; at an election the following year, Arturo Illía was elected President. Illía was strongly nationalist, and ingratiated himself with the Peronists by revoking the agreement made by Frondizi whereby Argentina allowed the USA to exploit her petroleum resources. This anti-American decision was intended to unite the country. Perón had done so by whipping up hatred for the British. Now, Illía achieved a similar consensus by hitting out at the United States. For a short while it worked, and Argentina rejoiced once more in the belief that she could govern herself. But the rejoicing was short-lived. Aware that Peronism might be about to creep back in by the back door, the military deposed Illía in another bloodless coup, and a new repressive and authoritarian regime under General Juan Carlos Onganía assumed power. One of Onganía's first acts was to order a political purge of left-wing students and professors in the University of Buenos Aires. The police made baton charges and political activists were rounded up. Soldiers were sent to stand guard outside lecture halls and another generation grew up to accept that no government could rule Argentina without the backing of the armed forces.

* * *

Soon after his last term at Quilmes, Jimmy received a telegram from Oxford University informing him that he had won an Exhibition to read Classical Greats at Oxford.

Anna was overjoyed, and set about gathering the family for a Christmas celebration. Luis was going to be on leave and Johnny wrote to say that he had been allowed a few days' holiday from the seminary and would be able to spend his first Christmas at home for two years. Marc had flown in from Miami to play in a tournament and promised to come out to the camp immediately afterwards. After much persuasion on Anna's part, Larry agreed to come home for the first time since his expulsion from school. Blanca and Jorge would be at Casa Nova, so it was going to be the first time the whole family had been together since the wedding.

But at the last moment, Luis cancelled. He rang up to say that because of the threat of subversive elements he was required to remain at operational readiness during the Christmas period. Whether this was a convenient excuse or not, nobody knew. He sent the family his love and best wishes and said that he might be able to fly over and give them an impromptu display.

There was the usual exchange of hospitality between neighbouring estancias. The Jowetts put on a ball at the big house, Ceci gave a smart dinner at Tijerita and there were asados here, there and everywhere. The three Jowett girls came out with their husbands and families; Amy Dalligan was out with Phillip and his wife, and Stiffy's elderly mother came out for one last visit to her beloved Argentina.

It promised to be a fairly happy Christmas at La Calandria. Anna made Tito promise not to fight with Larry, and everyone was put on their best behaviour. For a day or two, all went well; then the old animosity between Larry and Tito flared up again and everyone relaxed and behaved as they had always behaved, so that mealtimes were like a strange leap backwards in time, with the same old exchanges between brothers, the same brotherly teasing of Nikki, the same friction between Larry and his father, the same passionate argument over whether to go to midnight Mass on Christmas Eve or high Mass on Christmas Day – and the same old pastime of trying to persuade Anna to join the Catholic Church.

'No,' she would say. 'I was brought up a heretic, and a heretic I shall remain.'

On Christmas Eve the Jowetts came over for lunch and they had a lazy asado under the trees by the pool. That evening, the Stefenellis and their house party – including Botta, Lambretti, Ocampo and a senior naval officer called Emilio Massera – were coming to drinks, a social duty Anna was not looking forward to. Though she had not mentioned the fact to anyone, her health had deteriorated in recent months and she had taken to having an afternoon siesta every day. It was a practice she had long resisted but now, with plenty of servants to see to everything, she had at last succumbed. So after the barbecue she went up to her bedroom while Marc, Jimmy, Nikki and Belinda Jowett played doubles and the others lolled by the pool, dropping into the water from time to time to cool off.

It was a lazy summer afternoon. Hummingbirds were collecting nectar from the smoke bushes. In the trees behind the house, the ben-te-veo was telling the world, over and over again, that he saw it well. On the tennis court, Belinda and Jimmy were being soundly beaten by Marc and Nikki. Then, from nowhere, a silver monster roared overhead and climbed vertically into the cloudless sky. Luis had kept his promise.

The aircraft executed a faultless stall turn and then dived vertically, pulling out so low that its jet exhaust shook the upper branches of the eucalyptus trees.

The tennis game was interrupted and Anna came out to watch. The jet – no one had any idea what sort it was – roared round in a tight turn at low level and came overhead at less than a hundred feet, upside down. It looped, it barrel-rolled, it slow-rolled and performed an extraordinary manoeuvre in which it seemed momentarily to go completely out of control. And finally, to frighten them, Luis put down his undercarriage and flaps and made a slow approach as if he were going to land on the lawn, slamming on the power at the last moment in order to clean up and climb away before giving one last victory roll.

Then he was gone, and all that was left were a few faint whorls of smoke and a smell of burnt paraffin that hung about in the airless afternoon.

As Anna went back into the house she heard Tito say, 'Right, Larry. You can make yourself useful for a change. You'll find a brand-new Union Jack in a plastic wrapper on my desk in the office. I'd like it put up before our guests arrive.'

Larry was stretched out by the pool. He had on a pair of Bermudan shorts and was picking at his guitar. He gave no indication that he had heard what his father had said.

'Well get on with it!'

Larry glanced up. 'Sorry, Pa. It's against my principles. I gave up hoisting flags long ago.'

'I am telling you to get that bloody flag *up*!' Tito growled.

'Now, now,' Larry said. 'Watch the blood pressure.'

'For God's sake, Larry,' Marc said. 'It's only a bloody flag.'

'In that case why bother to put it up?'

'They always fly their flag when we go there,' Tito said. 'Why the hell shouldn't we fly ours when they come here?'

'Talk about "keeping up with the Joneses"; keeping up with the ruddy Stefenellis, more like.'

Jimmy closed a book and said quietly, 'I don't mind doing it.'

'No,' said Tito. 'Why should you? You helped with the asado. Larry's done stuff-all since he arrived except sit on his arse and twang a guitar.'

Larry played an arpeggio and said, 'And rather beautifully too, if I may say so.'

The Jowetts were being careful to keep out of the family squabble. Tito got off his sunbed. 'I'll put the bloody thing up myself,' he muttered, and went off in the direction of his office. A minute later he came out of the house with the flag. He attached it to the halyard and hoisted it halfway before a knot got stuck in the pulley. Cursing under his breath, he gave the rope a sharp tug, whereupon it parted and the flag and halyard fell on his head.

'Right, Nikki,' Tito said. 'You're the lightest. Be a real angel and climb up and thread it for me.'

Larry took up his guitar and launched into the Argentine national anthem.

Oid el ruido de rotas cadenas
Ved en trono a la noble igualdad!

'Trouble is, Dad's neither very *noble* nor very *igual*, is he?' he drawled, and abruptly changed to a syncopated rendering of 'Pomp and Circumstance'.

Lying on her bed under a single sheet, Anna heard some of the argument and singing through the open window and then the voices seemed to come from further and further away until they turned into a strange, waking dream in which they went on arguing interminably. Then she dreamt that Catarina had come into her bedroom carrying a steaming pan of something horrible – lights or tripe – which made a strange squeaking noise as it bubbled in the cauldron.

She woke with a start. Outside, someone was screaming.

She went to the window and looked out. Tito, Nikki, Marc, Larry and the Jowetts were crowding round something on the ground. She threw on her dress and ran downstairs. Their faces turned towards her as she came onto the verandah. Then she saw Jimmy. He was lying on the flagstones with his head round at a grotesque angle, and blood was pooling under his chin.

All arrangements for Christmas at La Calandria were cancelled and Jimmy was buried on Boxing Day in the dusty, windswept cemetery of Our Lady of Sorrows in Cadoret.

After the funeral, Anna seemed to crumple. Though she kept going and only very rarely showed her grief, within a matter of months she had aged visibly.

Tito did not believe in over-doing the mourning and told Anna that it was all a matter of self-discipline. Because of her restlessness at night they began to sleep apart, and days passed when they saw little or nothing of each other.

They were becoming estranged.

One Sunday morning at the end of January when Tito was in his dressing room clipping his moustache with a pair of nail scissors, Anna knocked on the door.

'Tito, we can't go on like this any longer.'

He continued to bend towards the mirror. 'So what do you propose we do about it?'

'I want to go home.'

'This is your home.'

'No it isn't. I don't belong here. I never have. I don't even feel that I belong to you any more. I want to go to *my* home. I want to see my mother before she dies and I want to find a school for Nikki.'

He turned back from the mirror, scissors in hand. 'We can't go anywhere this year. We'll go to Europe in sixty-eight as planned. March to August. That's a promise.'

'I don't want to go to Europe, Tito. I want to go to Scotland and I want to go now.'

He shook his head. 'We can't sell any ponies this season. There aren't any worth selling. Next year will be different.'

Her lower lip trembled. 'Do you always have to think in terms of profit, Tito? Couldn't you think of me, just this once?'

He laughed drily. 'Despite rumours to the contrary, Anna, I am not made of money. I cannot afford to be out of the country two seasons running.'

'In that case, can I take Nikki and we'll go on our own?'

'And interrupt her school term?'

'She doesn't have exams this year, but she does next. Besides, you said she could go to school in England for her last two years.'

'She's not fifteen yet. She needn't go until September next year at the earliest.'

'I would still like to take her. I'd like her to see several schools, not just the one you choose for her. I'd like her to meet my side of the family and I'd like her to see something of Scotland, too.'

He swung round, a vein pumping in his neck. 'All right, Anna. Go, for God's sake! Take Nikki and go. But don't ask me to pay your fare, because the money isn't there, do you understand? I'll take you to England next year willingly, but if you want to go this year you'll have to pay for it out of your own pocket.'

She opened her mouth to speak but then changed her mind and remained silent, standing in the doorway of his dressing room only a moment longer before abruptly turning and going back to her room.

A few days later Anna went by herself to Buenos Aires for a couple of days and when she returned she came into the office and told Tito that she had booked her passage to England and would be leaving on one of the Highland boats with Nikki at the beginning of March.

'Oh yes?' he said sarcastically. 'And where's the money coming from?'

'That's all settled. I've paid for the tickets.'

'What with?'

'I sold some jewellery.'

'What jewellery?'

'My jewellery.'

'You mean jewellery I gave you.'

'Yes.'

'What did you sell?'

'My gold chain. And my eternity ring.'

'That was my mother's ring, Anna. It was an heirloom. And I gave you that gold necklace in Paris in 1951.'

'I know that. You don't have to remind me.'

'You had no right to sell them.'

'Weren't they mine then? I thought they were gifts. You never told me they were on loan.'

'You know what I mean. Anyone else would have had the decency to mention it first instead of skulking off and selling them on the quiet.'

'Well what do you expect, Tito? You said I could go home to Scotland provided I paid my own way, when you knew fine well that I couldn't possibly afford to pay the fare on my own.'

She flushed, aware that in the heat of the moment her Scottish accent had been more pronounced. She would have preferred to be

198

able to keep silent and let actions speak louder than words. She hated arguing with anyone, and Tito most of all. Whoever 'won', she felt that arguments demeaned both sides.

'Where did you sell them?'

She shrugged. 'A jeweller on Rivadavia.'

'How much did you get for them?'

'Enough to pay our fares, and a bit over.'

'Well don't expect me to buy you any more bloody jewellery, will you?' he snarled. 'Because I'm not going to. Ever.'

After that, Anna began thinking seriously about a divorce. It wasn't the first time she had toyed with the idea, but now it seemed like a more serious possibility. But the thought was terrifying, and a week before her departure she went to Tito's bedroom in the hope of patching things up.

'I'm sorry,' she said simply.

'What for?'

'I should have asked you before I sold the eternity ring.'

He said nothing.

'Can we try again, Tito?'

He looked down at her. Her hair was almost white. She had undone it for the night and looked what he mentally termed a slummock. She held no physical attraction for him whatsoever.

'It's no good blaming ourselves is it?' she said. 'Or each other, for that matter.'

'I'm not blaming anyone.'

She began weeping silently.

'Come on, Anna,' he muttered. 'Buck up.'

She leant against him and, reluctantly, he held her.

'I'm frightened that we're drifting apart, Tito. I feel as if I never really knew you. As if there has always been a part of your life you never allowed me to see. Couldn't you change your mind and come with us? We could make a new start. On a sea voyage we'd have time to talk. Get close again. Couldn't we do that?'

'I can't leave, Anna. There's too much going on. Besides, you'll be all right on your own. Probably do us both good to have a break from each other.'

She tried to smile. 'Would you like me to sleep with you tonight?'

It was the last thing he wanted, but he gave in and said yes. It was a complete failure. He couldn't feel anything for her at all. She said it didn't matter and for an hour they lay on their backs, side by side in the darkness, listening to the dormilóns and the cicadas outside, until Anna took her pillow and tiptoed back to her room.

When she had gone he heaved a deep sigh and fell quickly asleep.

Anna and Nikki sailed on the Highland boat the following week and after a tearless farewell at the docks, Tito found himself at a loose end in Buenos Aires.

For once, he had no business to attend to, no meeting with Botta or Lambretti, no Lodge meeting, no secret assignation. Wandering along the soulless city streets he caught glimpses of himself in shop windows. He saw a man in dark glasses with a pot belly; a man in a lightweight beige suit and a Panama hat, a melancholy man who stared broodingly back at his reflection.

He went into a café and ordered himself a coffee and a large slice of chocolate cake. He sat by the window and watched the herds of people drifting by.

Well – she was gone. He had four months on his own. The boys were off his hands and the estancia practically ran itself under Stefenelli and the new cadet-manager they had taken on. So what would he do? Spend a bit of time at the Hurlingham, maybe. Play a bit of polo, perhaps. Mix in society a bit.

He wondered about Anna. There was just a chance that she might not come back. Would he mind? Not really. In fact it'd be quite a relief.

He finished his coffee and left. He wandered along Florida to the Plaza San Martín and sat on a bench under the trees by the monument.

His thoughts wandered back over the years. He remembered his father teaching him about farming, stock-breeding, riding, polo. And then the teenage years. School with Stiffy. Winning his first polo trophy. The parties. Ceci in a tennis skirt.

Magdalena.

He stared across the park at a nurse with a pram and a little girl feeding the pigeons.

He recalled the morning he had met Botta for the first time. March it was, same time of year as now. And wasn't it here in this park that he had killed time before going to see Rui about an annulment?

He closed his eyes and saw, involuntarily, Magdalena as she had been when he went to identify the body. He shuddered. Would he ever be able to erase that piece of horror from his memory?

'Tito, darling!'

Of all people, it was Emelda, a diaphanous Emelda in Indian silks and bangles. She sat down beside him and they touched cheeks.

'Darling, what on earth are you doing here – or shouldn't I ask?' He explained about Anna and Nikki.

'I didn't know they were going to England. Why aren't you going with them?

'Oh – pressure of work.'

She laughed her lovely, sensual laugh. 'Oh Tito – really! Pull the other one. So now you're all on your ownio are you? Poor sweet.'

He was flattered by her company. She was a good deal younger than himself and they had never had an affair. She had belonged to Stiffy and Stiffy had been – still was – his best friend. Mind you, that hadn't prevented him from fancying her. What was that joke about her that went the rounds of the Anglo-Argentine Community before the war? 'Here comes Emelda Dalligan; all members stand.'

At first, he was too interested in her cleavage to pay much attention to what she was saying, but after a while he realized that she was telling him about her chauffeur-lover Fernando, with whom she had just broken up. She was outraged. He remembered what Stiffy had said about her being a nympho, and felt the first stirrings of sexual arousal in months. He could see what Stiffy meant. Fernando had dumped her and she needed sex like a drug addict needs a fix.

He put his hand on her knee. 'What would you say to a spot of lunch?'

She giggled. 'Darling, I thought you'd never ask!'

He took her to a discreet little place that was owned by a member of his Lodge and they tucked into smoked salmon, sirloin steak and profiteroles.

'Do you realize, Emelda, that you and I have never been out together by ourselves before?'

'I *know*! We'll jolly well have to catch up, won't we?'

He leaned across the table and said very confidentially, 'Has anyone ever told you that you have the most amazing figure?'

She bubbled with sexy mirth. 'Frequently,' she said, and they locked knees under the table.

'What is it about you?' he chuckled. 'You make me feel thirty years younger.'

She borrowed his cigarette to light her own, making eyes at him while she sucked at it until the end glowed red. They took three hours over lunch and Emelda told him all the juiciest gossip about the British community, some of which went back thirty years. Did he know that Randy Jowett had kept a woman in Cordoba and that she had had two illegitimate children by him? Or about the sex orgies that went on during the school holidays in a certain famous girls' school?

'Tell me more,' he laughed. 'Tell me more.'

'And of course there's that priest of yours. Pellegrini.'

'What about him?'

'Can't you guess? Kinky as they come, darling. Rumour has it he's a tv.'

'A what?'

'Transvestite. Apparently he was caught being shafted by an altar boy during the Mardi Gras celebrations in Rosario a few years back, so they sent him out to the camp to cool his ardour. I thought everyone knew *that* one!'

She wagged her finger and scolded him lightheartedly about his affair with Chiquita, and over the coffee quizzed him about Anna. He told her how Anna had let herself go to seed.

'And you know what she did? She went off and sold jewellery that belonged to my mother to pay for her trip to Scotland.' He shook his head. 'Little blighter never even bothered to consult me.'

Emelda leaned towards him and lowered her voice. 'Do you know, I was always a little uncertain about Anna. I mean – she always did rather trade on one's goodwill, didn't she? She's never been, well, quite one of us, has she? So is this trip of hers a sort of . . . trial separation or something?'

He shrugged. 'We haven't discussed it in so many words but it might easily turn out that way.'

'Poor darling,' she said. 'I am sorry. But now tell me, what are your plans? You're not going to hide yourself away at Calandria all through the winter, I hope?'

'I'm just going to take it a day at a time.'

'That sounds very sensible.' She put her head on one side and wound her necklace round her forefinger. 'What are you doing for the rest of today?'

'Nothing much.'

'Like to do it with me?' She laughed and then sang into his ear in a musky, intimate voice, 'It's a lovely day today, so whatever you've got to do, I would rather like to be doing it with you . . .'

She clapped her hands in mock applause, which had the effect of summoning the waiter. When Tito had paid, her eyebrows jumped twice and she said, 'My place?'

They held hands in the taxi. Her apartment was on the Avenida Alvear. Going up in the lift they fell into each other's arms and the moment they were in the flat with the door closed she set about undressing him.

'Would you like a shower?' she asked. 'I think I would.' She kissed him again. 'You go in first and I'll come and join you.'

'Wizard,' he said, and headed for the bathroom.

They kissed wildly under the tepid torrent. She soaped him, she played with him, she kissed him, she massaged him with long, gentle fingers.

But something went wrong. In spite of all Emelda's skill and dedication, Tito Cadoret failed for the first time in his life to rise to the occasion.

They went into the bedroom and she tried again.

'Sorry about that,' he said eventually.

She put on a silk dressing gown. 'So am I.'

'Better call it a day, I suppose.'

'Yes. I suppose we had.'

There seemed nothing left to say. He pretended to be in no hurry to dress but in fact he could not escape from the ignominy of the situation quickly enough.

'Another day, when you're in the mood,' she said, and closed the door firmly behind him.

When he got out into the street, he stood indecisively for a while, then started walking aimlessly about the city, pausing at a street corner to watch an argument between a taxi driver and the driver of a collectivo, picking his way over the broken sidewalks and from time to time going into stark little cafés with rows of empty tables and chairs, to sit gloomily away from the window with only a cup of black coffee and a glass of toothpicks for company.

21

'I KNOW IT SOUNDS weak and feeble,' Anna said. 'But I don't think I can go much further.'

'Mummy!' Nikki said. 'We've only just set out.'

But Anna was sitting on a boulder and although she was making light of things, she felt awful.

They were out for a walk on the Pentland Hills with Ailsa and Douglas. It was early April; there were lambs in the fields and a biting north-westerly was ruffling the heather.

'You go on,' she said. 'I'll just go quietly back.'

'I'll come back with you,' Ailsa offered.

'No, I'll be perfectly all right. I'll just have a bit of a sit, then I'll wander slowly down.'

'I'll give you the keys,' said Ailsa, and added quietly, 'Are you quite sure you'll be all right on your own?'

'Yes, quite sure.'

She watched them go on up the hill, and after a while made the effort and started back down the path.

They had been in Scotland for two weeks. Anna's mother had been moved into an old people's home and on arrival in Edinburgh Anna and Nikki had stayed with her sister and brother-in-law in Corstorphine. Harriet and Brian had married a few years before. They were a homely couple who had no children of their own and were keen churchgoers. They had fixed ideas about how a fifteen-year-old girl should behave and were wary of Nikki's Roman Catholicism. Anna had planned to stay with them for a month, but realized very quickly that neither she nor Nikki would be able to stick it that long so, at Ailsa's invitation, they had come out to stay at Howgate.

The move came as a great relief. Ailsa and Doug had a large house and a relaxed attitude to the young, and on the first evening, over a kitchen supper, Ailsa told Nikki that she could have free riding if she was prepared to help out at the local stables. So Nikki was happy, and that was the main thing.

Anna made her way across a field of sheep and lambs and entered the Tullochs' garden via a wicket gate. She let herself in by the back door, took off her shoes and put her feet up on the sofa in the sitting room.

She was annoyed with herself. It was not the first time this had happened. The last time had been on the boat the day of the line-crossing ceremony when she had had a dizzy fit, and in spite of her protestations Nikki, who hated horseplay of any sort, had used it as an excuse not to attend.

She was going to start looking at schools for Nikki soon. Ailsa had said she could borrow the Morris Minor and had recommended Kerrmuir College, a girls' boarding school on the Fife coast of which Ailsa was a governor. It sounded just right for Nikki: it had an excellent academic record and plenty of sport and holiday activities. But what Anna liked about it most of all was that it was a Scottish school which meant, in her view, that it must be streets ahead of any other.

She lay on the sofa and thought about it all. During the trip over, she had started the long process of coming to terms with Jimmy's death. It seemed to her that there was an inevitability about it, just as there had been about Tim's. Death and Argentina seemed linked. No one who genuinely cared for others, no one who was sincere or gentle or loving or intelligent had much chance of survival over there. That was what made it so important to get Nikki settled properly in a school over here.

She didn't know why, but she felt an urgency about it. She was afraid that unless Nikki managed to break away from her present situation there was a danger that she would turn out like so many Anglo-Argentine young ladies: a spoilt, selfish, ill-educated, rich little bitch. But it was not yet too late. If she could just persuade Tito –

The back door bell rang. Not bothering to put her shoes on, she went to answer it.

The caller was a man of fifty or so, tall, heavily built with a kindly face and reddish cheeks. He was wearing faded corduroy trousers and a tweed jacket with leather patches on the elbows. When Anna opened the door to him he was looking at the potted seedlings in the porch. It was Angus. He held out his hands to her, and she went to him and he took her in his arms and held her.

She had heard some of his news from Ailsa. She knew that he was about to retire from the Army and was going to farm his land. She also knew that his divorce was pending.

She made coffee and warmed her back against the range while he told her about Rob, who was an engineer lieutenant, and Kate, who had left university and was working as a researcher for a television news programme. He asked about her family. She told him about her boys, about Blanca, about Jimmy.

She had forgotten what a gentle man he was, how thoughtful and how sensitive to her feelings. She found herself admitting things to him which she had once thought could never be admitted to anyone.

'So you've come to get away from it all.'

'More or less. I've got Nikki with me. I'm going to look for a school for her.'

'Nikki's your youngest.'

'Yes. She's fifteen.'

'Have you any schools in mind?'

'Ailsa recommends Kerrmuir College.'

'That's where Kate went.'

'Did she enjoy it?'

'It didn't do her any harm.'

She sighed. 'I would so like to see Nikki settled.'

'That was said with feeling, Anna.'

'Well, she hasn't had an easy childhood.'

They went through to the sitting room. She found herself telling him about Nikki and her suspicions about what might have happened four years before.

'Luckily she's very resilient. I'll say one thing for Nikki, she has tremendous guts – moral and physical.'

'Like mother, like daughter,' he said.

'I was never very courageous, Angus. Quite the reverse in fact.'

'You haven't changed a bit,' he said softly.

'Oh I have, you know. You can't live in Argentina without being changed by it. I'm a much harder person than I was thirty years ago.'

'How long will you be in Scotland?'

'Until the end of July.'

'So we'll see something of each other.'

'I hope so.'

He took her hands and held them. She tried to take them away, but he wouldn't let her. She said, 'I feel guilty about your wife.'

'Should I feel the same about your husband?'

She shook her head. 'There was never any need for anyone to feel guilty about Tito.'

'Anna –'

'What?'

He tried to say something but failed. Instead, he pulled her towards him and this time she gave way and let him take her in his arms again;

206

and while he held her, which was for a long time, she admitted to herself for the first time that the biggest mistake she had ever made in her life was to marry Tito Cadoret. Hugged tight in Angus's arms, her tears wetting both their cheeks, she felt as if she had come home at last.

'Do you know what I'm going to do while you're over here?' he said eventually.

'No?'

'I'm going to try and persuade you to stay here and never go back.'

She smiled sadly. 'We have a bird in Argentina whose call always says the same thing to me. "No going back." I've heard it practically every day since . . . since I had that telegram from you. It's a calandria. A mockingbird.'

The calandria was right. There was no going back, no escape from reality. What was done was done. She was married to Tito. It was her duty to return.

Yes, that was one way of looking at it, but there was another that was more persuasive. 'No going back' could mean that there was no point in trying to repair a relationship that had been faulted from the start; no point in returning to a husband who neither wanted nor needed her.

She talked to Ailsa about it and Ailsa urged her to make the break. It was now or never, she said, and proceeded to make everything as easy as possible for Anna to take the plunge. She said that they could stay indefinitely. She invited Angus to supper and encouraged Anna to accept when he invited her and Nikki to visit his farm.

Angus became a frequent visitor. He took to dropping in for coffee in the morning on the off-chance that Anna might be free for a pub lunch. And she was free. She went to visit her mother twice a week but otherwise she was completely free. He was on Army terminal leave and she was on holiday. His wife was living with her lover in Buckingham and Tito was no doubt pleasing himself with whoever took his fancy in Buenos Aires.

Anna came quickly to the conclusion that there was no point in trying to hide what was going on from Nikki. Nikki was no fool: though she hated discussing anything to do with her parents' relationship, she had made it known to Anna on the voyage over that she understood the situation very clearly and knew why they were going to Britain without her father. She was also perceptive enough to realize that the huge improvement in her mother's morale since their arrival at the

Tullochs could not be due solely to the change of scenery and the fresh air.

Nikki's morale improved, too. On a brisk, windy day at the beginning of May, Anna took her to visit Kerrmuir College, whose grounds ran down to the sea and whose local village was a little grey-stone fishing harbour where seabirds wheeled and seine nets were spread out along the harbour wall. On the way back, Anna asked her what she would think of the idea of starting there in September the following year.

'Well it would be better than going back to Michael Hamm. Anything would be better than those damn nuns.'

They drove through Auchtermuchty. Nikki said, 'I wouldn't mind starting this September.'

'I think your father would have something to say about that.'

'You don't *have* to give him the choice, do you?'

'What's that supposed to mean?'

'If you divorced him and married Angus.'

It was a shock to hear the possibility put so coolly into words.

'Isn't that what you're thinking of doing?'

'We can't always do what we want to do in this life, darling.'

Nikki blew her hair out of her eyes. 'Oh yeah? Where have I heard that before?'

They drove through Fifeshire and came to the new suspension bridge. It was a grey, windy day and the Forth estuary was flecked with white horses. The metal surface of the road bridge rumbled under the wheels.

'Would you be very upset if Daddy and I separated?'

'Probably. I mean – everyone is, aren't they? But that doesn't necessarily mean that I don't think you should.'

'What do you think I should do, then?'

'I don't know. I don't think it's fair to ask me that.'

They stopped to pay the toll.

'Well would you be very upset if you could never go back to Argentina?' Anna asked as they drove on.

'What do you *think*, Mummy? Of course I'd be upset. It's my home!'

There was a sudden blaring of horns and screaming of brakes. She was on the wrong side of the road. For ten or fifteen seconds, death was very near. The car careered back onto the left-hand side of the road, overshot, took the verge and spun to a halt. For a full minute, Anna sat behind the wheel, shaking. Then they drove slowly on to Howgate.

* * *

There was another factor, one that Anna had not discussed with Nikki. It was that she was becoming increasingly convinced that all was not well with her health.

She had mentioned her tiredness and loss of weight to Ailsa soon after her arrival, and Ailsa had made an appointment for her to see Dr Marklew, a specialist in gynaecology at the Royal Hospital. A few days after the visit to Kerrmuir College, Anna spent a day in Edinburgh being examined, interviewed and tested. Inevitably, while waiting for the laboratory report on the biopsy, she speculated on the result.

What if there was something seriously wrong with her? Wouldn't that be the best possible reason for staying on in Scotland? If she needed treatment she would be able to extend her visit with a clear conscience. But even that seemed a cowardly way out. Why should she need an excuse for doing what she believed to be the right thing?

And what was the 'right thing'? Did it exist? Whatever her physical condition and however badly Tito had behaved in the past, wasn't she still bound to him for better or for worse?

Ailsa said that she should stay on in Scotland whatever the verdict on her health. 'It's quite possible that emotional stress is the cause, you know. Doug's seen lots of cases where people have fallen ill because of unhappy marriages. You've made more than enough sacrifices. Why not snatch a bit of joy out of life before it's too late? Why not make two people happy instead of three people miserable?'

She found herself agreeing and disagreeing with Ailsa at the same time. It was all very well to imagine an idealistic second marriage with Angus, but the thought of never seeing Tito or her boys again was strangely frightening. It seemed to her that if she left her husband and married another she would be breaking faith with something that was of fundamental importance to her. It would be intrinsically, unforgivably wrong.

As the weeks passed, Angus and Ailsa chipped away at her resolve. Ailsa arranged for Nikki to spend four weeks of the summer term at Kerrmuir's, leaving Anna even freer to meet Angus and catch up on the lost years.

She would have liked to go for long walks with him over the Pentlands, but found that she didn't have the energy for more than a short stroll. 'Old age creeping on,' she said one day when they were out in the Landrover reviewing his flocks.

'Nonsense. You're still a spring chicken.'

209

He switched off the engine. They had stopped on the crest of a hill which gave a magnificent view of sweeping, granite-topped moors, the sun on a reservoir, a village nestling far below in the valley.

'Are you any closer to deciding?'

She shook her head. 'Not really.'

'I've said all I can. I love you, you know that. Let me look after you. Let me put right what went wrong, Anna. Let's be together as we always should have been.'

She looked up at a sparrowhawk hovering overhead. 'I want to say yes, but something inside me says no. A sort of instinct. I never thought I would feel this way. I can't explain it. I've even prayed about it. If only I could know what was right.'

'I know I can't put the clock back,' he said, 'but at least let me try to make up for what happened.'

'You weren't to blame. I was the one who tore up your letter without reading it.'

They got out of the Landrover. He took her arm and they walked a little way over the moor.

'Isn't it a question of whether to obey the spirit or the letter of the law?' he said. 'Legally, you belong to Tito, and legally I still belong to Wendy. But spiritually we belong to each other. Isn't that it?'

'I don't know what to think any more.'

They stood on a high point with the wind in their faces.

'I have a suggestion,' he said. 'A friend of mine keeps a cabin cruiser on the Caledonian canal. I could borrow it for ten days. We could be completely on our own. Just the two of us. What do you say?'

It rained almost incessantly the whole time, but the weather didn't matter. They were together, and though they kept off the subject of their future, both became increasingly confident that Anna would not return to Argentina.

'How can I possibly return to the monotony of the camp after this magnificent scenery?' she asked one day.

With rain storms sweeping down off the mountains from a Payne's grey sky, they puttered happily along, alone together for the first time in their lives.

And it was not platonic, it could not possibly be. There was a wide double berth in the stern of the boat and they made use of it, sleeping in each other's arms at night and spending whole afternoons in it while the rain pelted down on the deck above them.

They needed to splice their lives back together again and interweave every single thread of the past years. He had to know all about her children, her friends, her acquaintances, and she wanted to hear about his escape through the German lines and how he had made his way south through France to Spain, Gibraltar and freedom. He told her about Wendy, too: how they had been happy for the first fifteen years of their marriage, but how Wendy had one day revealed to him, at the height of an argument, that she had had a long-standing love affair with another man. After that, for seven long years, he had fought to keep the marriage intact.

'I think it was the only battle I ever lost,' he said quietly.

Anna told him about Rob's visit to Argentina. 'He was so like you were at the same age, Angus. I liked him tremendously. Quite what he thought of us lot I can't imagine.' Then she told him about Nikki, and her problem of shyness. That led on to the wider network of suspicion that was like a backdrop to life in Argentina: how there were parts of Tito's life that were a closed book to her and how he seemed to be in the pocket of his lawyer and his banker and his administrator.

'It's a different world out there,' she said. 'It's all appearance and no reality. If you haven't got money, you borrow it and find a way of not paying it back. And however much money you have, you always pretend that you've got more.'

On their last day, the sun shone. They returned the boat to its mooring and had lunch in Fort Augustus before driving south.

'Have you decided?' Angus asked.

'I think so. But I'll need an awful lot of help. I suppose I shall have to cable Tito. That's the part I dread. Actually having to tell the world that – that my marriage is a failure. That it's over.'

'What you must always remember is that there is nothing you need blame yourself for, Anna. You've been the best possible wife to him. You've stuck it out for nearly thirty years. There aren't many women who would have tolerated what you've had to put up with. And you won't have to go back, either. You won't have to meet any of them ever again.'

She sighed, shaking her head.

'You're still not sure, are you?'

'Not completely.'

'Well, don't rush it. We needn't say anything to Ailsa or Nikki just yet.'

'I'll have to within the next day or two. The boat sails a week on Thursday. I'll have to cancel the booking. And there's Nikki to think of. She must accept what I'm doing. I can't risk hurting her.'

'But you do want to stay, don't you? That's what you want isn't it?'

211

She nodded.

He took her hand across the table. 'There. I've got you. I'm never going to let you go.'

Ailsa was about to go out when they arrived back. 'Help yourselves to whatever you fancy,' she said. 'There's a letter for you on the kitchen table, Anna. Oh – and there was a message for you to ring the hospital.'

The letter was from Tito. She could almost hear his abrupt, sulky voice coming off the paper. It had been a long, wet winter, he said, and he had spent most of it in the camp. Jorge and Blanca had spent over a month up north setting up a fertilizer plant near the Bolivian border. He hadn't seen any of the boys since her departure. He'd expected at least one letter from her and wondered if the post office union had been up to its old trick of dumping UK mail in the River Plate.

Then there was some agricultural news – bovine footrot had struck again – and the letter closed with a reminder to let him know if she wanted to be met off the boat.

There was a PS. 'Catarina had a stroke last month and died in Laboulaye hospital last week.'

'I was so fond of her,' she told Angus tearfully. 'She was my only real ally when I was first out in the camp. She's been like a mother to me.'

Angus put his arm round her shoulders and comforted her; but at the same time could not help thinking that the death of a much-loved cook might persuade her finally not to go back to Argentina.

'Weren't you supposed to ring the hospital?' he said.

'Oh yes. I nearly forgot.'

When she got through she was told that Dr Marklew would like her to come in for another consultation, so she arranged to go in at nine o'clock the following day.

Dr Marklew's hooked nose and thick black hair gave him a Levantine look, but his accent was from Glasgow.

'I apologize, Mrs Cadoret, for asking you to come in at short notice. I'm afraid there was a rather longer than usual delay in obtaining the results of your tests, but they are now to hand.'

She sat on the upright chair in front of his desk and waited for him to go on.

Dr Marklew took off his pebble glasses, polished them, and put them on again. Then he opened the file on his desk and studied the report it contained. While he did so, Anna glanced round. The office was soundproofed and neat: an examination couch in one corner, a few shelves of medical books and a bar chart for the year 1967. On the cream distempered wall, the red second hand of an electric clock crept noiselessly round. It was almost nine thirty. Angus was going to pick her up at ten and they were going to drive to Kerrmuir College to collect Nikki. They would have lunch at Auchtermuchty and, if the time seemed right, Anna would break the news to Nikki that she intended to stay on in Scotland. Anna and Angus had agreed that Nikki should make up her own mind whether or not to return to Argentina.

Dr Marklew looked up. 'Now I regret to say, Mrs Cadoret, that the result of the biopsy reveals that all is not entirely well.' He looked at her in a way that was oddly frightening. 'Have you had a recurrence of the bleeding you described to me when we last met?'

'Yes, but – not a great deal, you understand. Just – spots really. Nothing very much.' She watched him look again at her notes. 'Perhaps you could just tell me what you've found out.'

'Yes,' he said quietly. 'Yes, perhaps that would be best.'

Angus had parked the Rover a block away from the hospital and had returned to the main entrance to wait for Anna. He had an instinctive dislike of hospitals. It seemed to him that every single person who went in and out of these doors was living on the edge of tragedy. He even felt threatened by the cheerful efficiency of the nurses and porters, doctors and cleaners.

He found an empty seat, thumbed through a copy of *Reader's Digest* and then threw it back onto the table and thought about Anna instead.

She hadn't said anything about her health to him, but there was a nagging doubt in his mind all the same. On their cruise together she had tired very easily – much too easily, he thought – and more than once he had suspected that she was in pain. But Anna was a stoic: she would never hint that there might be anything wrong, let alone complain.

He looked at his watch. Nearly quarter past ten. Whatever she was being told, it was taking a very long time.

'Tumours,' said Anna. 'Not fibroids.'

'No. Not fibroids.'

'Are these tumours benign?'

'I'm afraid not.'

Dr Marklew launched into explanations. As if from a long way away,

Anna heard him say that tumours were frequently caused by injury to the cervix during intercourse or childbirth. He noted the fact that she had had five children and one miscarriage. While he continued, she remembered how, in the early years of their marriage, Tito used to ride in from the fields and use her to achieve the relief he said he needed every day.

'As to treatment,' Dr Marklew was saying, 'we would recommend first a course of deep X-ray radiation.'

'How long would that go on for?'

'That would depend. Sometimes we use a course of radiotherapy as a precursor to surgery.'

'Surgery. You mean . . . hysterectomy?'

'Yes.'

'Do you think that will be necessary, Doctor?'

'Essential.'

She hesitated. 'Can I get one thing clear? You haven't actually said that I have cancer. But that's what it is, isn't it?'

'I'm afraid so.'

'Cervical cancer?'

'Yes.'

She reeled inwardly. While he went on to describe the facilities that the hospital could provide, she sat on the upright chair before his desk, her hands joined on her lap, her thoughts far louder than his words.

I am not ready to die, said the voice inside her head. It's not fair. It's not fair, please God can't you see that it's not fair? What am I to say to Angus? What am I to say to Nikki? I can't die yet. I mustn't die. He's wrong, he must be wrong. Cancer. Cancer. Me. Cancer . . .

He had asked a question.

'I'm sorry?'

'How long will you stay in this country?'

'I don't know. How long would the treatment last?'

He said it was difficult to forecast that exactly.

'So . . . it could go on indefinitely?'

'That's a possibility, yes.'

She took a little breath. 'What if I had no treatment at all, Doctor? What if I just left it to run its course?'

'I think that's out of the question, Mrs Cadoret. You must realize –'

'But I need to know. I must know what my choices are. I need to know how long you expect me to live.'

'Well, there is a possibility that it will go into remission.'

'I'm not interested in possibilities. I want to know the truth.' She appealed to him. 'Please. However uncomfortable.'

'Without treatment . . . it really is very difficult to say. It could be a year. Possibly two. Or . . .'

'Or?'

'It could develop very rapidly.'

'A month? Six months?'

'Well, possibly under a year.'

'And with the full treatment? X-rays and surgery?'

'Almost certainly longer. Perhaps up to five or ten years. Perhaps a complete cure. But . . .'

'But what?'

'I don't want to raise your expectations too high, Mrs Cadoret.'

'So what you're saying is that whatever I do, eventually, it'll win.'

He said nothing. There was quite a long silence. She said, 'If I choose to have treatment here in Edinburgh, that would mean several weeks of radiotherapy, wouldn't it? And then an operation. And – and at the end of it, no guarantee that it would work.'

'I think we can guarantee that the disease will spread far less rapidly if you undergo treatment and surgery, Mrs Cadoret. As an alternative to having treatment in this country, may I suggest that you fly back and start it immediately in Argentina?'

'I'm not flying. If I go back, I'm going by sea.'

'In that case I think you should know that if treatment is delayed, its efficacy will be seriously reduced.'

'It's already that bad is it?'

'Yes, I'm afraid it is.'

The red second hand moved on round the face of the clock. It was already past ten. Angus was waiting.

She sensed the same feeling of detachment she had experienced at her wedding. She reflected that, in a way, this was another sort of betrothal.

She heard herself say, 'I think, what I would like to do is keep going normally for as long as I possibly can.'

Marklew's eyes narrowed. 'Do you mean without treatment?'

'Would you think that very silly of me?'

'Not necessarily.'

'One more question,' she said. 'Do you think, if I went back to Argentina, it would be possible to – to let it run its course without telling anyone?'

He glanced up at her. In a previous interview she had told him something of her life in Argentina. He was an intelligent man. She had the impression that he had put more than two and two together.

215

'You would have to have a lot of privacy,' he said quietly, 'and you would have to be very brave.'

For a moment she saw in her mind's eye a picture of the person she might be in a year's time. God help me, she prayed silently. God help me to be brave.

Angus felt her hand on his shoulder and leapt to his feet.

'Sorry I was so long.'

He took her arm. 'All well?'

She smiled a tight little smile. 'I'll tell you about it in the car.'

Outside, the sun was glinting on the car roofs. They walked along in silence. He unlocked the passenger door and held it for her while she got in. Then he got in behind the wheel beside her.

'Well?'

She took a deep breath. 'The first thing I must tell you is that I've changed my mind. I'm going back after all.' She turned to him. 'I'm sorry. I'm so sorry.'

It was like an unexpected blow to the solar plexus. He was left winded, shocked. 'Why?' he asked. 'Why?'

She glanced down at their joined hands, then looked steadily into his eyes and told him, 'I've got cancer.'

They sat in the car and talked. She said that she wanted it kept completely secret. She would tell no one else – not Nikki nor the Tullochs nor her mother. She had thought of trying to keep it from Angus, but had realized straight away that it would be impossible.

So she told him everything. The probable cause, the choices open to her, the chances of a cure, the nature of the treatment.

'It would mean at least one operation and probably more, to say nothing of having to fight a physical and emotional battle which I shall almost certainly lose in the end.'

She turned to him.

'My darling – I don't want that. I would rather live out my allotted lifespan naturally than spend thousands of pounds trying to give myself a few more months of existence as an invalid. I don't want to be irradiated. I don't want to spend the rest of my short life going in and out of hospitals and clinics. I would rather – I would rather keep going normally for as long as I can.'

He was holding her hands in his. 'But why must you go back to Argentina?'

'Isn't it obvious? I don't want you to watch me die. I want you to remember me as I am now. And – and I don't think I could bear to

216

see you – coming into my room' – she began to break down – 'you know: with flowers and grapes and chocolates and – and asking me how I'm feeling today. I was never completely sure about getting a divorce. I – I asked God to tell me what I should do, and – well in a way he has, hasn't he? I must go back to Tito. I know I must. I wanted to be certain in my mind and now I am.' She saw his face. 'Oh Angus, darling. I'm sorry I cried. We mustn't cry darling. Don't – please don't cry . . .'

22

TITO WAS ON TOP FORM. 'Got some news,' he said as the chauffeur-driven Mercedes left the docks. 'Randy's selling up.' He glanced at her. 'Well, say something, Anna, if it's only goodbye!'

'You mean he's selling La Ventolera?'

'That's right. The whole shooting match. Going back to merrie England to savour the fruits of his labours, he says. He's a bloody fool of course, but don't tell him I said so. Doing it for Betty, I gather.'

'Who's he selling to?'

Cadoret winked. 'Give you one guess.'

'You mean –'

'Gave me first refusal, didn't he?'

'But – can you afford it?'

He laughed. 'Can I afford it? Can't afford not to afford it! Know what you're thinking. But there is a difference between paying for a joy-ride to Europe and purchasing property which will appreciate in value and give me a high return at the same time. Ventolera will wash its face within five years. Got to speculate to accumulate, mosca. And much safer to speculate with someone else's money. That's what they call gearing in the financial world. Of course my visit to Europe next year's off, so it's as well you went when you did.' He turned to Nikki. 'Well, you? How did you like bonnie Scotland? Haven't left your heart in the Highlands, I hope?'

Nikki feigned a dutiful amusement and said she hadn't.

'Glad to hear it. Very glad indeed.'

'I never thought Randy would sell,' Anna remarked.

'Neither did I. But he's had a bad winter. Had two truckloads of prime steers hijacked on the way down to the frigorifico in April and his bank foreclosed on him. Says he can't ignore the writing on the wall any longer. Can't afford to keep the place up but on the other hand doesn't want to sell to a native, so' – Cadoret tapped the side of his nose – 'special price for special friend.'

'I still don't understand how you can even contemplate buying it,' Anna said. 'With or without backing.'

218

'Yes, well there's quite a lot you don't understand when it comes to business, isn't there?'

The car sped on along the flat road out to Hurlingham.

'We saw a very nice school,' Anna remarked. 'Kerrmuir College. Right on the Fife coast. Lovely.'

'Yes? Oh, by the way. We've bought an aeroplane. Little twin-engine job. So things are looking up.'

He had booked them in at the Hurlingham for the whole of Camp Week. He was going to do the Palermo Agricultural Show and had tickets for the Hurlingham Winter Ball.

'So we'll be living it up for a change. Beef by day and balls by night. Just like old times.'

'I don't know if I'll be up to going out every evening, Tito.'

'Rubbish! You're back in Argentina now. Forget Little England. Get a bit of prime beef back inside you, that'll sort you out.'

They arrived at the club in time for egg sandwiches and champagne. Nikki went off to join the young, while Tito and Anna joined the Jowetts, Stiffy and Ceci.

'Anna, darling,' said Ceci, and kissed her warmly. 'You're looking wonderful. Lovely to have you back in our midst.'

They sat down in cane chairs under the trees outside the club-house.

'I expect Tito's told you the news?' Betty said. 'So sad. But we simply can't afford the upkeep any longer. If we don't do something soon the place will fall down about our ears. And as it was built by old grandfather Cadoret, we thought it would be nice if it went back to Tito. That's the only consolation really. Randy couldn't bear to think of it falling into the hands of some tricky Dicky who might turn it into an amusement park or a football ground. Do you know, there's a chap out near Sarmiento who's built a replica of Wembley stadium on his estancia. I ask you! At least with Tito holding the reins the place will be well looked after. Randy says that he wouldn't have let it go to anyone else – not even at double the price.'

Anna had not had her customary rest that afternoon, so after a while excused herself and went up to their room and lay down on the bed. When she woke up an hour or so later Tito had come in to shower and change for dinner. He stood at the foot of the bed and pulled off his tie. 'So what did you get up to in Scotland? See anything of that old flame of yours?'

'Yes, we did meet.'

'And?'

He was looking down at her, running his tie through his fingers.

She didn't want to lie about Angus, but on the other hand she saw no point in souring relations with Tito unnecessarily.

She smiled. 'I came back, didn't I?'

'Can't say I'm surprised. Grass is always greener, isn't it? Until you go and have a close look, that is. So now you're back. Well, we've got a busy year ahead. I plan to finalize the deal with Randy within three months. Then the whole place'll have to be gutted and refurbished. Like to be in by spring next year.'

'In? In where?'

'Where do you think!? Wouldn't buy the big house just to look at it, would I? My grandfather built that place and I intend to live in it. We can start again, you and me. New house, new chapter. That reminds me.' He opened a drawer. 'I got Jorge to do a bit of devilling for me. He found out which gaucho you sold that necklace and ring to.' He produced them and handed them over. 'There you are. I'd be grateful if you'd wear them, Anna. There's been a bit of talk. You know. About us. It'd be good to prove the grapevine wrong for a change, eh? Go to the ball and – you know. Show 'em.'

He came and sat down on the bed beside her. He took her hand and looked down at her with his blue, predatorial eyes.

'Don't know about you, but I wouldn't say no to a quick shower and a bit of the you-can't-bend-it. What do you think, Poppet? Am I in luck?'

He was not in luck. She explained that she had a slight problem in that department and that he would have to be patient. He looked grumpy. He said it took the gilt off the gingerbread. She said she was sorry but she couldn't help it.

She accompanied him to the Palermo Show on two days and they went to Ceci's Camp Week dinner party in Belgrano. At the Hurlingham Winter Ball, she experienced a curious sensation of déjà vu, as if she were new to Argentina all over again and being given the once-over just as she had been nearly thirty years before.

All her friends and acquaintances in the British community were getting on now. Randy and Betty were in their sixties and talking constantly of their retirement in England. Stiffy was still beset by worries about Emelda and was looking a lot older than fifty-eight. Ceci had dyed her hair. Even the fair Emelda – whose latest lover was a prize-winning novelist – was looking a little jaded, with crow's feet appearing when she smiled and her neck beginning to sag.

While the men gripped whisky glasses in liver-spotted hands, sucked at the damp ends of cigars and talked self-importantly about beef or alfalfa crops, the ladies shrieked with laughter, squabbled pretentiously, compared jewellery, shared confidences and bitched about each other's husbands or lovers. Watching them, listening to them, Anna felt more of an alien than ever before.

They flew out to La Calandria in the Beechcraft. Since Catarina's death, Piotr had turned to drink and now lived by himself in a hovel next door to the bar in Cadoret village. Marga and her husband had moved from Casa Nova to take their place. Things were the same, but things were different.

Anna had had plenty of time to think on the voyage over. Knowing that she had only a limited time to live gave her a fresh view of the world and life. She was more determined than ever to keep her secret: dying well was already becoming more important to her than living well. While Tito talked and thought almost incessantly about the removal to the big house, Anna meditated on her own removal to another place.

From now on, her path sloped downward, and she knew that she must walk down it with dignity to its end rather than being pushed backwards, fighting and scrabbling, to the inevitable conclusion. Death, she discovered, simplified questions of morals and duty amazingly. Providing you faced it, acknowledged it – even befriended it, death lost much of its terror and enabled you to see things with a startling clarity.

She regarded death not as a person but as a door. She had been given the privilege of life, and that privilege necessarily involved the obligation of death. She would go where Timothy and Jimmy and her father and Catarina had gone. If the door opened onto a black void of unconsciousness, then so be it – there was nothing to fear. If it meant a heightened awareness, a seeing face to face rather than through a glass darkly, there was everything to look forward to.

Her only slight anxiety was to see Nikki settled in her new school. But when she suggested the possibility of sending her to Kerrmuir College, Tito's reaction was entirely predictable.

'Over my dead body,' he said. 'Her name's down for Waltham Abbey, and that's where she'll go. It's the best Catholic girls' school in the south of England and it's only an hour away from London airport. Sending her all the way up to the north of Scotland's crazy. Apart from anything else, this Kirby place of yours isn't even Catholic.'

She put up the best fight she could. 'She'll be nearly seventeen by the time she goes, Tito. Kerrmuir College caters for Catholic girls, so it isn't as if she'll be brainwashed or anything. Besides, she's seen the place and knows what it's like and actually wants to go there. Isn't being happy at school just as important as having the right religious education?'

He shook his head impatiently. 'You agreed when we got married that all the children would go to Catholic schools. This Kerrmuir place isn't a Catholic school. So there you are. QED.'

She didn't have the energy to make any more of a fuss. 'I'm sorry, darling,' she said to Nikki later. 'But I did my best.'

Nikki laughed. 'I knew I'd never go there as soon as you said we were coming back to Argentina.'

At the end of March, Randy and Betty threw their last party at the big house. It was a sad, nostalgic affair, with the band playing tunes from the thirties and the guests trying to look as if they were enjoying themselves. In the space of thirty years, the British community at Cadoret had dwindled to a handful of people whose families had either left Argentina or had married Argentines and 'gone bush', as Ceci called it.

The evening was further marred by an ugly scene between Tito and Stiffy. Tito had drunk too much and became aggressive. The two men stood in the big entrance hall and started shouting at each other. Betty tried to separate them, but failed. Randy, for some reason, kept well clear.

'That is a bloody lie, Rathbone!' Tito shouted. 'Say that again in front of a witness and I'll have you for slander!'

Ceci, in navy blue velvet and brilliant red beads, tried to intervene. 'Now stop it, stop it, both of you. Just stop it!'

Tito ignored her. 'Go on,' he said to Stiffy. 'They're all listening. Say what you just said to me a minute ago.'

Stiffy was white-faced, and much quieter. 'Don't be so bloody idiotic, TC.'

'You accused me, Rathbone. You accused me of double-dealing. I want an apology and I want one now.'

'Well you're not going to get one.'

'Then I'll say it for you. What you said about me. That's fair isn't it? You accused me of buying Randy out under false pretences. Now will you apologize or won't you?'

Stiffy stood up. 'I did not accuse you of anything, TC. All I said was that it seemed odd to me that the bank that was backing you and the bank that foreclosed on Randy was one and the same. If you want to take me to court over that, go ahead.'

'That's right, wriggle out of it!' Cadoret shouted as Rathbone walked away. 'No guts that's your problem, Rathbone. No bloody guts!'

He collected Anna and they left the party early.

In the car on the way back he sat slumped in the back seat behind his driver. He turned a bleary gaze on Anna. 'Suppose you believe him like all the others do you?'

'Nobody would have had the first idea what the argument was about if you hadn't insisted on telling them, Tito.'

'Well the buggers know now, all right.' He looked out of the window at the passing fence posts. 'Fuck it,' he said suddenly. 'I don't give a shit.' He leant forward and bellowed in the driver's ear. 'Did you hear that, López? I don't give a fucking shit!'

'*Sí, señor*,' murmured the driver uneasily. '*Sí, sí, señor.*'

That was the watershed year of 1968, when a series of political tremors shook the world. Inflation was rising and currencies were being devalued. And now Argentina was hit by a new crisis. Britain, blaming her foot-and-mouth epidemic on Argentine beef, imposed an overnight ban on further imports. In the space of a year, Argentina's beef exports – her primary source of foreign currency – fell by seventy-five per cent. At the same time President Onganía's wage freeze and economic reforms became increasingly unpopular with the labour unions and resentment began to fester in the industrial centres of Santa Fe, Rosario, Córdoba and Buenos Aires.

Saigon was bombed. There was a rush on gold. Marches and demonstrations were held in Washington and London against the war in Vietnam. The US bank rate went sky high. Students rioted in Paris – and George Brown, Harold Wilson's Foreign Secretary, who only a year before had agreed with Sr Costa Mendez that Britain and Argentina should negotiate over the sovereignty of the Falkland Islands, resigned from office.

Anna heard about these alarms and excursions on the BBC World Service and read about them in newspapers and magazines, but she was left unmoved by them. Nor was she interested in the development of La Ventolera which now dominated Tito's thoughts and conversation.

She spent as much time as possible out of the house, sometimes in gentle communion with the ponies in the paddock, sometimes strolling alone in the park, pausing to watch the flight of a scissors bird or listen to the call of the ben-te-veo. She wrote a lot of letters: one a week to Nikki, one a month to each of the boys, her mother and Ailsa. To Angus, she wrote whenever she felt like writing, which was frequently.

He was the only person to whom she could pour out her thoughts and feelings and, as she explained to him, it was not necessary that he reply at the same length. But he did reply: not long letters, but gentle, loving letters which she paid the pony boy to deliver to her privately and which she kept in the little brown leather case she had brought out with her to Argentina.

One bitterly cold afternoon in June, she rummaged through her drawers and ended up sitting by the log fire in the sitting room, reading her old diaries. She had started keeping them soon after getting married, as one of several measures against boredom. Reading them now, she was shocked at the interminable round of social gatherings: the polo at Laguna Blanca, the parties at Ventolera, the lunches here, the bridge parties there and the little domestic crises that had occasioned dashes into Cadoret or Laboulaye to collect the vet or the doctor, or longer visits to Buenos Aires to see films, buy clothes, have one's hair done or visit the dentist.

She put all the diaries in a cardboard box and gave them to the gardener to burn. A few days later, she did the same with all her letters.

The contractors moved in at La Ventolera within days of Randy and Betty's departure for England, and one day at the end of June Tito took Anna over to see the work in progress.

It was far more extensive than she had expected. The house was being re-roofed, re-wired and re-plumbed and a French designer had been brought in to advise on colour schemes, furnishings and even the paintings to be hung on the walls. The peons' quarters had been knocked down to make way for a wide, cobbled yard with stables on three sides, and another area had been pegged out for the special sheds and enclosures in which the prize bulls Tito planned to breed would be kept. The park was being re-landscaped. An eighteen-hole golf course was being laid out and there was to be an airstrip with its own windsock and control hut. The polo pitch was to have a wooden pavilion and a raised stand for two hundred spectators. A new leisure wing was being built which would have a sauna, gym, massage cubicles, heated swimming pool, bar and disco. One of the few original parts of the house that would remain unchanged was the superbly sprung ballroom floor.

'Well?' Tito asked when the tour was complete and they were walking back to the car. 'What do you think?'

'It's very impressive. I'm not sure what Randy and Betty would think though. I'm sure they thought you were going to keep it as it was. I certainly did.'

'Randy can't grumble. No point in doing things by half measures.' She was feeling faint after the walk and was glad to get to the car.

He looked at her. 'You all right?'

'Yes, I'm fine now.'

'I know you're fine, you've told me a thousand times you're fine. Question is, are you fit, Anna? Haven't got some fell disease or anything, have you?'

She shook her head and laughed and said of course she hadn't. He looked at her searchingly. 'Not giving me the mushroom treatment are you? Not keeping me in the dark and feeding me horseshit by any chance?'

'Why would I do that?'

'You tell me, mosca, you tell me.' He looked at her again. 'Are you pining for that old flame of yours?'

'I'm missing Scotland a bit.'

'Well you won't have much time for that sort of thing when we move in here. There'll be a lot of entertaining, you realize that? I'll want you at my side.' He compressed his lips tightly and looked hard at her. 'Couldn't you – dye your hair or something?'

'Why on earth should I want to do that?'

'Make you look a lot younger, wouldn't it? Probably make you feel younger, too.'

'I'm quite happy as I am.'

He grunted. 'Maybe you are. But if we're going to do justice to this project, you're going to have to take more trouble over your appearance.'

'I didn't realize there was any project.'

'Well there is.' He started the engine and they drove down the newly surfaced drive. 'This place'll put Cadoret on the map. It's going to become a model estancia. A VIP conference centre. A place where statesmen meet to discuss world affairs.'

She couldn't help smiling. 'Is that why you want me to dye my hair?'

He set his jaw and looked angry. 'You can be very irritating when you've a mind, Anna. Did you know that?'

The last thing she wanted was for anyone – and particularly Nikki – to guess that anything was wrong with her; so although she did not dye her hair, she did have it permed and set, and made sure that

225

when Nikki came back from her last term at Michael Hamm at the end of July she was well turned out.

Nikki brought a school friend to stay for a week and then the two of them went south to the friend's estancia near Rawson, in the Chubut. Nikki was due to start at Waltham Abbey in the second week of September, and would fly to Britain to stay for a few days at Petworth with the Smythes before starting at her new school.

By the time Nikki returned from Rawson, Anna knew that her illness had made a significant advance. It took more and more of an effort to get herself out of bed in the mornings, and by midday she felt drained of energy. So the struggle was beginning. It was now a year since Dr Marklew had broken the news to her. He had warned her that without surgery she would be lucky to have as much as two years left. Had it been irresponsible of her to refuse treatment? Sometimes she suffered doubt and depression over it. The awful part was that one was completely alone. She didn't like to burden Angus with too many thoughts and feelings, and there was no one else to turn to.

Nikki's departure for England became a target date for her. Provided she could keep going normally until then, provided Nikki suspected nothing, everything would be all right. If there was one thing she dreaded now it was a prolonged illness and slow death. The thought of her children coming to sit by her bed and watch their mother die was horrific. All she wanted was to be allowed to slip away when no one was looking.

Nikki knocked on her door at six o'clock in the morning on the day of her flight to England. She was sixteen now: not so much pretty as striking, with a strong, good face and lovely light brown hair that fell in soft curls to her shoulders. She came in in her pyjamas and kissed her mother and sat on the bed.

'Did I wake you?'

'No. I've been awake for an hour.'

Nikki heaved a big sigh.

'I know how you feel, darling, but I'm sure you'll enjoy it once you're there.'

'Will I?'

'If you make the effort, yes. But not if you shut people out the whole time. You must make friends. Join in. Do things.'

Rain pattered against the window.

'Mummy – is anything wrong?'

'Wrong? How?'

'With you. I mean – all your tiredness. And you're not exactly overweight, are you?'

'Oh – I'm all right! Just getting a bit lazy in my old age. I tell you what – shall we go for an early morning ride? Just the two of us?'

'But it's pouring with rain!'

Anna threw back the bedclothes. 'Who cares? We haven't had a ride together for ages, have we?'

They saddled up Zapata and Violeta and cantered side by side along the broad earth track to the lake. On their way back the rain eased and the morning sun shone out from behind a leaden bank of cloud.

'I'm so frightened,' Nikki said suddenly when they were hanging up the tack in the saddle room. 'I feel as if something dreadful's waiting for me just round the corner.'

'It's because you're growing up,' Anna said. 'We have to be brave in this life. Women more so than men.'

Nikki turned her head quickly. 'I know.'

At the end of November Rui Botta called a meeting of his closest business associates to discuss the arrangements for the grand opening of La Ventolera. Soon after midday the first limousines and sports cars began entering by the steel security gates of his Olivos residence, a sprawling ranch-style building with black rooftiles and brilliantly whitewashed walls.

The terrace where Botta received his guests was bordered by potted geraniums and overlooked a sparkling azure swimming pool that shimmered in the sun. Cadoret arrived on the dot of twelve thirty, which was the time he had been invited. As usual, he had a feeling that he had been invited later than the rest. For some years now he had accepted the hard fact that the only thing that really counted with Rui Botta was national origins. So although Cadoret was a Catholic and although he was a third-generation Argentine, he had the disadvantage of having predominantly British parentage and could therefore never hope to be treated or trusted by Rui as were Jorge Stefenelli or Toni Lambretti.

That was not to say that Rui did not go through the motions. He embraced Cadoret, shook him by the hand and patted his back. He beckoned to a servant and invited Cadoret to take coffee or juice or whisky or grappa or maté or bottled water or whatever else he might want. He was welcomed as an equal. But he was not an equal and he knew it. This was a game played to Botta's rules, a game he was required to play, a game he did not much enjoy.

They sucked at their cigars and called each other 'che'; they congratulated each other on business successes, ribbed each other over sexual escapades, laughed at the misfortune, bankruptcy or sudden death of rivals and enemies.

At sixty Botta looked more than ever like a retired hit man. His pewter grey hair was closely cropped and his white ears lay flat against his bullet head. He wore a heavy signet ring on the little finger of his right hand, and sucked repeatedly at the damp end of a cheroot.

At length, he called the meeting to order. 'Okay boys, let's go. Jorge: we'll hear from you first.'

Stefenelli was immaculately dressed in an Italian suit, pointed shoes and impenetrable dark glasses. In his gentle voice he outlined the timetable for the grand opening. The VIPs – who included an admiral, two generals and a bishop – would arrive by air and would be met by Cadoret, dressed as an old-style estanciero. Cadoret would be accompanied by his wife, in the dress of a nineteenth-century Argentine gentlewoman. On arrival there would be champagne on ice at the polo pavilion and a reconstruction of a battle between gauchos and Indians, followed by a demonstration of gaucho skill with the lasso and other feats of horsemanship.

For the ladies, a fashion parade would be held on the lawn in front of the house, and after it the guests would join up for more drinks and canapés before lunch, which was planned to start at two and go on until five or six. After lunch there would be swimming, tennis or a work-out in the gym for the energetic, while for the over-fed or over-forties there were the private suites and rooms in which to siesta. For health addicts there were the sauna, the steam room and the services of qualified masseuses.

Before dinner there would be a son-et-lumière performance of excerpts from Martín Fierro's 'El Gaucho'. The ball would start at eleven p.m. There would be three bands and two cabarets. The party would continue until dawn, when a champagne breakfast would be served.

Botta was well pleased, and said so. Then he turned to Cadoret.

'I have only one misgiving,' he said. 'Your wife.'

She was sitting in the shade on the verandah when he arrived back the following morning. She had taken up watercolours again and was working on a study of a hummingbird collecting nectar from the smoke bushes. She looked up and took off her glasses.

'Successful trip?'

'Very.'

She washed her paintbrush in the jamjar of water and put it away and closed up the box. She had a strange, faraway manner that made him feel excluded.

He pulled up a chair and shouted for the maid.

'Anything for you, Anna?' he asked when Rosa appeared.

'My usual, please.'

'That's a fresh orange and a long cold beer.'

'Sí, señor.'

He eyed the girl as she went inside, then turned back to Anna.

'Did you have rain here yesterday?'

'A little. How was your meeting with Rui?'

'Not bad. He's worried about you.'

'Well, that's a change.'

The drinks arrived. He sprawled in his deck chair and looked out over the smooth lawn, the landscaped park, the solitary ghost gum rising out of the privet wood.

'You realize you'll be required to appear on my arm to welcome the VIPs when we open the big house?'

'No?'

'Yes you do, Anna. Come on, buck up. I told you.'

She inclined her head. 'I must have forgotten. I'm sorry.'

'Rui's concerned that you may not be the right person for the job.'

'I see.'

'It's very high powered, Anna, you realize that? It's not one of Randy and Betty's asados. The Bishop of Rosario's coming. And the naval C-in-C. Possibly el Presidente himself, but we have yet to receive a reply from the Casa Rosada.' He wiped froth from his lips with the back of his hand. 'We'll be the reception committee, you and me.'

She smiled faintly. 'In that case, I think I'd better resign.'

He shook his head. 'You can't do that, Anna. Not this time. You've got to play your part. Be Ladybird to my Lyndon. I've got to have a wife on my arm. Look like a spare prick at a wedding otherwise.'

'Well I'm sorry, Tito, but I don't think I'll be up to it.'

He slouched in his chair, the beer sparkling in the glass at his elbow. There was a long silence. Eventually he said, 'Why the hell did you bother to come back from Scotland?'

She said nothing, so he went on. He said what he had been wanting to say. The whole thing.

'You don't want to make this move, do you? That's what this is all about. You don't want to see me moving up in the world. You can't bear to think that I might actually be successful. That's what it is. You're frightened of success, that's your trouble, my little fly in the ointment. Always have been, always will be. That's why you hate Rui.

And Jorge. And Blanca. Same reason. Because they're successful. You made a hash of your personal life and you can't bear to see anyone else making a go of theirs. Least of all your husband. You've got a suburban mentality, Anna, that's your trouble. You can't think bigger than three-up, three-down. You're a little Scotlander, a wee Mary. All this nonsense about feeling tired and having days in bed . . . You've given up on life, haven't you? Your soldier-boy turned you down so you've come back here to mope and malinger and put the wet blanket on everything I do. Know what I overheard someone say at Casa Nova the other day when they saw you come into the room? "Keep death off the roads." That's the impression you give these days. No wonder Rui's concerned. We can't open Ventolera with you looking like the ghost of Christmas past, you know. I'm buggered if I'm going to let you sabotage my chances any longer.'

He glanced at her and was gratified to see that his words, like well-aimed missiles, had struck home. She was staring straight in front of her, fighting back tears. And then for some strange reason he actually felt sorry for her. It was as if he needed to hurt in order to love. Hurting her acted on him like a narcotic, a smoke that made you want another the moment you stubbed it out.

'Why did you come back last year?' he asked again. 'Why didn't you just stay on?'

She shook her head and said nothing. That irritated him. He would have preferred her to fight back. He was just about to say so when she pushed herself to her feet, stopped and then doubled up in pain and sat down again. She fought it for several seconds. Her face became damp with sweat.

'Anna, Poppet, perhaps I overdid it a bit just now –'

'It's all right. I'll be all right in a moment. Just a bit dizzy, that's all.'

'What is it? Don't say "nothing", because there's obviously something wrong. Are you ill?'

She bowed her head.

'You are, aren't you?'

She turned to face him, gritting her teeth. 'I didn't think I'd have to tell you – but, yes, I am.'

He stared at her. 'What is it?'

She made a little throw-away gesture with her hand. 'The usual thing. It's a woman's problem.'

He went over to La Ventolera a few days later. There was only a fortnight to go before the grand opening. Ranch fences were being painted

230

and potted plants placed in position. A removals lorry was unloading bedroom furniture. In the ballroom, the refurbished chandelier was being hoisted back into position on a block and tackle.

He found Jorge with the new major domo, an arty-looking young man in his late twenties called Bernado de Gasperi. He told them that Anna was ill but did not go into details because he didn't know any.

'So she won't be able to take part,' Stefenelli said.

'I'm afraid not. What do you think? I could ask Miss Jowett from La Tijerita to stand in. I'm sure she'd be happy to help us out.'

Stefenelli shook his head. 'No. We need someone with a bit of flare, Tito. Someone who's used to facing cameras. I'll ask Blanca. She'll jump at it.'

'But – you mean –'

Stefenelli laughed. 'No – not with you, with me! We'll take over as host and hostess. You can be the figurehead. The granddaddy. The old estanciero.'

'I like that,' de Gasperi said earnestly. 'Yes I like that a lot. The old and the new. Señor Cadoret can represent the bygone generation, and you and Blanca the new, Jorge. Yes – yes, I like that a lot.'

Cadoret was not heartened at the prospect of being cast as a symbol of a bygone age. Having been given the leading role in this publicity extravaganza, he now found that he had been relegated to a walk-on part.

His public wrangle with Stiffy had not helped matters much either. He was feeling increasingly isolated by the British community. He didn't feel as if he belonged anywhere. He was neither a dark blue Anglo nor a light blue Argie, though each side seemed to regard him as belonging to the other. Now, on top of everything else, he was conscious that control of La Ventolera was slipping out of his hands. He had been used by Botta and the members of the Lodge to pull a fast one over Randy Jowett, he saw that now. He was a small cog in Botta's vast money-making engine. However much he might like to disentangle himself from it, it was impossible. He was locked into the machine and there was no way out.

Then there was the question of Anna. He didn't know whether to believe that she was ill or whether she was just using illness as an excuse. Either way, he felt that she was keeping some sort of secret from him. That annoyed him because it made him feel at a disadvantage.

He even wondered if Anna might be feigning illness to gain his sympathy. But at the same time, he needed *her* sympathy. Since failing with Emelda he had remained celibate. Nights with a call-girl in Buenos Aires no longer appealed. For the first time in years, he felt lonely and insecure. He needed a relationship that was permanent and sincere. He wanted to be able to share his thoughts, his hopes and his fears. He wanted to love and be loved.

Anna was spending more and more of her days in bed. He took to going to her room in the evenings after dinner. He told her what he had been doing that day, asked her how she was feeling and then, because what he really needed to do was open his heart to her and tell her all his worries and guilty feelings, ran dry of things to say.

Nikki was due back from school on the day before the opening of La Ventolera. Anna resigned herself to the fact that she would not be able to travel to Ezeiza airport to meet her and asked Tito to go instead; but as there was a dress rehearsal scheduled for that day which he had to attend, he asked Jorge to arrange for Nikki to be met and flown out to Calandria.

When the Beechcraft touched down on the newly completed airstrip at La Ventolera, Nikki was not on board. Her plane had been delayed by twenty-four hours.

Tito drove over to Calandria to tell Anna. She was sitting on the verandah, having got out of bed specially for Nikki's benefit. She had had the girl in from Cadoret village to do her hair and was sitting in a deck chair with a pillow for her head. She looked small and ill and frail. Her hair had gone completely white.

'Sorry, but there it is,' he said shortly. 'You know what they say. "Time to spare – go by air".'

'Never mind,' she said. 'I'll see her tomorrow.'

'I'm not so sure about that, either. The Beechcraft's going to be ferrying VIPs most of the day.'

'Couldn't she come out on one of its trips?'

'See what I can do.'

She burst suddenly into tears. 'I was so looking forward to seeing her . . .'

He felt something frightening stirring inside him, something that he didn't understand. He sat down beside her and took her hand.

'I'm sorry,' she whispered. 'I'm sorry I cried, Tito.'

He wanted to say something to make her feel better. He wanted to reassure her in some way. He thought of saying 'I love you' but that was what every husband said in the romantic films Anna insisted on going to whenever they visited BA. He regarded 'I love you' as a formula, a cop-out. There was no machismo in 'I love you'. It was

232

a wet, effeminate sort of thing for a man to say. It had been said and sung so often and so lightly that it had lost its meaning. So what did have meaning? What was there to say?'

He glanced at his watch. 'Look, I can't stay now, Poppet. I'm wanted at the big house. I'll see you the day after tomorrow when it's all over, okay?'

She watched him stride off across the grass to the car and drive away, then she put her head back on the pillow and closed her eyes. It was a hot afternoon. A calandria was squawking in the trees by the pool.

Waltham Abbey wasn't as bad as Nikki had expected. She was taking Physics, Chemistry and Biology at 'A' level and to her surprise found she actually liked two out of three of her teachers. It was particularly nice not to have to switch languages every other day, or to listen to the weekly harangue about the Islas Malvinas or the iniquitous ban on Argentine beef or any of the other dirty tricks Argentines believed had been played on them by Britain over the past century or so.

She made friends. Beth Hartley, Philippa Wayne, Rissa Bax and Nikki Cadoret formed an easy quartet who spent most of their spare time in each other's rooms listening to records, comparing boyfriends and collapsing into uncontrolled hilarity at unpredictable moments and for little reason other than the fact that they found being sixteen a pretty hilarious experience.

One weekend in early October, Rissa, whose father owned Acecraft Yachts and was very wealthy, took her home to Emsworth and they went on a windy sail to the Isle of Wight in Mr Bax's ketch. Mrs Bax did not go because she was always seasick and had given up sailing a long time ago. Rissa had been sailing since she was eight and she and her elder brother Paddy introduced Nikki to coffee-grinders and goose-necks and other pieces of nautical black magic. Mr Bax (his name was Jeffrey) was like his daughter: small, dark haired and red cheeked with a bluff, jolly manner. Nikki liked him and Paddy enormously and the success of the weekend was made complete when Paddy held her hand as they walked back to the boat after having supper out in Cowes.

The term went surprisingly quickly. Nikki spent a couple of week-ends with Roger and Penelope Smythe, and at the end of term they came to the carol service to collect her. As soon as it was over she was whisked off to Heathrow airport and caught the plane for Buenos Aires.

She had changed into tight Wranglers and a cheesecloth shirt in the plane, and turned a few heads as she pushed her trolley of baggage

233

into the arrivals hall at Ezeiza airport. She was looking round to see if there was anyone to meet her when her name was called by a voice that sent a shiver down her spine.

'Nikki, sweetheart. You're looking great, honey!'

It was José Ocampo. He was going to Cadoret in the Beechcraft and had been asked by her father to meet her and take her out with him.

She adopted the coldest possible manner towards him and when he put his hand on her shoulder to guide her she shook it off, stopped and said, 'Would you like to go first, Colonel Ocampo? I'll follow you.'

He led the way to the private air departures and her bags were loaded onto the Beechcraft. Five minutes later they were airborne.

She said nothing at all to Ocampo during the flight, which lasted about fifty minutes. She turned away from him and stared out of the side window at the vast chequered plain that stretched out below. The sky turned crimson. The plane circled over the glimmering lights of La Ventolera and set down with a squeal of tyres.

They rolled to a halt. The pilot, a swarthy man known simply as Che, taxied back to the control hut, gunned the engines and shut down. Nikki expected her parents to be there to meet her, but there was no one. Che drove them over to the big house in his car.

'I thought we were going to land at La Calandria,' Nikki said.

Che laughed. 'And miss a good party? It's all happening here, tonight, chick. This is where it's at.'

Ocampo turned round in the passenger seat. 'If you want to go to La Calandria, I can take you.'

'I'd prefer to go with my father.'

'He'll be busy right now.'

'I'll ask him all the same.'

They parked. Che said, 'Will I see you at the party?'

She shook her head. 'I'm going to Calandria.'

'That's a pity. I could show you a good time.'

'I don't want to be shown a good time, thank you.'

She carried her two cases into the house and then went through to the verandah. On the newly laid lawn, an audience of a hundred or so was seated on chairs, and swarms of flies and moths were gathering round the spotlights that illuminated the trees.

There was a burst of applause, then an earsplitting howl of feedback through loudspeakers which stopped as suddenly as it started. The son-et-lumière performance of *El Gaucho* had begun.

* * *

234

The spotlights changed colour and the voice of the actor hired to recite the epic boomed in the gathering darkness. Bats and bugs flapped and zoomed overhead and cicadas trilled. Each verse was punctuated by the twang and shudder of an over-amplified electric guitar.

> *Tiemblan las carnes al verlo*
> *Volando al viento la cerda,*
> *La rienda en la mano izquierda*
> *Y la lanza en la derecha . . .*

> Your flesh would creep could you but see
>   The Indian horde come flying,
> With hair astream in their devilish flight,
>   Loose rein in left and lance in right,
> Like a whirlwind blast they're here and gone,
>   Leaving only the dead or the dying.

It went on and on – and on. Standing to one side, Nikki could see her father sitting in the front row with the VIPs. He looked somewhat ridiculous because he was dressed up as an old-style caudillo in bombachas and poncho with a big curved knife stuck into his belt of coins. He had grown his moustache so that it dropped either side of his mouth.

> To cap my troubles an Indian came
>   Spitting foam like a puma
> He rode at me like a howling gust
>   His lance at the ready to give me a thrust
> 'Christian!' he yelled. 'You're going to die
>   When this lance goes three-foot through ya!'

Eventually there was an interval. The master of ceremonies held the microphone close to his mouth and shouted a long, deafening appreciation of the rendition so far. He reminded the audience that this production was a world première and that it made a significant contribution to Argentine culture. He introduced the actor and the guitarist and announced that during the interval Bobby Doblas and his Tango Band would play a selection of Carlos Gardel favourites. Waiters appeared with drinks on trays. People stood up and asked each other how they were enjoying it so far. Nikki went over to her father, who did not look particularly pleased to see her. When she had been introduced to an admiral with cold eyes and a cowlick of dyed black hair, she turned back to her father.

'Where's Mummy?'

'At Calandria.'

'Why isn't she here?'

He shrugged. 'Not feeling too well.'

They had to shout above the noise of Bobby Doblas and his Tango Band.

'Can someone drive me over there?'

'I doubt it. I asked José to take you. Why didn't you go with him?'

She shook her head. 'I thought you'd be meeting me.'

'I'm tied up, you can see that. You've missed the boat, Nikki. Best thing you can do is stay for the party and go back to Calandria in the morning.'

'I don't want to stay for the party. I've been travelling for the last two days. I'd quite like to go to bed.'

He took her by the arm and led her to one side. 'Look, I'm busy, do you understand? This is business, not pleasure. You're a big girl now. If you want a lift home you'll have to fix it for yourself. I haven't the time to run around after you. Got it?'

'Got it,' she said, and walked away from him.

She made her way past outbuildings, avoiding a group of peons who were lying under a tree, drinking. She went to the paddock and having talked to the ponies for a few minutes to get to know them she chose the most friendly one and got up onto its back.

The recitation of El Gaucho had been resumed and the trees were illuminated once more. The guitar burped and stuttered and the voice of the storyteller boomed behind her. Then, in mid canto, the voice fell suddenly silent. There had been a power cut. When Nikki looked back, La Ventolera had been plunged into darkness.

It was a strange way to come home from school. Going along beside the wire fence, she wondered what her friends would be doing now. Probably watching television in their cosy little English homes. And here she was bareback on a horse with no name, miles from anywhere with the sky bursting with stars and the moon hanging upside down like a Christmas decoration in the northern sky.

She felt suddenly tired. The pony had decided that it didn't want to go for a night ride after all and required constant urging. It was a long way from Ventolera to Calandria, and by the time she reached the eucalyptus ride, the moon was well up and sending silver slivers of light down between the branches.

There were no lights on in the house. She guessed that the power was still off. She rode across the grass and tethered the mare and went round to the kitchen door.

It was locked, which was unusual. She knocked, then went round to the front door and knocked again. She stood on the verandah, wondering what on earth could have happened. It was extraordinary that none of the maids were in. Presumably they had all gone over to the big house to help.

She went round to the back of the house. Her mother's window was open. She stood for a few moments looking up at it and wondering whether to call her.

The insects trilled and a dormilón gurgled somewhere over by the pool. She went back to the servants' wing and looked in at the windows. She found one that was not properly shut and managed to get it open. She climbed in and tried the first light switch, but without success, then went along the corridor from the servants' wing to the kitchen and through the kitchen to the dining room and from there along the corridor to the hall.

The house was quiet, but not completely quiet. There was a noise coming from somewhere. She stood in the hall and listened. A shaft of moonlight came in through the window on the landing. She stopped at the foot of the stairs and listened again. Somebody was snoring.

She took off her shoes and went silently upstairs and along to the end of the passage. The door to her mother's room was ajar and the snoring was coming from inside. She was afraid to go in because she didn't know what she would find. Who could possibly snore as heavily as that? Her mother had never snored in her life. So did she have a man in there with her?

Heart thumping, she put her head round the door and looked in.

Her mother did not have a man with her. She lay alone under a single sheet on the large double bed. She was on her back, her mouth open. And she was snoring.

Nikki went into the room and stood by the bed. 'Mummy?'

She crouched by the bed.

'Mummy?'

But Anna did not awake. She didn't even stir.

Something was terribly wrong. She ran downstairs and picked up the telephone. It was dead.

She went back up to her mother's room. She took her mother's hand and tried again to wake her. 'Oh Mummy!' she sobbed. 'What's the matter? What's wrong?'

She decided to stay in the room until her mother woke up. There was an armchair by the window so she sat in it. Time passed. The patch of

237

moonlight on the floor changed shape and position. Her mother snored on: deep, rattling snores that were totally alien to her. Twice, Nikki's head nodded and she forced herself awake. The third time, just before she fell asleep, she had the thought that when her mother woke up she would have the surprise of seeing her sitting there in her room.

Cadoret had taken a liking to one of the masseuses, a redhead called Belita, and had already danced much of the night away with her.

The power cut had been a blessing in disguise because the ballroom had had to be candlelit which gave the whole place a far more romantic atmosphere than Bernado de Gasperi had imagined possible.

With Belita's expert assistance Tito relaxed and began to enjoy himself. The day's unquestioned success and the part he had played in it had given a much-needed boost to his morale and Belita's company added the perfect finish to a perfect day. She was one of the best-looking women he had had the pleasure of taking onto a dance floor in a long time and he had been confident of getting her into bed within minutes of meeting her. You could tell with some women. At least, he could.

So round about three in the morning he took her up to his room; and when the lights came on Belita was putting on an extremely good act, moaning and writhing and pointing her red toe-nails at the ceiling.

Nikki woke with a start as her mother's bedside light came on. She got quickly out of the chair and went over to the bed.

'Mummy?' she whispered. 'Are you awake?'

Anna's head was right back on the pillow and her mouth was wide open. She had stopped snoring completely. She wasn't making a sound.

Nikki sank to her knees by the bed and clutched at her mother's hand, the gentle hand that had painted birds and trees and animals, the hand that had soothed and comforted, the hand she loved so much.

'No,' she whispered. 'No! No, no, no, *no* . . .!'

But her mother did not hear. She was gone.

Part Two
NIKKI

23

ROB McNAIRNE HAD LITTLE FEAR of treading where angels might think twice about rushing in. He was not a brilliant engineer, but he didn't mind getting his hands dirty and he could tell when a Chief Tiff was flannelling. He had the moral courage to stand up to senior officers who bullied and to disregard subordinates who fawned. He was inclined to be scatterbrained and had difficulty getting up in the morning. In his dealings with women, his feet were of clay. If ever it came to a choice between an early return on board or a night of passion with a willing woman, Rob McNairne had the breaking strain of a chocolate finger.

For a few years he was prevented from developing any sort of permanent relationship with a woman by the custom the Navy has of putting to sea on Monday mornings. Then one day on a skiing holiday in Austria he met a large, forthright chalet caterer by the name of Clare Vanning.

Clare had oomph. She had sailed as a cook on a Fastnet race. She had acted as co-driver on a Monte Carlo Rally and she had come within a cat's whisker of marrying a member of the Royal Family and being turned into a Duchess.

She met Rob when he was hanging up his salopettes in the chalet drying room. She was the elder daughter of elderly parents. Her father was the Reverend Michael Vanning, vicar of a small country parish in Devon. Penny, her younger sister, had married a gentleman farmer and was doing very nicely thank you.

Clare played Rob as carefully as she might a two-pound trout. She tempted him, tickled him, cuddled and courted him, and when she was confident that she had hooked him, she kept the line so subtly taut that he never knew he had been angled, let alone hooked. He swam up to her, right into her net, and was gaffed and landed on the grass at the bottom of her father's leafy garden one hazy, lazy day in the summer of '69.

They were married during a thundery downpour and the reception was held in the grounds of Buckfast Abbey. There was a uniformed guard of honour and at the reception Rob's commanding officer, an urbane man with a reputation for skill at backgammon and crosswords, told him that he believed Clare would do him a lot of good.

He slapped him on the back. 'Just what you need, my lad. She'll sort you out in no time flat. Steady you down. Sharpen you up. Just exactly what you need.'

Rob McNairne sipped his champagne and said nothing. He was not sure that he wanted to be steadied down, sharpened up or done a lot of good.

Rob's parents divorced soon after he was married, and after a year in the Far East, the young McNairnes came to Edinburgh. It was the autumn of '71. Rob had been appointed assistant engineer officer to HMS *Lerwick*, an anti-submarine frigate with a fat, upright funnel, two guns at the front and a helicopter at the back. She was not a new ship, and soon after Rob joined her she spent several weeks at sea, skirmishing with Icelandic gunboats. While turning across the sea in a force ten, the ship took a large wave aboard which stove in the hangar doors and caused cracks to appear in the deck by the funnel, so the ship was sent into her long refit two months early.

Rob and Clare had been allocated a married quarter in North Gyle Gardens which Clare invariably referred to as North Gyle Ghetto.

They had been married nearly three years and some of the glamour had worn off. They had no children, Clare having announced early on that she wanted to wait before starting a family. Rob left the house at seven every morning and seldom got back before seven at night. Often he was tired and frustrated by the clock-watching and rampant bureaucracy in Rosyth Dockyard or the chronic lack of importance attached to engineering matters in the Royal Navy at large.

The life of parties and high-living Rob and Clare had known in Singapore and Hong Kong faded to a distant dream. Clare became bored and said so.

'Go and find yourself a job,' he told her.

So she did. She got full-time work as a personal secretary in Gribble Drossart, a Scottish merchant bank involved in financing North Sea Oil. She began moving in an entirely different social circle from that of her husband. She mingled with chartered accountants, senior executives and company directors.

She was twenty-eight and he was twenty-seven. They met over coffee in the kitchen in the mornings and over supper by the fire in the evenings. Rob read *The Times* and Clare read the *Financial Times*.

They were busy people, each striving toward some indefinable goal, each aware that their present situation was not exactly what they had wanted or expected from marriage, each unable to tell the other about their misgivings.

They did not argue or fight, they were too civilized for that. They ran their lives efficiently and amicably. They attended social functions at the naval shore establishments in Rosyth and Port Edgar and gave drinks parties for the people to whom they owed hospitality. They went to the theatre and the ballet. At Christmas, they went to stay with Rob's father at Howgate, and in the new year they took a week off and went skiing in Austria.

Soon after their return, Clare's mother rang up to say that her father had had a heart attack.

'I'm taking a fortnight off,' she told Rob when he came home that evening. 'You'll be all right on your own, won't you?'

He saw her off at Turnhouse airport the next morning. When he got back to the ship, which was lying at the bottom of a dry dock in Rosyth, he was met by Lieutenant Rick Mallard, the flag lieutenant to Flag Officer Scotland and Northern Ireland, or FOSNI for short.

They went forward to the wardroom, where the officers were finishing Stand Easy.

Mallard accepted a cup of coffee. 'I've come to ask you to help me out of a hole,' he said.

McNairne grinned. 'Where have I heard this before?'

Rick Mallard and Rob McNairne had joined the Navy together. They had even been on the same selection interview. Mallard was not as well organized a flag lieutenant as his admiral might have wished.

'The fact of the matter is, I've made a bit of a cockerel,' he said, and produced an invitation bearing the names Lieutenant and Mrs R. McNairne, which stated that Lady Pamela would be At Home that evening.

'Slipped down the back of my festering filing cabinet,' Mallard admitted. 'You should have got it six weeks ago.'

'Sorry mate,' said McNairne. 'But it's "much regret unable". I've just seen Clare off on the plane south. Her father's ill.'

'I see.' Mallard thought a moment. 'Could you come on your own?'

'Won't that throw your numbers out?'

'No, I'm top-heavy with birds. Doc Buchanan was invited but he's had to cancel. If I tell Lady P that you've cried off as well she'll go bananas.'

'But I haven't cried off.'

'You know what I mean. She's doing a wall of death as it is.'

McNairne looked sideways and sighed. 'All right. I'll be there.'

Mallard drained his coffee. 'God bless you, sir. You're a knight and gentleman.'

They left the wardroom and went back along the upper deck to the brow. Pneumatic hammers were going and a crane was dangling a replacement evaporator.

'Black tie, nineteen forty-five for twenty hundred, okay?'

'I'll be there.'

'Cheers, mate. I'll put you in for the OBE.'

'Don't bother,' said Rob, and saluted as Mallard went ashore.

It was the usual sort of flag officer's evening. Most of the guests were naval, though there were a couple of Crabs from Pitreavie and a senior dockyard matey and his tarty wife from Rosyth.

They gathered in a room furnished, curtained and carpeted to standards laid down as befitting a vice admiral. A petty officer steward in a white coat with blue piping on the sleeves and collar came round with the Sackville sherry, and Sir John and Lady Pamela mingled with their guests, putting them at their ease, introducing them to each other, breaking up little circles that seemed too well established and leading lonely-looking guests to come and meet so and so.

There was a seating plan but Rob failed to consult it until the last minute. He found his place and waited behind his chair until Lady Pamela was seated, then held the chair for the lady on his right. It was all standard routine up to that moment, but from then on everything changed.

'I think we know each other, don't we?'

She was about nineteen or twenty. Long, fairish hair. Rather a large nose, but a gentle face and lovely honest eyes.

A gavel banged and the chaplain said, 'For these and all thy mercies we give thee thanks, O Lord.'

They sat down. He looked at her place card. It was difficult to read because it had been written in old English script and was angled slightly away from him.

She had been reading his. 'Rob McNairne.'

'That's right.'

'You came out to Argentina in a ship about ten years ago.'

'Good Lord! Wait a minute –'

Then he remembered. The little girl with fair plaits, sitting down

244

opposite him at a breakfast table, helping herself to cereal, asking if he could ride.

She was smiling at him. 'I'm Nikki Cadoret. Do you remember me?'

'Of course I remember,' he mumbled awkwardly. 'Of course I remember.'

She picked up her fork and started on the prawn cocktail. 'Do start,' she said. 'Lady Pamela's looking.'

He felt as if they were secret agents who had met by chance and did not wish to be recognized.

'What on earth are you doing here?'

'I'm in my first year at university.'

'Edinburgh?'

'Yes. What about you?'

'Oh, I'm in a ship in refit. Very boring. What about your family? Are they still in Argentina?'

'My father and brothers are. My mother died three years ago.'

'Oh . . . I am sorry. I remember your mother well. She was very kind to me when I stayed with you.'

She nodded. 'Yes. She would be.'

'Wait a minute – my father knew her, didn't he? Didn't she come to Scotland a few years ago?'

'That's right. We both did.'

'That can't have been very long before she died.'

'It was about a year. We stayed with the Tullochs. Actually it was Ailsa who gave my name to the flag lieutenant here.' Nikki gave an odd little smile, a twisted, quizzical smile. 'I think she wants me to meet the right sort of people.'

'And you've gone and bumped into yours truly instead. That was a bit of hard luck. So what's university like? What are you reading?'

'I'm doing a degree in nursing.'

'I didn't know you could. I suppose you're living in some squat in the Cornmarket, are you, and eating spag bol at the Traverse every night?'

She laughed. 'Not exactly. I'm sharing a flat in Thistle Street.'

'There's a pub in Thistle Street isn't there? The World.'

'We live opposite.'

They talked non-stop through the hors d'oeuvre and the entrée. Every now and then their eyes would meet and he didn't even have to wonder what she was thinking, because in an extraordinary way he knew.

'You realize we're talking far too much?' she said when the main course was being cleared away by the naval stewards.

'I know. I must do my social duty and talk to the old bat on my left. How are you getting back tonight? Can I give you a lift?'

'No, it's all right. I've got a car.'

'Perhaps . . . I could bang on your door one of these days?'

'I can't stop you, can I?'

'No hope of a coffee this evening, I suppose?'

She looked at her plate for several seconds. Then she turned to him and smiled with those lovely grey-green eyes of hers.

'All right.'

Thistle Street is a narrow, dark street that runs parallel to George Street which runs parallel to Princes Street. It's a place where you can sometimes park your car, provided you are quick off the mark and good at reversing.

It was nearly midnight when Rob parked his Beetle outside Nikki's flat. He went up a narrow staircase to the third floor. Nikki let him in. She had put a woolly jumper on over her dress and had replaced her shoes with a pair of moccasins.

'You found us,' she said. 'Come in.'

The gas fire had been lit and there was a lamp with a Chinese shade that gave a gentle, golden light. A basket-chair hung from the ceiling, as did a large balsa-wood mobile in the shape of an albatross, whose wings went up and down when you gave its string a pull. The carpet was threadbare and covered in books, papers and records. As Rob entered, a girl in glasses and an oversize T-shirt appeared at a door into another room.

'Hullo, I thought you were asleep,' Nikki said.

'Well I'm not,' said the girl and looked myopically in Rob's direction.

'Rob this is Carol. Carol – Rob. Do you both want coffee?'

Nikki went into the kitchen to make it. Carol curled up in the hanging basket and swung gently to and fro.

'Are you in the Navy?'

'For my sins, yes.'

'I didn't know it was a punishment.'

'Put on the Mahler,' Nikki said from the kitchen.

Rob did so.

'You're at the university too, I take it?'

'Psychology,' said Carol. 'Before you ask.'

Nikki came in with mugs of coffee.

'Mahler,' said Rob, making conversation. 'I don't think I know anything at all about Mahler.'

'You don't have to,' Nikki said.

'You're not at ease, are you?' Carol said. 'What are you thinking about? Your wife?'

Rob leant back in the sofa, which had a poncho draped over it. 'No, I wasn't as a matter of fact.'

Nikki said, 'Don't take any notice of Carol. She's always like this, aren't you?'

'Why don't we meditate?' Carol said. She hopped down out of her swinging basket and sat cross-legged on the floor opposite Rob. 'It'll help you to relax. It's much better with three. Join hands and close your eyes. Mahler's perfect for it.'

Rob was not into meditation and had difficulty sitting cross-legged on a hard floor. But it was a good excuse to take Nikki by the hand. After a while he felt compelled to open his eyes and when he did so found himself looking straight into hers. They stared at one another as if hypnotized.

'Do you do that very often?' he asked when the symphony was over and Carol had allowed them to get up off the floor.

'Every evening,' Carol said. 'I find it therapeutic.'

'I probably need a bit more practice.'

'Carol goes and meditates in the park when it's fine,' Nikki said. 'I tried once. I got hit on the head by a football.'

Carol drained her coffee and stood up. 'Well – good night both. Have fun.'

The door closed behind her. Nikki said, 'We get on very well, but she's a bit intense.'

There was a silence.

She said, 'So you're married.'

'Yes. I would have told you.'

'I knew already. The Tullochs told me about you. What have you done with your wife? Clare, isn't it?'

'She's in Devon. I shouldn't be here, should I?'

She sighed. 'Oh . . . who cares? Put on another record.'

'What?'

'Anything except Wagner.'

He knelt among the records. 'Who's Fernando Sor?'

'He's the Beethoven of the guitar. Put him on.'

He did so, and the room filled with wonderful classical guitar music.

He sat down on the floor and leant his head against the arm of the

247

sofa. The music filled him with an impossible ache which he had never experienced before. After a while, he felt her fingers touching the back of his head.

'I have so much to say that I can't say anything,' he said quietly.

'I know,' she said. 'I feel exactly the same.'

The music flowed over him and through him and round him. Nikki was touching the back of his head, running her fingers up and down the nape of his neck.

'Do you have to get back to your ship or anything?'

'No. I have a dank little MQ to go back to.'

'What's an MQ?'

'Married quarter.'

The gas fire flared and the albatross soared gently overhead. Nikki was bending over him. Their lips touched.

'Would you like to stay the night?'

In the morning she came into his room with a cup of coffee and sat on his bed and they talked. She asked him what they were going to do about it and he said he didn't know. She said that she had never intended this; he said that he hadn't either but that it had just happened. She was in pyjamas still and he in his shirt. He held her in his arms and they said nothing for a long time because there was no need to say anything.

'I want to tell you something,' he said at last. 'This may sound absurd, but I never knew what it meant to be in love before.' He took her hands and faced her. He smiled, shaking his head. 'I'm . . . smitten. Head over heels.' He held her hands tightly. There were tears standing in his eyes. He heard himself say, 'There's no point in trying to hide the fact. I've never felt about Clare – or anyone for that matter – even a quarter of what I feel for you.'

He went to the window and looked down on the roof of his car parked in the street below.

She said, 'If it helps at all, I feel the same.' Then she came and stood behind him and put her arms round his waist and added, 'But I don't think it does help really, does it? If anything, it makes matters worse.'

It was Saturday. He drove back to the ship, attended captain's messdeck rounds and left again as soon as the hands secured at midday. He met Nikki at her flat and they had lunch in Edinburgh. When they emerged onto the street it was snowing.

'Where would you like to go?'

248

'Somewhere out of town. Somewhere by the sea.'

They headed over the Forth road bridge and along the Fife coast to the village of Crail, where they walked arm in arm along the beach, their heads bent against the driving snow.

'I nearly came here to school,' she said. 'My mother wanted me to go to Kerrmuir's.'

'Why didn't you?'

'My father wouldn't have it. He's a bit like that.'

She told him about Waltham Abbey. Going back for her second term after her mother died had been a nightmare.

'My work went down the drain. I didn't know what I was doing or where I was going. I ran away. We had a drama master who fancied me, so I took off. I thought I could hitch to London. I wanted . . . I just wanted to disappear. For ever. I never wanted to see that school or my brothers or my father – especially my father – again. But the police picked me up. I got as far as the roundabout.'

They stopped walking and he held her and kissed her. Her lips and cheeks were cold from the driving snow and there was snow on her Russian fur hat.

They started walking again.

'Then in the summer holidays I went on a fortnight's sailing holiday with a friend. We went over to St Malo and the Channel Islands, and on the way back I developed acute appendicitis. The yacht had a radio and they radioed for help and I was picked up by a helicopter and taken to the naval hospital in Plymouth. And when I came round from the operation I didn't want to live. But there was a junior naval doctor – a houseman I suppose – who came and talked to me. I never discovered his name, but I owe him a lot. He treated me as a human being rather than a desirable piece of skirt. He sorted me out. He convinced me that I was an individual. He made me want to work again. Live again. I'd wanted to be a vet or a doctor, but I wasn't brainy enough for either. I scraped enough 'A' levels to come here and do nursing. Am I talking too much, Rob? Stop me if I witter on.'

She obviously needed to talk. She said that she had never opened up to anyone before but was an inveterate bottler-up. She put her hand inside his coat pocket and interlocked her fingers with his and they walked along that wintry beach for miles. When they got back to the car it was getting dark.

'Do you know, I've never had a serious boyfriend?' she said on the way back across the Forth. 'Not one. And now look what I've done. I've gone and fallen for a married man. I feel so awful about your wife, Rob. I expect you do too, don't you?'

'A bit,' he admitted.

She blew her hair out of her eyes. 'I suppose really we ought to call it a day now. Ships in the night. What do you think?'

'I think we should make the most of the time we've got.'

He turned off the Corstorphine road.

'Where are we going?'

'I'm going to introduce you to the delights of North Gyle Ghetto.'

The house was cold and so were they.

Nikki looked round at the chintzy covers and family photographs. She came to him, shivering. 'I never knew guilt could be so exhausting.'

'Look at you,' he whispered. 'You're frozen.'

'Not frozen,' she whispered. 'Tense.'

'No need to be.'

'I can't help thinking about her.'

They looked at the photograph of Clare and himself on the windowsill. It had been taken when they were just back from honeymoon.

'You both look so happy together, Rob. I don't want to spoil your life. Perhaps I'd better go. Oh God, I don't know what I want!'

'I know what *I* want.'

'What's that?'

'You.'

She bowed her head, then looked up at him, then bowed her head again.

'I don't know what to say.'

'Don't say anything.'

He led the way upstairs and they went into the spare bedroom. 'I want to protect you,' he said. 'I want to look after you. I want to make love to you.'

'Rob – would it be enough – just to go to bed together? I'm so terrified that if we actually make love something will change. I'm afraid that I might never be able to let you go.'

He held her face in his hands. 'I promise that we won't ever do anything that you don't want to do.'

'That's the most wonderful thing any man has ever said to me,' she replied.

Part of him understood what was happening, knew that he was being unfaithful and foresaw the horror and heartache of a broken marriage. That was the logical part, the part that passed exams, the part that had got him into the Navy, the part he used every day. But Nikki had made the illogical, irrational part of him far stronger. She made him feel like a schoolboy again. He had an extraordinary urge to write poetry and sing. Suddenly, the Royal Navy was reduced in his eyes to a futile game of boy scouts in long trousers. Nothing mattered but Nikki. He found himself daydreaming during the first lieutenant's weekly planning meeting. He was late for captain's requestmen and defaulters. He forgot to sign the night rounds book. From being a keen young engineer officer, he was transformed into a sighing Romeo. The only thing that mattered was when and where he would next meet Nikki and for how many hours and minutes they could be together.

He guessed that something had once happened to her – she never said what – that had made her man-shy. After her sailing accident she had set herself the target of getting into university and had put everything else aside to achieve that aim. She told him about an uncle she had never met who had been a doctor and had been killed in an horrific incident in a wilderness called the Chaco in Argentina. Her ambition was to go out there and work on the same mission as he had done.

'I want to do something with my life,' she said. 'I don't want to fritter it away like my mother did hers.'

'Aren't you being a bit hard on her?'

Nikki shook her head. 'She was always the first to admit that she had wasted her life. She used to say that the only thing there was for a woman to do in Argentina was breed. She should never have married my father. She should have married yours. You didn't see them together did you? They were made for each other. Anyone could see that.'

He touched her fingertips. 'Like us?'

'Probably.'

That was the first time that he put it into words and told her he loved her. It came out of its own accord. With Clare, it had always cost him an effort to say 'I love you.' But Nikki was different from Clare. She made him ache with love. He felt entirely in tune with her, as if they had belonged to each other since the beginning of time.

Having declared himself, he realized that something had changed fundamentally in his life. He was living a deceit. The realization kept him awake at nights until he took a decision that whoever else he deceived, he must never deceive himself. He would not pretend to himself, nor kid himself that his actions were for motives higher than was the case.

He was in love with Nikki, that was all there was to it, and when you were in love you had a choice: to smother love for the sake of

251

conventional morality or flout convention for the sake of love. He had already embarked upon the latter course and was committed to it. Though he had not actually made love to Nikki, he had been to bed with her and had therefore become an adulterer. He had no choice now but to deceive Clare and keep his secret; and if Clare ever found out then he would just have to face the consequences.

One evening they came back late to the flat on Thistle Street after seeing a play at the Traverse theatre club and having a candlelit spaghetti bolognese supper. They sat on the floor and listened to records and talked.

They could talk for hours about anything and everything.

She told him more about her extraordinary family. About her step-sister Blanca, who owned a fashion boutique in Buenos Aires and lived an entirely separate life from her husband; about the circle of Italian Argentines in which her father now moved. She told him about Marc, her polo-playing brother who had once boasted to the press that he needed a woman a day to keep his eye in on the polo pitch.

Then she told him about Jimmy. 'Remember how you put that flag up at La Calandria? I watched you. You got a rope from the tack room and tied it round the chimney to support the mast. Jimmy didn't know about that sort of thing. He just crawled out along the mast or yard or whatever you call it. I saw the staple beginning to pull out of the side of the house; there was nothing I could do' – she closed her eyes, reliving it – 'and ever since I suppose I've always known that if you'd been there, he wouldn't have died.'

The next day he called into the married quarter on his way into Edinburgh from the ship and while he was there the phone rang.

'Hullo, it's me,' said Clare, and her voice faltered. 'Listen – Daddy died yesterday morning. The funeral's on Thursday. Is there any hope of your being able to come down for it?'

'I will if I possibly can,' he said. 'But it is very short notice.'

'I tried to phone you last night. Were you duty or something?'

'Yes I was,' he said quickly.

That was the first lie.

He drove to Thistle Street and broke the news to Nikki. She clenched her fists and looked out of the window and said in a strangled voice, 'I've been dreading this moment.'

'So have I.'

'Does it mean I won't see you again?'

'I don't know. No, why should it?'

'But this is where it starts, isn't it? The other woman.'

He put his hands on her shoulders. 'I don't know what's going to happen, but I do know that I'll never stop loving you. Love doesn't stop or run out, does it? If it does, it was never love to start with.'

She leant against him.

'I feel so bloody guilty.'

'Do you think I don't?'

'Perhaps we ought to make a clean break now, Rob. Once and for all.'

'Could you do that?'

'I don't know, but I think we ought to try. Don't you?'

He flew south for the funeral. The service was held in the country parish church Mr Vanning had served so well for twenty years. Practically the whole village turned up. Mr Vanning was spoken of as an upright and warm-hearted man, a loving husband and father and a dedicated and caring parish priest.

Rob held Clare's hand and stared down as the coffin was lowered into the grave.

'Thank you for coming down,' Clare said two evenings later when they were home again. 'Having you there made all the difference.'

When she got into bed he could not help making mental comparisons. Clare was noticeably heavier, hotter, thicker – and older. Where Nikki was tentative, questioning, hesitant, gentle, Clare was confident, assured, forthright. If Nikki was a startled roe, Clare was a blundering heifer.

'Have you missed me?' she asked suddenly, and pulled her head back to look at him.

'Of course I have,' he said, then hid his face between her breasts.

The strange thing was, in a way, he had missed Clare. He liked her as a person. He enjoyed her company, in bed and out. They suited each other physically and temperamentally. As she had said on the day they got engaged, they made a good team.

But, he reflected, when you are in a team it is not a good idea to be in love with the other members, even if it is a team of only two. Love was not good for efficiency. Love was late for appointments, forgot to post letters, burnt the toast. Love was more than just not having to say you were sorry. Love took the whole complicated jigsaw of morals and ethics and threw it into the wind.

Love didn't care where the pieces landed.

*   *   *

253

'Rob,' said Clare on Monday evening when he arrived back from the ship. 'You remember when I phoned you the day after Daddy died, and you said you'd been duty the night before?'

He threw his cap onto the kitchen table and unbuttoned his reefer. 'Yes?'

'You weren't duty, were you?'

His stomach fluttered unexpectedly. The last time he'd felt that was when he was a midshipman doing an air-experience course with the Fleet Air Arm and the instructor had put the plane into a fully developed stall.

'What?'

'I said – you weren't duty, were you?'

He stared at her, blinking.

'I washed your jeans today,' she said. 'And found these.' She produced two ticket counterfoils for the Traverse Theatre and held them out on the flat of her hand as if offering sugar lumps to a stallion.

He stared at them. He had received a note from Nikki in reply to his that morning. She had agreed to meet him the following afternoon. There was a ship's sports afternoon and he was going to play truant.

'Oh.'

'Why did you lie to me?'

'I didn't lie –'

'For God's sake, Rob! Funny sort of duty if you've got time to bomb off to the theatre.'

He felt his heart thundering. 'Listen – I didn't want to upset you. You told me your father had died and then asked me if I'd been duty. So I said yes. It – came out automatically. Just a white lie, that's all.'

'Who did you take?'

'What?'

'Don't say "what" every time you don't want to answer a question. Who did you take to the theatre? The duty petty officer?'

'No, surprisingly, it was not the duty petty officer. Now I'm going to go and change, if you'll excuse me.'

She barred his way. 'Who? Who, Rob? Who did you take to the Traverse that night?'

'Look. I had to help Rick Mallard out the other day. He'd made a cock-up over the invitations and was short of a man for one of Lady P's dinner parties. I found myself sitting next to someone I'd met years and years ago when I was a midshipman. We got talking, and I took her out to the theatre. Once. End of story.'

'Her. You took her out to the theatre.'

'Yes.'

'What's her name?'

He shook his head. 'Does it matter?'

'Of course it bloody well matters!'

He sighed. 'Her name was Nicola Cadoret. I met her nearly ten years ago in Argentina. Her parents were very kind to me and had me to stay. The least I could do was repay a little of their hospitality. So I took her to the theatre. There. Now do you want to know anything else?'

'How old was she when you met her in Argentina?'

'I dunno. About ten.'

'So she's about twenty now.'

'Something like that, yes.'

'Good looking?'

'Not particularly.'

'But you liked her.'

'Yes. Yes, I liked her.'

'You liked her enough to lie about her.'

'That's just absurd.'

Clare did not often cry, but when she did he found it a most painful experience.

'Sweetie, you're making far more of this than is necessary. Nothing happened. I just took her to the theatre, that was all.'

'But why did you have to lie to me?'

He hung his head. 'I don't know. I'm sorry. I shouldn't have.'

She said she didn't know what to think because it was so totally unlike him to lie. She wanted to know more and more about Nikki. She wanted to know everything. She got out of him that Nikki was at the university, that she was doing a degree in nursing, that her mother had died a few years before and had been friendly with his father.

'You mean before your father's marriage broke up?'

'Yes. That's why they invited me to stay when I was in Argentina.'

'So she's an old friend of the family.'

'No, I wouldn't say that. Just a – a –'

'Just an old flame.'

'For God's sake! She was ten!'

'That's not too young to start, believe me. I had my eye on boys – and men – before I was ten. She's probably been carrying a torch for you ever since.'

'I can assure you she hasn't.'

'Oh? So you did discuss it, did you?'

He pushed past her, went upstairs, changed and came down for supper. The interrogation was resumed over shepherd's pie.

'Was that the only time you saw her?'

'No, I told you. I met her at FOSNI's dinner party.'

'Apart from that. I suppose you met her at the weekend, did you? What was it, lager and smorgasbord at the Copenhagen? Or a pie and a pint at the World? Touching knees under the table? Soulful glances over the best bitter?'

'Look – this isn't improving things –'

'I don't want to improve things,' Clare shouted, and her eyes protruded in anger. 'I want to get at the *truth*!'

Nikki picked him up in her Mini. They drove out to Crail. It was a clear, crisp February day. May Island was visible on the eastern horizon. They sat on the harbour wall and dangled their legs. He put his arm round her shoulders.

'Clare knows.'

'Oh God,' she said. 'Is it very bad?'

'It isn't very good.'

'Rob, the last thing I want to do is wreck a marriage. Anyone's marriage. But least of all yours.'

He shook his head.

'We should stop seeing each other. Shouldn't we?'

'Should, shouldn't.' He glanced at her and then looked out to the harbour entrance where a fishing boat was chugging in with gulls wheeling and crying around it. He spoke to himself as much as to her. 'It's all meaningless, isn't it? I just want to be with you, that's all I want. I was never in love with Clare – or anyone else for that matter. Getting married to her . . . just seemed a good idea at the time. The trouble is, if you've never loved someone you don't know what it's like, do you? You don't know what you've missed so you don't know what you might be forfeiting by getting married. So . . . you go and marry a nice girl like Clare Vanning and then – bang! – Nikki Cadoret comes along and it's too late. You can't undo love. You can't un-love someone. I can't, anyway.' He turned to her. 'What do you think?'

'I feel sorry for Clare.'

'You're so calm, Nikki. That's what I love about you.'

'I'm not at all calm inside, believe me.'

'But you're at peace with yourself, aren't you?'

Nikki gazed out to sea. 'Not in the way you think. I . . . bottle things up.'

'Tell me.'

She shook her head. 'Nothing to tell really.'

The fishing boat had tied up alongside the quay and men in yellow thigh boots and coarsely knitted sweaters were unloading a meagre catch. He watched them and thought about Clare. When she wasn't interrogating him about Nikki, when they were on good terms, he enjoyed her company. They went well together. They *did* make a good team. Hadn't he always wanted to be a good husband? Hadn't he always promised himself that he wouldn't make the mistakes his mother and father had made? Then he thought about Nikki. He owed her no debt of affection. Was that why he felt so irresistibly drawn to her? Was that why it was so unthinkable that they should try to break apart? If he had any guts he would tell her now, gently, quietly, that they must not see each other or write to each other again. She would accept that. He knew she would. But could he bring himself to do that? The answer was no. He simply couldn't do it.

He sought her hand and held it tightly. The harbour, the boats, the horizon, the gulls – all became fogged and blurred.

She got down off the wall. 'Come on,' she said quietly. 'Let's go for a walk along the beach.'

Two weeks later Clare and Rob went out to Howgate to stay for the weekend with Rob's father. Rob's sister Kate and her husband Allan, who was in the Royal Highland Fusiliers, were also staying. Kate was comfortable, conventional and pregnant. She and Clare had shared a flat in London together before they were married and Allan and Rob had been at Fettes College together. The four knew each other well and were good friends.

Angus had ordered a huge joint of best Scottish beef for Sunday lunch and had invited the Tullochs and their son Paul and his wife and three children. They were going to be twelve for lunch.

Clare was a first-rate cook so she donned a butcher's apron and took charge in the kitchen while Kate, who knew which silver and glass to use and where everything was kept, saw to laying the table and arranging the seating.

Not long before one o'clock, when a log fire was roaring in the hearth and delectable smells of roast beef and Yorkshire pudding were coming from the kitchen, the telephone rang. Rob answered it.

'Angus?'

'No, Rob. Hullo, Ailsa.'

'Your voices are so alike! Listen – would you mind if we brought one extra for lunch?'

'I'll ask the cook. Clare! Ailsa says can they bring one extra?'

'Of course they can,' Angus said from the study. 'The more the merrier!'

'I heard that,' Ailsa laughed. 'We'll be right over.'

'Who's the extra one?'

'Surprise,' Ailsa said, and put the phone down.

The guests drove up in two cars ten minutes later. Angus went out to meet them in the drive. Children and red setters spilled out onto the gravel and there was a round of handshakes and kisses.

'First time we've all got together in years,' Angus said, shaking Doug warmly by the hand. 'And who's this? Wait a minute – it's Nikki, isn't it? Ailsa, my dear, what a splendid surprise! Come along in out of the cold, all of you. Rob, I've got someone here you haven't seen in years! Nikki Cadoret from Argentina. Remember?'

'Yes, of course –'

'Yes, of *course*,' cut in Clare, sweeping into the hall from the kitchen. 'Of course! I've heard so much about you, Nikki – and all of it good, of course. What a thrill to meet you at last. No, I won't shake hands, my hands are wet. I gather you and Rob saw quite a lot of each other while I was down south, isn't that right?'

'Well –' Nikki started.

'Yes,' Rob said rather loudly. 'We bumped into each other at the admiral's.'

Clare looked from one to the other. 'And at the Traverse, wasn't it?'

'I didn't realize you'd met,' Ailsa said.

Angus pulled a pipe out of his jacket pocket and blew into it. 'Nor did I.'

'There are lots of things you don't know, Dad,' Clare returned. 'Isn't that right, Robert?'

'Well what the hell did you expect me to say?' Clare hissed when they were up in their room that night. 'I suppose you wanted me to pretend, did you? Well I've got news for you, buster. If you think I'm going to start covering your tracks for you, think again.'

'You've wrecked the whole weekend.'

'*I've* wrecked the whole weekend? That's rich. That is really rich.'

'There was no need to behave like that. All those pointed remarks at lunch. You embarrassed the Tullochs and you nearly reduced Nikki to tears.

'Ah, poor little Nikki! What about me, Rob? What do you think I felt like? What sort of hell do you think I was going through?'

'But you made it worse. For yourself, for all of us. There was no need for it. Do you think I wanted Nikki to be there? Do you think she would have come if she'd known we were going to be there?'

'I've no idea what Nikki wants – apart from a certain part of your anatomy. She might have thought you'd managed to get rid of me again. For all I know the two of you might have hoped to turn it into another of your romantic meetings. Or you might have planned it together to inflict the maximum amount of pain on me.'

'Well we didn't. Neither of us had any idea this was going to happen.'

'Oh? How do you know she didn't know? Have you been meeting her again? Or do you make long, passionate telephone calls to her every morning from the ship?'

'Don't be so bloody ridiculous.'

'How am I to know it's ridiculous, Rob? How am I to know what to believe and what not to believe? How am I to know, ever again, whether you're telling me the truth?'

And then they both broke down and wept in each other's arms and she made him promise that he would never see Nikki again, or write to her or phone her or contact her in any way – ever, ever again.

'I promise,' he said. 'I promise.'

'Is it over? Can you promise me that it's over?'

'Yes. Yes, it's over.'

'Then make love to me,' she whispered, and drew him to her, and demanded more of him that night than she had ever demanded before, so that he was left exhausted and drained and emotionless. Afterwards, lying awake into the small hours listening to the wind howling in the slates and the grandfather clock downstairs striking the quarters and the halves and the hours, he saw the bleak truth of his situation for the first time. He had broken something that could not be repaired. Whatever he promised to Clare, Nikki would always come first. One day, sooner or later, he would have to see her again.

The clock struck four. He was missing Nikki already. He longed to be alone with her so that he could talk to her, reassure her and be reassured by her.

It was not over. It would never be over, never until his dying day.

As the Edinburgh winter turned reluctantly into spring, HMS *Lerwick* was put back together again, set to work, cleaned, painted and polished. During this time, Rob continued to meet Nikki whenever possible, but that wasn't often and was usually only for snatched half-hours in her flat on afternoons when he was able to get away from the ship. They exchanged letters and notes instead. He wrote direct to her flat and she wrote to him at his ship. There were long letters in which Nikki thought on paper, expressing all her feelings of love, apprehension and guilt; there were shorter notes telling him where she could meet him and when, and there were the notes she left for him in the flat, notes like 'Had to dash out. Shan't be long. Pimms in the fridge. Love you. N.'

He didn't have the heart to destroy them. He kept them in a locked drawer in his cabin and often took them out to re-read them.

He was careful to cover his tracks and provide himself with an alibi for Clare when she asked him where he had been or why he was late. He needed those alibis: Clare interrogated him frequently and at unpredictable times. Suddenly, for no apparent reason, she would fire a trick question at him. 'How was the traffic in Edinburgh?' she might ask when he had said he had come straight from Rosyth; or 'When did the meeting end?' when he had supposedly been held up on board. But there were other questions too, questions she would ask him before they got up in the morning, when his brain was half-awake and she could catch him off-guard. 'How often did you screw her?' she would challenge, or 'Did you do it the way we do it?' Such questions burnt him emotionally.

The opening shots would be fired in bed before they got up. Then, when he came down to breakfast, the torment would start in earnest. They would stand like boxers, toe to toe in the kitchen, she demanding to know every last detail, he dodging and weaving every barbed question she hurled at him.

'How many times do I have to tell you?' he would say. 'We never made love. Do you hear me? Nikki and I never made love.'

Clare perfected the art of hitting him where it hurt and Rob learnt how to lie easily and convincingly. They trained each other in the art of verbal combat. Each hated what was happening yet each felt compelled to carry it through. Every time she caught him out, their marriage took another lurch downwards. Each time she began interrogating him, he threw up still higher defences against her. The more he lied, the more she interrogated. The more she interrogated, the more he lied.

Sometimes they reduced each other to tears and would stand in the kitchen – it always seemed to be in the kitchen – weeping exhaustedly on each other's shoulders.

Then there would be a rapprochement that would last a few days or possibly a week. Clare would make love to him in the way she believed he particularly liked. He would pretend to enjoy it but

260

she would instinctively see through his pretence; they would have another sleepless night; in the morning she would ask another of her questions.

'Her breasts are smaller than mine, aren't they?'

'Why can't you leave it alone?' he whispered. 'Can't you see that we're both wounded? Why must you pick the scab off every single time? Why must you make it bleed, and bleed and bleed?'

'You hate me, don't you,' she whispered. 'I saw it in your eyes last night. You hate me, but you haven't got the guts to say so.'

She threw back the bedclothes and stamped out to the lavatory and he lay on his back and, weeping, admitted it to himself. 'Yes, yes,' he whispered. 'I hate you. I hate you.'

HMS *Lerwick*'s delayed re-commissioning ceremony eventually took place on a windy day at the end of June. The officers and ship's company had worked night and day for a week to bring the ship's appearance up to the required standard, and when they fell in on the dockside the barrels of the guns were oiled and gleaming; the guardrail stanchions were pristine white; the decks had a fresh coat of green, and the ship's crests on the three-inch rocket launchers and anti-submarine mortars were freshly painted in white, blue and gold.

The white ensign flapped noisily in the wind and the Royal Marine band played excerpts from *South Pacific*. FOSNI arrived in a black Vauxhall with his flag flying from the bonnet. The guard presented arms and the band played a musical salute.

The commissioning service was shared by three chaplains who took it in turn to lead the officers and men in prayer. The captain and a junior seaman read the lessons. They sang 'Eternal Father Strong to Save' and repeated the Naval Prayer.

There were drinks and a buffet lunch in the wardroom afterwards. Clare and Rob were making a special effort. Clare got amusingly drunk. She kicked off her shoes and flirted with the first lieutenant.

Rob was talking to Lady Pamela when Clare came up.

'Can I have the key to your cabin? I've sat on a vol-au-vent.'

He produced it. 'You know your way, don't you?'

'Should do,' she said, and added, 'It's all right, Lady P. I'm his wife.'

Rob turned back to the admiral's wife, who began telling him about the banyans they used to have on Lantau Island when her husband was on the staff of C-in-C Far East Fleet after the war. Five minutes later, Rob felt a touch on his arm and turned to find Clare standing before him, her eyes blazing and in her hand every letter and note he had ever received from Nikki. The key to the private drawer in his desk was on the same ring as the key to his cabin.

'You bastard,' she said, and the conversation in the wardroom died suddenly away. 'You shitty little bastard.'

She threw the letters on the carpet at his feet and left the wardroom. He gathered the letters up and pursued her down an accommodation ladder and along the deck, aft to the brow. She was in her stockinged feet and the back of her red trouser suit still bore the marks of a squashed mushroom vol-au-vent.

'Clare! Wait!'

She waited for him at the head of the brow where the officer of the watch, the quartermaster and the bosun's mate stood ready to salute. She waited for him, but as he came up she stepped up onto the end of the brow so that she could look down on him, with the sideparty saluting beside him.

'Fuck off, McNairne.' She spat her words at him. 'Fuck off out of my life.'

She drove fast through Rosyth dockyard and ignored the policeman at the gate when he signalled her to stop. All the way into Edinburgh, horns blared after her. She drove through red lights, clipped a parked car, missed a woman on a zebra crossing by inches.

She had found Nikki's address on one of the letters. She drove down Thistle Street and parked outside. She went barefoot up a narrow flight of stairs and banged on a black door with a brass door handle.

It was opened by Carol, who blinked at her through steel-framed glasses. Clare pushed past her and found Nikki reading a book on the sofa. She was eating a green apple. Her hair was long and loose about her shoulders. Her feet were tucked under her, she was surrounded by books. The record player was on.

Classical stuff. Bloody guitars. The very music Rob had been crazy about for the past three months.

The balsa-wood albatross soared gently on the current of air made by the opening door.

'I think I'll make some coffee,' Carol said, and disappeared into the kitchen.

Clare looked at Nikki and her brain automatically registered the reasons why Rob had fallen for her. It was not that she was glamorous or even particularly good looking. Her nose was too large and her breasts were too small. But she had something else, something Clare had seen in other women but knew she did not possess herself. It was an indefinable quality, a gentle femininity, a warmth of expression, a look of intelligent understanding. No wonder he'd been knocked sideways.

Nikki put her book aside. 'Would you like to sit down?'

Heartburn brought back the bitter taste of semi-digested pastries, peanuts, champagne.

'I found your letters.'

'Oh.'

'He told me it was over. Weeks ago. He's good at most things, you know, but I never knew how good he was at lying. He's a real expert. Did you know that?'

Nikki looked down at her hands. 'I never intended this to happen,' she said. 'Neither of us did.'

'I suppose you think you love him, do you?'

A kettle whistled momentarily in the kitchen.

Nikki shook her head and said she didn't know and that she had never wanted to take Rob away.

'I came to tell you you could have him.' Clare was suddenly blinded by tears. 'But why should you? Why should you? You never promised to love, honour and obey him, did you? I did. You never made a home for him. I did. You never cooked and cleaned and kept house for him or met him when his ship arrived back or had his car serviced or mowed his lawn or listened to him banging on about the bloody Navy. I did, damn you. I did.'

Carol appeared at the door, a mug in either hand.

'Would you like some coffee?'

Clare felt herself being lifted up on a breaking wave of anger. 'Yes I would very much like some coffee. Thank you. Coffee is exactly what I would like. Here you are, Nikki, Nicola, whatever your name is. Here you are.' She took both mugs from Carol and swung them so that the coffee splattered across the wall, the prints, the albatross, the poncho and Nikki herself.

Weeping, she ran out, down the stairs, slipped on the bottom step, recovered and went out to the car.

She drove fast out of the city. Going along the main road past the zoo she pulled out to overtake a line of slow-moving traffic. As she did so, a lorry emerged from a side road to the right. She was doing well over fifty miles an hour. There was little time to brake and no room to swerve.

24

CAROL SAT CROSS-LEGGED in her basket, swinging gently to and fro. The room was candlelit and smoky from joss sticks that smouldered in empty wine bottles.

'The search for the ox,' she began, in a faraway, hypnotic voice. 'The ox, the symbol of ultimate nature. The search for the ox, the decision to search, the decision to follow a path, the path to direct knowing. The searcher is at first looking for something only vaguely apprehended. She has no proof of its existence, only her intuitive feelings that the ox exists and must be found. And when she finds the tracks at last, the tracks of the ox, she sees in them the first direct evidence that the ox exists.'

Libby was lighting the joint. She sucked the smoke in through her teeth and let out a gentle, 'Aaah . . . !'

'She follows the tracks,' Carol went on in her soft, mesmeric tones, 'for a lifetime perhaps. But though she may never glimpse the ox, she knows that there is no other path to be followed, no other way but to continue the search . . .'

Carol, Nikki and three girlfriends had been to see a play at the Traverse and had returned to Thistle Street to smoke grass and meditate. While Carol continued along her mystical path, the others reclined on floor cushions.

Nikki felt a touch on her arm and accepted the roach. She drew deeply and inhaled fully, and a little while later when she heard someone laughing it took her a moment to realize that that person was herself.

'And now, out of the corner of her eye, the searcher glimpses the ox for the first time. She enters a new phase, a phase of knowing that the ox is omnipresent. After this first glimpse her task becomes clear. She must catch the ox, tame it and ride it home . . .'

For the first time in three weeks Nikki's black despair began to break up and dissolve. And she was still laughing. Why? She was laughing because she was laughing. She was laughing because it didn't matter. Rob was only a man, after all. Viv and Jo were close to her, their arms around her, supporting her, their eyes laughing, their hands reaching out with love.

'. . . gradually coming, coming to a deeper, more intimate, more subtle relationship, so that the ox is a tool for ploughing the field of enlightenment no longer, but a companion, a free companion . . .'

Cool fingers slipped in over her breasts and went back and forth over her nipples, bending them this way and that; and the words went on and the roach came round again and she floated upward.

'. . . now the disciple, who has become a sage, reaches the realization that disciplines were never necessary, for enlightenment was always at hand. Everywhere is the ox, and the ox is everywhere. She has ridden the ox home; the self is alone and yet forgotten. She has approached the threshold of pure consciousness and knows that there is no enlightenment because enlightenment is all around. Nothing is holy because all is holy. All is sacred because nothing is sacred. She has returned to the source of all thought, all consciousness . . . the profane has become sacred . . . the seeker merges with the phenomenal universe. She becomes the clouds. She becomes the mountains. She becomes the waves and the pine trees. This is no phantom, no dream. It is the true manifestation of the source of all love, all power, all thought, all knowledge . . .'

There were lips on her lips. Hair was falling like a tent about her face.

'And now, with helping hands, the seeker enters the marketplace. She has become a cheerful villager who wanders from place to place. The gate of her cottage is open but not even the wisest can find her. She has entered so deeply into universal experience that she can no longer be traced. She has seen the intrinsic Buddha in all life. She has seen him and in seeing she brings all with whom she has contact into bloom.'

Nikki arched suddenly, her body shaking like a stretched bow.

'The ox!' Carol whispered. 'The ox . . . !'

When she opened her eyes and looked at the cracked plaster of the ceiling, her headache was so intense and the feeling of nausea so revolting that had the means been readily at hand she would willingly have ended her life. It was a sense of despair that was blacker and more impenetrable than anything she had ever known.

Everything had gone wrong. All over again.

She heaved her legs off the bed and put her bare feet on the floor. Bleakly she gazed about at the mounds of clothes, records, empty bottles, full ashtrays, books, papers, envelopes – even a syringe, which was something she had not seen in the flat before.

She lurched with a sudden urgency out of the room towards the bathroom. Vomit sprayed painfully through her nostrils and then shot with surprising velocity out of her mouth.

She stood shivering at the bathroom window and looked out at the chimneypots and back yards. A woman in curlers was emptying a bucket into a dustbin. A tortoiseshell cat was sitting on the roof of a coalshed, eyeing a pigeon that strutted on a window ledge. Through a downstairs window she could see a man in braces reading a paper.

She closed her eyes and immediately saw the startling green of the pampa stretching away to a bar-flat horizon. She saw a long straight earth road going to vanishing point between endless wire fences; thunderheads rising purple and mauve into a distant sky. She heard the creak of a windpump, the thud and whinny of ponies cantering, the cries of peons working a herd.

She was sick again. Afterwards, shivering and sweating and feeling like death, she knew that she must get away, right away. She must escape now, before it was too late.

There was plenty of time to think on the plane. While other passengers read or watched the movie or slept, Nikki sat staring into the darkness, her thoughts leaping back and forth between the recent and distant past, trying to fit the haphazard events of her life into some sort of order or pattern.

She had only been back twice since her mother died. After going back to school (whichever direction she travelled between Britain and Argentina always seemed like 'going back') she had spent most of her holidays either with the Smythes, the Tullochs or friends.

Since her mother's death she had exchanged the occasional letter with her father and Johnny, the only one of her brothers who seemed to have the remotest concern for her well-being. She had also kept in touch with Ceci, who never failed to mark her birthday with a card and a cheque; but of Marc, Luis and Blanca she had heard little, and of Larry, nothing.

She looked out of the cabin window into the darkness. Far in the distance, tiny lights twinkled on a mainland. They were flying southward off the coast of South America.

While the Boeing buzzed on through the night, she began to see that without a central aim in life she would be condemned, year after year, to continue bumping into destiny, shying away from it, knocking at doors only to be turned away.

She forced herself to think about something other than herself.

Why was it that other families were so close-knit, or at least kept in touch and saw each other occasionally? On her mother's death her family seemed to have exploded outwards from the home, each member taking a different direction.

And why was it that none of them – herself included – seemed able to achieve a real maturity? Individuation, Carol had called it. None of them seemed able to individuate, become themselves, or make close relationships.

Marc she identified in her mind with Argentine machismo: the endless need to prove himself and win acclaim on the polo pitch or tennis court. Johnny was dedicated to a self-denying obedience to the Church, Luis to a mindless, spotless, soulless militarism.

It occurred to her that each of her brothers seemed to represent a separate section of Argentine society. She played with the idea, turning it over in her mind. Yes. Marc was sport, machismo and big business. John was the Church. Luis was the military. Even Jimmy had had his place, for Jimmy was dead, just as doubt and gentleness and respect for academic achievement were dead in Argentina. Larry? Nobody knew much about Larry. He had gone to earth. He was a subversive.

And what of Blanca? What motivated her? Blanca had always been an enigma. A Peronist – of course, that was it. Yes, Blanca was the Peronist of the family, and every good Peronist was motivated by feelings of jealousy or hatred or revenge or all three. Blanca's jealousy and hatred and revenge were those of Argentina: they were the same feelings of resentment that had been consuming the nation's soul for so many years. It was a jealousy at not truly belonging: in Blanca's case to the family, in Argentina's to the larger family of nations.

But hadn't there always been something more than mere jealousy in those dark smouldering eyes of Blanca's? From the moment of their first meeting – that cold Judas-kiss on the day she had travelled by train out to Cadoret with Ceci – Nikki had regarded Blanca as a threat.

And me? she wondered, slipping off into a doze. Where do I fit in? I'm the little gringa, aren't I, the Anglo-Argentine, the type Blanca's lot loves to hate. I'm the Islas Malvinas. I belong to Argentina but I've been captured and occupied by the filthy British . . .

When she awoke, the plane was in the descent and the captain was making an announcement. They were about to land at Rio where they would remain on the ground until ex-President Perón, who was returning to Argentina from exile in Spain that day, had landed at Ezeiza.

Some sort of political trouble was expected. There was going to be an indefinite delay.

25

OF THE THREE ORIGINAL PROPERTIES built by George Cadoret, La Tijerita was the smallest and the most attractive. No golf course, swimming pool, water tower or outhouses cluttered the view. Built of red brick that was now covered by creeper, it had been designed and built by the same architect who had designed the Hurlingham clubhouse, which it resembled, though on a smaller scale. One of its most attractive features was its landscaped lawns. They were so vast that from the bay windows of the drawing room you could hardly detect the fence that divided the park from the pampa, so that you had the impression that the grounds had no limits and extended the length and breadth of the country.

'I love my Tijerita,' Ceci said when Nikki went to tea with her soon after her arrival back in Argentina. 'More and more. When I was younger I always thought the camp was boring.' She sighed. 'But I was the one who was boring, not the camp. Here at La Tijerita I have my books and my record player and my ponies. I can be at peace. But then one never fully appreciates peace until one has experienced conflict, does one?'

They were having tea from the trolley in the sitting room before a roaring log fire. Outside, a chilly drizzle was falling. Camp winter at its worst.

'But now tell me, dear. How do you find your father?'

It was a loaded question. Nikki's arrival home had been a painful experience: she had been shocked at how much older her father appeared. She had always known him to be a forthright, energetic and overpowering man, a father who had for many years kept his sons under his thumb and his daughter at arm's length. Now, something seemed to have been knocked out of him. He had a hollow-eyed look that was half apologetic, half ingratiating, like a dog that knows it's done wrong. He had been out in his Ford truck when she arrived, and when he returned and found her already at home he had broken down, hugging and kissing her and treating her like a returned prodigal.

'I think he might be rather lonely, Aunt Ceci.'

268

'And I think you are quite right, my dear. But it's entirely his own fault. He hardly stirs from Calandria these days. I've invited him over here for meals any number of times but he always manages to make some excuse or other. Of course, he's hardly been seen in the British community since your mother died.'

'I'm not sure if he sees himself as part of the British community any longer, Aunt.'

That was another change Nikki had noticed: one of her most vivid childhood memories had been of her father shouting at them to speak in English. It had become a family joke. Larry had taken a delight in adopting the latest Argentine slang to taunt his father into fury. But these days Tito was speaking more Spanish than English. 'Got to move with the times,' he had said when Nikki commented on it. 'Can't kid ourselves any longer that because we're British we own the place, because we aren't and we don't.'

Ceci put the teacups on the trolley. 'Yes, well, you know what people have been saying about him. That he's gone bush. Walking about in that silly hat all the time and keeping his bombachas up with that ridiculous tirador. It's all very well for a young man to go criollo, but at your father's age it's undignified and silly. What's more, it's lost him friends. Friends are so important, aren't they? Especially at his age. No, your father's being a very silly billy. He has no friends at all these days and he's brought it all on himself.'

'He does have some friends, Aunt. I think he sees a lot of the Stefenellis and the people at Ventolera.'

Ceci gave one of her little snorts. 'Those people aren't friends, they're – what was that expression I heard dear Stiffy use the other day? Chupa-medias. Sock-suckers.' She sighed. 'But now tell me about yourself. How are you getting on at university? When do you expect to qualify as a nurse? There's a desperate shortage of trained nurses, you know. The British Hospital will snap you up the minute you show your face out here with a qualification. Is that what you'll do? Work for the BH?'

'I don't know. I may not go back.'

'What do you mean?'

'Well . . . I'm not sure if I'm suited to nursing, Aunt. If I can find a good job while I'm out here I might stay.'

'Now Nikki – that's just defeatist rubbish! Of course you're suited. What would your mother say if she could hear you now? The trouble with you younger generation is you have no stick-at-it-ness. Argentina needs young people with backbone, my dear. If you love this country at all, you'll go back to Edinburgh, get yourself qualified and come straight back and work. You'd have the world at your feet. You could get any number of top jobs anywhere in the country.'

'I don't want a top job, Aunt. I want to do something worthwhile.'

'Go and work with the indios. I had the Bishop of Salta staying here only two weeks ago. They're crying out for qualified nurses up at Embarcación. You could go and work at Misión Yuchán where your uncle was.'

'But I'm not an Anglican. I'm not even a very good Catholic any more.'

'I made the change and never regretted it. You could do the same. You're an intelligent girl Nikki. I'm sure you're not really taken in by all that hocus-pocus about the Virgin Mary are you? All these ridiculous little roadside grottos to the Difunta Correa.' Ceci referred to the unbeatified saint who had died at the roadside suckling her baby because no one would stop to give her food and water. She giggled suddenly. 'You know what dear Stiffy calls her? "Defunct Fanbelt". Isn't that delicious? No, if you ask me, the Roman Catholic faith is a dead weight fastened to the leg of every nation it infests. Look at the difference between Protestant North America and the Catholic south. If Catholic countries hadn't had to gild so many churches with gold leaf and line so many Popes' pockets over the past three hundred years they'd all have a lot more prosperity and stability – including Argentina. Look at the massacre at Ezeiza the other day when you arrived. And it's all done in the name of the Virgin Mary or the Sacred Heart or Our Lady of Passion.'

Nikki smiled. 'You realize I'm going to Johnny's ordination next week?'

'I did hear, yes. Your father sent me an invitation but I refused. What a waste of a good young man. You see there's another example of what the RC Church does to a nation. The celibacy of the priesthood skims the intellectual cream from a society. Do you realize that practically every nineteenth-century statesman, scientist and military leader in Great Britain was able to trace his descent from the clergy? But in a Catholic country, that can't happen. Tragic. Oh no, my dear. Don't talk to me about the Roman Catholic Church, thank you very much. That's a subject I can get really heated about.'

The maid came in to collect the trolley, and Aunt Ceci digressed to air her views on the difficulty of finding good staff and the changes she had seen in the camp over the years. 'The parties we used to have before the war, dear – now they were really something. But of course one can't organize anything worthwhile these days with only a man and a dog. No, I'm afraid it'll be a very long time before Argentina sees good days again, Nikki.'

'Actually I was going to ask if you would like to help me organize a party, Aunt.'

'Oh yes? Who for?'

'Well, Johnny's coming down from Córdoba for a few days after his ordination, and Daddy wants to get the family together. We could ask some of his old friends from the British community too. What do you think?'

Ceci liked to be thought of as 'with it'. 'Darling,' she said, 'what a perfectly *fab* idea.'

There wasn't much to do except ride and read at La Calandria, so Nikki had plenty of time in which to gather the family. While her father toured the estancia or lunched at La Ventolera or attended meetings of the farmers' association, CREA – which Larry had said stood for 'Crazy Rustics Empoverishing Argentina' – she sat in the office at La Calandria trying to contact brothers, friends and relations on the telephone.

She ran Marc to earth in Miami.

His voice echoed in the telephone receiver. 'Who?'

'Nikki! Your sister!'

'Bloody hell! What do you want?'

She could almost see him glancing at his watch and wondering how far the peso would fall before he could get her off the line.

'We're having a family party at Calandria. The first weekend of September. Can you get here for it?'

He muttered 'shit' under his breath. 'What's it in aid of?'

'Johnny's being ordained. Haven't you had a letter from Dad?'

'Probably. Look, I can't speak now. Why don't you ring me this evening about seven?'

'For God's sake, Marc, you can make it if you want. Can't you make the effort?'

'Well . . . no promises.'

'Just say you'll try and be here then. Will you?'

'Okay,' he said, and rang off.

Then she tried Luis. He was an Air Force major on the central air staff and seemed to be permanently in conference.

'*¿Qué?*' he said when she finally got through to the officers' mess and he had been summoned to the phone. She explained all over again. He said he would have to clear it with his Brigadier.

'When can you let me have an answer?'

He was vague at first but then suddenly changed his tune. 'Can I bring some friends?'

'What sort of friends?'

He laughed. 'The usual sort of friends. Girlfriends. Do you think I'm homosexual or something?'

She said no, she didn't think that, but how many friends did he intend to bring?

'As many as you like, chinita. A boyfriend for you, if you want. Perhaps three or four so you can choose. Would you like that?' He laughed again and was still laughing when they were cut off. She was unable to get back to him.

Blanca was easier to contact but she wanted to take over the party and run it at La Ventolera.

'That wasn't the idea,' Nikki said.

'No, but mine's a better one. Calandria isn't big enough for a proper party.'

'It's only a family thing, Blanca. Just the immediate family and a few friends.'

'Not if we have it at LV. If we have it at LV we can build it into something. It could be good publicity. We could have a ball.'

'Dad doesn't want a ball. He wants an informal party. Close friends and family.'

'Well I'm not his family so he won't want me,' Blanca said, and hung up. Nikki rang her again straight away. 'Look. Could we compromise? We could have a lunch party for the family at Calandria and the ball at LV in the evening.'

But Blanca, like Luis, had changed her tune. 'You must ask Bernado if you want to have a party at LV,' she said abruptly. 'That sort of thing's got nothing to do with me.'

'But I wasn't the one who suggested –'

There was a click. Blanca had rung off.

Lastly she tried Larry, but with no success. All she had was the number of a bar where he had once played the guitar, but dialling that resulted in a torrent of abuse from a man who sounded drunk, called her a whore's daughter and told her to get off the line because he was waiting for a call.

She sat alone in the office and looked disconsolately at a sepia photograph of a bull that had won a prize for her grandfather in 1926.

How naive she had been to think that she could bring the family together again. It seemed that they were united only in their desire to be disunited. Brother hated brother and step-sister distrusted

272

step-sister. She had heard the same querulous note of suspicion in the voices of each of the three. 'Why should I?' they seemed to be saying. 'What's in it for me?'

The party looked increasingly as though it was going to be a non-starter. The whole point of it was to reunite the family, and if she couldn't do that there didn't seem much point in trying to assemble those of the British community who were still prepared to give her father the time of day.

She sat at her father's desk and tried to summon the energy to go on, but winter in the camp was already having its depressing effect on her. She looked at the long line of estancia diaries on the bookshelf beneath the picture of the prize bull. The first bore the date 1882. Feeling bored and depressed, she picked one out at random and began reading the neat, copperplate entries.

Bleeding horses for grass staggers . . . cutting ingrowing cows horns . . . moving asoleada heifers . . . tightening fences . . . parting reject animals for matadores . . . put rodeo into maize in no. 3 . . . rained heavily during siesta . . . half-day fiesta . . . polo at Laguna Blanca . . .

The days and weeks and months and years went on and on and on, season following season, life changing yet remaining the same.

When was it that her mother had first come out? Just before the war: 1938 or 1939. She took out the 1939 diary and began searching the pages. She found the first entries in her father's writing, each one neatly entered with comments about the day's work, the weather and the daily rainfall. Then she found an entry that read:

Peones revising, earthing up trough in No. 8, skinning dead animal. Parted 4 consumo steers. Loaded 150 steers for Avellenada. Two men fetching hay. Collected provisions, children and nurse from Cadoret.

June 8th 1939. The day her mother came out to the camp with Blanca and Luis. Nikki sat back in the revolving chair and remembered how her mother used to tell them the story about coming out to Argentina to work with the Indians in the north: how her brother had been killed and she had stayed on instead of going straight back and, after staying with Aunt Ceci, had gone to look after Blanca and Luis with Gangan at Hurlingham before taking them out to the camp.

'What a journey that was,' she used to say. 'We had a sleeper compartment over a wheel and Blanca was sick in the night, and when we arrived at Cadoret station there was no one to meet me and I sat in the ticket collector's hut and drank maté with him until your father arrived.'

Nikki's eyes filled with tears. If only she could pick up the telephone and dial another number, a number that would put her mother on the line. If only she could hear her voice again, her quick, encouraging way of speaking. 'Nikki?' she would say, just as she always did when she rang her at school. 'Hullo, darling, is that you? How are you getting on? What have you been doing today?'

She sat at her father's desk in the room that had once been the nursery, and let the thoughts and memories of her childhood take over. She re-entered the land of 'if only', that sad land of sighs and sunsets . . .

'Hullo, what are you doing here all by yourself?'

Her father was standing at the door.

'I've been trying to fix up the party. I've spoken to Marc, Luis and Blanca so far.'

'Get anything out of them?'

'Luis said he might bring some friends. Marc said he'd try to get back for it. Blanca said we should have a big party at Ventolera.'

He came and sat on the desk beside her. The light was almost gone. The sky had turned yellow and black.

'I was looking at the old diaries.'

'So I see.'

In the silence, his breath whistled in his nostrils. He looked down at the diary and nodded to himself. Then he said, 'Would you ever consider living here and running this place, Nikki?' He seemed to struggle inwardly, and gave a sudden, angry sigh. 'My grandfather built this house. He built La Ventolera and he built La Tijerita. I thought – years ago – I thought I could reunite it. What a hope!'

There was a long silence. Nikki said, 'But – eventually . . . won't Calandria be shared equally between us?'

He shook his head and looked out of the window at the dying day. 'Doubt it. Very much doubt it.' Then he got off the desk and walked away a few paces, turned, and came back. 'I don't think I've got all that long, Nikki. I don't know if you've learnt anything at that university of yours about irregular heartbeats, but I've got one and sometimes in bed it seems to stop for so long that I wonder if it'll ever start again. I dream about flying practically every night. They say that's caused by a dicky heart, don't they?'

274

He was afraid of death, that's what it was. She knew she should feel sorry for him, but she couldn't and had to pretend.

'Oh Dad!'

He held out his hands to her and she went to him to comfort him. He held her in his arms and sobbed embarrassingly, saying how much he missed Anna, how he longed for one of his family to marry and give him the joy of seeing his grandchildren before he died.

She told him that lots of people had irregular heartbeats and that it didn't necessarily indicate heart disease. She said that worrying about it only made it worse.

'You've got years and years ahead of you, Dad. I'm sure you have.'

He nodded to himself in the way he did, his breath whistling in his nose, a little out of breath, his jowls hanging in folds, his white moustache stained nicotine yellow.

'Could probably find you a job, you know,' he said. 'You could live here. And – and when I'm gone, well, you'd be able to stay on. Maybe find yourself a husband and the two of you could run Calandria.'

'Daddy, I'm training to be a nurse, not an administrator.'

'Your mother was a nurse. A child's nurse. But she loved Calandria. She loved her ponies and her garden and you children. She loved Argentina too, in her way. If you could find a husband who loves the land, Nikki, if you could have a few sons to take over from you –' He broke off, shaking his head. Then his mood swung back under the shadow. 'Take no notice of your father. No one else does. No, off you go and – and get yourself qualified and marry an English stockbroker and settle down in suburbia. Who cares about this place? Who cares about the family?'

Although Nikki cared about both the estancia and the family, it seemed unlikely that she would be able to do much about either. La Calandria was a changed place. She didn't recognize the maids or the dogs or the administrator or the foreman or the peons. Now that Botta was running the two estancias, La Calandria had been relegated to the position of a satellite that had little use apart from that of an overspill dormitory for the larger functions that were held at La Ventolera.

It was as if the house had lost its soul. The family atmosphere that had always prevailed while her mother had been alive had vanished. But something else troubled her about Calandria. At first she thought that it was just the camp winter – a factor renowned for driving people to the whisky bottle. But it was more than that. There was an oppressive feeling in the house. She never heard anything go bump

275

in the night nor did she see grey ladies flitting about the corridors at dusk, but there was something else, an indefinable presence that sometimes made her feel intensely depressed.

One afternoon when she was alone in the house she opened the piano stool in the drawing room and looked through her mother's old music scores. At the bottom of the pile were some even older ones which had belonged to her grandparents. Having nothing better to do, she opened up the piano and began to amuse herself by picking out some of the tunes. She found the score of 'Ain't We Got Fun' and smiled over the words: 'Ev'ry morning, ev'ry evening, ain't we got fun . . .'

The moment she began to pick out the notes, she experienced a chilling sensation that sent a huge shiver down her spine and raised goosepimples on her arms and legs. She stopped playing and turned quickly, convinced that someone had entered the room. Nobody was there. Terrified, she ran out of the house. It took a strong effort of will to return inside.

Two days before Johnny's ordination, Nikki drove with her father up to Córdoba. They checked into the Hotel Sussex and arranged to meet Johnny in town for lunch the following day, but her father ate something which upset him in the night, so it ended up as lunch for two under a trellis in the dry Córdoba sunshine.

Johnny was going prematurely bald. He was thirty-three, the gentlest of her brothers, with rimless glasses and an enquiring manner. At the beginning of the meal there was some question of whether he would have wine or water to drink. Nikki settled that by telling him that he wasn't a priest yet and might as well make hay while the sun shone.

Halfway down the bottle, conversation became easier and she found herself telling him about Rob.

Johnny was a good listener. She hadn't talked to anyone about Rob and found great relief in doing so. They were made for each other, she said. She had never felt so calm, so safe, so much at peace with herself and with the world as when she had been in Rob's company.

'So what went wrong?'

'His wife found out. She came to the flat, lost her rag and then went and smashed up her car.'

Johnny looked aggrieved. 'You didn't tell me he was married.'

'I didn't want you to prejudge it.'

'Do you feel guilty about it?'

'Of course.'

'And you want to be rid of your sense of guilt.'

'Wouldn't you?'

He looked at her and shook his head. 'This may sound trite, but I would never have expected you to take up with a married man.' He smiled sadly. 'Not my innocent little sister.'

She lit a cigarette. 'I haven't been innocent for a very long time.'

'So what now?'

'I don't know. Part of the reason I came out was to discover what I want to do. I've got another year at Edinburgh and need two more in a teaching hospital to get my state registration. Dad's conducting a not very subtle campaign to get me to stay on at Calandria. He's worried about his heart.'

'That sounds like emotional blackmail.'

'Do you think I should go back to Edinburgh?'

'Seems a pity to throw two years away. There's plenty of good work for nurses. You'll be more value qualified than unqualified. I hope to get a parish in the Chubut. You could do worse than come and join me.'

'Aunt Ceci suggested I go and work at Misión Yuchán.'

'As a Catholic?'

She looked directly at him. 'I've lapsed. I haven't been to Mass for ages.'

He leaned across the table and took her hand, holding it tightly and shaking it to emphasize his words. 'Then unlapse. Go to confession. Start again. No wonder you're uncertain what you want to do. You don't need a sermon from me to know that.'

He poured more coffee for them both.

'If you went to confession this afternoon that would be the best gift you could possibly give me for my ordination. Nothing would give me greater pleasure than to be able to give you the blessed sacrament at my first Mass. Will you do it for me, Nikki?'

Outside the main door to the cathedral was a woman with one hand out and a baby at her breast. Nikki went in, put holy water on her forehead and joined the short queue of people waiting for confession.

The salt in the holy water made her forehead itch. When her turn came she was deliberately blunt, terse and to the point. She didn't manufacture anything. She used no euphemisms, nor did she show any emotion she did not feel.

'I fell in love with a married man with whom I was sexually intimate on many occasions, Father. It's over now, but I still love him.'

The act of saying those words seemed to be a betrayal. It seemed to give a hostage to honesty too: the morals of what had happened still confounded her; it was still difficult to believe that she should not love as deeply as she loved Rob.

She saw the priest's head move closer to the grille.

'Go on.'

She tried to go on. She tried to tell him everything. She wanted to make a good confession for Johnny's sake. But the act had become meaningless to her. She was conscious of a necessity to play a part and collaborate with the shadowy figure behind the grille in a performance. She was unable to fake sorrow for feelings and activities that had been so spontaneous and so deeply rooted in her emotional self. How could anyone quantify a sin? How could anyone say how many years in purgatory you would have to suffer for taking a drag of marijuana or loving a Rob McNairne?

She left the confessional and ran out of the church into the dry, white sunshine.

'God be merciful to me, a sinner,' she whispered, and threw a handful of silver to the beggar at the door.

The party for Johnny was cancelled for lack of support. Blanca said she didn't want to come and Marc sent a cable to say that an important polo match had come up and that he would be unable to attend. Though no one said so directly, most of Tito's friends in the British community had turned their backs on him after the sale of La Ventolera, and his Argentine circle had no desire to mix with Anglos.

Tito took the whole fiasco as a personal affront. But what was worse, he began pressurizing Nikki to stay on at Calandria.

'It's been done before,' he would say. 'There was an English girl managing an estancia up near Córdoba in the fifties as I well recall. She could do it, Nikki. Why not you?'

A week or so after Johnny's departure some VIPs visited La Ventolera and she and her father were invited to help entertain them at dinner. They drove over a little after nine and were escorted through the grand hall and two sumptuously decorated ante-rooms to a parlour full of middle-aged men in dark suits, each supplied with a leggy escort girl.

While Tito went to pay homage to Rui Botta and be introduced to the Minister for Social Welfare, Nikki was welcomed by Jorge Stefenelli.

'Ah, look who it is,' he gushed, advancing upon her with open arms. 'My little Nikki! How are you, sweetie? You're looking fabulous. Come and meet some lovely people.'

278

One of the lovely people was Colonel José Ocampo, now a senior member of the Dirección General de Fabricaciones Militares. Another was Licio Gelli, visiting Argentina on business. A third was Admiral Massera, another associate of the DGFM. The last and youngest by far was a blond naval flag lieutenant who undressed Nikki with his eyes and took it for granted that she would fall at his feet.

The evening proceeded on its brittle way. Conversation at the dinner table was dominated entirely by the men. It consisted largely of a series of unfunny stories and wisecracks at which those who knew what was good for them, which was everybody, laughed heartily. At one moment when Nikki looked along the table, every single guest was grinning in ersatz good humour.

After dinner the ladies left the men to sit over their brandy and cigars and went to take coffee and chocolate mints in the large drawing room. Hanging over the fireplace in a heavy, gilded frame was the portrait of Magdalena Salgado which Tito had commissioned thirty-five years before and which Blanca had rescued from an attic in La Calandria soon after her marriage to Jorge. It was the sort of picture that commanded instant attention, and the ladies, desperate for a safe subject of conversation, clustered round to admire it.

'She's so like you, Señora Stefenelli!'

'Oh no, I think your bone structure is much finer than hers, Señora Stefenelli!'

'Is she still alive, Señora Stefenelli?'

They turned back towards Blanca. She was nearing forty now, an imposing woman whose marriage to Jorge was nothing more than a business relationship. She inhaled from a black cigarette through a jade holder and looked upon her guests with disdain.

'No she is not alive. She was murdered on my fifth birthday. Raped and murdered in front of my eyes.'

There was a shocked silence. Somebody whispered, 'How terrible!'

'Yes,' Blanca said. 'How terrible, how terrible.'

'Did they ever find the culprit?'

'No. No, they never found him.' Blanca's eyes blazed. 'But one day I will find out who was responsible. Somebody gave the order to do what they did. One day I shall find out who that man was. And when I do –' Blanca stopped. When she continued, she did so very softly and calmly, but her voice contained a quality of ruthlessness that made Nikki shiver. 'I shall see to it that he pays for his crime.'

That September the caretaker government that had replaced Héctor Cámpora held elections and Juan Perón was swept back into power with his third wife, Isabelita, on his arm. For a few weeks Argentina was carried along by a flash flood of optimism. An expansionist policy was predicted by the pundits and moves were being made to bring about a social pact between the two major unions.

Tito was optimistic for a quite different reason.

'Excellent news,' he said to Nikki one afternoon when they met for a drink before dinner. 'I've discussed it with Jorge and he's made me a very generous proposal. We've got the go-ahead.'

Nikki looked at him blankly. 'The go-ahead for what?'

'Your managership. Jorge has agreed to double your allowance on the condition that you agree to become a cadet-manager.' He beamed with parental pride. 'So there you are. What do you think of that?'

'I'm not sure.'

'What d'you mean you're not sure? It's a magnificent opportunity. Give it a couple of years and you could be the administrator. Jorge said that he wouldn't normally consider a woman for the post but that José Ocampo spoke very highly of you. He thinks you would do an excellent job. You won't ever get a better opportunity than this.' He smiled tearfully. 'Never thought it'd be you that would take over from me. Always thought it'd be Marc. Or Luis. But not my little Nikki. Of course, you made quite an impression the other night at LV. I knew Rui was impressed, and Admiral Massera's flag lieutenant was obviously very taken with you. So you see. It was worth going, wasn't it?'

'Daddy – I don't want to be a cadet-manager. I want to be a nurse.'

'And spend the rest of your life emptying jerry pots and giving enemas? Come on, Nikki. Have a bit of sense. You've had your fling at university. You've found your roots, done your own thing. Okay. Now it's time to start thinking responsibly. There is such a thing as duty, you know. Even in this day and age. And there's something else you must take into account. You can't expect your allowance to continue if you turn this offer down. Jorge made that quite clear, and I must say I think he was quite right to do so.'

She said she would sleep on it, but in the event slept very little. At breakfast the following morning, she told him her decision. 'I've decided to go back to Edinburgh.'

He looked balefully up at her from his eggs and bacon. 'Is that your final decision?'

'Yes.'

'What about your allowance?'

'I'll just have to manage.'

He attacked his fried egg. Without saying a word, he managed to place her in the wrong.

'You make me feel like a traitor,' she said.

'That's your rotten hard luck, isn't it?'

'I have thought about it, you know.'

'Glad to hear that.'

'And I shall be back.'

'Oh yes? When?'

'As soon as I'm qualified. Probably in three years' time. Perhaps for holidays too. If I can afford it.'

'To do your daughterly duty?'

'It's not like that at all. I want to get a proper qualification so I can do a proper job of work.'

'Which means that running this place isn't a proper job, I suppose? That's what you could be doing. In a year or so. You could be running Calandria. Thirty thousand hectares.' He drained his coffee and wiped egg off his mouth. 'What do you expect me to say to you? You've been offered a job that's practically unheard of. A woman administrator.' He stood up, rolling up his napkin and fitting it into its silver ring, his lips beginning to quiver as he lost his temper. 'Just like your mother, aren't you? Soft as butter on the outside and hard as nails in. Go on then. You go off back to Edinburgh and be a nurse. Who cares what happens to this place? Who cares what happens to all I've slogged my guts out for over the last forty years? Not you, obviously. No – off you go. Back to your boyfriend, whoever he is. No one else gives a shit about me, so why the hell should you?'

She spent the rest of the day on horseback and then lay awake throughout another night, listening to the tap of creepers against her windowpane and the sudden whistling of the wind.

In a way, she was grateful to her father for flying off the handle and trying to twist her arm financially. She couldn't help thinking that had he taken a gentler, more understanding line she might have been more inclined to stay on. It was his attempt at what Johnny had called emotional blackmail that did it. He was holding a gun to her head and saying, 'If you love me you'll stay, and if you don't stay I'll die while you're away and you'll be sorry for the rest of your life.'

Yes, that was it. That, and the remark about her being soft on the outside and hard in. How utterly, utterly wrong could a father be about his daughter? Only she knew how raw and tender and easily hurt she was inside herself and how difficult she found it to camouflage that sense of vulnerability and appear outgoing and confident to the world. As for being 'just like her mother' – she wished she could have more of her mother's integrity, her steadiness of purpose, her sense of fair play.

Her father had the grumps all that day and the next and preserved a glowering silence throughout all meals. It was like being eleven years old again except that her mother and Jimmy were not there to share the load.

Ten years ago she would have been frightened by his surliness. Now she was simply angered by it. Had she been five years younger she might have gone to him, apologized and backed down. But she was twenty-two, not seventeen. The house made her feel depressed and the thought of living under the same roof with a man who could veer so violently and unpredictably between cheery bonhomie, maudlin self-pity and quivering fury horrified her.

She made up her mind to return to Edinburgh and, without telling her father, used the office telephone to reserve a flight. She wondered how to break the news to him. However carefully and tactfully she wrapped it up, she knew that it would cause another explosion of anger, self-pity and vituperation. Though her father was not a highly intelligent individual, he had an uncanny knack of twisting what you said to his own advantage, and she could no longer be sure that he was able to control his temper. All she could be sure of was that, whatever she said to him, he would do everything in his power to force her to stay on until she had missed her matriculation date. The only way to convince him that she meant what she said was to vote with her feet.

As she said in the note she left for him, she saw no other way to avoid more recriminations and bad blood. She said that, provided he took a bit more exercise and watched his diet, she was sure that he would last many more years yet. She said that when she had qualified as a nurse she would be back in Argentina, this time to stay.

'. . . please forgive me, but I just can't face another row with you like the one we had. I feel as if I am being torn apart. You were right: I do belong in Argentina – I feel that very strongly – but at the same time I know that if I am to be any use to this country I must get a nurse's qualification first. I think it would be very selfish of me to take the soft option and stay on at Calandria as a cadet manager. Please understand, and please believe that I *do* care.

With lots and lots of love,
Nikki.'

She added a PS to say she had borrowed the Humber and would leave it at Cadoret station, then put the note in the envelope and propped it up on his desk in the office where he would see it as soon as he came in.

She arrived by train at Once station at four that afternoon. Posters of Perón yelled from every corner. She took a taxi down Corrientes and along Maipú to the Gran Hotel Dorá. Spring had come and the streets were crowded. The Jacarandas were blooming and children were walking home from school in their white overalls. She left her luggage at the hotel and walked along Florida, mingling with the crowd, revelling in the bustle of the city after the void horizons of the camp.

She walked on and on along the shopping precinct and came eventually to the Plaza de Mayo, where a huge Argentine flag flew from a tall flagpole and the Grenadiers stood guard outside the Casa Rosada like toy soldiers in their polished boots and shakos.

She was waiting to cross the road and continue into San Telmo when she heard shouts from the Plaza behind her. A youth was dodging his way through traffic as it came round the corner by the Ministerio de Bienestar Sociale.

Police cars appeared from nowhere, sirens screaming. People stared. Plain-clothes men were running across the Plaza, jumping the low fences and hedges, cutting across the flower beds, brandishing guns. Two shots were fired. They echoed back and forth across the Plaza like thunderclaps.

It was over as quickly as it had begun. The youth gave himself up and was bundled into the back of a Ford Falcon and driven off at high speed. Within a matter of seconds, it was as if nothing had happened. The toy soldiers still stood outside the Casa Rosada; the Argentine flag still flapped lazily in the evening breeze; the traffic resumed its flow.

Back at the hotel, there was a message for her at the desk to ring a Buenos Aires number. She went up to her room on the top floor and dialled. A woman answered without giving a name or number.

'Yes? Who is it?'

'Nikki Cadoret.'

'Just a moment. Don't hang up.'

She waited for some while, then: 'Hi, Nik!'

Of all people, it was Larry.

'How did you find out where I was?'

'Oh – through the grapevine, you know. I rang Dad and found you'd just left. I gather you've been over here for three months. Why didn't you contact me?'

'I tried. I rang Puccini's.'

He groaned. 'Who the hell gave you that number? I haven't been inside Puccini's this decade.'

'It was the only one in Dad's address book.'

'Well sod him. I gave him our new number six months ago. How long are you in BA?'

'I'm flying from Ezeiza tomorrow.'

'Shit. Look – I'm singing at De Quincey's on San Lorenzo tonight. You know the Viejo Almacén? De Quincey's is in a cellar bar about fifty metres further on. It doesn't liven up until after midnight, so why don't you come about eleven while we're still quiet? I'll bring Adriana and we can talk.'

'Who's Adriana?'

'Christ, didn't Dad tell you anything?' Larry laughed, and Nikki guessed that Adriana was with him at the phone. 'We got married last March. Adriana's my beautiful darling wonderful wife.'

The entrance to De Quincey's was unmarked. A steep staircase led straight down from the street. At the foot of the staircase was a heavily soundproofed door. Nikki went inside and was greeted by an atmosphere thick with cigarette smoke. While she stood peering into the gloom there was a shout and she saw Larry sitting with a group at a table in the far corner.

She was introduced first to Adriana, a petite Jewess with lovely dark hair and kind, intelligent eyes. Larry was quite obviously devoted to her, and she treated his excesses with bright-eyed amusement. The rest of the group were musicians or students or artists or academics of some sort – the intellectual set which her father despised. Nikki found them far from despicable. They welcomed her like a friend, provided her with wine and empanadas and engaged her in close conversation about her political views. They wanted to know what people in England thought about Argentina, whether she supported CND and how she thought Apartheid could be done away with in South Africa. Her answers sparked off separate discussions. Cigarettes were lit from cigarettes, rumours and news about friends and enemies were swapped and a heated discussion developed over whether the social and economic crisis could be solved without recourse to armed revolution.

'Are you involved much in politics?' Adriana asked.

'Not at all. I'm not politically minded.'

'Well you should be,' Larry said.

'Apathy is the enemy of education,' remarked a bearded university lecturer. 'Apathy closes the mind and kills the will to learn.'

Adriana leant across the table to make herself heard. 'And you know what causes apathy? Ignorance and fear. I'm a journalist, Nikki. I see apathy every day. We've got to a situation in this country where people are so frightened of speaking the truth – or even being seen carrying a newspaper that publishes the truth – that the official censor isn't needed any more. People censor themselves. They do the government's dirty work for them.'

Larry joined in. 'It's not just in the arts or the media, either. Apathy stultifies intellectual growth. It smothers individuality and chokes freedom of expression and inventiveness – in the sciences as well as the arts. People are so frightened of saying the wrong thing – even by mistake – that they prefer to say nothing. Either that, or they leave the country.'

'But what is there to be frightened of?' Nikki asked. 'I mean – surely the government can't lock up the entire staff of *La Prensa*, can it?'

There was bitter laughter.

'They don't have to,' Adriana said. 'The state controls the DGFM and the monopoly industries and the monopolies control the advertising where the papers make their profit. The government can pressurize a paper by threatening to cut off its advertising revenue. It could put *La Prensa* out of business tomorrow if it wanted to. But it can do better than that. It can control the media. It can make sure that every newspaper in the country becomes a voicepipe for the government.'

A record was playing a song about Vietnam and some of the people at other tables were joining in.

> . . . and it's five, six, seven, open up the pearly gates.
> Ain't got time to wonder why – we're all gonna die . . .

Larry and his group left the table to set up their instruments. Soon after, they launched into their programme to the enthusiastic applause of all present. Watching him perform so confidently and with such easy humour and rapport, Nikki wondered what her father would have said if he could see Larry now. In the plane coming over she had thought to herself that each one of the family lacked maturity. But Larry seemed to her to be the exception. He was doing what he was good at, he had married for love and he had the courage of his convictions.

The show went on until five. At the end, Larry tried out some of his subversive numbers. One which went down very well was set to the tune of 'Obla-di, Obla-da' and was aimed at the shadowy López Rega, who controlled Perón and Isabelita.

> López Ré, López Ré, López Re-gaaa!
> La reputa que te parió-oo!

Afterwards, Larry and Adriana took Nikki to breakfast at a snack bar before driving her back to her hotel in their beaten-up Peugeot.

They exchanged addresses and telephone numbers in the hotel foyer. 'Come back soon,' Adriana said. 'We need people like you.'

They hugged her and said goodbye. Adriana was so warm and genuine that it was like having a real sister for the first time in her life. 'Take care, won't you?' she said as they got back into the car.

She watched them drive away until the car was out of sight, and was in tears when she turned to go into the hotel.

Adriana had always wanted to be a writer of children's books but when she was offered the job of editing her university magazine she jumped at it and in that way entered the world of political journalism. It was through journalism that she met Larry. Her first article to be published was a review of one of his shows. In it, she said that his was 'one of the few brave voices speaking out against censorship in Argentina today'. Larry saw the review, remembered Adriana and invited her out. In the weeks that followed they could hardly bear to be out of one another's company. Their friends teased them for their romantic, bourgeois love affair. They even laughed about it themselves.

They were not the sort of people you would have expected to hold the estate of matrimony in very high esteem. But sometimes love is stronger than ideology. Sometimes people want to give permanence to their relationship so much that marriage is the only way to do it. They marry because they want to be married. This was the case with Larry and Adriana. Theirs was a marriage of like minds. From the day they became one, neither of them once regretted the decision. They were simply devoted to each other. It was quaint, but it was true.

It was also just as well. In Argentina, you needed the love of a close and happy relationship to keep on an even keel during those turbulent years of the seventies. Within weeks of Perón being sworn in as president, the world oil crisis that had been precipitated by the October War was fuelling inflation. The much-vaunted social pact was falling apart at the seams. The bubble of national optimism had burst. In a wave of strikes and demonstrations, the workers shouted for better wages and conditions, an end to state corruption and a return to union democracy.

The only way to national liberation, claimed the left-wing Montoneros, was the achievement of socialism through Peronism. The only way to national liberation, the right-wing generals said, was the total destruction of the Left. Both sides counted on Perón's support but only one could receive it.

Working behind the scenes, López Rega pushed ahead with the process of turning the country into a totalitarian, fascist state. Bit by bit, then chunk by chunk, the freedoms that most of the Western world took for granted were chipped away. First a Law of Redundancy made it possible for the state to dismiss university staff whose political views were considered too radical. Then a Law of Compulsory Arbitration outlawed the right to strike. And then, in a move against left-wing provincial governors, an Act of Obligation to National Security gave the federal government the right to intervene in the internal affairs of the provinces and appoint governors of its own choice. To tighten the grip of the military, this last power was exercised to the full, and generals and admirals with no political experience were appointed as governors to a large number of provinces.

The Montoneros had hoped that Perón would move the country towards socialism. When they saw the big sticks of fascism being brought out, they were first alienated and then driven underground; and as the contradiction of a people's president who turned against the people became more acute, so kidnappings, subversion and violence spread. Violence spawned violence. Right-wing paramilitary groups and death squads like López Rega's guerrilla police group, the Triple-A, came into being and the flames of civil war fanned out across the country.

Then it happened, the event people had been dreading. Perón died and Isabelita was installed as his successor. From the start, everybody knew that she was only a puppet, and everybody knew who it was that worked her strings.

That was the day the crowd in the Plaza de Mayo sang Larry Cadoret's version of 'Obla-di, Obla-da'. It was also the day that the apartment where he and Adriana lived in the Buenos Aires district of Once was ransacked.

For a few weeks after Isabelita became president, a faint hope remained that, after all, a woman might be able to soften the harsher repressions of López Rega's strong-arm policy. But the hope was short-lived. The attacks on newspapers, radio stations, cinemas and the homes of writers, journalists and intellectuals who spoke out for human rights and freedom of speech made it increasingly obvious that far from making life easier, López Rega's glove puppet was making matters far worse.

The flames of civil war crackled and roared. After a brief armistice, the Montoneros went underground and declared all-out war on Isabelita's new regime. The ERP stepped up their guerrilla operations, attacking military and industrial targets and financing their war through kidnappings.

The response of the generals and admirals was to demand more freedom of action. No government could last long without the backing of the military, and Isabelita's was no exception. Theirs was a demand she had no power to refuse even if she wished to. So she gave them all the permission they wanted – *carte blanche* to act as they saw fit in order to win the war against the ERP and the Montoneros.

On her authority, terrorism became a legitimate instrument of government. The dogs were roaming the streets again: this time it was going to be more difficult than ever to bring them back under control.

In February of 1975, Adriana discovered she was pregnant. Though they could ill afford it, Larry took her away to the seaside at Pinamar for a holiday. They spent a week under canvas there, with the South Atlantic rollers crashing on the shore and the seabirds balancing on the gusts. They put away their watches and lived by the sun. They ate fish barbecued within minutes of being caught and bought salad and fruit and wine from the village. In the evenings they sat on the sand outside their tent and watched the March moon rise over the sea, while Larry tore at Adriana's heart-strings with the strings of his guitar.

They made a pact with each other not to talk about the political situation. They ate and slept and sang and made love and bathed in the ocean, and at the end of their week they knew that there had never been a holiday like it and would never be again.

Driving back to Buenos Aires, both were conscious that now they were to be parents they would have to face up to a new dimension of responsibility. Until now they had been prepared to risk their liberty for the sake of freedom of speech. But should they risk the liberty of their unborn child?

'We always said we would make no compromises,' Adriana said. 'Why should we compromise now?'

Larry had never imagined that fathering a child could strike so deeply into his emotions. For two years he had lived under the shadow of sudden arrest, abduction, interrogation and murder. Both he and Adriana knew and were known by the media world in Buenos Aires. Adriana had written articles that would almost certainly have resulted in arrest had she been a man, and only an instinct for knowing how far he could go had kept Larry out of trouble. So far, apart from the single ransacking of the flat, they had been left alone by the forces of the government. But how long could it last?

'I think we should move,' he said.

'Where to?'

'Away from Buenos Aires.'

'You mean run away.'

'No. Move.'

'*Where to?*'

'Córdoba. Salta. Or the Chubut. Somewhere where you and the baby will be safe.'

'What makes you think we'd be any safer in the Chubut? At least in BA they know who we are and we know who they are. If we move out, they'll be far more suspicious. We'll be swapping the devil we know for the devil we don't. And anyway, where else can we earn any sort of living?'

He allowed himself to be persuaded – Adriana was the one with common sense – and they stayed on in the apartment.

But they did make compromises. As the baby grew inside her and began to make itself felt, Adriana became more circumspect about what she wrote. She said nothing to Larry about it, and Larry said nothing to Adriana about the fact that his group seldom sang a protest song these days. Both knew what was happening. The government forces, official and unofficial, were infiltrating the universities and clubs and discos. If you wanted to survive, you had to make compromises.

Slowly, each of them edged towards the very apathy they had once condemned. They were not afraid for themselves, only for each other and the baby.

Daniel was born by forceps delivery at the end of October 1975. He was a healthy and vigorous baby and was without blemish apart from a purple birthmark on his head which would be quickly covered when he grew some more hair. In an attempt at reconciliation, Larry wrote to his father to tell him he was a grandfather and sent him a snap of the baby. Adriana sent several of him to Nikki, who was completing nurse's training at the University College Hospital in London and who wrote back a long, warm letter of congratulations.

'We're going to have lots more,' Larry would tell his friends, and

Adriana would smile the smile of a woman who has had the pleasant surprise of discovering that when love is truly present, having a baby is the most wonderful privilege and experience.

After the baby was born, Adriana did most of her work at home and relied heavily on the telephone. When it began to make odd noises, she realized that it was tapped. It was a bit of a joke at first. There wasn't much they could do except be reasonably careful. Nevertheless it didn't make life any easier. Adriana couldn't go out to interview people as she used to, and quite a few people came up to the apartment instead. Both she and Larry knew that this was dangerous, but they had a living to earn and neither of them really believed that anything very serious could happen to them.

At three o'clock one morning when Daniel was six weeks old, they were arrested.

Fifteen armed sailors in boots and combat gear smashed the door in with their rifle butts. They came into the bedroom wearing wigs and false moustaches and scarves on their heads so that they could not be identified.

They shouted a great deal. They shouted '¡Viva la Patria!' and called Adriana a Jewish whore. All her papers, notebooks and press cuttings were removed as were Larry's three guitars and all his music scores and lyrics. They were stripped naked and pushed against the bedroom wall. Larry was hit across the jaw with a rifle butt and one of the sailors drew swastikas with a felt-tip pen on Adriana's breasts.

Daniel woke and was crying but Adriana was not allowed to have him. When she pleaded to be allowed to take him with her they spat in her face and told her to shut her filthy Jewish mouth. When Larry tried to put up a fight, he was punched in the face and kneed in the crutch.

Bags were put over the prisoners' heads. They were hustled down the stairs and into a truck, which sped off through the city at high speed, its tyres squealing on the corners.

26

Rui Botta's seventy-second birthday fell on 29 February 1976 and was celebrated at huge expense at La Ventolera. A steer was roasted in its hide and young lambs were barbecued. An internationally known American singer and an Italian film star were part of an all-star cabaret booked to entertain the guests after dinner.

Botta was a happy man, but Jorge Stefenelli had already taken steps to make him happier. Jorge was the heir-apparent to Rui's fortune and it was well known that the old man had long wanted to see Jorge and Blanca start a family so that the inheritance might not be dispersed. But Blanca was barren, and the marriage loveless. Almost from the start, Jorge had sought satisfaction with mistresses, while Blanca's life was even more solitary and private than previously.

The decision to adopt a baby had been taken by Jorge. He presented it to Blanca as a *fait accompli*. She would be the adoptive mother and could play as large or small a part in his upbringing as she wished. Jorge had contacted José Ocampo, who had spoken to Massera. There were plenty of babies available for adoption, and Blanca was shown several before she settled on a beautiful, fair-haired baby boy whose only blemish was a purple birthmark on his head.

In his speech to propose a toast to his uncle, Jorge avoided the embarrassing details and announced that there was one more birthday surprise. Then he snapped his fingers and a nurse in high heels came walking down the banqueting hall with an infant in her arms.

'Uncle Rui,' announced Jorge with a flourish, 'meet your great-nephew.' A quaver of emotion entered his voice. 'Rui Stefenelli, meet the greatest great-uncle of them all.'

The band struck up 'Happy Birthday'. With tears of happiness streaming down his face, Rui Botta held the baby in his arms, acknowledging the standing ovation of the guests.

Blanca moved forward to take the baby back from her father-in-law. She had only had the child for a week, but was already becoming strongly possessive.

* * *

One afternoon in early September when Cadoret was sitting at his desk staring disconsolately at the faded photographs on the wall, Stefenelli called up on the radio to say that he and Toni Lambretti were flying out that afternoon and would be coming over to Calandria for a meeting.

Cadoret wondered what this could be about. Whatever it was, he had no reason to feel optimistic. Now that Nikki had gone he had been thrust very much on his own company, and in the evenings was inclined to brood. He knew he should take Nikki's advice and give up eating steak because it was bad for his heart. He also knew that he should give up driving round the estancia in the truck and get onto the back of a horse again. But you couldn't cover the distance on horseback you could in a truck, and getting a pony saddled up was too much of a bother what with one thing and another. Besides, time was precious in these days of cost-effectiveness. You needed to be in the office a lot more. There wasn't time to be trotting over the pampa enjoying the fresh air. There was an ever-growing mountain of paperwork to get through and he seemed to lurch from crisis to crisis. His pony boy had been stopped on the road by the traffic police and asked for 'colaboración' only the other day and had had his papers confiscated because he had been unable to pay up. Then a week or two before that another truck of prime steers had been hijacked on its way down to Liniers for auction – to feed some guerrilla gang, no doubt. But there was no point in complaining to the police because the chances were high that they were in on the hijack in the first place.

As it was a warm evening, he received his guests on the verandah. The three men sat and drank whisky. Stefenelli opened the conversation with an unusually solicitous enquiry into Cadoret's health. Tito said he was well.

'You don't find it at all lonely living here on your own?'

Cadoret tipped his deck chair. 'Why should I? This is my home.'

'But I think you would be a lot happier in an apartment,' Lambretti said.

Cadoret took another slug of Old Smuggler. 'Can't agree with you there, Toni. Lived all my life in the camp. I'm a landmark. Isn't that so, Jorge?'

'We have a problem, Tito,' Lambretti persisted. 'You know what it is?'

'Don't tell me, let me guess,' Cadoret sighed. 'Interest rates.'

'Interest rates, yes. But not just interest rates. There is the matter of arrears of interest and interest on arrears.'

Cadoret felt his pulse quicken. 'Look – how many times have we

292

been through this? We agreed a plan only last year. You extended the period of repayment and agreed to freeze the rate at thirteen per cent on the outstanding sum –'

'Exactly,' said Lambretti. 'That is exactly our problem.'

'So what are you proposing now?'

Lambretti spread his hands. 'Let's talk this out as brothers, Tito. I don't have to tell you how much we've done for you in the past. Back in the old days at the Banco Pergamino. Then later the personal loans we raised to keep you afloat. And latterly the very generous assistance of the Banco Ambrosiano. Down the years, we've been good friends to you. Don't spoil things now, okay? You know as well as we do that if we were now to demand a proper rate of interest on your loans, you would end up on the street within a week. We could break you. That's true isn't it?'

Cadoret glowered. 'Go on.'

Stefenelli appeared not to be listening. He reached his hand out to a tortoiseshell cat that had appeared on the verandah and was rubbing itself sensuously against the leg of the table.

'Okay,' Lambretti said. 'We want to make you a proposition, Tito. We'd like you to move out of La Calandria and relinquish the title. In return –'

'Now wait a minute –'

'No, Tito. You wait a minute. In return we'll set you up in an apartment in Buenos Aires for your retirement. Somewhere nice. The apartment on the Avenida Quintana, so you can have coffee at the Biela every morning. We'll pay your rent and we'll give you a pension –'

'I'm not retiring! You can't force me –'

'Tito, my friend. Listen to me. Before you say anything more, think about it. You'll never get a better offer than this one.'

Tito stared bitterly out across the park. 'This is my house,' he said. 'I inherited it legally from my father who inherited it legally from his.'

Stefenelli stopped trying to seduce the cat and lit a cigarette with a wax match.

'You inherited it, yes.' Lambretti twirled the ice in his tumbler. 'But you chose to use it as collateral to raise a loan. I myself arranged that loan for you when the Banco Pergamino was in existence. I don't have to remind you of all that. Down the years we've been very useful to you, Tito. Rui and I – we've stayed loyal. Now it's your turn to prove your loyalty to us in return.'

Lambretti left his deck chair and strolled on the semi-circle of paving stones beneath the flagpole. He stood with his back to Tito and looked westward at the beginnings of another multicoloured sunset.

'Why are you looking so angry, Tito?' Stefenelli asked quietly. 'It was always on the cards, wasn't it? You don't own this place. All you own is a mortgage which you can't repay. You're only here because of our generosity. We've kept you afloat for thirty years. If it hadn't been for Uncle Rui and Toni here, you would have been out on your neck back in '45.'

'Look,' Cadoret said. 'Nikki's coming back to Argentina in a couple of weeks. Jorge — you were enthusiastic about taking her on as a cadet-manager. Can't I stay on long enough to see her into the job?'

'I thought you said she was going to work as a nurse?'

'Yes, but I think I can persuade her to change her mind, and if you can give me a few months' grace, well — I might be able to raise a loan in order to pay off some of the arrears. Couldn't you just give me that chance?'

Lambretti turned on his heel. 'Okay. Let's say we give you six months in which to recover your position —'

'That would be marvellous!'

'What would happen, Tito? I'll tell you what would happen. Calandria will be making a bigger loss than it did in the past six months and you will end up owing Banco Ambrosiano more than you do today. In which case, we could no longer be able to make you the generous offer we are making you now. Are you willing to take a risk like that?'

Cadoret thought wildly. 'Give me a couple of months then. Give me eight weeks. Even six weeks. At least give me some sort of a chance.'

Lambretti returned to the verandah and sat down. 'You realize we're talking about arrears and interest of two hundred thousand US dollars? Who's going to lend you that sort of money?'

'At least let me try, Toni. At least let me try.'

There was a brilliant flash of colour as a bird swooped between the trees.

'Four weeks,' Lambretti said. 'I'm prepared to let my offer stand for four weeks. If you can pay off your arrears of interest by then and give me an acceptable guarantee that you can continue payments promptly in future, then perhaps we can come to some other arrangement. Failing that' — Lambretti gave a very Italian shrug — 'I think you know what will happen.'

Stefenelli looked at his watch. 'We have a meeting, Toni.'

'One other possibility,' Tito said as they went across the grass to

294

the car. 'If – if I could raise a bigger loan, I still have the right to redeem the mortgage altogether, isn't that right?'

Lambretti looked at him sideways. 'It would have to be a very big loan, amigo.'

'But if I could?'

'Yes, in theory, you could redeem the property. But it is only a theory, isn't it? Unless you've been deceiving us all these years about the state of your assets.'

Stefenelli got in behind the wheel of the Mercedes and slammed the door. 'If that were to prove the case there would be a quite different sort of price to pay,' he said. 'But I think you know that too, Tito, don't you?'

While the shadows extended and the first nightjar began chuckling, Cadoret strolled about on the grass at the back of the house. In the peons' kitchen, one of the women was singing off-key. Wherever he looked there were reminders of his childhood, his youth, his married life. Memories of parties and asados, birthdays and Christmases, dances, fiestas, weddings, christenings. There were memories every-where: the tennis courts, the swimming pool – even each individual tree, because his father had been a great tree-planter and he had tried to follow his example. This was the old ombu where the children had had their swing and he had himself played as a child. This was the conifer where Johnny and Marc had found the comadreja the day he and Anna arrived back from England. He stopped, staring at it, remembering.

Another memory of Anna, an extraordinarily clear one of their honeymoon: it was of Anna winding up the gramophone and putting on a record of Harry Lauder. He could hear the scratch of the needle and that faint, faraway Scottish voice which Anna said sounded as if it were calling to her from across the oceans.

> I have heard the mavis singing
> His love song to the morn
> I have seen the dewdrops clinging
> To the rose just newly born . . .

What was the other one she had played at that awful place on the Paraná river? 'Keep Right on to the End of the Road.' He was nearly at the end of his road now. Was there any possible way of delaying the inevitable? It seemed unlikely. Only death could extricate him from the hold that Botta, Stefenelli and Lambretti had on him. The cruellest irony of all was that if he drew on the capital in his Coutts account he would sign his own death warrant. He would be found guilty of deceiving the Lodge, and the penalty for that was the running noose about the neck, the throat cut across, the tongue torn out by the root . . .

But he had lost much more than mere property. He had become isolated from his family and from his friends. Was there nothing at all that he could salvage from the wreckage?

He became suddenly aware of a need for reconciliation. Yes, that was what he needed above all. Reconciliation. An easy conscience. Peace of mind.

In the yard beyond the peons' quarters, the foreman was ringing the seven o'clock bell to mark the end of the working day.

He turned and went back into the house.

Stiffy Rathbone hadn't spoken to Tito Cadoret since their argument at Randy and Betty's farewell party at La Ventolera. He was surprised therefore – and not particularly pleased – to receive a telephone message to call Tito on the telephone. He considered ignoring it, but his friendship with Tito went back a long way.

'Stiffy!' Cadoret shouted over the sound of radio music. (Though El Palenque was only a few leagues from La Calandria the telephone line was an appalling one.) 'Good of you to call back! How are you?'

'I'm well, thank you.'

'Good. Good. Look – er – I've been thinking. I don't know about you, but I'd like to – to bury the hatchet, so to speak.'

'Oh yes?'

'Yes. What do you think? Could we give it a try?'

'I suppose we might.'

'Oh, wonderful! I'm so glad. Look. I – er – wondered if we might meet?'

Rathbone closed his eyes. 'All right.'

'Great! What about lunch at Laguna Blanca some time? On me, of course. When are you free?'

They met outside the clubhouse at midday, Tito in a brass-buttoned blazer and college square; Stiffy in drills and brogues. Rathbone was surprised to see how much weight Cadoret had put on. Cadoret had forgotten how lame Rathbone was.

Stiffy had just bought a brand new Ford Falcon, so that gave them something to talk about for the first uncomfortable minutes. All the police and security forces – official and unofficial – drove around in Ford Falcons.

'If you can't beat 'em, join 'em, eh?' Tito remarked.

Stiffy grunted. 'Something like that.'

They strolled across to the polo pitch and watched the morning match. In recent years the club had been taken over by Argentines.

'Changed a bit since our day,' Tito remarked.

Rathbone agreed that it had. They watched the rest of the chukka in silence.

'Look,' Tito said as the bell rang. 'It wasn't really my doing, you know. Buying out La Ventolera. My hands were tied. I had no choice in the matter.'

They stood side by side and watched the teams thunder up and down the pitch, shouting and cursing and whirling their sticks. While they watched, Tito talked.

'I'm in hock, old boy. Been in hock since before the war. When they say jump I have to jump. You must know how it is. Do you think I wanted them to take LV off poor old Randy like that? No way. No way. But there was nothing I could do, d'you see? These people are big, Stiffy. They're very big. A chap can't argue the toss with them. Have to play ball or face being kicked out of the game. Sometimes you play ball and still get kicked out. That's what's happening to me. Been given my marching orders. They want me out of LC and there's no way I can stop them.'

Stiffy didn't feel sympathetic. Cadoret's outpouring sounded suspiciously like an exercise in self-justification and whatever he said now couldn't alter the fact that his behaviour over La Ventolera had been despicable. But Cadoret was not the only one who needed to talk, and over lunch, when they had finished a bottle of wine and Tito had told Stiffy about his heart, Stiffy told Tito about his divorce.

When those topics had been exhausted they moved on to politics, in which Stiffy took an active interest. Stiffy had a financial interest in the *Buenos Aires Herald*, and was appalled at the way the Ministry of Information was gagging the press and persecuting writers. Earlier that year the novelist Haroldo Conti had joined the growing list of those who had disappeared. Books had been burned in Córdoba, and the Swiss correspondent of *Der Bund* had been arrested and expelled.

'I heard about Larry and his wife,' Stiffy said. 'Have you heard any news of their whereabouts?'

'Only that they were being held by the security services. Had it coming to them, mind you. They were both subversives.'

'How do you know?'

'Oh – information received.'

'Have you done anything about it?'

'No point, is there? How else are we to beat subversion except by arresting subversives? Just because he happens to be my son –'

'I think there's every point. I think we should all make as much noise about these disappearances as we possibly can. You know they've made it illegal for newspapers to report deaths and abductions without official permission? Absolutely appalling. I tell you, TC, we're not far off being a Nazi state right now. God knows what's going on under cover. You can't open your mouth in a collectivo without wondering who might be listening. All you can read in *La Prensa* these days is foreign news. The *Herald* seems to be the only paper with enough guts to publish even a small part of the truth about the graft and corruption.' He refilled their glasses. 'You know who I blame?'

'Who's that?'

'The Freemasonry. If we could get rid of that lot this country might just have a chance of survival.'

'Watch your voice, old boy,' Tito said. 'You never know who's listening.'

'If I can't speak freely in my own club where can I speak? I don't give a damn who's listening. The trouble with Argentina is that we're all living in fear. It's time people stood up for their principles. That was your mistake, TC. If you'd stuck out against Botta and Co. –'

'My hands were tied. I told you, Stiffy. I had no alternative.'

But Stiffy had gone off on another tack. 'Wait a minute . . . where did I see that –'

'See what?'

'I know where it was. My godson's regimental mag. That's right. Colonel Ocampo. He's in with Botta, isn't he? And he's also some sort of arch-wizard in the Freemasonry.' Rathbone put his knife and fork down. 'You're not in it as well by any chance, are you, TC?'

'Do you think I'd have told you all this if I were?'

'Perhaps not. I wouldn't mind betting Botta and Co. were though. Has that ever occurred to you? Might explain a lot, don't you think?'

'I've never seen any evidence to support it.'

Rathbone snorted through flared nostrils. 'Yes, but the men in aprons don't exactly broadcast their allegiance to the world, do they?'

'Suppose not.' Cadoret cleared his throat. 'Actually – there is one way that you might be able to help me. But it would mean my sharing a confidence with you which I haven't shared with anyone before.'

'Oh yes?'

Cadoret paused while the waiter removed their plates.

'Would you be at all interested in getting money out of the country?'

Stiffy looked at him quickly. 'What sort of shady deal are you up to now, TC?'

'Not shady at all. Absolutely clean and above board. Thing is –'

'Go on.'

'Can I take you into my confidence, Stiffy? This is absolutely confidential, you understand that?'

'My word is my bond,' Stiffy said. 'I've never broken it, and I don't intend to. So if there's anything crooked about what you want to suggest I don't want to hear about it.'

Cadoret wiped his moustache nervously. 'Thing is, I can't afford interest repayments on my loan to the Banco Ambrosiano, so they're foreclosing on me –'

'And you want a loan –'

Cadoret leant across the table. 'Can we please keep our voices down? No, I do not want a loan. I have a fiduciary account with Coutts in London which Botta doesn't know about and must not know about. It's my life-saver, see? If all else fails I can go and live in Britain. But I don't want to do that. I can't open a new bank account in this country without running the risk of Botta finding out, but if – if you wanted to increase your external capital, well, I wondered if we could come to some arrangement.'

'You mean – I pay off your loan in Argentina and you pay me back into an account in Britain?'

'Just that. Yes.'

'Mmm,' said Stiffy. 'I'd have to think pretty carefully about that.'

'It would pay you handsomely to do it,' Cadoret said. 'The peso's practically in free-fall right now and we could arrange matters so that you would get the very best possible exchange rate.'

'What sort of sum are we talking about?'

'You mean you are prepared to consider it?'

Perhaps it was the beginning of old age: Stiffy needed reconciliation, too. He leant back in his chair. 'Well, I suppose I might. After all, what are friends for?'

Late that evening, Cadoret returned to Calandria, having dined with Stiffy at El Palenque for the first time in years and having agreed arrangements for a confidential quid pro quo exchange of funds in Argentina and London.

It was nearly midnight, but for once he did not feel tired. He walked up and down in the hall until Rosa came along to find out if there was anything he wanted.

'No, no. Go back to bed, Rosa.'

He went along to the office and paced about, still churning all that he and Stiffy had said in his mind. Perhaps, perhaps it might be possible to hang on long enough to turn things round. Perhaps he might be able to persuade someone else – Ceci perhaps – to support him with another loan elsewhere, somewhere that Botta could not reach. He'd had a bad year, yes, but he'd had bad years before. If he could just turn this corner and get the estancia back into profit . . .

The telephone rang. Who on earth wanted him at this hour?

'Cadoret speaking.'

'Daddy it's me. Nikki.'

'Sweetheart! Where are you? When did you arrive?'

'I'm in BA. I tried to ring you earlier –'

'I've been out all day. Wonderful to hear you! When can I expect you? Would you like me to have a plane collect you?'

She hesitated a moment. 'No – that's what I wanted to tell you. I'm going up to Salta tomorrow.'

'You're what?'

'I'm going straight to Salta, Daddy. I'm needed up north right away. Didn't you get my letter? I did say that I wouldn't be able to spend long in the south.'

He felt a sudden pain in his chest.

'Daddy?'

'Go on then!' he shouted. 'Go on up to Salta! See if I bloody well care!'

27

THREE WEEKS AFTER lunching with Stiffy at Laguna Blanca, Tito
Cadoret was summoned to Buenos Aires for an interview with Rui
Botta.

He arrived at Rui's residence in Olivos in an optimistic frame of
mind. He had completed the first currency exchange with Stiffy and
had told Toni Lambretti that his old friend had agreed to come to his
rescue with an interest-free loan. For the time being at least, he was
off the hook.

After a long wait in an adjoining lobby he was eventually shown
into the large open-plan room that overlooked the pool.

He was received, but not welcomed, by Botta and Ocampo.

'Sit down over there,' Ocampo ordered. He obeyed.

Beyond the sliding bullet-proof glass doors, two men in dark suits
stood guard, their backs to the room. At Botta's feet, an elderly cocker
spaniel was licking itself.

'Take a look at that,' Ocampo said, and flung a copy of the
Washington Post in Cadoret's direction. 'Letters page.'

Cadoret was not familiar with the *Washington Post* and Botta's baleful
silence made him nervous. He fumbled with the newspaper for some
seconds.

When he found the right page, a letter immediately caught his
eye. It accused Freemasonry of having infiltrated Argentine politics,
big business and industry at the highest level and suggested that
much of the widespread corruption in Argentina could be 'laid on
the doorstep of Masonic Lodges'. It went on to cite the example
of 'a longstanding friend' who since the war had been 'systemati-
cally bled white of all his property and inheritance by a group
containing at least one senior member of the Freemasonry.' The
letter was signed E. Rathbone and the address given was Estancia
El Palenque, Cadoret, Argentina.

Cadoret felt his bowels loosen. He was unable to prevent himself
breaking wind.

'Well?' Botta asked.

'I said nothing to him that broke my Obligation.'

'But you admit that you have met him.'

'Yes.'

'What else did you tell him?'

'Nothing. Nothing at all. Only that I was short of funds.'

Botta sat motionless and silent for a long time. At his feet, the spaniel stopped licking itself. Its teeth chattered as if it had a bitter taste in its mouth.

'Okay, my friend,' Botta said eventually. 'If you haven't broken your oath, you'll be glad to prove your loyalty. Rathbone's in town right now. Give him a warning. Take him to Alfredo's. We'll keep a table for you. Tomorrow. *Sin falta*. We'll be listening, Tito. Make sure you tell him, yes?'

Alfredo's was a steak house on the Avenida Costanera. Rathbone arrived in his Ford Falcon which he parked at the roadside alongside a few other cars, including a police Ford Falcon, whose occupants had taken a table for three and were noisily enjoying lunch. Rathbone was shown to a table under the vine trellis overlooking the road. Beyond that, the Plate estuary glinted dully in the sun. From time to time jet airliners roared overhead on the approach to Jorge Newbury airport.

Soon after Stiffy had been shown to a table for two, Cadoret showed up in a taxi. He seemed strained.

'You all right?' Stiffy asked when they had ordered.

'Fine,' said Cadoret.

'What's all this about? Business or social?'

'Bit of both.'

A waiter took their order.

'Any further news of that lovely daughter of yours?'

'No. No further news.'

'According to Ceci she's already gone up to the mission. She's a brave girl. You ought to be proud of her, TC.'

'Yes. Yes, I am.'

'You sure you're all right, TC? You look a bit white about the gills.'

Cadoret smiled awkwardly. 'Something I have to tell you. Bit tricky.'

'Well if you don't tell me, I won't know, will I?'

'It's that letter of yours to the *Washington Post*.'

'Ha!' said Stiffy. 'Fame at last! I didn't expect anyone to pick that one up.'

'Well they did.'

'Who did?'

'People.' Tito glanced at the police officers. One of them was speaking into a hand-held radio. 'You realize you're playing with fire, don't you? These things don't go unnoticed.'

Rathbone snorted. 'I wouldn't have written to the press if I'd wanted it to go unnoticed.'

'Well it's put me in a bit of a spot, I can tell you. I'd have appreciated it if you'd let me know you were going to write that letter.'

'I didn't mention you by name.'

'People put two and two together.'

Stiffy waited for a jet to go over.

'People?'

'You know what I mean.'

'Do I get the impression that you've been detailed off to put a flea in my ear, TC?'

'I don't know what impression you're getting. All I'm saying is that you're skating on thin ice.'

'Well it all goes to show, doesn't it? There I was, thinking I was striking a blow for freedom. I thought I was helping you.'

'I need that sort of help like I need a hole in the head.'

'That wasn't the impression you gave me the other day. You looked like a man who could do with a spot of moral support. You looked like a frightened man, TC. Still do, come to that.'

'I'm not frightened,' Cadoret said quickly. 'You're the one who should be frightened.'

There was a squeal of tyres in the distance and the sound of an engine at high revs.

'Oh?' said Rathbone. 'Why's that? Do you know something that I don't know?'

'Look,' Cadoret said, raising his voice. 'If you know what's good for you, you'll shut up, right? Otherwise someone might just come along and shut you up. Now do you get the message?'

At the table where the police officers were lunching, conversation had stopped.

'My God,' Rathbone muttered. 'They've really got you by the balls, haven't they?'

The steaks arrived. Rathbone pushed his away. 'Was this why you dragged me out here? To warn me off?'

A car hurtled past going out of town. Immediately, the policemen stood up from the adjoining table and a sergeant came swaggering over to where Cadoret and Rathbone were sitting.

'Whose is the Ford Falcon?'

303

Rathbone said, 'Mine.'

'We have to use it.'

'Haven't you got a car of your own?'

The sergeant held out his hand. 'Give me the keys.'

'On what authority –'

The sergeant pulled out a gun and called him the son of a whore.

Rathbone handed over the keys.

When they had driven off, Rathbone turned to Cadoret. 'I suppose it would be too much to ask you to act as a witness to that?'

'I'm sure you'll get it back,' Tito said.

'I wish I was. So now we know where they get all these Falcons you see being driven around with no number plates. From mugs like yours truly, that's where. Well I'll not stand for it. I'd recognize that thug anywhere and I'm going to report him. And if you want to call yourself a friend of mine, TC, you'll back me up.'

'I am your friend,' Cadoret said. 'And if you've got any sense at all you'll drop the whole bloody thing.'

Rathbone stood up. 'Goodbye, Cadoret. I've had enough of your advice. Just tell your minders whoever they are that I've got the message. And don't bother to ask me to lunch again, because I won't come.'

Rathbone reported the commandeering of his car to the police authorities that same afternoon, but got little sympathy from them. It was explained to him that in these difficult days it was up to citizens to collaborate as fully as possible with the police in order that the war against subversion could be won. He was again advised to take no further action.

A week after the incident, he wrote a letter to the *Buenos Aires Herald* to complain about the treatment he had received from the police. In the letter he said that he would recognize the police officer who took his car. The letter was published. The following day, when he was walking along the Avenida 25 de Mayo towards the English Club, a police car drew up alongside him.

'Sr Rathbone?'

'Yes?'

'We found your car.'

Rathbone's face lit up. All was forgiven. 'Excellent news! Where is it?'

'Parked on the Autopista Acceso Norte. Do you want it back?'

'Well, of course!'

'Get in then.'

The car was driven at speed out of the city and onto the autopista that goes out towards Hurlingham. When they were passing through a shanty-town area, a Ford Falcon came into sight, parked on the hard shoulder. The police car drew to a halt fifty yards or so ahead of it.

'It's all yours,' the sergeant said, and Rathbone was left standing on the hard shoulder with the traffic whipping by. He limped back to his car and looked in. They had given him his car back and the keys were in the ignition. He suspected a trick of some sort, but didn't want to wait around because that stretch of road was renowned for hold-ups and robberies.

Telling himself that having the courage to speak out had won the day after all, he got in behind the wheel and turned the key in the ignition.

The Ford erupted in smoke and flame.

When the fire had been put out, pictures were taken of the burnt-out wreck and the charred body of its occupant. Later that week it was identified in a press release as that of Sr Esteban Rathbone. Rathbone, said the press release, had had his car stolen by subversives the previous week. The accident was unfortunate as Sr Rathbone had only received his car back that day. It had been recovered for him by the untiring efforts of the city police.

Stiffy had always been a popular member of the British community, so his funeral was well attended. Tito went to the service and sat at the back of the Anglican Cathedral, but after the service the open hostility of old friends in the British community decided him against going to the cemetery for the burial and he turned off the route on the way to Chacarita.

Buenos Aires was unusually sweaty that day. He drove aimlessly about the city for an hour or so and when he was sure the burial would be over went to Chacarita to visit the grave alone.

As he approached he saw that the diggers had arrived to fill in the grave and were throwing the wreaths into a wheelbarrow.

He watched them from a distance for a while and was about to leave when it occurred to him that he had never once visited Anna's grave, which was also in the British Cemetery. He went to the keeper's office to discover its whereabouts and having done so made his way along the lines of headstones and crosses.

There were fresh flowers on the grave. Seeing Anna's name and the words, 'greatly beloved mother to Blanca, Luis, John, Marc, Larry, Jimmy and Nicola' wrenched him emotionally and he was weeping at the graveside when he heard his name called.

It was Ceci.

'Hello, Tito.' She sounded apologetic. 'I stayed on after the burial.'

'Was it you who brought the flowers?'

'Yes, but they come from Nikki.'

The name ANNA seemed to burn into his heart as deeply as it was engraved in the white marble. When Ceci slipped her hand into his a new, larger wave of sorrow broke over him.

'Oh Tito, darling!'

He fumbled for a handkerchief and blew his nose.

'Come back to the house,' she said suddenly. 'Come back to Belgrano. Will you?'

She didn't know what had prompted her to put her hand in his, nor did she know why she had asked him to come back to the house. Driving through the city, she experienced a sense of inner turmoil that was not far removed from panic.

But was it so surprising? She had been terribly hurt by him all those years ago. He had done more than wound her: he had disfigured her whole life. Even now, nearly forty years on, she had a recurring nightmare about being engaged to Tito Cadoret and being unable to break it off. He had been the cause of her massive loss of confidence, a loss from which she had never fully recovered. He was the cause of her nervousness. He had caused her disillusionment with the Catholic Church and had planted inside her a life-long fear of men. He had caused her to lose the ability to form true and lasting relationships and – yes – to be afraid of her own emotions. And now she had slipped her hand back into his after all these years. She had asked him to 'come back'.

She drove the car straight into her garage and went quickly up the steps into the kitchen. She looked at her face in the hall mirror and did some first-aid with a handkerchief. She was still at it when she heard his car outside.

She went to the door and saw him, distorted through the spyhole, standing outside in his black suit. She saw his white hair and white moustache. His red face.

She opened the door to him and tried to smile. He came in and she shut the door behind him. And then suddenly she knew that he was every bit as apprehensive as herself and a moment later he was holding her as he used to hold her long, long ago, when they were twenty-five and life was fun and there was nothing to fear. He was holding her and they were both weeping, weeping for the past, weeping for each other, weeping for their lost youth, the life they might have shared, the children they might have had, the things that might have been.

'Come on, this is just silly,' Ceci said eventually. 'I don't know about you, my dear, but I could do with a cup of tea. I think we've both had quite enough emotion for one afternoon, don't you?'

She told him to go into the sala and take his jacket off and sit down. Ten minutes later she brought a tray in and they sipped Earl Grey and smiled at each other in bewilderment and began, tentatively, to find their way back – not only to each other but to the selves they had left at what Ceci called the roadside of life so many years before.

'Do you realize that this is the first time we have been alone in each other's company in nearly forty years, Tito? Oh – where has all the time gone? Where has it gone?'

Tito balanced his teacup on his knee and made wondering noises.

Every sentence she uttered that afternoon seemed to be attended by a following of wistful dots. 'What a very strange thing life is, don't you agree, Tito? When one thinks what might have been. And how much time one simply wastes, doesn't one?' She put her head on one side. 'I've forgiven you, you know. It took a long time, but I have forgiven you.'

In reply, he muttered something unintelligible which was intended to sound apologetic.

She reached out and patted his hand.

'We must do this again,' she said when he got up to leave. 'It's so silly to waste what time we have on this earth, don't you think?' And then she held out her arms to him and asked for another hug and called him a sentimental old thing, and he couldn't help admitting to himself, as he drove away, that it had been very comforting to be cosseted by Ceci and that he wouldn't at all mind seeing her again.

A week later, when they were both out in the camp again, he rang her at La Tijerita.

Her nervous laughter echoed over the party line. 'Tito! I thought you'd forgotten all about me.'

'Well – of course not. Look – er – I wondered if you'd like to meet one of these days?'

'Tito, darling, I'd simply love to.'

'Great! When are you free?'

'What about this evening?' Ceci giggled shrilly in a way that took him straight back to flat chests and silly dances. Pure nerves of course, but that was Ceci for you. 'Come about eightish and we'll have some sups. Would you like that?'

He drove over to Tijerita that evening in the old Humber Hawk, which he now kept carefully preserved in a garage and only took out on special occasions.

When he arrived, Ceci was in one of her tizzies. She didn't know whether she should be sitting down, standing up or throwing cartwheels in the hall.

'Tito, darling,' she said, and provided him with a damp cheek to kiss.

Talking all the time, she led the way through to the drawing room, whose French windows were thrown open to the evening sky.

'Here you are, you can make yourself useful and do the drinks,' she said. 'That's fresh lime for me in the jug and the whisky in the decanter's real J&B because Nikki brought it out on the plane, kind girl. Have you heard from her recently? I had a note from Diana Dalligan the other day and she said everybody thought the world of her.'

Having a conversation with Ceci was like sitting at the bottom of a verbal waterfall.

They sat at either end of the sofa and, while the sun sank flaming to the horizon, Ceci talked relentlessly on. She talked about Stiffy, she talked about Nikki, she talked about the tour of Tierra del Fuego and the Falkland Islands she planned to make in the new year; and eventually she got round to asking about himself.

'So what's the latest at Calandria, my dear? My capataz said he heard you'd had foot-rot the other week after the rain.'

'Not foot-rot. Bit of bloat –'

'Bloat! Not too catastrophic, I hope?'

'Not at all.'

'So you're still afloat are you?'

He smiled. 'Just about.'

Ceci put her head on one side and sighed. 'It really is so silly, isn't it, Tito. I mean – you sitting all alone over there and me sitting all alone over here. We really must see lots and lots more of each other.'

'Not so sure I'll be living at Calandria very much longer.'

'My dear, why ever not?'

'Looks as though I shall have to sell up.'

'Sell up? La Calandria? Tito, I don't believe I'm hearing this! Who to, for goodness sake – oh, silly question. Botta's lot I suppose. Why you didn't give him his marching orders long ago I simply cannot comprehend. Anna couldn't stand Stefenelli. Nor could Nikki for that matter. But then I think we women are a lot shrewder than you men give us credit for, aren't we? If you'd listened to Anna a bit more over the last twenty or thirty years, I think you might be in a healthier financial position than you are today, Tito Cadoret. Oh look! Sunset. There. Gone!'

There was an amazing silence for all of ten seconds.

'Now if I ask you a serious question, Tito, will you promise to give me a serious answer?'

He wondered what was coming. 'All right.'

Ceci took a little breath as if about to speak, hesitated, breathed out, took another little breath and said, 'You've never told me this, and I've never asked. Perhaps I shouldn't ask now. But – why *did* you let yourself get mixed up with Botta?'

'Should've thought that was pretty obvious,' he said.

'Well it isn't, and please don't go grumpy on me, Tito. There must have been a good reason for going to Botta in the first place, and there must have been a much better reason for staying with him all these years and letting him live off you. There was, wasn't there?'

He nodded.

'Why can't you talk about it?'

With the sun gone, the sky had gone an amazing mixture of blues and purples, and the night insects were beginning to clatter and ring. Far away, on the very limit of the horizon, an express train rushed northward.

Ceci came and sat with him on the sofa. 'You've lost so many friends, Tito. But you never lost me, did you know that? Oh, I've told myself that I hated you often enough, and for a long time I believed it. But you've always had a special place in my heart. I've watched what's been happening to you these last few years since Anna died and I've longed so often to offer you my help. You see – you've cut yourself off from your friends, Tito. That's a terrible thing to do. Friends are so, so precious. I want to help you, darling, but how can I if you won't take me into your confidence?'

'Helping yours truly is a dangerous business these days,' he said gruffly, and went to the drinks trolley to replenish his glass. 'Look what happened to Stiffy.'

'But poor Stiffy acted very foolishly. Even I know that you don't argue with the police. He was courting disaster. But you don't have to do that, do you?'

He came back to the sofa and sat down. 'Don't I?'

'Of course you don't. So why not talk about it? Why not share it with me? It was all because of Magdalena, wasn't it? I mean – that's

309

what everyone always said, but no one's ever heard you admit it, have they? It did have something to do with her, didn't it?'

He sat with his elbows on his knees and looked down into the whisky glass. 'Yes. Yes, it did.'

'Were you – did you know Magdalena was going to be murdered? Was that it?'

'I didn't know beforehand. I – I thought –'

Ceci took his hand. 'Go on, Tito. Please don't stop now.'

'I went to Botta on José Ocampo's recommendation. He said he could get an annulment for me.'

'At a price.'

'Yes. He sent me along to Toni Lambretti and they raised a loan on the security of Calandria.'

'And then –'

'Then Magdalena was murdered. I asked for the return of my loan, but they told me that it had been made as a gift to the Church and that gifts weren't recoverable. They made it look as if – as if I had had Magdalena murdered. I was threatened with legal proceedings by the police. I was placed in a position that – that if Botta didn't support me, I didn't have a leg to stand on. He had the power to clear my name or – or send me into the dock as an accessory to murder.'

'But – you didn't have anything to do with the murder, did you?'

'Nothing at all. All I wanted was an annulment.'

'So it was blackmail.'

'A subtle form of it, yes. I tried to change my lawyer then, but they – they had a hold on me by then. I was . . . trapped.'

'But . . . surely you could have proved your innocence by showing where the money had gone?'

'I tried to do that. But the loan had passed through the account Lambretti had opened for me, not my regular bank account. It had been paid into a numbered account abroad. I had no way of proving who had received it or what it had been used for. They had me over a barrel.'

'And ever since –'

'I've had to pay them interest out of earnings. The interest rate leapt when war broke out and every time I defaulted they increased the loan to cover the interest owing. Then after the war we lost out again on the repayment of war credits by Britain so they raised new loans in my name to make more money but they always managed to keep me in debt to them. I've never been able to repay them.'

Cadoret's mouth clamped shut. He hadn't planned to tell Ceci all this, but now that he had, the telling of it had churned him up

310

emotionally and he had an extraordinary feeling that it would be very easy to break down and cry.

'Oh, Tito, darling,' Ceci whispered. 'If only you'd never got mixed up with that Magdalena woman in the first place. If only, if only, if only!'

'Bit late for that now, Ceci.'

'Listen,' she said. 'You've made a start. Now go on. Tell me everything. Share it with me. I have my faults but I'm not a gossip, so whatever you say will go no further than these four walls. Please tell me, Tito. Will you?'

He sighed. 'It's a long story.'

Ceci folded her arms and sat back in her chair. 'Go on. I'm not going to say another word until you've told me the whole thing.'

He told her a lot, but he did not tell her everything. He made no mention of the gift of his best polo pony to a police officer, nor of the perks his association with Botta had provided: the free lunches, the association with the rich and the famous, the unlimited use of call-girls. He said nothing about the numbered accounts operated in his name by Lambretti, or the exchange of funds he had arranged with Stiffy Rathbone. When it came to explaining the sale of La Ventolera, he made himself out to be no more than a puppet.

'I'm not even a cog in their machine,' he said, and laughed bitterly. 'More like a ball bearing. I go round and round in circles and when I finally crack I'll be easily replaced.'

Ceci sighed. 'My poor, poor Tito. You sound as if you've been needing to talk about this for years.'

'Oh – I awarded myself the MBE a long time ago. Know what that stands for? Member of Botta's Empire. Once you're an MBE, they've got you. There's no escape.'

The maid came in and announced dinner. They moved through to the dining room and ate by candlelight. Halfway through the meal, a gust of wind blew in through the open window and a dented brass vase of flowers fell over on the polished table.

'What worries me most of all,' Cadoret said when the emergency was over and the spilt water mopped up, 'is that if I'm forced to relinquish ownership of Calandria, and if Botta purchases El Palenque, which seems very likely now Stiffy's out of the way, you'll be surrounded here at Tijerita. He'll even own a majority shareholding in the access roads. It'll be just a matter of time before you're forced out, Ceci. And when that happens, they'll have made a clean sweep. They'll have the entire original Cadoret estancia – all ninety thousand hectares of it.'

311

'I must say I hadn't foreseen that possibility,' Ceci said quietly. 'Is there really nothing one can do?'

'Not much. Botta has big business behind him. He has contacts with the heads of the armed forces and with Videla himself. I've never known him fail to get his hands on a piece of real estate once he's set his mind on it.

'But surely there must be some way to stop them. Come on, Tito, where's that hit-and-score spirit you always used to have?'

He smiled to her across the table. Although there was much about Ceci which made him feel impatient, there was also quite a lot about her that he liked. Perhaps it was all a part of this need he had for reconciliation – he didn't know.

'Well, if they start making noises about purchasing La Tijerita, you know you can count on me for support. Though I'm afraid that isn't worth a great deal these days.'

'That's very sweet of you, Tito. All the same, I think I should have a chat with my attorney, don't you? If Botta's got his eye on my beautiful Tijerita, I think Hugo Ferreyra ought to know about it.'

He met her frequently after that first evening together. They lunched on Sundays at Laguna Blanca and took it in turns to play host for supper two or three times a week. As Christmas approached and spring gave way to summer, Ceci set about improving Tito's lifestyle. She persuaded him to eat less beef, do without a cooked breakfast and cut his daily consumption of wine and whisky. She also got him on the back of a horse again and he enjoyed the experience so much that he gave up using the Ford truck for travelling about the estancia.

'Want to ask you something,' he said a week before Christmas when they were out riding on her land.

'Your wish is my command!' she replied.

'I want you to be my wife.'

Ceci reined in her mount. The two horses stood head to tail, swatting the flies off each other's faces.

'Why, Tito?'

He appeared to make an effort. 'Because I love you. Because I need you. Because I think we could make each other happy.'

She smiled and blushed and wept a little. The horses' tails swished to and fro. From its perch on a fencepost, a little owl swivelled its fluffy head and fixed them with an unwavering stare.

'Do you want my answer now?'

'If you can give me one.'

'It is because you love me, isn't it, Tito? It wouldn't be a marriage of convenience? I couldn't bear that.'

Cadoret's horse shook its head suddenly.

'I think he heard me, didn't he?' Ceci laughed.

'I do love you,' he said. 'And more than that, too. I'd like to be able to make up for – for – everything. I want to clean the slate, my dear. Start afresh. I can't do that without your help. So, will you help me?'

She surprised him then. She tilted her head and looked at him sideways and said, 'Yes, on two conditions. First, that we're married by Anglican rite, and second that you break with Botta completely and take Ferreyra as your lawyer.'

He blinked rapidly. 'I – I don't know if that's possible.'

'All things are possible, Tito. It'll just take a little courage on your part, that's all.'

'But I'm in debt to them. I can't turn my back on them.'

'We'll pay off the debt. You and me. We'll do it together, darling. We'll put the two estancias in our joint names. We'll turn the tide on them. I've talked to Ferreyra about this. He says the only way to defeat these people is through mutual trust.'

'I wasn't making a business proposition, Ceci. I was asking you to be my wife.'

'I know, and I'm touched and thrilled by it. But in our position, one simply can't separate the question of estates from the question of marriage. We can't assist each other financially without the sort of mutual trust that can only be found within marriage, and we can't hope for any marriage worthy of the name without complete financial trust in one another. Surely you must have thought about all this before you asked me?'

'Well, of course –'

'I'd love to say yes, Tito, and let you whisk me off my feet like a twenty-one-year-old. But life can't be like that any more, can it? It's not that I don't trust you – I do. But I must protect what is mine. I know you wouldn't dream of – of using marriage for your own gain, but at the same time, I can't trust Botta not to use you against me in the same sort of way as he used you against Randy. You do understand that, don't you?'

They trotted back to the house in silence and, when they had handed their mounts over to the pony boy, walked back to the house together. 'Listen, darling,' Ceci said. 'Say you agree, now, to break with Botta and his gang. Tell me, now, that you intend to sever all ties with them, and in return I promise that the day

313

the deed is done, I shall be yours. Can I give you a fairer answer than that?'

'Suppose not.'

'Well? Will you break with them?'

'I can't do it on my own, Ceci. I'll need support. Every sort of support.'

'I will give you *all* my support, of whatever kind, my darling. Whatever I can do or give to help you get free from that lot, is yours. Come here, I want to hug you, poor Tito. I want to hug you and love you and look after you and make you happy. All you have to do is say you'll let me. Is that so very very difficult?'

He shook his head. She took his head in her hands and kissed him smackingly on the lips. 'There. Cheer up! It won't be nearly as difficult as you expect. See?'

Hugo Ferreyra was an engaging young attorney, nearly bald, with large spectacles and a gentle manner. His reputation for fighting hopeless causes was well known in Buenos Aires Province: he was a champion of the Madres de Mayo, the mothers of the Disappeared who wore the names of their lost children on white headscarves and who demonstrated outside the Casa Rosada every Thursday.

Tito and Ceci sat in his cramped and cluttered office in Laboulaye, gave him the relevant facts and figures and asked his advice on how best to protect La Calandria and La Tijerita from being absorbed into Botta's empire.

The plan that was finally hammered out relied heavily on trust. It involved a transfer of funds from Cadoret's Coutts account to Ceci's in Switzerland, which, combined with a further sum raised by Ceci, would be sufficient to redeem the mortgage on La Calandria and pay off all interest and arrears of interest. Cadoret would at the same time resign his directorship of all companies in which Botta had involved him, and would wind up his account with the Banco Ambrosiano and his numbered accounts abroad.

They were also to make new wills in favour of each other and would each take out substantial insurances on their lives.

'I suggest you wait until the new year before making your move,' Ferreyra said. 'In the meantime, it might be worth your while to inform the British Consulate of your intention to redeem the mortgage, so as to make it as difficult as possible for our friend Botta to pull any tricks. Also, I think you should delay any announcement about your intended marriage until after the financial arrangements have been completed.'

Ceci looked at Tito. 'We could do that as soon as I come back from my tour, couldn't we, darling?'

'That sounds like a very good idea,' Ferreyra agreed. 'It'll give me time to finalize the paperwork and tie up all the loose ends. But do remember, please, both of you, that the arrangement you are entering into must be kept strictly confidential until the whole plan is launched.'

They shook hands with him and departed. 'I think that's the best morning's work you've done for a *very* long time, Tito Cadoret,' Ceci said as they drove off.

He accelerated out of the town. 'Can't say I'm looking forward to having to give Rui his marching orders.'

'You must just stand up to him, Sweet. Present him with a *fait accompli*. It's all perfectly legal. He's got no grounds for complaint whatsoever. Goodness knows, he's manipulated you for long enough. It's high time someone manipulated him back.'

'Well I hope it works. We'll be a pair of bankrupts if it doesn't, *sin duda*.'

She patted his knee. 'Oh you! Don't be so pessimistic.'

There had been heavy rain in the night and the earth road had turned to mud. Spinning the wheel this way and that to keep the car on the crown of the road, Cadoret wondered how he could sell the idea to Botta. One thing was certain: there was not a hope of putting it across as a *fait accompli*. No, the only way he might conceivably convince them would be to show them what might be in it for the cartel, and the one way of doing that was to offer them the bait of more land. So what if he told Jorge and Rui that he might be able to use marriage to Ceci to help them get their hands on La Tijerita? It would be back-door purchase all over again – just the sort of deal they relished. It might also win him back some much-needed credit with the Lodge. But he would have to play his cards extremely carefully. It would be all too easy to offer them La Tijerita and then see La Calandria slip from his grasp.

'What are you doing for Christmas?' Ceci asked suddenly.

'Nothing much.'

'Well then come and spend it with me at Belgrano. That's an order, Tito. I won't take no for an answer.'

It was the happiest and most restful Christmas season he could remember. They spent it quietly at Belgrano and at Ceci's invitation he stayed on in order to see in the new year with her. They went to the theatre, picnicked at Tigre, watched polo at Hurlingham and in the evenings played Scrabble, at which Ceci won so consistently that she eventually gave him a handicap of fifty points.

'Never mind, Tito,' she would say, pouring the letters back into the bag. 'You had all those i's, didn't you, and I was pretty jammy to get "quizling" on a triple-word square, wasn't I?'

Then she would brew a pot of catchamai tea to give them both a good night's sleep and later, when he emerged from the bathroom in his silk dressing gown, she would kiss him good night.

She took charge of him with brisk authority. She put him on a fat-free diet and took him riding in Palermo park every morning. But she did more: she made him feel loved and needed again. For that he was grateful, and content to listen while she talked.

And how she could talk. She had a habit, born of years of loneliness, of carrying on two sides of a conversation at the same time so that apart from the occasional grunted agreement it was scarcely necessary for him to join in.

'Now guess where we're going for New Year's Eve,' she said. 'No of course you can't possibly guess, can you? So I'll tell you. The Sheraton, that's where. We'll dance the night away. I've booked a table for two.'

The Aljibe Bar was on the top floor of the Sheraton. Its ceiling was hung with massive glass crystals and its picture windows presented the most stunning view of the city, which sparkled and roared far below. Outside in the balmy December air, a band in pale blue tuxedos played Latin American dances and tangos.

The moment they took to the floor together Ceci remembered how wonderfully they had danced together in their youth. Tito Cadoret and Ceci Jowett – hadn't they once been the only couple in the British community that everyone knew must get married, they were so well suited?

At ten to midnight, Tito excused himself. 'Just going to see a man about a dog,' he said.

'Well don't be long, darling. We're almost into '77.'

By the time he got back Ceci was looking worried because people were crossing arms and preparing to sing 'Auld Lang Syne'. They joined the throng moments before midnight began to strike.

She flushed suddenly. 'Oh golly!' she exclaimed. 'I've just had a thought. We're in a leap year, aren't we?'

'Not for much longer.'

'I know, silly. So is it definite then? Will you marry me?'

'I will!' he said.

Midnight struck. They began to sing.

*　　*　　*

They agreed to keep their engagement secret until after Ceci's return from her tour of the south. Over cucumber-and-scrambled-egg sandwiches at the Dorado boat club – one of their old haunts of pre-war days – they fixed a date for a quiet wedding in the third week of March.

'It'll be an autumn wedding for an autumn couple,' Ceci said.

She had considered cancelling her holiday altogether, but had decided that as she had tried to take it so often before and had been so often frustrated, this time it was now or never.

He saw her off from Jorge Newbury national airport, and she gave him some last-minute instructions in the departure hall. 'Now you're to keep up the riding and keep off the whisky, do you understand, Tito? I want you to be looking fit and youthful when I come back, see? Oh, I'm *so* looking forward to it. I know – let's go straight to the Sheraton, shall we? After I've landed. We can go up to the roof bar and you can put the ring on my finger and we'll go public with champagne. What do you think? Isn't that a perfectly marvellous idea?'

At the last minute, she confessed to a premonition of death. 'So silly,' she said. 'But I always get it before I fly. I've always been convinced that I'll die in an air crash.'

'Oh – you'll be all right.'

She smiled damply. 'I know. I'm just being a silly Ceci.'

Her flight was called. They embraced; she held his hands tightly; they embraced again; she said, 'I love you so much, Tito,' a declaration which never failed to make him feel uncomfortable. 'I'll be staying with the Governor at Stanley, so you can write to me there,' she said finally, and kissed him once more before going out to the plane.

He stayed to watch the jet lift off the runway then drove back to Ceci's house, where he was going to spend a night before returning to the camp.

After a solitary supper, he glanced once more through the draft wills and agreements which Ferreyra had prepared for them, and then he took all Ceci's old photograph albums down from the bookshelf and indulged himself in nostalgia.

The albums went back to the early twenties when Ceci and he had been in their teens. But there was one album smaller than all the rest which he discovered was full of snaps of Anna. Each snap had a caption in white ink: 'In the garden at Belgrano'; 'Shopping in BA'; 'Picnic at Tigre'; 'First riding lesson'; 'Tennis at Hurlingham'; 'Watching polo'; 'Grip with the knees!'; 'Off to the Colón'.

He sighed, and turned the last page of the album. Inside the back

317

cover was a posed portrait photograph of Anna in her wedding dress, taken before the wedding.

Anna looked out at him with those searching eyes of hers and he felt suddenly touched. He had forgotten – perhaps he had never realized – just how young, how tender, how lovely his Scottish bride had been.

28

THROUGH THE LONG HOURS on the overnight coach from Córdoba, the thought had never been far from Nikki's mind that she was following in the footsteps of the uncle her mother had talked about so often; so when the sun came up and she looked out and saw the Andes rising up to the west, she was aware of an unfamiliar sense of destiny. She was making the journey her mother had always wanted to make. She was beginning an entirely fresh chapter in her life.

'Nikki Cadoret, I presume?' said a voice behind her when she was waiting for her baggage to be unloaded. She turned. It was Phillip Dalligan, looking colonial in a khaki shirt, shorts and desert boots. He picked up three of her four bags and led the way out of the bus station to a Ford that had seen better days.

He was a very easy man to talk to. Quiet, slight of build, unassuming.

'The last time we met,' he said as they drove through the pleasant suburbs of Salta, 'was that Christmas when Aunt Annelise died, remember? Since when there've been a few changes for both of us. How do you view the prospect of working at Misión Yuchán?'

She said she was looking forward to it.

'Joan and Neil are certainly looking forward to having you with them. What news of the family? Your father still hale and hearty?'

'I think so. I've only spoken to him on the phone. I decided to come straight up here without visiting him on the way. That sounds awful, I know, but –'

He glanced at her. 'You don't need to explain. I'm a black sheep myself. My mother has never forgiven me for leaving the Catholic Church.'

Diana, Phillip's rather formidable wife, welcomed her into their sixth-floor apartment, which was filled with a delicious smell of freshly baked bread and roasting coffee. Diana was more overtly evangelical than her husband, who was several years younger and definitely under her thumb. She had converted him to Protestantism five years before. As he wryly admitted, that had been no mean feat.

Before they started breakfast Diana said, 'Shall we give thanks?' and said grace, adding a prayer of thanks for the new worker who had been called into the Lord's service. This caused Nikki to wonder, momentarily, who she could possibly mean. Phillip then read a portion from the *Daily Light*, after which Nikki, who was ravenous, fell upon the rolls and coffee.

After breakfast Phillip took her to meet the Anglican Bishop of Salta, a tall, softly spoken man who had lived most of his life in the north. He encouraged her to learn the local dialect of Wichi Thamtes ('people words') as quickly as possible, then handed her over to his assistant, who showed her how to operate a radio and advised her to visit the hospital at Embarcación on her way up to Misión Yuchán.

The following day, Diana took her to a muddy quagmire on the city outskirts called the Barrio. This was the shanty town. Nikki was introduced to some of the people. One Bolivian family had been tempted south by promises of land and had ended up destitute. The husband had found a job on a building site but had started spending his wages on drink and had left home. His wife, her elderly father and three teenage daughters were trying to earn money by cutting the fat off bones taken from the waste-bins of the local abattoir and rendering it down to make lard. They were using an electric stove they had found on a tip and had connected it to the overhead electric cable with a pair of spring clips.

'Completely illegal of course,' Diana said. 'But what else can they do? Mind you, they pay another sort of price. A little girl was electrocuted last month. She was standing barefoot on mud, ironing her father's pants.'

They looked in at the moth-eaten Pentecostalist tent, where hollow-eyed women and children were gathering in expectation of a bowl of soup in exchange for church attendance.

'What hope is there for them?' Nikki asked.

Diana looked at her quickly. 'Plenty. There's always hope in God's love, Nikki. Shall we go back now?'

On the way to the car they passed a naval school for young ladies. 'The Navy's quite powerful up here,' Diana said. 'That's because the governor of Salta is an admiral. It makes me so angry . . .'

'Angry?'

'When I see these smart girls in their blue suits marching up and down within a stone's throw of so much poverty . . .'

'It's obscene, really.'

'Yes. That is exactly what it is. Obscene.' They got into the car. 'But do be careful,' Diana continued as they drove back. 'It's all right for

320

you and me to voice our feelings in private, but however strongly you feel, never do so in the hearing of anyone who you can't be completely certain of. And whatever you do, don't try to be a heroine by speaking out. It isn't worth it. All that will happen is that you will be arrested for subversion and we'll lose another worker. That's what happened to your brother and his wife, wasn't it?'

'I don't know,' Nikki said. 'Nobody does.'

Armed police were checking each vehicle when Nikki arrived by bus at Embarcación two days later. She had expected to be met, but as no one showed up she went and sat in the shade of the trees in the central square, where martial music was being played over loudspeakers and children came marching out of school at midday in their blue and white overalls.

Neil Hemmings drove up in a Chevrolet truck an hour later, having sprained his thumb while changing a wheel on the way. He was approaching fifty: large, bald, talkative and pleased to see her.

'I've got to pick up diesel and fertilizer, have the puncture repaired, do some shopping for Joan and collect the medical supplies from the hospital,' he said. 'Oh – and collect the mail and post some letters. Don't let me forget.'

They went to the hospital. Nikki met a doctor who made a pass at her. 'I think you must be crazy,' he said. 'I could find you a really good job here. Why waste your qualifications on the indios?'

'I don't think they will be wasted,' Nikki said. 'The greater the need, the greater the importance of the work. Don't you agree?'

The doctor laughed condescendingly and patted her bottom. 'Come back and tell me *that* in three months' time, Sweety, and I might just believe you!'

Neil's thumb was badly swollen and painful, so Nikki drove. It was a long, bumpy ride over a dirt road full of potholes. When they pulled up in the clearing in front of the two bungalows and the clinic at Misión Yuchán, the big eucalyptus trees were black against a scarlet sunset and bats were wheeling overhead.

She stepped down from the truck and looked about her.

'What's that humming noise?' she asked.

'Oh – that's the wind in the church windows,' Neil said. 'I don't even notice it now.'

The church bell rang every morning at seven o'clock. Prayers were led by Esteban, the Indian deacon, and were said in Wichi Thamtes. The days when the white missionaries conducted the services were

321

over: Neil, Joan and Nikki sat in the congregation with the handful of Wichi who still remained loyal to the mission.

Wichi Thamtes was difficult to learn. It had no relationship with English or Spanish and Nikki was not a natural linguist. But it was important that she learn it as quickly as possible in order to function as a nurse. With the help of Liliana, the Indian auxiliary, she could treat the common ailments, but there were a lot of illnesses that did not have obvious symptoms. The men were easier to treat than the women, because most of them spoke a little Spanish. But even if a Wichi woman understood Spanish she was unlikely to admit to it because that would mean that she had learnt it from a criollo man, which implied that she had slept with him, which was taken to mean that she was a prostitute.

Her bungalow consisted of a kitchen, a bathroom, a sitting area and a bedroom. Food was not plentiful, and she had to resign herself to feeling permanently hungry. On Joan's advice she baked her own bread. Breakfast consisted of a home-made roll and instant coffee with powdered milk. Joan said that one became accustomed to the reduced diet after a time, but Nikki found that difficult to believe.

After breakfast each day she started work at the clinic, which was in a hut next door to her bungalow. She found the professional isolation frightening at first. The most important thing she had learnt during training was when to refer a case to a doctor. There was no doctor at Misión Yuchán, and because of lack of equipment or drugs, many of the methods she had been taught were impracticable. She had radio contact with Salta twice a day but apart from that she was on her own. There was no bus or rail service that came anywhere near, so that if the need arose to take a patient to Embarcación the only way was to go down by road in the Chevrolet. Fortunately that situation did not often arise: the Wichi would do anything to avoid being hospitalized in Embarcación because they knew they would be treated like dirt there.

Most mornings were taken up in treating minor ailments in the clinic — cuts, abrasions, thorns in feet, abscesses, ringworm. Occasionally a criollo would be brought in with knife wounds from a fight (the criollos did a lot of fighting). But the biggest enemy was diarrhoea and vomiting among the children, and the commonest entry in her case-book columns was 'd & v'. The babies with d & v became dehydrated very rapidly and once they were past the point of no return there was nothing she could do to save them. Two babies died in her first three weeks at the mission. She prepared an emergency pack of sugar-saline solution and an intragastric drip and carried it with her when she went visiting; and she started a campaign to persuade mothers to bring their children to the clinic at the first sign of a tummy upset.

It was a constant battle to convince the people of the need for cleanliness. They simply could not comprehend it. There was a large puddle round the main village well in which black swine wallowed and where the dogs came to drink. The women spent hours chattering to each other while drawing water; their children played all around; the dogs licked their bottoms, each other and the children's faces and the bugs went round and round. It was pointless to try and persuade them that the dogs should be kept away from the children or the fresh water supply, because the Wichi were so soft on their domestic animals.

But they were not always soft. One day she was called out to see to a little girl who had been savaged by a dog. When she had stitched up her face, given antibiotics and made the child comfortable, the father, one of the village's keenest hunters and owner of the dog who had bitten her, beckoned Nikki to follow him to the bottle tree in the centre of the village to show what he had done to his daughter's attacker. It was hanging by the neck – a big dog. The rest of the pack lay around licking and scratching and looking sorry for themselves. They seemed to have got the message.

One of her most insidious enemies was the vinchuca, alias the reduviid bug. It was a large flying beetle, black with yellow-striped edges. It had a nasty smell. You heard them buzzing in the darkness and then suddenly they would drop to the floor. The bugs lived in crevices in the huts and did their dirty work at night. They bit the soft skin – usually a child's eyelid – which would be swollen by morning. The child would have flu symptoms for a few days and then the swelling and the fever would clear up of their own accord and nothing would happen for years. But the damage to the nervous system of the victim was done. The large bowel might cease to function or the oesophagus might swell up. If the nervous system regulating the heart was affected, the result could be a very slow pulse and a very sudden death. Like the vinchuca, the victim suddenly dropped.

TB was common. There were times when she felt that all she was achieving was to build immunity to the antibiotics she was using. The three-month course of streptomycin, followed by a two-year course of Nicotibina and PAS tablets would have been a challenge to the most self-disciplined of patients, but swallowing twelve large tablets a day was too much to ask of the Wichi and, unless she supervised them personally, most courses of treatment were abandoned within a few weeks. Then, usually, word would come back to the clinic that the patient was seeing the curandero.

*   *   *

Anselmo was well into his seventies. He had innumerable wives, children, grandchildren and great-grandchildren, and he exerted a powerful influence upon the people at Misión Yuchán. He was a wealthy man, and made a lot of money from private consultations. When Nikki arrived at the mission, Joan advised her to have nothing to do with him. But one day on her rounds she discovered that Anselmo had been telling the TB patients to throw away their PAS tablets.

'I'm thinking of confronting him,' Nikki said to Joan that evening.

They were sitting outside the bungalow after supper. Joan was one of those people who always had to have something to do and was mending one of Neil's shirts which had gone at the shoulder seam.

'What would you say?'

'I don't interfere with his patients. Why should he interfere with mine?'

'I wouldn't advise it,' Neil said.

Joan knotted the cotton and bit off the end. 'We tried confronting him some time ago. He laughed in our faces. No, I'm convinced that prayer power is the more effective solution. After all, you wouldn't go along to Satan and ask him to stop interfering, would you?'

'Here's a true story,' Neil said. 'A couple of years ago when Esteban was made a deacon, Anselmo put him under a curse. Esteban lost a sister, a granddaughter and his father all in the space of a month. Then his wife became ill. Esteban fell victim to acute depression. So Anselmo sent for him and said that if he didn't give up being a deacon, he'd lose not only his wife but the rest of his family, one by one and then he would die himself. Esteban came and told me and we prayed about it and discussed it, and eventually he went back to Anselmo and said, "Look, my father and my sister and my granddaughter are all in heaven, and if my wife dies she will go there too. But if I do what you say, I won't go to heaven when I die and I won't see my wife and family again."'

'What happened?' Nikki asked.

'Within a week, Esteban's wife was on the mend and all his depression had gone. There hasn't been a day's illness in the family since and Esteban has never looked back.'

There was a time of heavy rain. The village turned into a sea of mud and the road to Embarcación became impassable. The clinic ran dangerously low on essential drugs and Nikki felt the beginnings of panic. What if there was an epidemic? What if someone had a bad accident? She voiced her worries to Joan, who said, 'You just have to learn to have faith, Nikki. The Lord provides. He always has, and he always will.'

Two days later a man from the neighbouring village of Carboncito arrived on foot with the news that his son Emilio was ill with paralysis. Could she come at once to save his life?

Carboncito was three leagues away. After a difficult ride on horseback through mud, Nikki arrived at the village to find the boy paralysed from the neck down. The villagers crowded round the door while she examined him.

She asked the mother how long her son had been in this state. The woman was very frightened. 'He went hunting and was caught out in the monte during the storm two nights ago. He spent two nights out and when they found him he couldn't walk. Emilio and my sons carried him back and put him on his bed.'

She shrugged hopelessly and burst into tears.

Nikki had no idea what might be wrong with the boy. All she knew was that he had been chilled and that he was very thin. She prayed silently, 'God, help me to do the right thing.' But there didn't seem to be a 'right thing' to do. The only possible cause she could think of might be the chilling so, working on the premise that it was better to do something than nothing at all she decided to treat it by injecting Vitamin B. This had the effect of impressing the onlookers if nothing else.

'Keep him warm,' she told the mother. 'Give him hot maté to drink with plenty of sugar.'

There was no question of riding back to Misión Yuchán that day so she accepted an offer of a bed for the night. The weather had cleared, and that night the village held a dance, which was an opportunity for the village girls to choose boys for trial marriages, the theory being that if a girl got pregnant and was happy with the situation, the boy would be invited to go and live with her family.

She couldn't sleep for the noise and eventually gave up and watched. There was a big bonfire and much shouting and stamping of feet. The boys danced in a chorus line so that the girls could choose their husbands. They picked the ones they fancied and ran off with them into the monte.

When the noise finally subsided, she returned to the hut and managed a few hours of fitful sleep before dawn.

The sun came up. It was going to be a fine day. She got up and went to look in on the patient, but he was not on his bed. She found the boy's mother talking with other mothers by the well.

'Where's Emilio?' she asked.

A big smile: 'Gone out hunting with his daddy,' came the answer.

The weeks turned into months. She became gradually more fluent in Wichi Thamtes, and took to having conversations with Esteban, who was an amateur bone-setter and a great source of Indian wisdom and folklore. The only person, apart from Anselmo, who she regarded as an enemy was the young schoolteacher, Basilio, who was neither part of the mission nor the village. He was the only person at Misión Yuchán in the pay of the government, and was particularly scornful of Neil's efforts to help the Wichi run their own agricultural scheme.

'Missionaries will never teach these people to organize anything,' he told Nikki one day. 'The best thing you people can do for them is pack up and leave them to run their own lives the way they want to.'

'Then why do you stay, Basilio?'

'Because I have to *earn* a living, unlike you.'

Neil advised Nikki to be careful of what she said in Basilio's presence. Whether he had anything to do with the visit of the police, no one ever discovered, but one Sunday morning when they were coming out of church a Jeep drove up and a sergeant and four piled out and demanded to see all the missionaries together. Nikki was questioned as to her qualifications, place of birth and parentage. Then the sergeant turned to Neil.

'We understand you've banned the singing of the national anthem. Is this true?'

Neil picked up a church hymnbook and turned to the back, where a copy of the national anthem – in Spanish and Wichi – was pasted inside the back cover. 'Anybody who wishes to sing the national anthem may do so at any time of day or night,' he said.

The sergeant seemed satisfied by that and he and his men spent the rest of the morning sitting outside the pulperia drinking lemonade and flirting with the village girls.

But there was a sequel to the visit, because a few days later Juanita, a girl of thirteen who sometimes helped at the clinic, committed suicide. She had gone missing from school and was found dead by Liliana, lying behind the schoolhouse. She had taken her life the Indian way by eating honai, a pale green, striped fruit that grew in the forest and was only edible if boiled in several changes of water. Liliana said that Juanita had been going with a man in the village, but the affair had cooled, so when the police arrived she had flirted to make her man jealous. But it had had the opposite effect and he had dropped her completely.

'She ate the honai to make her man feel bad,' Liliana told Nikki.

Another death that was very painful was that of a baby not ten days old. His mother brought him to the clinic saying that he couldn't suck. Nikki got the mother to express some milk and got a little into the baby, but the next day was called out early in the morning and found that he had gone stiff and was arching backwards in his mother's arms. It was then that she recognized, too late, the symptoms of neo-natal tetanus. The baby had been delivered by Liliana under her supervision, and the tetanus had probably been caused by dirty instruments to cut the cord.

Feeling depressed, she went and prayed in the church by herself that evening, and while she was there heard a slight thud on the floor followed by running feet. When she got up to leave the church she found a dead bird on the floor by the pulpit. Its stomach had been opened and a crude wooden phallus had been inserted.

The succession of infant deaths continued regardless of her efforts. The first complete sentence she learnt in Wichi came from the hymn they sang at every child's funeral: *Hap natsas lewet han ihi*, There's a home for little children.

The cemetery was a sad place, full of vizcacha burrows and rotting wooden crosses. When she first arrived she searched it for a monument to her uncle but found none. Joan and Neil knew nothing about him, so one day when she was talking in Wichi to Esteban she asked him if he had ever heard of Dr McGeoch.

Esteban looked as if he had seen a ghost. 'How do you know about him?'

'He was my mother's brother, Esteban. Do you remember him?'

'Oh yes,' said Esteban looking more ashen than she thought possible in an Indian. 'I remember the English doctor and his wife. I was a boy when they came to Misión Yuchán. I remember them very well.'

She invited the old man back to her bungalow that evening and shared a gourd of yerba maté with him. When she asked why there was no memorial to Dr McGeoch at Misión Yuchán, Esteban became agitated and began telling her about every petty grudge and feud in the village over the past forty years. It seemed that he was willing to talk about anything at all except her uncle.

'But – do you know how my uncle died?' she asked. 'Is it true that he was killed by wild animals?'

Esteban bowed his head. 'No. Not wild animals.'

'What then?'

'Dogs.'

327

'*Dogs?* What dogs?'

'Hunting dogs from the village.'

'So it wasn't an accident?'

Esteban shook his head. There was a silence. Across the clearing, a dead leaf slipped and rolled along, blown by the evening breeze. In the eucalyptus trees, a ben-te-veo was repeating its call over and over again.

'Please tell me about it, Esteban. He was my uncle. No one ever knew how he died.'

So, haltingly and with sorrow, he told her the story of how Anselmo had put a curse on the doctor and his wife; how they had sought to educate the Wichi in matters of health just as she was doing, and how Dr McGeoch had finally brought the anger of the villagers down upon him by shooting a bitch and crushing the puppies underfoot.

'I saw him do it with my own eyes,' Esteban confessed. 'I was out early one morning and I saw him shoot the dog and kill her young. I ran back and told my mother, and my mother told Anselmo and before the sun had set the doctor was dead.'

She would never have believed, before coming to Misión Yuchán, that good and evil could be so easily and readily identified. She became quite thankful for the witchdoctor's presence in the village, because Anselmo's charms and curses provided daily proof of the evil that confronted them.

There was no doubt in her mind now that she was fighting a battle. It was a battle against spiritual as well as physical disease. It was the same battle that her uncle, her mother, Jimmy, Larry and Adriana had fought. She counted it an honour to join their ranks.

Her talk with Esteban did much to clarify her views. Now that she knew how her uncle had died, something had been unlocked for her. She began to understand her mother's attitudes more fully. She found a new sense of purpose. In an odd way, she felt that she could draw strength from the knowledge of what her uncle had worked for and why he had died.

Thanks to the old Indian deacon, she found a new confidence and a new sense of purpose. For the first time in her life she felt that she was doing something useful.

29

THE LAST CONSIGNMENT of the season's market-ready steers, destined for the meat-packers in Buenos Aires, was being loaded thirty at a time onto long-wheelbase trucks. The herd had been corralled and the peons were wheeling their ponies this way and that, shouting and whistling and making trumpeting noises to force the beasts out of the corral, along the manga and up the ramp to the lorry.

While he watched the loading, Cadoret's thoughts went ahead to the work to be done in the coming weeks. With the sales of steers completed, the next operation on the calendar was the weaning of calves and the first foot-and-mouth injections. Then there would be earmarking, parting female calves and the calving of last May's heifers. In April he'd start buying in new stock with the profits from the grain harvest. No more Brangus: once he was free of Botta and back in the driving seat he'd return to the Blacks which his father had bred with such success. In May the heifers would go to the bulls and the May heifers would replace the finished cows. He'd buy in more troops in July if he could afford it. And he should be able to afford it too, because there would be no more interest to pay Lambretti, and Tijerita and Calandria would be able to pool resources and operate as one.

Once loaded to capacity, each truck was weighed on the platform and the weight punched on a ticket for the driver to hand in to the agent at Liniers. That done each vehicle drove off along the earth road, its wheels throwing up a heavy spray of mud as it went.

Still thinking about the future, Cadoret rode back to the house. Trotting across the polo pitch he actually laughed aloud at the thought of being his own boss again. Freedom, that's what it was. No more fear. No more having to defer to some know-all twenty-two-year-old manager put in place by Stefenelli. His thoughts were so loud that he muttered to himself under his breath. 'I'll fatten 'em on short oats. I'll make a comeback. Enter a beast or two at the Palermo show. Get back into the stud business. Do Camp Week. Hold my head up again. We'll be unbeatable, Ceci and me. We'll crack 'em down the middle . . .'

* * *

He had expected to hear from Ceci's attorney within a week or so of her departure, so when three weeks had passed and he had received no word he tried to contact Ferreyra by telephone. His call was answered by a recorded message which invited him to leave his name and number, but as he was phoning from La Calandria and had just heard the tell-tale click that meant someone was listening on the party line, he hung up without giving either.

Instead, he drove over to Laboulaye to call personally on Ferreyra. He was met by the attorney's wife. She opened the door a crack and whispered to him that the office had been ransacked by the security forces and that her husband had been taken into custody. All his letters, case notes, documents, wills and contracts had been seized.

Two days later Stefenelli called round.

They met in the office. Stefenelli had been on an extended holiday and looked suntanned, healthy and opulent.

'Good news,' he said. 'We've got the government grant for the Rinconada project. We'll start building within a month and the factory should be in full production by the spring.'

This was a project that had recently been launched in Cadoret's name. It was one of many, from which Cadoret had learnt to expect little return. Land had been bought for a song in the poor area of northern Jujuy and a furniture factory was to be built with government aid. Cadoret knew that little furniture would actually be manufactured. Instead, the factory would be used as a cover for a refining centre and staging post for Bolivian cocaine. If previous experience was anything to go by, the project would operate for a year or so then go into sudden liquidation, probably at a declared loss.

'So how was your Christmas?' Stefenelli asked. 'I understand you spent it with Miss Jowett?'

Cadoret was surprised that Jorge should know this, but then reflected that he and Ceci had probably been seen together in public by Stefenelli's informers. It was best not to make any secret of it.

'That's right. We – er – seem to have got together again.'

'In more ways than one, it seems.' Stefenelli sat on the desk and swung a foot. 'Are congratulations in order, might one ask?'

Cadoret had agreed with Ceci to say nothing about marriage or property plans until Ferreyra had given the go-ahead. But with Ferreyra disappeared, everything was now uncertain.

'Well not exactly that –'

'I do believe you're blushing, Tito. What have we here? Is love in the air?'

He tried to look amused. He had an uncomfortable feeling that Stefenelli knew more than he was prepared to reveal.

Stefenelli crossed his legs, revealing a pair of black and gold silk socks. He lit a cigarette and blew smoke into the fan which was directed at Cadoret's face. Suddenly, any trace of humour in his manner was gone.

'What sort of fools do you think we are, Tito?'

The old heart started hammering again. 'Don't regard you as fools at all, Jorge.'

'No? Then why have you gone behind our backs with Miss Jowett?'

'Am I not allowed to have any private life at all?'

'Not when it comes to dealing in property to which you own no title. That's what you have been doing, isn't it?'

Cadoret did some fast thinking. 'Wait a minute, Jorge – let me explain. You stand to gain out of this –'

'With the British Consul being dragged in on Miss Jowett's side? You've been conned, Tito. By a woman, what's more.'

'Nothing's been finalized –'

'And nothing will be finalized, I can promise you that, my friend.'

Cadoret stared at the blotter on his desk.

'I understand you and Miss Jowett plan to marry.'

'We haven't announced it.'

'But you've tied things up very nicely all the same, haven't you? Mutual beneficiaries, joint ownership of title, loans without interest. Financially, you're as good as married already. We know all about it, Tito. We've got your number.'

Cadoret heard himself say, 'You can't stop me getting married.'

Jorge got off the desk and stubbed out his cigarette. 'Tell Miss Jowett the wedding's off. Otherwise –' Stefenelli drew a thumb rapidly across his throat. It was a secret sign.

Cadoret stood up. 'I can't contact her. She's touring in the south.'

'Send her a cable.'

'I have no address for her. Besides, she'll be in the Falklands by now –'

Stefenelli whipped round. 'In "the Falklands"? Where are "the Falklands", Tito? I've never heard of "the Falklands" before.'

'The Islas Malvinas.'

'I see. Visiting property that's been stolen by the English. And when she comes back she expects to steal some more, no doubt.' Stefenelli walked away, then spun on his heel. 'We've got all your papers. Your wills. Your financial agreements. We've also got the title deeds to Tijerita. That doesn't leave you with many cards to play, does it?'

331

Cadoret lunged after him as he turned to go.

'You've got my money and my house and my land. But you can't take away my right to marry. That's one thing you can't do.'

Stefenelli removed Cadoret's hand from his shoulder. 'Perhaps we can't,' he said softly. 'But I think we may be able to make it more difficult, don't you?'

'I will marry her,' Cadoret said. 'Whatever you do.'

Stefenelli winked, and smiled, and patted him on the shoulder. 'We'll see,' he said. 'We'll see.'

He told himself that he would marry Ceci come what may, but was unable to rid himself of a feeling of foreboding.

He wondered whether he should try to contact her. But what could he say? If he referred to Ferreyra's disappearance he would be breaking the law, and as Ceci was staying at the Governor's residence while at Stanley, anything he might say, whether on the telephone or in a telex, would certainly be intercepted and passed back through the intelligence network to the security forces. Having sought contacts in high places for so long, he was now entangled in the strings he had once endeavoured to pull. Having friends like Admiral Massera and Colonel Ocampo meant that he was condemned to have his every action watched. For the first time, he became aware of a possibility that his life might be in danger, that he might suffer the same sort of fate as Stiffy Rathbone.

Being unable to think of anything positive to do, he decided to do nothing. For a while, nothing happened. Then, on the Saturday following Stefenelli's visit, he was rung up in the office by Botta himself.

'Jorge tells me you and Miss Jowett plan to get married. Is that right?'

'Yes, that's right.'

'So you haven't changed your mind.'

He felt his heart begin to labour. 'No. And I don't intend to.'

'In that case you're a fool.'

'Is that all you rang to tell me, Rui?'

'I rang to give you another chance, Tito. And I'm still prepared to do that.'

He surprised himself then. He said, 'Go to hell,' and put the phone down.

He felt an immediate sense of exhilaration. He didn't understand why he felt the way he did at first, but then it dawned on him that he had at last broken free. All his life he had put property

332

before conscience. He had become enslaved to material things and the vanity of success. Now, for the first time in his life, he had managed to reverse those priorities. The extraordinary thing about it was that he was aware of a certainty and a peace of mind that he had never experienced before. He *knew* that what he had done was right. There was no question of it. He had promised Ceci he would marry her and this time he was determined to keep his word.

Two mornings after Botta's call, when he was at breakfast, the maid brought the telephone in so that he could take a personal call, long distance.

'Mr Cadoret?'

'Yes?'

'Phillip Dalligan here. I'm speaking from the Bishop's office in Salta.'

He had no idea why a Dalligan should be ringing him, let alone from a bishop's office up in the north. Then he made the connection. Nikki.

'I'm afraid I have bad news. We heard on the radio telephone from Misión Yuchán that your daughter was arrested late last night.'

'Who by?'

'As far as we know, members of the security forces.'

'But why? On what charge?'

There was a pause at the other end of the line, then: 'We have no idea why she's being held or where or who by, Mr Cadoret. I'm sorry. We'll let you know immediately we hear anything further. In the meantime we're all praying for Nikki here, and I'm sure you will, too.'

'Yes,' he muttered. 'Yes, I will.' He rang off and was still sitting at the table with the telephone in his hands when Rosa came in to clear away the breakfast.

'Shall I take the telephone, sir?' she asked.

'No, leave it with me,' he said, and dialled a number.

Botta's chuckle echoed over the line.

'Tito! I was wondering when you'd be in touch. So tell me, what can we do for you?'

'The one memory of the Islands that I shall carry with me to my dying day,' said Ceci as the taxi pulled away from Jorge Newbury airport, 'is that of the relentless, screaming, buffeting wind. It is like an animal, that wind. It whines and it growls, it barks and it howls. It leaps out at you with claws and teeth. Yes. That's what I shall always remember about the Falklands. The wind. The awful, crying wind . . .'

333

She had hardly stopped talking from the moment she came into the arrivals hall. Looking a little like Barbara Cartland in diaphanous pink, and followed by a porter who wheeled her matching luggage along on a trolley, she had flung herself into Cadoret's arms, told him she loved him to the end of time and had then embarked upon the long litany of things she had been saving up to say to him over the past five weeks.

'And of course one can hardly begin to describe the sheer variety and multiplicity of the wildlife, my dear. Priceless little rockhopper penguins by the thousand. Cormorants, steamer ducks – do you know that there are no mammal predators on the Islands? Wonderful, wonderful seals of course. Bull seals, elephant seals. And albatrosses, of course. They call them Molly Mawks over there. Great skuas. And those lovely brave little birds – oh! I can't for the life of me remember their name – which come in on the waves and leap up vertical precipices. Tito, darling, where are you taking me?'

'The Sheraton.'

She went pink with happiness. She held his hand and kissed him and snuggled closer. 'Darling! You remembered! Kind, thoughtful boy!'

He looked uncomfortable. 'And – how was Tierra del Fuego?'

'Absolutely breathtaking. You would think that you were on a different planet, Tito, honestly. And do you know, I never realized before how travel gives you an entirely new perspective on things. I wouldn't have missed this tour for the world. I feel like a new woman, do you know that? It's been far more than a tour – more like a spiritual experience. A renewal. Oh, are we here?'

'Looks like it,' he said and having summoned a porter to take charge of her luggage, escorted Ceci into the hotel.

They held hands in the lift. 'What a lovely romantic thought this was of yours, darling,' she said, and gave his hand a squeeze.

They stepped out on the top floor and made their way to the same table by the window in the Aljibe Bar where they had sat on New Year's Eve. On the roof garden, the band was playing 'Moon River'.

Ceci settled back with a sigh. 'You know – I'm glad I went, but I'm so *much* gladder to be back with you, Tito.'

'It's very good to see you,' he said.

A girl in a flared miniskirt asked them if they would take drinks from the bar.

'What would you like?' Tito asked.

'Well – I think champagne, don't you, darling?'

He agreed and, when the girl had gone, turned back with a look of agony on his face which Ceci did not notice because she was gazing out over the sprawling city.

'So what's been happening?' she asked, and patted his knee. 'Tell me all about everything.'

'I'm afraid it's not very good news,' he said. 'Ferreyra was arrested a couple of weeks after your departure.'

Ceci's eyes opened wide and her head went back in surprise. 'Why on earth didn't you cable me, Tito?'

He shook his head. 'It would only have made matters worse. You see – I think Botta was behind it. I have no proof, but he's found out about us.'

'You mean – the deal.'

'Yes.'

'But not our marriage plans?'

'No, he knows about that as well.'

Ceci shook her head and laughed nervously. Her fingers fluttered about, patting the back of his hand. 'Well – it needn't make any difference, need it? We're not going to let Botta upset our plans, are we?'

Cadoret looked down at the traffic crawling along the Avenida del Libertador. 'That's what I told him.'

She gripped his hand. 'Good for you, Sweet. Good for you.'

The champagne arrived. He waited while the cork was pulled and the wine poured, and when the bottle was back in its bucket and the waiter had gone, he turned to her. His face had lost all its usual colour and there were beads of sweat standing on the loose skin of his cheeks.

'Ceci, my dear – I have something terrible I must tell you.'

'What?' she said faintly.

'Something happened which – which I'm not allowed to tell you about.'

'Who says? Botta?'

'Yes.'

'But Tito we agreed! We said –'

'Ceci you are going to have to be very patient with me. You must understand. They've put me in an impossible situation.'

'What are you saying, Tito? What are you trying to tell me?'

He looked down at the champagne fizzing in the glass and said, 'I can't marry you.'

She sat stock still and closed her eyes. 'What do you mean?'

'It's Botta. He's – he's made it impossible for me to marry you. I can't tell you why because if I do, well, I can't tell you. I'm sorry.'

335

'No,' she said in a sort of dry croak. 'No, Tito. Not again. Not all over again.'

'I have no choice.'

'Why? Why?'

'I can't tell you why. Perhaps one day I shall be able to. Perhaps you will understand why from events, I don't know. But now – I just can't tell you. I'm sorry, Ceci. Believe me I am sorry . . .'

But Ceci was not listening to him. She was gazing out over the city and a tumult of memories was rushing through her mind. It was as if the road of her life – she had always thought of life as a road – had suddenly petered out ahead of her and she had no further to go.

She stood up and looked nervously about her. Then she took off her shoes. It was a silly thing to do, but something that went right back to her childhood, because she had always been able to run faster in bare feet. And now she needed to run.

She ran between the tables, past the people who turned and stared. She ran out onto the roof and past the band; and she knew that now she had started running, she must not stop, not stop for one instant. Keep going, keep going, she told herself, and was hardly aware of vaulting onto the balustrade.

High, high on the castle. I'm the queen of the castle, get down, you dirty rascal . . .

Then everything slowed down. She was standing on the balustrade with the city spread out beneath her and the gentle breeze of Buenos Aires was billowing out her pink dress.

She heard a voice calling to her. It was her father's voice, the father who had died when she was ten years old, the father she had loved so much. 'Ceci!' he called. 'Ceci!'

'Coming!' she replied – and she plunged forward, out and away from the cares of this world, out and away from Tito and the terror and tragedy and filthiness of life, out and away, and down and down, with her dress flapping like a broken wing round her head and her reflection in the hotel windows following her down and down and down, all the way down to the final smack of bone and flesh.

A group of young people – the jet set – were arriving at the hotel. The men were excited because they had just seen a woman jump from the top floor. They were laughing and whistling and whooping as they came in by the glass doors and crossed the lobby to push the call buttons for the lifts.

When the first lift arrived, an elderly man with white hair and a white moustache and a grey face stepped out. They pushed past him and crammed in.

'Yeeehaaa!' shouted one of the men as the lift doors closed, and smacked a fist against his palm.

30

SNOW HAD COME EARLY to the Hampshire village of Bishop's Waltham. By New Year's Day it was three inches thick in the paddock where Rick and Zoe Mallard intended to hold their annual families' football match. But there was no question of cancelling. The New Year's Day football match in the Mallards' paddock had become a tradition, and the naval families of Hampshire's 'navy-blue belt' who attended it took a delight in braving the elements.

Rick and his three sons spent the morning getting the glühwein ready, laying the barbecue and clearing the snow from the drive, a task they were still completing when the first guests arrived.

The Rovers, Peugeots and Volvos backed up against the hedge at the front of Park Cottage in a neat row. Muffled and scarved commanders, toddlers, teenage daughters, prep school boys, golden retrievers and cheerful wives spilled out onto the snowy gravel. There was a lot of Happy New Year-ing and kissing, during which Ian Ringrose's Jack Russell, Scrap, shot off in pursuit of the Mallards' ginger tom, which stood spitting at bay with its back arched under a snow-laden copper beech.

'Don't worry about Mussolini!' Rick shouted after Louise Ringrose, who was floundering after Scrap up to the top of her green wellies in snow. 'He's perfectly capable of looking after himself!'

Parents and children made their way down past the fruit cage to the paddock, and Rick's younger brother Vanden – a wild, freckly, overgrown schoolboy who was a captain in the Paratroop regiment and was known universally as 'Van' – organized everyone into teams.

There were about twenty a side and the ages ranged from three to forty-three. Most of the fathers were commanders and all of them had either served in the same ships or had been to the same schools or through Dartmouth together.

The paddock sloped down to the boundary fence, so there was a tendency for the side playing downhill to score the most goals. Some of the West Downs prep school boys had to be restrained from playing too rough, and four-year-old Penny Courtenay, whose father had just

338

heard that he was to be promoted to captain, was led off proudly bearing a bloody nose without so much as shedding a tear over it.

At nineteen goals all, Van Mallard received a pass from his youngest offspring and made a determined push up the hill through the snow until only Rob McNairne and six-year-old Lucy, the McNairne's only child, stood between him and the goalposts. Lucy was plucked out of the way by her mother just before the titans clashed. Van caught Rob off balance with a shoulder charge which sent him sprawling on his back in the snow before going on to score the winning goal.

Everyone cheered everyone else and then it was time for glühwein and hot dogs.

'Thought you were taking that a bit seriously, Van,' Rob remarked when their glasses were full.

Van was the only army officer present and regarded naval officers as smoothies. 'No point in playing a game unless you intend to win,' he growled.

The old friends gathered. They were all members of the rising generation of naval families, a loosely knit élite, a culture within a culture, a club within a club. They lived in villages like Meonstoke and Droxford and Soberton and Swanmore and Corhampton. Most of the husbands were ship captains or first lieutenants or staff officers. Their wives met on school runs, at dinner parties, speech days and the official cocktail parties that were held aboard their husbands' ships, and their children went to the same boarding schools and the same birthday parties.

But that year after the Mallards' football match, there was a slight sense of unease among the naval officers who stamped their boots in the snow and sipped their hot wine. Though Margaret Thatcher's election victory two and a half years before had been hailed as the end of the Navy's wilderness years, the appointment of John Nott as Secretary of State for Defence had sent a shiver of apprehension down the spines of naval people.

It seemed that the process of emasculating the Royal Navy, started in the sixties under a Labour government, was now to be completed under Thatcher. Though never stated in so many words, Nott's message was clear and uncompromising: Britain could no longer afford to maintain a first-rate Navy. The last of the old capital ships – the aircraft carriers *Ark Royal* and *Hermes* – were to be scrapped or sold. The brand new mini-carrier *Invincible* was to be sold to Australia. The days of the amphibious support ships *Intrepid* and *Fearless* were numbered, and the frigate fleet was to be cut by a quarter with immediate effect.

But life had to go on, and the talk at the Mallards' party on that first day of 1982 was of the latest promotions and appointments rather than politics, and of a frigate captain who had recently been relieved of his command for failing to bully the dockyard into completing his ship's refit adequately and on time.

When the hot dogs and glühwein were almost finished and Zoe had gone into the house to fetch the mince pies from the oven, a red Mini came scrunching up the snowy drive and parked under a tree which sent down a white, powdery shower as the driver – a nursing sister wearing the navy-blue uniform cloak with a scarlet lining of Queen Alexandra's Royal Naval Nursing Service – stepped out and made her way down to the crowd of guests who warmed their hands at the brazier and sipped their hot wine.

'Sorry I'm late!' she said, self-conscious at being the only person in uniform.

At the sound of her voice, Rob McNairne turned quickly. It was Nikki Cadoret – or rather, Sister Nicola Cadoret, QARNNS.

She had been sitting with a bag over her head, naked, when the guard kicked her in the back and told her she was to be transferred. She had been told to take a shower and given clothes to wear and had been marched into an office where an Air Force major tried to make her sign a statement admitting that she had worked for the People's Revolutionary Army.

When she refused, the major took a different line. He said that he had it in his power to get her released. He tempted her with food and privileges and promised that if she agreed to cooperate with him her situation could be improved immeasurably. He spoke with suavity and persuasion. He said that they could be good together and that if she agreed to work as his personal assistant and act as an undercover agent to infiltrate the Madres de Mayo, she could live very comfortably as his mistress. He left his chair and came and stood behind her and tried to fondle her breasts, but she lashed out and broke his sunglasses.

She was dragged outside and pushed into a helicopter in which another detainee sat with his head in a bag and his feet set in a lump of concrete. The helicopter took off and flew low and fast and when it was over the Paraná River she was made to watch as they pushed the other prisoner out of the door.

'Now will you reconsider your decision?' the major asked when the helicopter landed back, but she refused to speak, having already made up her mind that it would be better to die than cooperate.

She expected to be taken out and shot, but she was put into another helicopter and when they landed she saw with amazement that they were at Ezeiza International Airport.

'You're a brave kid,' said the young officer who drove her across the tarmac to an awaiting jet. She recognized him by his shoes, which she had glimpsed from underneath the bag in her weeks of imprisonment. He had tried often and hard to have sex with her but she had always fought him off. He gave her back her passport and had the effrontery to pat her on the back and wish her good luck. 'No hard feelings, okay?' were the last words he said to her.

And then – it was like a dream – she found herself going up the steps of the jet. An air hostess in a pleated tartan skirt was helping her to her seat by the window and the aircraft captain was welcoming his passengers aboard this British Caledonian aircraft, and hoping that they would all have a pleasant flight.

The plane rushed down the runway and into the sky. It climbed swiftly. Nikki looked down out of her window and, for a few brief moments, caught a last glimpse of Argentina.

Then the reaction began to set in. She sat with her head bowed and the tears streamed down her face. After a while, one of the air hostesses came and sat beside her and Nikki broke down. The hostess – Nikki never discovered her name – took her in her arms and comforted her.

She went back to the missionary society and was for a while supported by them; but the situation was unsatisfactory. She found it impossible to talk frankly about her ordeal and when it was hinted to her that she might have invited trouble by becoming involved in Argentine politics, she saw that she must break with missionary work and try to start a new life.

She returned to nursing and for a few months worked at the Middlesex Hospital in London; but no sooner had she started than she found herself being pressurized to take part in industrial action for more pay. She had never had the slightest interest in politics and when she saw an advertisement for the QARNNS, the prospect of becoming part of an organization with a tradition of service and excellence appealed to her. So she applied, was called for interview and within a year was commissioned. Now, she was working at the Haslar Naval Hospital in Gosport.

'Come and meet everybody,' Zoe Mallard said. 'Who don't you know?'

Rob, Clare and Lucy left immediately. 'Will you contact her?' Clare asked as he drove back to their married quarter on Portsdown Hill.

He braced himself for the conflict to come. 'Of course I won't.'

'Why "of course"? I would have thought if there was any "of course" about it, it would have been of course you *will*.'

He said nothing. Lucy was in the back. He had no wish to fight with Clare in front of her.

'You'll certainly have ample opportunity, won't you?'

'Why?'

'For God's sake, Rob! Do you really expect me to believe that you'll sit on board in your cabin every evening for the next three weeks without once picking up the telephone and getting in touch with her?'

He glanced in the driving mirror. 'I would much rather we talked about this some other time.'

'Yes, I bet you would.'

He was silent again. How long was it now? Summer of '72, that was when Clare had had her car smash. Almost ten years. Ten years of carefully stitching together what had been broken, ten years of admitting that he was to blame, ten years of reassuring Clare that he loved her. Ten years of trying to convince himself that he had never loved or been loved by Nikki.

Clare had had a miscarriage as a result of her accident. It had added to her shock and distress. She had broken more than bones: on the day she came out of hospital, Rob had been told by the hospital almoner that unless he pulled out all the stops to help his wife recover mentally as well as physically, there was a danger that she might descend into a state of chronic depression.

It had been a long, hard struggle and there had been many setbacks on the way. Over and over again, usually when he was just beginning to think that the whole ghastly episode was finally behind him, something would happen or something would be said to remind Clare, and all her bitterness and recrimination would come pouring out again. Now, as he turned off the A27 and began the climb up Portsdown Hill, he made up his mind that he would not permit Clare to open that old, deep wound again.

He had good reason, too: he was at an important stage in his naval career. Three weeks before, he had been appointed at short notice as Squadron Marine Engineering Officer of a guided-missile destroyer squadron. At about the same time he had completed the purchase of a seventeenth-century farmhouse in Devon, just outside Plymouth. He would be moving Clare and Lucy down there within the week and having done so, would then return to his ship, attend a week's Damage Control refresher course then sail for a six-week work-up at Portland during which his department would come under the close scrutiny of the Flag Officer Sea Training's staff.

'I would like a quick word behind a closed door,' he said to Clare as they were getting out of the car, and when they were alone in the dining room where teachests were full of wrapped crockery and pictures were stacked against the wall, he set about reassuring her all over again.

'I feel nothing for her whatsoever,' he said. 'I don't want to see her, I don't want to meet her, I don't want to have anything to do with her. Will you please accept that?'

Clare regarded him bitterly. 'I don't have much choice in the matter, do I?'

'Yes you do. You do have a choice. You can say yes for a change. Can't you? You can say, "Yes, I believe you and I trust you."'

'But I don't believe you, Rob. I don't believe you and I don't trust you.'

He looked out of the window at the white roofs of Cosham, with Portsmouth Harbour, Gosport, Lee-on-Solent and the Isle of Wight beyond.

'Do you think you ever will be able to trust me?'

'I doubt it.'

'But don't you see that you would be much happier if you could?'

'I don't expect to be happy any more,' she said. 'Not really happy, the way I was once. You killed all that. It's no good trying to get it back, because it just isn't there any more. Now if you don't mind I want to get on with the packing.'

Nothing he said could convince her that he did not intend to take up with Nikki again. For a full week he tried every possible way of reassuring her. When he suggested he take her to London to see a show she poured scorn on the idea. When he offered her breakfast in bed she said no thank you, she wanted to get up and wash her hair. When he told her that he loved her she put on a hard, ironical smile and turned away from him with a snort of contempt. No, she did not want to talk things out; no, she did not want to go for a walk on Old Winchester Hill; no, she did not wish to make love. By the time the day of the move came, he was beginning to believe that she actually enjoyed making everything as difficult as possible.

The move went as smoothly as could be expected, and they spent a final strained weekend together in their new home. They had hoped to move before Christmas, but it had not been possible. As a result there was a long list of things to be done – doors to be repaired, tap

343

washers to be replaced, pictures to be hung, the washing machine to be plumbed in – that he could have done himself but which Clare would now have to see to.

'I've been thinking,' she said after lunch on his last day at home. 'Why don't you get in touch with Nikki after all?'

He looked at her. 'Are you serious?'

'Yes, I'm serious.'

'You really think that would be a good idea?'

'Well you'd look her up if you were free, wouldn't you? If I wasn't in the way you two would have married by now. So why not get in touch?'

'What are you saying? Do you want to split up?'

She laughed. 'Well I don't want to go on the way we are, Rob, that's for sure.'

'I've tried very hard, you know.'

'Oh – I know. That's been quite obvious. But you shouldn't have to try, should you? It should come naturally. Do you think I enjoy the way things are now? Do you think I enjoy listening to you trying to patch things up the whole time when I know you can't stop thinking about Nikki?'

He shook his head. There was a long silence.

'All the same,' he said eventually, 'I don't see how meeting her's going to help either of us.'

'At least you'd know one way or the other, wouldn't you? I mean, if you fell into each other's arms on the spot we'd all know where we stood. We could get on with a divorce. On the other hand, it's just possible that the two of you might not hit it off. In which case you'd be able to come back and behave like an ordinary husband and father for a change instead of giving me all this ersatz love for breakfast, dinner and tea. Doesn't that make sense?'

'I don't know,' he said sullenly. 'I don't know anything any more.'

She drove him to Plymouth station. 'See you when I see you,' she said, and left him standing on the bitter, windswept platform.

After dinner on board the following Saturday, when his ship was alongside at Portsmouth and most of the other officers were either at home with their wives or on a run ashore with the weapons-electrical officer, Rob gave up reading through his departmental orders and decided to take Clare at her word. He put his coffee cup down, looked at the phone on his desk for a few moments and finally picked it up and gave the dockyard operator the number of the QARNNS mess at the Royal Naval Hospital, Haslar.

Suddenly her voice was in his ear.

'Sister Cadoret speaking.'

'Nikki,' he said. 'It's me. Rob.'

She was silent for so long that he thought they might have been cut off.

'Are you still there, Nikki?'

'Yes, I'm still here.'

'I was wondering if you'd like to meet?'

Again she was silent.

He said, 'It would be very good to see you again.'

He heard her sigh, then: 'No, Rob. I don't think so.'

He frowned. There was another silence. 'How are you?'

'Oh – all right.'

'Are you off-duty now?'

'Yes.'

'I could jump on a ferry and come over to Gosport.'

Another silence.

'Would you like me to?'

'I'm not sure.' He heard a catch in her breath. 'Yes, I suppose I would.'

'Look – I tell you what. I'll leave it to you. I'll take a walk down to Railway Jetty and come over on the ferry. You've got a car, haven't you? So – so if you're there to meet me, we can take it from there. Okay?'

The longest silence of all, this time. Then: 'Okay.'

'In about half an hour then.'

'All right. Rob –'

'What?'

'If you decide not to catch the ferry after all, I'll understand.'

'I'll see you very soon,' he said, and they rang off.

He changed out of mess undress. He threw on corduroys, a tweed jacket, a trench coat and a tweed hat and went out of his cabin and aft along the upper deck to the brow.

The officer-of-the-day and the quartermaster came to attention at his approach. 'I'll be ashore for a couple of hours,' he told them, then raised his hat as he went over the side and walked briskly away with his hands in his coat pockets, through the dockyard, past Nelson's *Victory* and out through the main gate.

The Gosport ferry came alongside with a scrunch of tyre fenders. It was a clear night with a bitterly cold wind. He looked back at the lights of Portsmouth as the ferry moved away from the jetty, then turned to look forward to the lights of Gosport and the submarine

345

base. He felt as if he were leaving one life behind and starting a new one.

The ferry slowed, turned and went alongside. He walked up the ramp from the pontoon landing stage and out past the ticket kiosk to the end of Gosport High Street.

He stood for a few minutes wondering if she had decided not to meet him after all. Perhaps her car wouldn't start. Perhaps it would be better to turn round now and catch the next ferry back across the dark oily water to Portsmouth. Perhaps it would be better to forget about her once and for all.

Then a Mini came round the roundabout and drew up five yards from him. Nikki reached across to unlock the passenger door. He got in beside her and they gazed at each other, each startled by the other's presence, each unsure what use to make of the moment, now that it had arrived.

They drove out of Gosport. 'Where are you taking me?' he asked.

'A pub, I guess.'

They went past the naval school of engineering on whose staff he had been working until only a few weeks before.

'It's been a long time,' he said, and she replied, 'It's been a very long time.'

They found a forgettable little pub near the railway on the edge of Fareham. They sat down in their coats by a fake coal fire in the saloon bar and looked at each other. She said, 'I don't think we should be doing this.'

'Why not?'

'Second time round. It never works.'

'You sound as if you know.'

A train rumbled over the bridge. 'I feel like something out of *Brief Encounter*.' She smiled sadly. 'It'll only end in tears.'

'I rang you at Clare's suggestion, believe it or not. She was the one who suggested I should look you up.'

'She was probably interested to see if you would. Anyway, how are things in that direction?'

'All right, I suppose.' He sighed heavily. 'No they're not. They're not all right at all. In fact they're bloody.'

'In that case I don't see how meeting me's going to help.'

He turned a beer mat round and round on the table, then looked up. 'You've changed, Nikki.'

'I'm older. Bit wiser too, I hope.'

'How long have you been in the Quarns?'

346

'Just on three years.'

He reached out and pushed back a lock of her hair to reveal a burn scar on her neck. 'How did you do that?'

She smiled quickly. 'Oh . . . some silly party.'

He put his hand over hers and they were silent. In the far corner of the bar, a fruit machine flashed its lights and regurgitated ten coins in rapid succession.

'I gather you've just been promoted?'

He nodded.

'So things can't be all that bad.'

'Success as a naval officer doesn't necessarily mean success as a person.'

'That sounds like a quotation.'

'"Love means never having to say you're sorry?"'

'Something like that.'

She lit a cigarette.

'You never used to smoke.'

'Well I do now.'

'Did I drive you to it?'

She smiled and shook her head.

'Tell me then. What's been happening to you?'

She looked away. 'Oh . . . nothing very interesting. I worked on a mission in the north of Argentina for a bit but it didn't work out so –'

'What?'

She shrugged. 'I came back to England. Took the Queen's shilling.' She looked at him quizzically. 'You're going grey, Rob.'

'And thin on top.'

'And you've got a daughter.'

'Yes.'

'And you've just moved house.'

'Where did you find all this out?'

'Rick told me.'

'Did he . . . say anything about Clare and me?'

She shook her head. 'Are things very bad?'

He suddenly found himself telling her much more than he had intended. About Clare's long and difficult recovery after her accident; about her anger over losing a baby; about the strain he felt of having to accept the blame for it all; about the way Clare had of allowing the wound to heal only to open it up, over and over again.

'I'm to blame – I know that. I've admitted it to Clare and I've apologized – I don't know how many times. But I don't think there

347

is anything I can say or do that will change things now. I thought Lucy would improve matters. We both did. But if anything, she makes matters worse. A mother and a daughter can form a formidable alliance, you know. There's very little I do or say that's right these days – as far as either of them are concerned. I just don't know what the way out is. There seems no way out. When Clare suggested I should contact you I thought – well, maybe she's right.'

'I don't think she would have really wanted us to meet, Rob.'

'But that's the trouble, you see. She will not say what she means. Everything is in a sort of code. Still. What about you? Any men on the horizon?'

'If there are, they don't get any closer.'

'Why not?'

'I don't let them.' She smiled quickly, then looked aside into the slowly rotating red glow of the fake fire. 'Anyway, I'm not sure if I want to get married any more.'

'I'd marry you tomorrow if I could.'

'That's what they all say.'

She had a new way of smiling. It was a reluctant, lopsided smile that contained hurt and anger.

'Things could change,' he said. 'And I have a feeling that they are going to, too. Coming across on the ferry this evening I had a sort of premonition. I feel as if I'm about to begin a completely new stage in my life.'

She rested her chin on her hands. 'All I know is, I don't want to be the cause of you and Clare breaking up.'

'You wouldn't be the cause. I would. And anyway, I'm beginning to think that it might be for the best.'

She looked at the table and shook her head. 'No, Rob. Please. Don't use me as an excuse. I did enough damage the last time round.'

'Listen. It wasn't you that did the damage. Clare and I were getting bored with each other before I met you in Edinburgh. I sometimes think that meeting you actually prolonged the marriage. Clare wouldn't have had that accident and I wouldn't have felt obliged to try so hard with her. She would have found some chartered accountant or stockbroker to take her skiing every winter.' He smiled sadly. 'And with a bit of luck, I might have found you.'

They sat in silence for a while, then she said she ought to be going back. Before getting into the car, they walked along by the head of Fareham creek. It was low tide. Boats were lying at all angles in mud berths. An icy wind was whistling in the rigging and making loose halyards tap and ring against the masts.

He took her arm. 'I haven't asked you anything about your family. Or Argentina for that matter.'

'I don't know much about either. I haven't been back for four years.'

'Your father still alive?'

'When I last heard, yes. He's retired now.'

'And your brothers?'

'One of them married and they had a baby –'

'Oh, that's good news –'

'No. It isn't. They were disappeared.'

'What do you mean?'

'They were abducted when the baby was six weeks old. Nothing's been seen or heard of them since.'

'Oh no! That's terrible!'

She shrugged. 'That's Argentina.'

'What of your other brothers? Do you hear from them?'

'Not a lot. There isn't much point in writing. You can never guarantee that letters will be delivered.'

'So . . . have you got any plans to go back?'

'I don't have any plans at all. I gave up planning years ago.'

'What's happened to you, Nikki?'

That angry smile again. 'Life.'

He took her in his arms.

'I love you,' he whispered. 'I've always loved you.'

She pulled away from him. 'Don't,' she said. 'It's not worth it.'

On the way back to Gosport he asked her if they could meet again the following day. 'It's the last chance we'll have for some time. We sail on Monday for Portland and immediately after the work-up we sail for Springtrain.'

'What's that?'

'NATO exercise.'

'I don't think we should meet again, Rob.'

'Well may I ring you?'

'What's the point? Why not just go back to your wife?'

They drew up at the end of Gosport High Street. They sat in the car and stared at each other just as they had done when they had met two hours before.

'I don't know what to say,' he muttered.

'Don't say anything. Just walk away. Think of Clare. Think of Lucy. Think of yourself for that matter.'

He heaved another deep sigh.

'Go,' she whispered, and kissed him on the cheek.

He got out of the car and stood looking in at her.

'Keep safe, Nikki.'

'You too, Rob.'

The passenger door didn't shut properly. 'You have to slam it,' she said. He did so and, with a final wave through the window, turned and strode away to the ferry.

Clare had just arrived home from doing the school run with Lucy when the phone rang.

It was Rob. 'We're in. How's things?'

'Fine. Do you want to be collected?'

'Well I suppose I could get a taxi –'

'No, it's all right. I'll come and pick you up.'

'I can't get off much before six. Come and have a drink on board. Bring Lucy if she'd like to come.'

'I can't very well leave her, can I?'

'Suppose not. How are you?'

'I told you. Fine.'

'Lucy's new school still okay?'

'Yes.'

'Right well – see you about six?' He gave her the ship's berth and directions how to find it, then rang off.

Clare returned to the kitchen and began buttering malt bread for Lucy's tea.

She didn't really want Rob home. In the space of eight weeks she had sorted out the house on her own, fitted herself and Lucy into a new routine and settled into a way of life in which Rob played no part. That was what you had to do as a naval wife. It was the only alternative to spending a life in tears, either longing for your man to come back, adjusting to his presence or dreading his next departure.

In the old days – the days before Rob picked up his Argentinian girlfriend, before the marriage fell apart – she used to get tremendously excited about his arrival back from sea. Hearing his voice on the phone, going down to the ship, having drinks on board in the wardroom – it had acted upon her like an aphrodisiac so that by the time they arrived home she could hardly get between the sheets with him quickly enough.

Not any more: the only reason for looking forward to having Rob home now was for his value as a handyman to fix things that needed fixing before he took off again in his ship.

She stared out of the kitchen's latticed window at the daffodils and jonquils that were bursting into flower in the apple orchard and told herself that she should be grateful for what she had. This house was beautiful – there was no doubt of that. Its old ship's beams, its inglenook fireplaces, sagging ceilings and whitewash, its rambling garden, orchard and paddock fulfilled a dream. What was more, she was financially secure: Rob was successful in his career and she had inherited capital from her mother. Lucy was happy at her new school. She was learning to ride and Clare had decided to give her a pony for her seventh birthday.

Rob had just finished his work-up. In a week's time his ship would sail in company with other ships on a cruise (it was called a group deployment these days) that would take them through the Mediterranean and the Suez Canal to India and the Far East. They would be visiting Gibraltar, Naples, Alexandria, Djibouti, Colombo, Singapore and Hong Kong. Rob had already suggested that she pack and follow during the deployment – leave Lucy with friends and come out to Gib, Singapore and Hong Kong while the ship was in port.

Ten years ago she would have leapt at the chance.

But now? No. Being the middle-aged wife of the SMEO was hardly the same as being the newly married bride of a randy lieutenant. Besides, the Royal Navy of 1982 was a different animal from the Navy she had known in the early seventies. There would be no escaping for idyllic weekends on Lantau Island; no twisting at the Go Down at three in the morning; no late-night street suppers; no trips up-country in Malaya; no nights of bliss in Government Rest Houses or midnight skinny-dips on beaches that shone like silver under a flaxen moon.

All that was gone for good. It was part of a Navy that was no more.

No thanks, she thought. I'll stay home and teach Lucy to ride. Then the phone rang again.

'Me again. Look, if it'd be easier for you, I can get a lift back with the doctor. He lives in Plymstock so it's only five minutes on for him.'

'I'm perfectly willing to collect you, Rob.'

'Well – which would you prefer?'

She felt suddenly impatient. This was typical of Rob. He was for ever deferring to her. 'All right, I will take a decision for you. I will bring Lucy and collect you at six o'clock.'

'No,' he said in his decisive naval officer's voice. 'If you're going to be in that sort of frame of mind, I'd rather you didn't come on board at all. I'll come with Doc Haines.'

'Fine,' she said, and they left it at that.

They drove up in a Landrover, Rob in a tweed suit, Haines still in his surgeon lieutenant's uniform, with red between the two gold stripes on his sleeve.

They both looked as if they could do with a good night's sleep. 'This is Ian, our tame doctor,' Rob said, getting out of the Landrover, and she liked him immediately: a man with an honest smile, hair that was nearly black, blue eyes that twinkled when he smiled. She sighed inwardly. Rob had been like that, a long time ago.

'Come in for a drink,' Rob said, but Haines said no, he wouldn't, and Clare knew that he was itching to get home to his wife.

The Landrover drove off. She followed Rob into the house. In the hall, he dumped his grip and kissed her tentatively.

'Good work-up?' she asked.

'Excellent. The engineroom department got a "Good" which in Portland terms means almost perfect. Everyone's very chuffed.'

They went into the sitting room where a log fire was burning and Lucy was curled up on the sofa watching television.

'Hullo Lucy! How's you?'

Lucy was on the plump side. She glanced back over her shoulder and said a cool hullo.

Clare went into the kitchen. Rob followed.

'What about you?'

'Me?'

'Well – how's everything?'

She shrugged. 'Under control. We've had our work-up as well, Lucy and I.' Then she turned and caught him off guard. 'Did you contact Nikki?'

'What?'

'You heard.'

'I'm going to make myself a horse's neck,' he said. 'Gin and tonic for you?'

'No thank you.'

While he was out of the kitchen she held onto the edge of the sink to stop her hands shaking.

He came back with his drink.

'So you did see Nikki, did you?'

'At your suggestion, yes, I did.' He leant against the stainless-steel rail of the Aga. 'And before you run away in auto, may I get a word in edgeways?'

She sighed. 'I would rather you didn't. I don't want a shouting match and I don't want another long string of excuses.'

352

'What do you want?'

'What do I want?' She breathed out and shook her head. 'I'll tell you what I want. I want an end to all this. I want it to stop. That's what I want.'

They stood in silence.

'Would you like me to turn round and go back on board?'

'I wouldn't mind.'

'Sure you don't want to hear about my meeting with Nikki?'

'Quite sure.'

'It was your idea, wasn't it?'

'What was?'

'Practically the last thing you said to me before we left for the station was, "Why don't you look Nikki up?" That's what you said.'

'I suppose it didn't occur to you I might be forcing you to make a decision?'

'It might have helped if you'd said what you really meant.'

She snorted. 'You astonish me sometimes.'

'Well. I'm glad I evoke at least some feeling in you. I rang Nikki because you said you thought it would be a good idea, right? You can't deny that. And I still think it was the right thing to do. She – sorted me out. You may find this difficult to believe, but she told me to go back to you.'

'And that's why you're here is it? Because Nikki told you?'

He coloured. 'I can't do a thing right, can I? I could have lied to you. I could have denied meeting her. You encourage deceit, Clare, did you know that? Look. We've got a weekend together –'

The words she had rehearsed in the past hour said themselves. They came tumbling out, charged with a hateful emotion. They were words she had never thought to say, words that a part of her disagreed with but which had to be said all the same.

'No. We haven't. I'm sorry, Rob, but we haven't. If you don't understand what I feel now, you never will. Do I have to spell it out for you? We've come to the end. You asked me what I wanted and I told you. I want this to stop. I want to be on my own. I want you out of this house. I want you out of my life. I want you to get on your bike and go, Rob. Now. I want you to go *now*.'

Then she walked out of the kitchen and he was left alone, shaking his head and clenching his fists, and Lucy's school paintings on the wall went out of focus and in the next room on the television someone was talking about some diplomatic question over the landing of scrap-metal dealers on the island of South Georgia.

31

BOTTA TOOK POSSESSION of La Tijerita after Ceci's death, but although Cadoret was allowed to stay on in residence at Calandria, he did so in disgrace.

From that time, his relationship with Botta and the cartel changed completely. His last few responsibilities were taken from him and he was put on a small allowance and given a housekeeper, a moody woman called Angelita, whose husband had left her and who believed that the world owed her a living. She vented her spleen upon Cadoret, slapping his meals down in front of him with an ill grace and leaving his bed unmade and linen unchanged for weeks at a time.

1980 and '81 were difficult years for Botta. After the collapse of Michele Sindona's Franklin National Bank a fake kidnapping to get Sindona out of New York was staged and when evidence turned up the following year that Licio Gelli was implicated, Gelli's country house in Tuscany was raided by the Italian police. Gelli had gone when the police arrived but he had left behind him a P2 membership list. Along with several other Argentines in influential positions, Botta's name was on that list, and the day the scandal broke he died of a heart attack.

After the burial, walking at her husband's side past the memorials in the cemetery of Recoleta, Blanca turned to Jorge and said, 'I want Calandria.'

'Take it,' he replied. 'It's yours.'

A week later, on a wet morning in November, a chauffeur-driven Chevrolet came splashing up the avenue and Blanca, looking as if she had just stepped off a fashion parade, alighted. Her high heels clacked in through the hall and along the passageway and as she entered the breakfast room a waft of Chanel entered with her.

Cadoret was having breakfast. He scrambled to his feet, egg yolk on his lip.

'Blanca, my dear! How splendid to see you –' he started, then stopped dead as if he had seen a ghost, for Blanca had brought

354

Rui with her, whom Tito had not seen since he was a babe in arms. Rui was five years old now, and the image of Larry at the same age. Cadoret couldn't take his eyes off him but did not have the nerve to comment.

'Will you have some coffee?' he offered.

Blanca ignored the question. She looked round the panelled room at the familiar landmarks of her childhood. 'You're moving out,' she said. 'I want this place.'

She enjoyed his reaction. His mouth fell open.

'This is very sudden, Blanca –'

'It isn't sudden at all. Jorge was going to move you out five years ago but you hung on. Well now your time's up. I'm not prepared to wait.'

The little boy held onto Blanca's skirt and looked round the curve of her hips at the old man.

Cadoret said, 'How long have I got?'

'I want you out by noon.'

'Noon? Noon when?'

'Noon today. I'll have a car sent round. Take Angelita with you. The apartment on Quintana's vacant. You can live there.'

'You want me out in three hours?'

'Yes.'

His hand shook. He steadied himself with his fingers on the edge of the table. 'I've lived here all my life and you want me out in three hours.'

'Yes.'

'What about my things?'

'You won't need much. The apartment's furnished.'

'Blanca,' he pleaded. 'Please. Give me more time. Please.'

She tossed her head. 'You've had more than enough time. I'll come back at noon to see you off the premises.' She turned on a high heel and left him standing there in tears.

The little boy hung back. He gazed at his grandfather and saw that he was crying.

Tito reached out and pulled the boy gently towards him. He pushed his fair hair aside and found the birthmark. The lingering suspicion about Rui's identity turned suddenly into a certainty.

'Daniel,' he said, and spoke in Spanish. 'Your name is Daniel.'

He released the boy and Rui turned and ran to catch up with his mother. He put his hand in hers and climbed into the back of the Chevrolet and the car doors slammed and they drove away down the wet avenue. Rui held his mother's hand and separated her fingers one by one, looking at her long, shapely fingernails that were painted a startling blue.

The car went slowly along, mud splattering noisily in the mudguards. Herds of cattle grazed in the fields on either side. Rui looked up at his mother.

'My name isn't Daniel, is it, Mummy?'

The apartment on the Avenida Quintana was the same one in which Magdalena had stayed with Blanca and Luis after separating from Tito. It was on the fourth floor of a block that had been at first owned by Cadoret, then taken over by Botta and now annexed by Stefenelli. Over the years, it had been allowed to fall into disrepair and was now badly in need of refurbishment and redecoration. Soon after Tito moved in, the only other tenant was evicted, so that Cadoret and his housekeeper became the only residents in the block. Angelita was given a flat on the ground floor, where she acted as concierge as well as housekeeper and minder for the old man on the top floor.

The move knocked the last of the stuffing out of Cadoret. He fell into a sterile existence of getting up late, lunching at the English Club, sleeping it off in the afternoons and sitting with a glass of Old Smuggler before the television set in the evenings.

One Sunday he treated himself to a trip on the train to Hurlingham. So much had changed. Retiro station was a filthy, dangerous place with beggars squatting at every corner, the trains breaking down, the service unreliable. In the heat of summer it was no longer safe to rest your arm on the open window ledge when the train was standing in a station because to do so risked having your watch snatched off your wrist. In the rush hour the trains were so full that people rode on the roofs and running boards. Sexual abuse of women had become commonplace, as were hold-ups in which passengers were relieved of valuables at gunpoint. On the way back, when Cadoret was waiting on Hurlingham station, a train went slowly through with a youth standing on a carriage roof yelling and waving his penis at the people on the platform.

Much had changed at the club, too. It was no longer the exclusive meeting place for the British it had once been. Wealthy Argentines had moved in and the place swarmed with teenagers. The golf clubhouse had been bombed by guerrillas in the seventies and had not been rebuilt. There was now a swimming pool and a crèche, and a new fad called 'short tennis' was all the rage. Polo was still played, but to Tito it seemed that the fun had gone out of that, too.

He heard little news of his family. As far as he knew, Luis was still in the FAA, though he didn't know his rank; Johnny, the last time he had heard, was working as a chaplain on an airbase in the Chubut; Marc was living with a mistress in Miami.

Of Nikki he knew even less. He had written to her after her enforced removal from Argentina but had never received a reply.

Having lost so much he no longer hoped for what he could not have; instead, he tried to find some sort of peace of mind. Even that was elusive. Though he tried to reassure himself that it had not been his fault that Nikki had been held in custody or that Ceci had leapt from the roof of the Sheraton, lingering doubts remained. Though he told himself that he had acted for the best at every stage in his life, he could not shake off an awareness that he had missed opportunities to escape from the snare in which he had become entangled; and sometimes, usually in the small hours when his own snoring jerked him suddenly awake, he wondered whether it might have been possible to have lived another sort of life, a life in which he might have retained the affection and trust of his wife and family, a life in which loyalty to his Lodge might have taken second place to loyalty to the community of which he was a part, a life that might have ended among friends rather than in the company of has-beens like himself who filled the empty hours with games of bidou or found a sterile entertainment in the swapping of schoolboy jokes over the fairy toast and Wilde's Sauce in the dining room of the English Club.

Then one April day towards the end of the summer, the staggering news broke that commandos had landed on the Malvinas. The blue and white flag flew over Puerto Argentino. The Plaza de Mayo, blocked only yesterday by angry crowds demonstrating against Galtieri's economic policy, was today blocked again with exultant people chanting 'Argentina! Argentina!'

The news changed everything. It was as if every man, woman and child in Argentina had been given the chance to turn over a new leaf and begin again. The country was united in a way Cadoret had not seen since the days of Perón and the descamisados. This new sense of unity produced a manic upswing of national confidence. United, the country could not fail. Anyone who read the newspapers knew that England had cut back her Navy and that her last patrol ship in the South Atlantic was to be withdrawn. Wasn't that the clearest possible sign that the English were at last washing their hands of the islands they had seized illegally nearly a hundred and fifty years before? It seemed inconceivable that they would sell off half their fleet one year and then resort to military action the next; and even if they had a late change of mind, they would certainly need support from the USA, which, if the latest friendly overtures to Argentina from Ronald Reagan's new administration were anything to go by, would not be readily forthcoming.

It was like a walkover at soccer. The opposition hadn't bothered to turn up, so the cup had gone by default to Argentina.

In the first heady days, the conquest brought out the best in people. It was seen as the cure for all Argentina's ills, the turning point of her history. From that day forward, the nation would turn its back on the tragedies of past years in order to march proudly into a new age, to take its rightful place as one of the great nations in the world.

On the morning after the news broke, Cadoret descended in the lift and took a walk along to the Biela for coffee. The park at Recoleta was crowded with excited people. Youths were linking arms, shouting and dancing. Children were waving flags. He experienced a torrent of emotion. It was impossible not to feel proud. Yes, it was right and just that Argentina should reclaim islands that were so obviously hers. On the street corner a man was selling flags on sticks, so he bought one and as he went on across the park encountered a television crew who pointed a camera in his direction. He waved his flag for them and shouted '*¡Viva la patria!*' – and that same evening caught a fleeting glimpse of himself on the television news, a white-headed symbol of the old guard, waving a blue and white flag on a stick.

He gripped his whisky tumbler and stared at the mob shouting and chanting on the small screen.

Suddenly he knew that he was old.

32

MAC LOGAN SAID THAT the fact that a hospital ship had been comman-
deered and that they were actually painting red crosses on its funnel
and sides was a sure sign that Maggie Thatcher meant business. Mac
was a naval surgeon who had done a loan appointment to the Aussie
navy in the early seventies and had seen action in Vietnam. Nikki was
convinced she had met him before. He was thin and bronzed with a
moth-eaten beard and a quietly rebellious manner. 'The moment they
start shipping chaplains and medics out,' he said, 'you can bet your
boots they're getting serious.'

They were storing ship at Gibraltar. The QARNNS sisters were
working alongside the nurses, and Mac and a couple of the housemen
had joined in. They had formed a human chain and were passing
cardboard boxes up the gangway. On the quayside, naval vans,
staff cars and lorries were going back and forth. In the harbour,
ammunition and fuel lighters were being manoeuvred alongside the
warships which had been arriving in the last few days.

'Can you see Maggie climbing down?' Mac asked. 'I certainly
can't.'

He was next in line to Nikki. She had a feeling that he might have
recognized her, too. More than once, as she passed him another
carton of blankets or dressings or Lucozade, she had been aware of
his glance.

The supply of boxes had dried up. There was a delay while the
next stores lorry took the place of the last. Mac took another long
hard look at her, then snapped his fingers.

'Got it! I know where I've seen you before. We have met before,
haven't we?'

'Well – I did have a feeling –'

'You've got an appendix scar, right?'

'How do you know?'

He grinned, shaking his finger at her. '*I* was the duty junior
houseman at Stonehouse when *you* were lifted off a yacht in the
middle of the Channel with a perforated appendix one summer

afternoon a long time ago. We had a long talk one morning when
you were on the mend. Remember?'

The packing cases started coming up the chain again and they talked
while they worked. He remembered a surprising amount about her:
that she had once had plans to be a doctor, that she had been brought
up in Argentina, and that her mother had died a few months before
her emergency operation.

'You've got a good memory,' she said.

He shook his head. 'Not a bit of it. I just fancied you, that's all.' He
sighed. 'And now I'm a married man with four kids and a mortgage.
Coming to the lunch-time piss-up in HMS *Rooke* today?'

Stewards were serving gin-and-tonics and horses' necks when she
entered the shorebase wardroom, and she was just accepting a drink
from a silver tray when she felt a tap on her shoulder.

It was Rob. As always happened when she met him, she felt a
sudden lightening, a softness for him.

'I thought you were on your way to the Far East!'

'So did we until last week. How are you?'

'All right. You?'

'So-so. Clare's given me the shove.'

'Oh Rob! I'm sorry. Was it . . . because of me?'

'No. Not you. Me.' He glanced round. 'Look – we can't talk now,
can we? Are you free this evening?'

She shook her head. 'I've got to go to a duty dinner at the Baiuca.
Our glorious leader's trying to instil a bit of *esprit de corps* into the
naval party.'

'Christ,' he muttered. 'We sail tomorrow.'

Their eyes met. She felt a sudden flash-flood of love for him.

'I – I really need to talk, Nikki. Couldn't we meet later? After your
dinner?'

'I'll try and get away early. I'll meet you at the ship as soon after
eleven as I can.'

He smiled his sad smile. 'Your place or mine?'

'I think it had better be mine, don't you?'

They met on the quay a little before midnight and walked to the end
of the breakwater. The moon came out from behind the Rock. Across
the bay, the lights of Algeciras sparkled like jewels.

They stood and kissed and she felt his cheek warm against hers.

'Did you ever read *A Farewell to Arms*?' he asked suddenly.

'Of course.'

360

'That's what I would like to do now. Steal a boat and row across the lake with you. Start a new life. Just the two of us. Let the rest of the world go hang.'

She leant against him.

'We could do it, you know. Not right away. But soon.' He pulled away and deliberately looked into her eyes. 'We're right for each other. I know we are. I've always known we were. You know it, too. Don't you?'

'Yes, but –'

'But what?'

'This is the worst possible time for either of us to make any sort of commitment.'

'Are you frightened of getting hurt?'

'Of course.'

He released her and stared across the Straits. 'That's Tangiers over there. Those lights. And the Atlas Mountains beyond. We could go there. If we really wanted to. We could just hop on the ferry and go. Do you understand what I'm saying?'

'I think so.'

'First decide where you would be, then do what you have to do.'

'Who said that?'

'Does it matter?'

'Not a bit,' she whispered, and at the same moment they turned to each other again, and wept in each other's arms.

On the way back along the breakwater he said suddenly, '*Will* you marry me? When I'm free? Don't answer that straight away. Think about it. Write to me. Will you?'

She stopped walking in order to face him.

'Rob, can I ask you something?'

'Anything.'

'Well, you may find this difficult to take, but I don't think we should rush things. Going straight from Clare to me might work, but it might also be a recipe for disaster. I want us both to be quite sure before we commit ourselves. Clare only gave you your marching orders a week or two ago, didn't she? And everything's in a turmoil. Anything may happen in the next month or two – especially if this thing comes to blows, which it probably will.'

'So what are you saying?'

She sighed. 'I don't *want* to say it but I think I must. I think we ought to hold off at least until this thing is over. I don't think we should write, either. Not for a month or two, anyway. The situation's so romantically charged, isn't it? Both of us going off to war, both longing for someone

361

to love. The moonlight on the bay, uniforms. It's all too much. It would be so easy to plunge into something and find ourselves emotionally over-committed. I need time, darling. You do too. I don't want you on the rebound, you're too important to me for that.'

He stared absently across the ruffled water.

'How long do you want to wait?'

'They're saying we'll be away for six weeks.'

'So I can write the first letter in six weeks' time?'

'No need to set it in concrete.'

'I may feel compelled to write to you.'

'Well, I can't stop you. But I think it's for both our good. Don't you?'

They walked on, and reached the warships that were berthed alongside. They stood under the sharp, dark bow of a guided-missile destroyer whose fans and generators made a steady, whispering hum.

'Keep safe, and write to me in six weeks,' she whispered, then kissed him lightly on the lips before walking away down the quay, back to her ship.

Clare thought the Falklands crisis was the best thing since Scrabble. It was shaking the country up and uniting the British people in a way that they had not been united since 1945. It was giving Britain one more chance to stand up to a totalitarian bully and defend the weak against the strong. It was providing a long-overdue reinforcement of the old values of service, duty, honour and patriotism.

But if it was doing great things for Great Britain, the crisis was doing even greater things for Clare McNairne. At first, when the crisis broke, she found herself in a quandary. Having just sent Rob packing, she suddenly felt proud of him and his ship in a way she had not felt for many years. There was no question of staying aloof from this. The only possible decision was to throw herself into the task of supporting the wives and families at home with all her energy.

This new-found interest did wonders for her. Her oomph came back with a woosh. She contacted the Family Welfare organization in Plymouth and volunteered her services. She spent hours a day touring about in the car visiting wives, organizing meetings and self-help groups and explaining the rules about sending letters or telegrams to the men who were serving in the South Atlantic.

She included Lucy in her new campaign, and helped her write a letter to the stokers' messdeck of Rob's ship, the final version of which read:

Dear Stokers!
We are all proud of what you are doing. I saw your ship on TV
and it looks great. Yesterday I bought a T-shirt with my pocket
money and it says STICK IT UP YOUR JUNTA!!!
     Come back safely. Hugs and kisses from
     Clare McNairne
     (Aged 7)

But helping the men of the task force at second hand was not enough
to satisfy Clare. It was all very well to encourage other wives to write
regularly and often to their menfolk, but should she not practise what
she preached? She began to see that in pushing Rob out of her life she
had deprived herself of a unique opportunity. This was no time to be
an estranged wife. Her place, emotionally, was at her husband's side.
He would need her support more than ever at this time, and if she
stood by him now, she was sure she could put an end, once and for
all, to his restlessness and yearnings after the little Argentine bitch
who had played so huge a part in wrecking their lives.

The more she thought about it the more convinced she became, so
a week or two after the task force had sailed she turned off the radio,
sat down at her seventeenth-century oak bureau and began a letter
to her husband.

Nikki had not actually volunteered to sail with the hospital ship. What
had happened was that in a weak moment she had remarked that she
wouldn't kick up a fuss if she was sent because it would at least make
a change from working on a men's medical ward, and within fifteen
minutes of saying so she was standing in the matron's office at RNH
Haslar being told that her knowledge of South American Spanish
might prove invaluable and that her name had been added to the list
of volunteers.

From the start, the party of naval consultants, surgeons, nursing
sisters and nurses that flew out to Gibraltar was led by an oligarchy of
indecision and suspicion. The people from Haslar hospital felt cautious
about those from Stonehouse. The consultants were determined to
maintain their status and remain purely as consultants. The sisters
and nurses rebelled against the petty rules introduced by the senior
QARNNS officer, and the P&O complement resented the presence on
board of officers and men from the Royal Navy and Royal Marines.

Everyone was uncertain of his or her position. The sisters felt
overworked and underpaid and didn't see why they should have to
be changed and seated by eight p.m. sharp for dinner every evening.

Within days of embarkation, shipboard romances began. Because there was a Medical Officer in Charge, a senior QARNNS officer, a lieutenant commander in command of the naval ratings and the ship's P&O Master, there were effectively four separate bosses, each with his or her own organization, within one hull.

Nikki had a first-class cabin to herself, with three berths and an adjoining shower. She had been put in charge of the wards (which had been converted from children's dormitories) on B, C and D decks and while the ship steamed south she and her naval nurses worked long hours to complete preparations to receive large numbers of wounded men. But while the naval party struggled to turn a children's cruise liner into an operational hospital ship, the P&O ship's officers insisted on prolonging the pretence that this was just another pleasure cruise, complete with dances and cocktail parties and competitions to guess the distance run.

The ship called in at Dakar to land the captain, who was seriously ill, and to take on board a replacement. Steaming southward through the tropics, exercises were held at any time of night or day.

They stopped at Freetown to take on water and fuel and mail, but there was no mail and morale sagged and, after sailing, the atmosphere on board became increasingly tense. The news from Washington and London and Buenos Aires was all bad, and the probability of a shooting war was turning into a certainty. Attendance at lectures on casualty reception, treatment of burns, fire fighting and flight safety was compulsory. At Ascension Island, they cleared mail but again received none. There was no shore leave. They looked across the harbour at the volcanic mountains, watched the helicopters scurrying back and forth between the warships and supply ships at anchor. They admired the sunsets, and then went below to shower and change in time for the nightly ritual of dinner.

After leaving Ascension, a new crisis arose. There was only a very limited capability to make fresh water on board, and it was announced in the ship's daily information sheet that if everyone continued to use water at the present rate, the ship would run out completely in ten days. Strict rationing was introduced, and the senior QARNNS officer announced a limit of one one-minute shower per day for all women on board.

Nikki started a letter to Rob.

My darling,
 I can't wait any longer. I simply must write to you. I won't post it until we agreed, but this way I shall at least have something

worth sending when the time comes. Also, if I don't write to someone about this awful ship I think I shall burst. Do you know, the senior Quarn (we call her Oggle) actually banged on my bathroom door just now and ordered me to turn my shower off because she had timed me *with a stopwatch* and I was ten seconds over the limit?!

I wonder how things are with you, darling. I think of you practically every minute of the day. There are so many things I long to talk to you about. Sometimes I wish I hadn't been so disciplined about not writing, but I suppose that deep down inside me I know it was a good decision. This will be the longest six weeks of my life. I watched you sail, darling, the morning after that night, but I didn't see you, so I suppose you were down in the bowels of the engineroom or something. There is something so dreadfully final about a warship sailing – the way you put on speed as you clear the harbour and dwindle rapidly to a grey smudge. I watched and watched, and then got a sound ticking-off from Oggle for setting the nurses a poor example. I don't think she likes me very much.

The trouble with this ship is that we are nearly all strangers to one another. The only thing that unites our various cliques is suspicion and distrust of other cliques. I get on very well with the sisters in my watchkeeping union – Viv Robinson has a quite hilarious sense of the ridiculous – and there are one or two surgeons I like, including a chap called Mac, who I told you about back in our Edinburgh days. He was the one who talked me back to sanity after my emergency op when I was seventeen. But overall, the atmosphere on board is bloody, with a hugely complicated pecking order and everyone pecking away like anything. We lesser mortals are united against our leaders (what an admission!). The MOIC is a pleasant enough man but rather ineffectual and certainly not a leader; Oggle has a raging sense of her own inadequacy. Roger, our tame aviator two-and-a-half is a particularly raw piece of meat in a very iffy sandwich. We have our moments, but in general the morale is definitely shaky. We have a determinedly unfunny entertainments officer who keeps trying to make me play Call My Bluff on the ship's radio, but all I feel like doing when I'm not working is sitting here in my cabin and writing to you.

So it's started. When I was at school in BA we went on a conducted tour of the *Belgrano*. It seems incredible that she's been

365

sunk. Why? Why? I feel powerless and furious. I want to bang my fists against Mrs Thatcher's chest. She simply cannot realize what she's done. The Argentine forces are amateurs against the Brits. They haven't a hope. I've lain awake for nearly five hours and it's the middle of the night. I've been thinking about my father and my brothers. I don't know what any of them are doing, but any of them could be involved. Johnny was down at an Air Force base in the Chubut the last time I heard and Luis is still in the FAA. Even Marc's in the arms trade, so I suppose he's making loads of money out of the whole ghastly business.

Darling, please keep safe. I can't bear the thought of you being hurt. I'm going to see if I can get an hour or two's sleep now, so goodnight and may God keep you. How I *hate* this killing. How I hate this fighting. Why I ever volunteered to join the QARNNS I don't know. The uniform I suppose. The possibility that I might one day be required to enter a war zone and treat injuries never entered my head.

We were called to action-stations and soon afterwards the helicopters started landing aboard and the stretcher bearers brought our first cases down the ramp to Casualty. You find out the name of the ship that's been hit when you cut away their clothes. It was the *Sheffield*. One moment we were playing doctors and nurses aboard a converted cruise ship. The next, the horned beast of war had barged in. Until you see battle injuries and the pallor of shock on their faces and the young, muscular bodies ripped and bruised and burnt – you have no concept of the horror of it.

We are very busy now. I stole five minutes after coming off watch this morning and went up on deck. This wind. It hits you in the face, doesn't it, cuts you in half, screams. And then falls suddenly to a horrible low moaning like a wounded animal that has been left to die. I love watching the albatrosses. How they glide and soar and swoop low over the waves.

We are in a NOSH box. Bet you don't know what NOSH stands for, so I'll tell you: Naval Ocean-going Surgical Hospital. So there you are. Our NOSH makes MASH look like a model of sanity and organization. We're in three watches and get one eight-hour stretch off every three days. One of the watches changes at 2000, the time by which we have to be changed and seated for dinner in the mess. This was obviously a crazy arrangement so the four of us agreed among ourselves to change it. That worked fine until Oggle found out and put a stop to it. 'If I start allowing unofficial routines, Sister Cadoret, I may as well kiss discipline goodbye.' (If *only* we could kiss her infernal discipline goodbye!)

We have the men from *Sheffield* and *Coventry* in the wards now, and the intensive care unit and surgical wards are in use. I was required to go and talk to an Argentine pilot today. Two broken legs and back problems after ejecting from a Mirage. We got on fine at first. He was very pleased to speak Spanish and I told him about my childhood and life at Calandria and my brothers, but when I asked him about his family he suddenly clammed up on me. It was like a curtain coming down over his eyes. He thought I was trying to pump him for information. It really upset me because I wasn't doing anything of the kind. Nothing I said would convince him. He just looked at me and gave me his name, rank and number. I suppose that's what war does.

We go to flying stations every morning and then stay at fifteen minutes notice to receive casualties. The part I hate is hearing the announcement that casualties are on the way. You hear the first helo stuttering on the landing pad and then the first patients come in from Casualty and you have to brace yourself to see more horrific injuries, to smile, to reassure, to stay calm, serene and do what you've been trained to do. The burns patients are the most difficult to look at and treat normally. You would have thought that part of our training would have prepared us to cope with the horrors we see almost every day now. But I suppose if we had been forewarned none of us would have stayed in.

Just heard about Van Mallard. What a waste of a fine, brave man.

I wonder what you are doing, darling Rob. We've had a briefing from Roger, so I know about the landings. Actually, I hated that briefing because he made it sound like a load of fun. Lots of overgrown schoolboys playing with toys they don't fully understand.

Today we left our box and went inshore for the first time to pick up casualties from Ajax Bay. While we were inshore we were visited by Argentine aircraft. They had a *very* good look at us but must have seen our red crosses and mercifully left us alone. Quite eerie though, knowing that they could blast us out of the water if they chose to.

The MOIC, Oggle and the consultants continue to behave as if they were on some sort of pleasure cruise. Meanwhile the surgical

367

teams and nursing staff are being worked into the ground. Rules about only doctors prescribing antibiotics and giving morphine have been conveniently shelved. So has the one about two sisters being present to check dosage.

We're running a shuttle service daily now, collecting casualties from shore and retiring to the safety of our box. The ships are being bombed almost every day and our workload is rising. There's an insidious feeling around that the Argentines could just get lucky and sink some major ships. We could even be defeated. In an odd sort of way, part of me (the Argentine part, I guess) hopes that we will be. I think Britain *needs* to be defeated.

I talked to a sub lieutenant off the *Sheffield* who told me about the anti-submarine war. He said that there's carnage going on among the whale population because whales give submarine-like echoes and every echo is attacked, just in case. I wonder what the whales think about it.

We anchored in Grantham Sound last night and I went on deck at dawn. There was snow on the hills and a cold wind. Sheep and cattle grazing. And people. Civilians. They were standing on a hillside and we looked at each other and I waved and they waved back and I felt suddenly tearful and couldn't stay up there any more, so I've come back to finish off this letter to you. I won't post it yet but will start another immediately. It's always nice to have more than one letter, isn't it?

Darling Rob, I love you and I am longing for you. I cling, still, to the memories of the quiet moments we have spent together. There is a dreadful temptation to say 'When this is all over' which I shall resist. But we will, won't we?

My love, always,
Nikki.

In April, Tito's lift broke down. In fact it wasn't the lift but the door on the fourth floor, which had been damaged by the removals men who came to take away the furniture Blanca had said he didn't need. It couldn't be closed properly and the lift wouldn't work unless it was fully shut, so Tito was faced with having to climb four flights of stairs every time he came back from an excursion to the English Club; but that wasn't such a disaster because the Malvinas crisis had caused a big shake-out of loyalties in the British community and Tito, along with several others, had decided to let his membership lapse and wasn't likely to lunch there ever again.

Soon after the sinking of the *Belgrano*, he had a heart attack. It was only a very minor one, but he was quite sure it was a heart attack because he had a very nasty chest pain and felt sick and sweaty and thought he was going to die. He rang for Angelita but she was watching the war news on the television, which was what everyone did all day, and either didn't hear the bell or ignored it.

He just had to manage on his own, which wasn't so very unusual because that was what he had been doing for some time now. He lugged himself to the bathroom and took some aspirin and stayed quiet and didn't have any whisky that evening; and the next day, though he still felt a bit odd and shaky, he went downstairs and along to Recoleta where he had a cup of weak tea instead of his customary black coffee, and the waiter came and talked to him about the news that the *Invincible* had been sunk. Everyone was celebrating that day: walking slowly back along Quintana he could hear radios and televisions going full blast with the news of how the FAA was winning the war by sinking British frigates and aircraft carriers; and overhead the endless procession of military transport aircraft going in and coming out of Palomar airbase continued and there was a marvellous grim determination among everyone because Argentina had at long last done what she should have done long ago. This was it. Britain was going to get its comeuppance once and for all.

But Tito now had a personal battle on his hands, and that was the Battle of the Lift. Workmen had taken the broken door away for repairs. They told him it would take up to three weeks, but after his heart attack it was out of the question to go up by the stairs so he bribed a workman to make the lift work without the door. That was a real triumph and he celebrated with his first glass of whisky since his attack. It was so good that he had a second and a third with the result that he became maudlin. None of his children ever contacted him and he wanted to see them before he died.

He sat in his chair and turned on the television, which didn't work very well because the picture slipped the whole time, but the sound was okay so he watched the news, which said that the troops were well established and dug in, that morale was high and that the successful outcome of the coming battle was in no doubt.

Then there was another résumé of the news of the sinking of the *Invincible*, which the British were still claiming, in spite of all the evidence to the contrary, had *not* been sunk.

He got up to go to the lavatory but on his way he had a little warning pain in his chest (he got quite a lot of them these days) and because he was frightened of having another attack he sat on the floor in the hall and waited for the pain to pass.

He sat there for quite a while, wondering about life and death and thinking about his children. Where were they? What were they doing? He hadn't heard from any of them for a long time.

He sat muttering to himself, wiping dribble off his chin with his sleeve and making little mental plans that were forgotten as soon as made. Eventually he got himself to the lavatory and back to the sitting room. He couldn't be bothered to turn the television off, so he left it on although it was only football, and when he had closed his eyes for five or ten minutes he made an effort and started a letter to Nikki.

After the landings, Rob's ship spent several days in Bomb Alley. The whole task force was keeping Greenwich time, which meant that British forces were always three hours ahead of the Argentines and had plenty of time to prepare for the daily attacks. For days at a time he saw no light of day, because his action station was in HQ1, the damage-control headquarters of the ship. Danger was a great leveller. People learnt very quickly to throw themselves on the deck when the raids came in and the close-range anti-aircraft guns opened up. Also, the peacetime heroes, the sportsmen and the prima donnas in the ship's company were very quickly displaced in popular esteem by others who were often quiet, insignificant people. The assistant manager of the canteen made a name for himself on the port Oerlikon gun. A scrawny chef metamorphosed into the ship's Terry Wogan and did *ad hoc* interviews and game shows for the ship's radio. One of the electrical ratings had an action station inside the top of the funnel, where he had instructions to fire a chaff rocket if ever a red light came on – but it never did. A couple of others had to be locked in the Sea Wolf missile magazine during action stations and were only let out at the end of the day when the last of the raids had departed.

The ship was hit by a bomb that failed to go off during one attack. It bounced off the sea and entered through the ship's side, leaving via the flight deck. Miraculously, no one was killed and the damage was quickly repaired, so that within twenty-four hours the flight deck was available again for helicopter operations.

After a while, time seemed to lose its value. Some days seemed like weeks and some weeks like days. The ship went to the rescue of HMS *Coventry* when she was sunk, and Rob witnessed her end when she rolled over and showed her daisy-petal propellers before slipping away beneath the surface. The survivors were given a wonderfully warm reception on board, with gifts of clothes and bunks given up and the chefs and stewards working flat out to provide hot food and drinks. In the middle of war, the men on board discovered a new dimension of love in their lives – it was that particular form of love for one's fellow human beings which can only be experienced in time of real adversity.

In between stints in Bomb Alley, the ship did goal-keeping for HMS *Invincible*, which meant providing anti-aircraft missile defence for her. It involved steaming fast in close company with the aircraft carrier and being ready to fire missiles or chaff rockets at a moment's notice in order to bring down attacking aircraft or seduce Exocet missiles from their target.

One night the two ships steamed at top speed all night in close company towards the coast of Argentina, and a Sea King helicopter was launched which never came back. After that time, prior warning of air raids taking off from Punta Arenas was always timely and accurate.

There was a shortage of mail at first, but when it came it did so with a rush. When Rob went up to the wardroom to collect his, there were twenty-two letters, each envelope consecutively numbered, from Clare.

He took them to his cabin and opened them up. She begged his forgiveness for throwing him out; she told him that all was forgiven and forgotten; she sent him all her love, all her warmth, all her encouragement and hopes and prayers and blessings. For over a month he had been sleeping less than six hours in twenty-four. The tension and the responsibility had taken their toll. Reading Clare's letters (and Clare knew how to touch him, still) confused and upset him. Having been bombed by Argentine aircraft he was now being love-bombed by Clare. In spite of his agreement with Nikki not to write, he was disappointed that she had kept to the agreement and regretful that he had as well. He wanted to break down and cry but knew that it was not yet time to permit himself that luxury; so instead he dammed up all the emotion inside him, tried to stop thinking about Nikki, and flung himself back into the business of war.

My darling,
    Here I am again, wondering what you're doing, longing to be with you, aching inside for you, having conversations with you in my head, making plans for us both, sending thought messages

to you . . . and at the same time trying to keep sane in the ghastly atmosphere that still prevails aboard this ship.

We had a large intake of Paras the other day – the bloody fruits of Goose Green. Up to now I've felt tremendous respect for all the casualties we've received, but this lot are definitely different. They are loud, arrogant and disobedient. Under the Geneva Convention, no weapons are allowed on board, and as each batch of soldiers arrives they have to surrender any knives or guns, which are then ditched over the side. But these Paras have concealed knives and bayonets on them and some have been found under pillows. They are also determined to have a go at the Argentine patients on board, so we have to keep them out of harm's way down on D deck. The Paras seem to think they take precedence over all other regiments in the British Army. They also resent being nursed by women. Not a nice bunch at all, but I suppose the more efficient you are at killing, the less pleasant you become as a human being.

That reminds me of something you said: 'Success as a naval officer does not necessarily mean success as a person.'

By contrast, yesterday I comforted an Indian boy with severe abdominal injuries. He was crying and calling out for his mother. He was from Mburucuya in Corrientes province. I sat with him and held his hand and he just sobbed and sobbed. He was terrified that the English would eat him, because he had been told that if he was ever taken prisoner that was what would happen to him.

Then I went off watch, did the usual high-speed wash and change (we have a better water supply now) in order to get up to dinner by eight. We'd just started dinner when in came Mac Logan in No. 8's, having been in theatre most of the day. There was a very pregnant pause, then the MOIC asked why he had not changed for dinner. Mac ignored him and went on eating, whereupon the MOIC ordered him to go and change, to which Mac replied, 'Piss off.' There were murmurs of support – I think that but for the fact that we had patients on board, there might actually have been a mutiny. Quite a nasty business. MOIC told him to go to his cabin and change immediately into mess undress, so Mac shovelled a bit more food down him (I don't think he'd eaten since breakfast) and departed. The latest rumour is that he may be court-martialled when we get back to UK. What a way to run a railway.

* * *

I write this in snatches in between, so forgive it if it's a bit disjointed. I wonder if you have any time to write. I don't suppose so. But it looks as though a final battle is approaching, so I hope soon that I will be able to send this off to you. I don't think I'd better until I hear from you, because I am *determined* not to twist your arm in any way, or use war as a means to an end.

You may not believe the latest drama. I was sleeping in my cabin this afternoon and woke up suddenly to find Oggle rummaging in my private drawers! I was very sleepy and asked something like, 'What are you doing?' She was extremely tight lipped. 'I am conducting a search, Sister Cadoret, that is what I am doing.' Then she gave me one of her stares and announced in a sort of low shudder, 'A bayonet has gone missing.' I boggled momentarily, then realized that she was searching my drawers because she thought I might have pinched it. I was more than a little cross and regret to say that I descended to sarcasm. 'Oh I *see*,' I said. 'That explains everything. I mean – if I saw a bayonet lying around, the temptation to nick it would be irresistible. I've always wanted a real bayonet for my very own.' No witnesses of course, so I was fireproof. She gave me an old-fashioned look and flounced out.

Now mail has arrived, the first in weeks, and everyone seems to be deluged with it except me, so I am feeling very blue. But I console myself with the thought that this thing really will come to an end fairly soon, and that then we can pick up the threads again and make a *real* start. It's a bit like a dream really, and I don't like to think about it in case it doesn't come true. I have decided definitely not to send these two letters to you until I have heard from you. Darling, you won't get cold feet, will you? No, I know you won't, but sometimes I torture myself with the possibility.

Another nasty little aspect of life on board this NOSH is the homely little paragraphs inserted daily by the Entertainments Officer in Today's Arrangements, the P&O information sheet. Today's offering, entitled Historical Yesterdays, gives us the origin of the Guillotine which is described, quote, as 'a happy little device which could separate someone's head from their body in record time!' unquote. That might be all very well if we really were on a pleasure cruise, but it's hardly suitable aboard a hospital ship, especially when one of the patients is a badly shocked and traumatized boy from HMS *Ardent* who keeps telling and re-telling the story of how, after the bombs fell, he saw the severed head of his best friend roll across the deck.

One of my nurses has come to me in a bit of a panic. She is pregnant. The father is a medical attendant on board one of the support ships and he wangled a night on board while we were at Ascension. Do you know, darling, I actually felt envious of her. I remembered what you said at Gib about doing a Hemingway and rowing off together into the moonlight. Why on earth didn't we?'

1st June. We've been at sea for six weeks, so I suppose I could post these letters to you. Something holds me back. Fear, I suppose. I'm terrified of being hurt. Please understand.

There was another fight in the dormitory where the Paras are today. They simply do not respond to gentleness. I suppose it has been deliberately pounded out of them. I can't help thinking that if you gave them the chance they would be every bit as bad as Admiral Massera's torturers in BA. I met him at a dinner party once, you know. It seems like a million light years ago.

Heard today that the march on Port Stanley has begun. Fighting in the hills and a steady intake of casualties, mostly bullet and shrapnel wounds. We've had another briefing from Roger about the conduct of the war. It went in one ear and straight out of the other. I am becoming increasingly pacifist. I find the whole business of war and killing physically repulsive. You do too, don't you?

The people I pity most are the Argentine conscripts. One we've got on board has never seen snow before and has no idea where the Islas Malvinas are. He was suffering from severe exposure when he came to us. The reason for this was not so much that he had been living in a wet trench for over a month but because he had been driven by hunger to raid a warehouse, and had been caught and punished by his platoon commander, who had staked him out in his underclothes on the freezing ground overnight. It's an old gaucho punishment they used when they were massacring the Indians.

I think there may be mail on the way, and I'm getting impossibly excited. I sort of *know* you will have written by now. People are talking about the 'final push' (why are military expressions *so* lavatorial?) and the end seems to be in sight. Well, I'm writing when I ought to be sleeping, so goodnight, my darling, and perhaps tomorrow I shall have a letter, no THE letter, from you. God bless you, keep safe. I'm feeling quite tearful now, probably tired. Sleep.

The mail came but not a lot and there was no letter from you. Then immediately after that we had a huge intake of patients and I have had no time to write for five days.

It was quite awful. The helicopters came aboard one after another in a long succession. We took over 180 patients in one day, nearly all of them burnt. They were victims of the bombing at Bluff Cove. The stretcher cases went straight to the burns unit and an overflow ward. Walking wounded, pain-racked, shocked, bewildered, came down the ramp to Casualty. Black faces covered in Flamazine. Black hands held aloft, as if in surrender. A nauseating smell of burnt flesh.

I went down to my B deck ward and was greeted with an incredible sight. Staff and patients everywhere, milling about. I was supposed to 'take over' the ward, but that was clearly impossible. Patients were pouring down the stairs, many with their burnt hands in plastic bags. They are mainly Welsh Guardsmen. They hadn't fired a shot and had been waiting to get ashore when the bombers turned up.

First we had to empty the dormitories of patients who were recovering from operations or who had older injuries. This included several Paras, and of course they kicked up a row. I had to be very sharp with their sergeant, who is the only person they will readily obey. We opened more dormitories and the new admissions were shepherded in. Tough, stoical Welshmen, quite uncomplaining – gentlemen every one. Their officer kept insisting that his men should be treated before himself. Most of them would have gone straight into intensive care normally, but as it was we decided whether a man should go into a top or bottom bunk by whether he had a usable hand with which to help himself up.

I should have spent at least five minutes with each man to reassure him and settle him in, but there was no time for conventional nursing. They all needed high fluid intake and high-protein diet. All we could do was pick out the illest and send them to other wards where they would receive better attention.

No one went off watch – we just worked straight through. When we had got them onto their bunks we started dressing the burns. I can't find words to describe it. Imagine thirty men in a room, each with face and hands fried to a crisp like burnt bacon.

And the smell to go with it. And the sense of inadequacy. And the need to keep calm and never allow your thoughts to show on your face.

We worked solidly through the day, evening and night, and even then some of the men had to wait nearly forty-eight hours before receiving treatment. But they were quite wonderful. I never heard a single whisper of complaint from anyone.

Then there was the monumental task of the drug round, which became a non-stop operation throughout the day. There were no prescriptions. It was up to me to give what I thought best. I loaded myself up with quantities of Omnipon, Temgesic, antibiotics and eyedrops and set out. Visited the people in each dormitory who were in most pain first and gave them Omnipon. That took most of the day. Then started giving antibiotics, eyedrops and ointment. In most cases their hands were useless and they had to be helped to do everything. We got the more able cases to help their chums – helping them to drink half-hourly, eat, wash etc.

Their sheets should have been changed several times a day but we couldn't do that so the exudate from their burns leaked into the bedclothes. These men are quite wonderful in their acceptance of suffering. It's very humbling.

Inevitably other patients lost out on treatment, and had to fend for themselves for a while, with the result that I am in trouble again. The cause of it was the Paras. I was cornered by their sergeant, who told me that his men were heroes and that they had fought while the Welsh Guardsmen hadn't and that his blokes deserved preferential treatment. I tried to explain that their injuries were no longer as serious as the newcomers' but was then subjected to a stream of abuse and called a two-faced Argie cunt. Well. I baled out fast, and soon after was sent for by Oggle and reprimanded for failing to give the Paras sufficient attention. I exploded – fatigue I suppose. I said that if she and the consultants could have brought themselves to muck in and do a bit of practical doctoring and nursing, the situation would never have arisen. She looked at me balefully and said, 'I did not hear that, Sister Cadoret.'

Oh darling, there's just been an announcement that a helicopter is on its way to us at this very moment with twelve bags of mail and I know with total certainty that there *will* be a letter from you this time, so I am not going to write another word until I have opened it . . .

There was a letter. She collected it from her pigeon hole in the mess and took it down to her cabin to read slowly and quietly.

Nikki, my darling,

I am going to hurt you, I know, but I have decided that it is better to hurt you now in a lesser way than to make believe that the happiness we always hoped for could happen. But the truth is that it cannot. Though I love you with all my heart, though I long to share my life with you, marry you, have children with you; though I know we were made for each other from the beginning of time, I also know that present circumstances forbid it.

I shall try to explain. After we sailed from Gib I was convinced that this time Fate, or whatever it is that determines things in this life, really was working on our side. I knew (and still know) that we were perfect for each other. I was certain that leaving Clare had been the best possible thing to happen – for Clare, for you, for me, for us. Then, four weeks out of Gib, I received twenty-two letters from Clare and have gone on receiving letters from her, one for each day with no exceptions, ever since. Darling, I know I don't love Clare as I love you, but I still have affection for her, feel responsible for her and for Lucy, and I think I feel guilty about what I did to her when we were in Edinburgh. Having all these letters from her has confused me and upset me. I love you no less, but I feel that I have a duty to pick up the burden I thought I was finally rid of when she gave me my marching orders in April. I am torn between my head and my heart. It is an agonizingly hurtful experience because I know that whatever choice I take I must hurt one of you.

So, with infinite regret and sadness, I have decided that I must do my duty as a husband and a father. The time for being pulled in opposite directions is over. You were right to insist on a pause during this conflict. Our meeting in Gibraltar was too impossibly romantic, and it would have been a huge mistake to rush things. Clare would still have written those letters. I would have suffered from much more guilt and would have been far more torn, and inevitably our love would have been damaged. This way, at least we can hold onto the fact that our love was and is real and always will be. That is something that is a fact, something that can never be taken away.

It is tempting, and would be very easy, to make some sort of promise or hold out some sort of hope that at some time in the future we may meet again when we are both free. But I'm not

377

going to do that, I'm going to give no hostages to fortune. (I always wondered exactly what that meant — now I know!)

There is little more I can say. My heart is breaking, Nikki darling. I know we are repeating what happened to our parents, and I also know that there is nothing I can do to stop what must happen happening. I know that you would insist on my going back to Clare (but I am not using that as a reason) and I know that if I left her now I would break her totally. That I simply cannot do. It would be like murder.

Please forgive me, Nikki. I love you always. Deeply. Totally. Too much, perhaps. But it simply cannot be. I don't want to stop this letter because it is the last time I shall write to you or try to make contact with you. I think it is better that you don't write back.

> Forgive me Nikki.
> I love you for ever.
> Rob.

Before the sun came up, the islands were a low black line on a howling horizon. The boat deck was deserted. She stood at the rail and let the wind blow the tears backwards out of her eyes. Slowly, the outline of the islands hardened and the sky lightened in the east. A seabird swooped close to her. She watched it balancing on the gusts, flapping its wings, turning downwind, then turning again to fight its way back. It seemed that this bird knew she was there, knew that she needed comfort. She found herself watching it, wondering about it, trying to imagine what it would be like to be a bird. Did birds have souls like people? She didn't see why not. What sort of bird was it? A stormy petrel. One of Mother Carey's Chickens.

Suddenly it flapped awkwardly, was caught in a gust and came down with a thud on the deck behind her. It was stunned momentarily, but then began to flap about to regain its freedom. She felt a sudden, deep affinity with it. Her heart went out to it as it flapped and hopped, trying to get airborne and regain its freedom, but every time being blown back against the ship's superstructure.

She began trying to corner it in order to relaunch it. She talked to it. 'No need to be afraid, darling. I'm not going to hurt you. Please. Please let me help you . . .' But each time she got near, the petrel managed to flap its way past her, and she was despairing of catching it when she felt the presence of someone behind her, and when she turned saw that it was Mac Logan.

378

He shepherded the squawking bird towards her until it could no longer escape. She seized it, pulled its wings to its side, felt it pulsing with life through her woollen gloves. Then she went with Mac round the superstructure to the lee side and launched it over the side and watched it fly away, and when she turned back from the rail, Mac was there and his eyes were full of tears, and she went into his arms and she knew that at that moment he needed her as much as she needed him and they clung to each other and howled.

33

CLARE'S TRIUMPH WAS COMPLETE. She had scored a stunning victory against all odds. Unaided, Britain had won back the Falklands; singlehanded, Clare McNairne had won back Rob.

And now he was on his way home. She bought a new outfit, had her hair done, paid the earth for a session with the beautician and obtained a dockyard pass so that she could be waiting for him on the jetty when his ship berthed.

She took Lucy. On a blustery day in July, they parked the car on Plymouth Hoe and waved from the shore as the grey ships moved up the Hamoaze. Bursting with pride, they waved again as the ship came alongside; and up on the bridge-wing Rob, in his best uniform, lifted his cap and waved back.

It was a perfect moment, a moment she knew she would always remember.

After a tearful reunion in the wardroom, she drove him straight home and put his dirty things in the washing machine. She gave him malt loaf and shortbread for tea and gazed at him in undisguised adulation.

'Now you're to tell us *all* about it, Rob,' she said. 'We want to know every last detail, don't we, Lucy?'

There were less joyful homecomings. On a cold day towards the end of June, a group of senior officers watched as tugs nudged the SS *Canberra* alongside the aluminium-ore jetty at Puerto Madryn. The heaving-lines snaked across and the berthing hawsers were secured. The gangways were placed and after a short delay a small group of junior officers disembarked. Among them was a priest, Padre Cadoret.

After stepping off the gangway he knelt on the jetty for a few moments, crossed himself and said a prayer of thanksgiving.

The troops – four thousand of them in this consignment – began to disembark. They wore no helmets and carried no weapons. Most were conscripts who had been recalled for service in the Malvinas – boys of twenty or twenty-one. They came down the gangways in single file, saluted the group of officers and followed on along the jetty. The disembarkation took place in complete silence. The men were not formed in squads nor did they march. The only sounds to be heard were the footfalls going along the jetty, and the cry of gulls overhead.

A line of covered lorries had drawn up to collect them. One or two of the men kissed the ground as they stepped onto Argentine soil. Quite a few crossed themselves. A few looked defiant. But for the most part they came ashore without showing relief or joy or any emotion whatsoever.

On the outskirts of the town people had gathered at the roadside and when the convoy was held up they threw packets of biscuits, chocolate and cigarettes to the men in the lorries.

The troops were assembled in a large shed before being taken from Puerto Madryn to the military airbase. They had been forbidden to speak to the public, but a few of them ignored the order and managed to slip out of the shed and give their names and the telephone numbers of their next of kin to the people outside the wire who had come to see the return of the defeated army. In this way, the first news that the boys were on their way home reached the civilian population.

Spring came again to Buenos Aires: in the city parks and plazas there were circular pools of pale blue petals under the Jacaranda trees. Christmas was approaching and the annual rush to the seaside had begun. In Palermo park people were riding, jogging, walking dogs, sunbathing or strolling by the lake. Up and down the Tigre waterway the ferries and pleasure craft went to and fro with picnic parties. On the River Plate, yachts leaned over in the gentle breezes.

Right across the city, in the streets and slums and coffee bars and restaurants, the porteñas talked about the war. Just as a person who has been injured in an accident needs to talk about the experience, so the people of Argentina needed to talk about what had happened. They needed to discover how and why their military government had led them into such a débâcle; why they had been bombarded from morning to night with radio and television reports that had led them to believe the nation was winning battle after battle and heading for a glorious victory; why the USA had sided with Britain instead of Argentina; why the Navy had been beaten by a navy they had been led to believe was run-down and disillusioned.

The whole nation was bruised and tender – not just from the Malvinas war but from the years of repression and internal conflict that had preceded it. In city suburbs, country towns, shanty towns, villages and Indian compounds there were families that had been torn apart. The youth of the nation was filled with anger and bitterness. Hidden away in the military hospitals there were men with broken bodies and broken spirits. In the minds of thousands of young soldiers there were memories of cruelty and cowardice on the part of their leaders that they could never forgive and never forget.

At the end of November, Johnny Cadoret received a letter from his father asking him to come and visit him. The old man said he had had a heart attack and was lonely and depressed. He said that he never saw anything of his family from one year's end to the next.

Johnny decided that it was time to do his filial duty, so, two weeks before Christmas, he took a few days' leave and came north to Buenos Aires where he stayed with a fellow priest in the officers' quarters at the Campo de Mayo barracks. After some difficulty with the city telephone system he managed to get through to his father's apartment on the Avenida Quintana and made a date with him for lunch the following day.

He arrived at the street door soon after one and rang the appropriate bell. After a long delay, the sound of breathing came over the intercom, then his father's voice.

'Who is it?'

'Johnny.'

'Come up.'

In a room off the marble-floored lobby, Angelita sat watching television. She eyed the priest as he went by.

Going up in the lift Johnny braced himself for what was to come. This was duty, not pleasure.

His father looked shrunken and frail.

'Johnny,' he said, and his false teeth clicked when he spoke. 'Well, don't stand there. Come in.'

The apartment was large but sparsely furnished and unwelcoming. A smell of stale cigarette smoke hung about the place and the walls had turned nicotine yellow. In the corner by the window stood a television whose bare leads were stuck straight into the wall socket without a plug. A single armchair, its arms well worn, was placed before it and next to it was a low table on which were a bank statement, a detective novel, a nearly empty bottle of Old Smuggler, a full ashtray and Cadoret's half-moon reading glasses.

Cadoret wore an old lightweight suit and a frayed Hurlingham club tie with a pin. He was out of breath and his facial skin had gone soft like a woman's. There was a large, dark, leathery mole on his forehead and the skin under his eyes fell in blue-grey bags of wrinkled skin.

'Well how are you, Johnny? What've you been doing with yourself?'

Johnny had been helping battle-traumatized young men to return to normality, but such work was confidential and he was forbidden by army regulations to discuss it.

'Oh – the usual sort of thing, Dad. One never has much spare time as a parish priest.'

'Well.' Cadoret panted for a moment or two. 'You're looking older, I must say. Past the forty mark, eh?'

'That's right. Forty-two last June.'

'Lost your hair too, I notice.' Cadoret stood and panted again. He reminded Johnny of an old dog that can only just support itself on its legs and really ought to be put down.

'I wrote to all of you, you know. After my – my little attack. I wrote to Luis, Marc, Nikki, Blanca . . . Yes. But only you replied, Johnny. Grateful to you on that account. For taking the . . . for taking the trouble.'

'That was the least I could do,' Johnny said.

'So. We'll go out to lunch, right?'

Cadoret patted his sidepockets and looked vaguely about him.

'Have you lost something, Dad?'

'No. No, I don't think so. I'm – I'm summoning my courage to ask you a favour, Johnny.'

'What sort of a favour?'

Cadoret turned to him with fear in his watery eyes. It was a look that Johnny had seen before, especially among the elderly or those close to death. He lifted his head and two folds of skin stretched like foresails between chin and neck. When he spoke, phlegm rattled in his throat.

'I'd like you to hear my confession, Johnny.'

Johnny knew immediately what sort of confession it would be, and he shrank from hearing it. He did not wish to be burdened or involved in any way with his father's lifetime of sins. Becoming a priest had been his way of escaping from all that. Each member of the family had made a similar escape. For Johnny, becoming a priest had been his way of breaking free from his father's continual striving for wealth, position and property. His decision had pleased neither of his parents: his mother had always abhorred the concept of the priesthood and his father had presumed that he would go into a more profitable occupation. But unlike his brothers, Johnny had no passion for polo or flying or music or literature. All his childhood he had been aware of the conflict between his parents, and all he had ever wanted was to escape from it and live a life of peace and harmony. That was all he wanted now.

'Why me, Dad? Why not another priest?'

'Because you're my son. Because –'

Though he was unable to go on, Johnny had an idea of what he had left unsaid. His father wanted what most people in Argentina wanted at that time. He wanted to be loved; he wanted to be reconciled; he wanted to be valued and needed and comforted. He wanted to be made to feel special and to be told that what had happened was not his fault. He wanted to be forgiven, absolved, set free from the lingering sense of guilt, the nagging uncertainty that he might in some way have cooperated with Fate in bringing about his own downfall. And now he thought – along with so many others – that the Church could put his life back together for him with a few whispered prayers and the sign of the cross made over him.

'Dad,' he said. 'It's not a good idea for a son to hear his father's confession. I could do it, but it wouldn't be the best way – for either of us. I wouldn't be able to advise you as freely as I could if I were not your son. There might be things which you would find difficult to say to me or which I could not say to you, as my father.'

Cadoret regarded him for a moment, then turned abruptly away. 'Thought you might like to do it for me,' he muttered. 'Just this once. Always said I'd ask you one day, remember?'

'I think that was a joke, wasn't it?'

'Maybe it was,' said Cadoret. 'But it's not a joke now. Never mind. Forget it.'

Johnny controlled his exasperation. It was the old emotional blackmail again.

'Look, if you think it really would help, couldn't we do it another time? We're going out to lunch now. We're going to relax. I'm not in the right frame of mind for it, even if you are. So can we take a rain check?'

'Until when? Tomorrow?'

So he'd got his way, as usual.

'All right. Tomorrow.'

'Excellent,' said Cadoret and immediately began getting himself ready to go out, collecting his glasses and cigarettes and wallet from the table by the chair.

'There we be. All set. Spectacles, testicles, wallet and watch. Do you want to piddle before we go?'

'No, I'm all right, thank you.'

'In that case I'll have one for you.'

Johnny waited in the hall. Cadoret emerged zipping his fly. 'Bingo,' he said and, blowing off an accidental fart, led the way out of the apartment.

The safety door to the lift shaft had been removed. 'How long has it been like this?' Johnny asked as they stepped in.

'Since before the Great Malvinas War. They took it off for repairs. Said the lift would be out of action for a couple of days, but after three weeks said they'd lost it and couldn't get hold of another. I tipped a bloke to get it to work without the door and it's been like that ever since.'

'It's bloody dangerous.'

'Strong language from a man of the cloth, Johnny.'

'Yes, well I'm on holiday at the moment.'

'Anyway. Can't do without it. My lifeline, this lift.'

'When did you last remind them about it?'

Cadoret gave a short hollow laugh. 'I'm the only resident in the building. They're not going to take any notice of me.'

'But it's outrageous –'

'Of course it is, but that's old age for you, Johnny. Just wait until you're my age and see if anyone takes any notice of you.'

They stepped out on the ground floor and on their way through the lobby Johnny stopped to have a word with Angelita, who was eating an empanada.

'That lift is a serious hazard,' he told her.

Angelita shrugged and spoke through a mouthful of pastry. 'It's not with me, Padre. It's with the contractors.'

'The lift shouldn't be in use while the door's off on the fourth floor.'

'I know that, Padre. But the old man can't get up the stairs without it.'

'All the same I think you should report it again. Will you do that?'

'Sí, señor. I'll report it again.'

'Lazy cow,' Tito remarked, and accepted his son's arm as they went into the street.

It was only a couple of hundred yards to the restaurant at Recoleta, but Tito could only walk very slowly, so there was plenty of time for him to tell his son about his heart, which was badly on the blink, the skin cancers on his forehead and the backs of his hands, the difficulty

385

he had getting comfortable in bed because of his piles and the problem with his waterworks, which meant that he seldom slept more than one hour at a stretch.

'And now some sort of damned fungus has got at my toenails which are falling off one by one. I had a chiropodist look at them a year ago but he managed to turn one septic and I ended up on antibiotics. And look at that,' he said, stopping to hold out one hand which shook visibly. 'Parkinson's I'd say, wouldn't you?'

'Oh I wouldn't have thought so. What does the doctor say about it?'

'Doctor? I can't afford to pay a doctor these days. Still. Enough of my organ recitals.'

They sat down outside at a table with a white and green parasol. Tito unfolded a napkin, put on his reading glasses and looked at the menu.

'Right. This one's on me, Johnny, so don't stint yourself.'

When they had ordered, Cadoret began to talk. He talked like a man who has been starved of company for a long time. It was a long, relentless, self-pitying monologue. He said that he had been dealt a rotten hand of cards from the start and had never quite managed to pull the sticks out of the fire. 'That was why things never worked out at home, Johnny. Did you know that? Because I was under pressure all the time. That was the reason. And your mother could never see it. Always thought she knew best, Anna did, when in fact she didn't even know what was going on. Nobody did. That was the trouble. I had the whole thing on my back. And now here I am at the end of my life and my children won't talk to me. Luis has disowned me. Marc's shacked up in Miami with some Lebanese tart. And Larry's been desaparecido'ed as far as I can make out. I doubt if I'll ever see Nikki again. I've written asking her to come out but I doubt if I'll ever get a reply out of her.'

Cadoret topped up his wine glass. 'But you know which of you children hurts me the most?'

Here it comes, thought Johnny. Me.

'Blanca. She's the only one of you that's not my child, but she's the one who manages to hurt me most of all. Always has done, too.'

Cadoret opened his wallet, took out a colour snap and laid it down on the table by Johnny's plate.

'Take a look at that.'

Johnny looked. The snap was of a woman and her baby.

'Who is it?'

'That's Daniel, my only grandson, and that's his mother. See the mark on the baby's head? Right, now have a look at this one.' He took another, larger photograph from his inside pocket. It was of a baby naked on a rug. 'Same baby, wouldn't you say? Same features, same strawberry mark.'

Johnny compared the two and nodded. 'Yes. I'd say so.'

'I know so. And you know who this is? Blanca's adopted son Rui, that's who. He was with Blanca when she came to Calandria to chuck me out. Spitting image of Larry at the same age. Need I say more?'

Johnny compared the two snaps again. He shook his head. 'What are you going to do about it?'

'Not much I can do. I'm a prisoner in that place, and that cow you talked to is my gaoler. No. I want you to have these, Johnny. I want you to hang on to 'em and use them when the time comes. Will you do that for me?'

'But . . . short of making a direct accusation, I don't see what I can do, Dad. Does Blanca know about it?'

Cadoret appeared to summon strength. 'That's another thing I wanted to talk to you about. If she does know, the chances are she's done it deliberately for . . . for revenge. If she doesn't – well, either way, sooner or later, she must be told.'

'And Daniel, when he's old enough.'

'Yes. But I'll be gone by then.'

Johnny shook his head. 'You have to be extremely careful in cases like these, Dad. You have to put the child first every time.'

'That's why I'm handing it over to you, Johnny.' Cadoret appeared to summon his strength. 'And . . . it's not as straightforward as it seems. Something else I need to tell you. Thought I could tell you about it in confession. Thought I could get it out of my system that way. As it is . . . it's about Blanca's mother. You know she was murdered? Yes, of course you do. Well, I don't know who committed the crime, but I know how it came to be committed. Blanca's never known the truth. I've always kept it from her. This is where I need your advice. Should I tell her? That's the question. I'll be lucky to see another six months on this earth and I want to die with a quiet mind. I want to tie up the loose ends, make my peace with – with whatever God there may be. And . . . I'm beginning to think I'll never be able to do that until I've told Blanca what I know. I've thought about it – God knows I've thought about it. And I've come to the conclusion that's the only way.'

They broke off while the waiter served them.

'I can't very well advise you if I don't know what it is you're thinking of telling her,' Johnny said.

'I know that.' Cadoret had become suddenly breathless. He reached for the wine bottle again, hesitated a moment, muttered 'bugger it' under his breath and topped his glass up.

'Only tell me if you really feel you must,' Johnny said quietly.

Cadoret champed his false teeth. 'I need to square up the account, Johnny. You'll understand what I mean when you've heard what I have to say.'

He launched into the story of his engagement to Ceci in the thirties and his marriage to Magdalena Salgado. After a while, Johnny felt that his father had forgotten his presence and was simply rehearsing aloud what had been tormenting him for forty years. He tried to listen impassively, but when Tito told him about bribing a police officer he couldn't help showing surprise.

'What with?'

'The best pony in my caballada.'

'But why?'

'On the understanding that the case would be dropped. I had no alternative, Johnny. He had me by the short hairs.'

'Who else knows about this?'

Cadoret laughed and shook his head. 'All the people you'd expect to know and a good few others besides. I shouldn't tell you this, but – oh, to hell with it! I'm a Freemason, Johnny. Yes. Have been for years. Did you hear about Calvi, the Vatican banker? The one who was found hanging under Blackfriars Bridge last June? He used to come to Ventolera. We're all in the same Lodge. We're all owned by Licio Gelli, alias "Luciani" after the Pope he had murdered. I've mortgaged my soul to them, that's what I've done. I've mortgaged my soul to P-Due.' Cadoret stopped a moment to drink more wine. He set the glass down on the tablecloth and turned it slowly by the stem. Then he looked steadily across the table at his son and added quietly, 'If they find out what I've just told you, they'll kill me.'

'Did you . . . ever tell anyone else?'

Cadoret's eyes lifted momentarily. 'Not about being a Freemason, no. But Ceci knew quite a bit about the financial side.'

'And she committed suicide.'

'Yes.'

'Because they found out you'd told her?'

'More or less. They discovered we were going to get married and that she planned to buy back La Calandria for me. They raided her lawyer's

388

offices and disappeared him and the next thing I knew, Nikki had been abducted and Botta was telling me that if I wanted her released I had to break all contact with Ceci. What else could I do? That was what broke Ceci. It was the second time I'd done it to her, you see. They forced me to make an impossible choice, Johnny. Between Nikki and Ceci. They'd have disappeared Nikki if I hadn't caved in. And . . . I didn't know Ceci was going to jump off the roof, did I? Was that my fault as well? And now they're waiting for me to die. They've banned me from the Lodge, branded me as worthless . . . why they don't just bump me off and have done with it, I don't know. Mental torture probably. They're good at that. Probably gives them a kick to see me like this. It does things to you, you know. It does things to your mind. It makes you suspicious. It makes you stop trusting people. You begin to think that everyone's against you. Watching you. You get nightmares. I . . . Some nights I wake up screaming.'

'And you think you should tell Blanca all this?'

'Not about P-Due. About Magdalena. I wrote Blanca another letter, you see. Last week. I told her I could give her new information about her mother and I asked her to come and visit me. And . . . and this morning, just before you arrived, she telephoned and said she would call in this evening.' Cadoret shook his head. 'Do you know, she's never once been inside that apartment since she was a child? And now she's agreed to come and see me.'

Johnny saw fear in his father's eyes again.

'Do you want me to be with you when she calls?'

'No,' Tito said quickly. 'No, I must see her alone. But I'm still not sure whether I should tell her. And . . . there's something else I must tell you. Blanca's always wanted revenge, you know. Anna used to say she was full of anger and that until she found out who murdered her mother and saw them brought to justice she would never be at peace in herself. Do you see what I'm driving at, Johnny? About the baby? Do you understand now?'

'What exactly do you intend to tell her?'

Cadoret bowed his head.

'You may find this difficult to believe, but I loved that child. She was a little fiend, but I loved her.' He looked up with tears streaming from his eyes. 'I've needed women all my life. But all my women have come to grief. If I can see Blanca again . . . If I can just explain –'

'But *what* would you explain?'

Cadoret closed his eyes for a moment, struggling inwardly.

'If I tell her anything at all, it'll be that – that the person to blame for her mother's death, is me. That's what I need to tell her.' He mopped his eyes with a handkerchief. 'I want to do one honest thing, one brave thing in my life, Johnny. Before I die. I want to make a clean breast of things. A . . . a sort of salvation, I suppose. But if I tell her, she might take revenge – not on me but on – on the baby. Am I a fool, Johnny? Am I just a frightened old fool?'

For the first time in his life, Johnny Cadoret felt sorry for his father. He was old and ill and confused and lonely, and he wanted to save his soul. He had resigned his membership of the English Club and had lost all his friends. He had a housekeeper who treated him like dirt and his allowance had been so eroded by inflation that he was close to the breadline.

'No,' Johnny muttered. 'No, Dad. You're not a fool.'

They sat for a while longer over the coffee, then Cadoret asked for the bill.

'Damn,' he said, looking into his wallet. 'I've left my credit card in the flat.'

'That's all right, Dad. I'll pay.'

'I wouldn't bloody well hear of it. I told you it was my treat and I don't welch on my promises. Besides, my American Express goes out of date next week and they won't renew it. Here you are, boy. Take my key and nip back and get it for me. It'll be on the table by the chair. Either there or on the bedside table.'

When he returned, Cadoret paid the bill and then accepted Johnny's arm for the slow walk back along the broken sidewalk to the apartment.

Angelita was waiting for them at the street door when they arrived. She was about to go out. Cadoret looked embarrassed. 'We'll have to say goodbye here, Johnny. She doesn't let me have visitors when she isn't in the building. You're late as it is. I'll see you before you go back south, won't I?'

'Yes, of course –'

'And about telling Blanca –'

Johnny shook his head. 'I wouldn't, Dad. She'll only misunderstand.'

Tito wanted to say something else to his son. He was not sure exactly what he wanted to say or how he could say it; all he knew was that he wanted to be able to show Johnny that he loved him. But it was beyond his ability to put that into words. All he could do was stand there mumbling conventional clichés of farewell.

'Great to see you, Johnny.'

'You too, Dad. Look after yourself, won't you?'

'I will.'

'Sure you'll be all right?'

'Quite sure. You go.'

'And about hearing your confession –'

'Don't worry about it. I'll take a taxi some time and go to Our Lady up the road.' Cadoret gave a little laugh. 'Where I married your mother.' His false teeth champed. 'Perhaps if you could just give me a blessing, Johnny . . .'

He took off his panama hat and, while Angelita tapped her foot and rolled her eyes upward in impatience, bowed his head for Johnny to say a blessing and make the sign of the cross over him. Then father and son embraced for the last time before the priest turned and walked off along the Avenida.

Angelita banged the front door shut behind her. Cadoret went along the marble lobby to the lift which he found padlocked with an 'out of order' notice hanging on the handle.

He stood at the bottom of the stairs and cursed. This was obviously Angelita's doing. She hadn't liked being told what to do by a priest and she was having her own back.

There were four double flights to climb. He stood and looked up the staircase and the challenge of climbing them unaided filled him with a grim determination. It would be a real achievement to get to the top. Something he could do entirely on his own, without help from another soul.

He set out slowly, taking it a step at a time. Halfway up the first flight he sat down to rest and when he set out again he found it easier to climb, very slowly, on all fours.

When he finally reached the top landing, he sat on the top step and laughed to himself in triumph, then took the front-door key out of his pocket and heaved himself to his feet.

He fitted the key in the lock but it refused to turn. He took it out and held it in the palm of his hand and stared at it. It was the wrong key. Johnny had given him the wrong key back when he came from collecting his American Express card.

He sat down and leant against his front door and wondered what to do. Angelita was out so there was no hope of getting a spare key from her. Then it occurred to him that Johnny would find that he had the wrong key sooner or later and would return. So the answer was to sit it out.

But there was a more pressing problem, and that was a full bladder. He held it for a while, but soon began to suffer increasing discomfort.

He didn't want to do it on the stairs or outside his own front door, but there didn't seem anywhere else.

Except the lift shaft.

He breathed out in relief and felt very much better for it. Then he took off his jacket and folded it up to make a pillow for his head. He sat leaning against his own front door but after a while he stretched out full length.

He awoke with a start. It was completely dark and his own front-door bell was ringing above his head. He got quickly to his feet and made himself dizzy as a result. The bell was ringing but he was unable to answer on the intercom or let the visitor in because he was the wrong side of his own front door.

'It'll be Johnny,' he thought, and the thought was so loud in his mind that he didn't know whether he spoke aloud or not.

The bell rang again, insistently.

He was confused because he had just woken from a complicated dream. It was dark and he couldn't find the landing light switch. He fumbled for it with his hands against the wall and the front-door bell rang and rang and rang and suddenly he remembered that Magdalena was coming to see him that evening.

'What am I thinking about?' he muttered. 'Not Magdalena. Blanca. Blanca.' Yes, only Blanca could ring a bell in that imperious way. But what if she went away? What if he was left here in the dark all night on the landing?

He was suddenly terrified that she would give up and go away. Johnny could only bring him the key to his apartment, but Blanca held the key to something far more important. It was the key to peace of mind. The key to a clear conscience. That was why it was so important for him to see Blanca and talk to her. He needed to tell her the truth about her mother's death. He needed to say to her, 'I was the man who paid to have your mother murdered.'

'Must confess it,' he muttered. 'Not to a priest, not to Johnny but to Blanca herself. Whatever the consequences. Must confess it. Must take the blame, once and for all. The only way. The only way . . .'

He shouted downward into the darkness. 'Hang on! Hang on! I'm coming straight down!'

34

NIKKI WAS AT SEA for three and a half months altogether and the only time she got ashore was one afternoon when they laid on a special trip into Stanley for the non-combatants and she went for a snowy walk along Port Stanley's single main street. She got talking with one of the locals and was invited to tea by Miss Maggie Jowett, a second cousin to Aunt Ceci. Maggie had met Ceci a few years before when she was on her visit to the Falklands. She had lived in Argentina as a child and had gone to nursery school with Stiffy Rathbone. She knew all about the Cadorets and Dalligans and Rathbones and lots of others besides. Nikki was treated to a long trip down memory lane (Maggie needed to talk) and when the time came to leave had difficulty tearing herself away without appearing rude. She sprinted down to the landing stage and got there just in time to see the boat halfway out to the NOSH, so she waved her arms at a passing Sea King (you could do that in those first weeks after the ceasefire) and hitched a lift. Nikki arrived back on board half a minute before the liberty boat to face another ticking-off from Oggle.

The homeward voyage seemed to take an age. It was a strange time. The ship had hung around at anchor off Port Stanley for weeks while the Argentine troops were shipped back and the patients recovered sufficiently to be transferred by ambulance ship to Montevideo for flight back to Britain. Then just before they sailed, when the wards were all packed up and they were painting out the red crosses, a Sidewinder missile went off ashore and took the legs of several men with it and they had a sudden aftertaste of it all, like heartburn after a heavy meal.

On the way home, in the tropics, the nursing sisters used to sit in the sun and chat. It was a limbo between war and peace. Nikki got to know Mac Logan a lot better during that time. Nothing at all had happened after they fell into each other's arms that morning when Nikki rescued the stormy petrel. They laughed about it and agreed that it was just a human necessity to hold on to each other at the time and had meant nothing at all. They used to sit in deck chairs on the boat deck and talk. He was a great reader and they swapped paperbacks.

She told him about Argentina and eventually about Rob too, but not everything. He told her about himself. He had been due to leave the Navy in May but had agreed to stay on for Operation Corporate. Now, like everybody else, he could hardly wait to return to his family and get on with the rest of his life.

Towards the end of the voyage back Nikki realized that something was beginning to happen between them (or to her, at any rate) so she backed off and made sure she was not at Mac's side when the ship docked at Southampton. She saw him go ashore and meet his wife and children, but after the first glimpse of them had to look away.

She had expected to be among the first off the ship, but when the moment came to leave, she felt terrified and was one of the last ashore. There was no one to meet her and she didn't want to be accosted by the media and asked asinine questions about what it was like or how frightened she had been. So when almost everyone else had gone ashore she crept off the ship and into the bus that was going to Haslar naval hospital, where she sat on her bed and looked at her unpacked luggage and wondered what to do next.

While she was sitting there, one of the nursing sisters who had not been to the South Atlantic came in and asked her if she would do her weekend duty, now she was back from her little holiday.

Nikki told her what she could do. She threw a few things in a bag, got into her car and drove away into the country. She spent a night in a pub in the New Forest. She had never felt lonelier in her life.

She couldn't let go, that was the trouble. Not being able to let go, not being able to cry. That, and feeling guilty to be alive and unmarked when so many were dead or scarred or burnt or crippled. And something else, too: from the moment she stepped ashore she had felt different from everyone else. She felt that no one who had not been where she had been — emotionally as well as physically — could have the first idea about what she had experienced, however clearly it was described to them. She no longer felt that she belonged anywhere or with anyone. It was as if there was a language barrier between her and everyone else who had not been to the South Atlantic with the task force.

It was late summer: although there had been sirens and fire-hose fountains and red-white-and-blue balloons to welcome them, and although people had thrown streamers and waved and cheered, the real celebration of the victory was over.

'Oh, are you lot back as well?' people said. 'Did you have a nice

time? Must have been a bit of a jolly for the nurses wasn't it? I mean
– all those men!'

All the nursing sisters were interviewed by the Matron in Chief. They
went up to London for it and were called in one by one. When Nikki's
turn came and she was asked if she wished to comment on any aspects
of organization or morale, she declined, thinking that once she started
she would probably only dig a deeper hole for herself than she was in
already.

'Nothing at all, Sister Cadoret?'

'No, Ma'am. Nothing at all.'

The Matron in Chief gave her a quick look, but that was all.

Later, Nikki wondered if it would have helped if she had said
something. The trouble was, they had never been encouraged to
be open about what had happened, and in any case she was an
inveterate bottler-up. There had been a briefing about security before
the ship's arrival at Southampton. The authorities were obviously
terrified that someone might spill the beans about the near failure
of morale aboard the hospital ship. The nursing staff were told that
if they were ever approached by the press for information they must
refer all such enquiries to their commanding officer. They were told
that although they might not be aware of it, their experience had
been unique in British naval history. There were things they had seen
and heard which, taken in isolation, might seem innocent enough but
which put together could be of use to a potential enemy. That was why
it was necessary to preserve a closely guarded silence about their part
in Operation Corporate.

It was this over-secretive, authoritarian attitude that had much to
do with the problems Nikki and others suffered afterwards. In
Nikki's case, she felt that her silence was required because what she
had witnessed was not so much of use to a potential enemy as an
embarrassment to the government.

Knowing she had to keep secrets made it difficult to share what
she had experienced with others. Not having anyone close to share it
with didn't help matters either. There were a lot of weddings after the
Falklands War between people who had been out there and 'spoke the
same language' – and quite a few existing marriages were placed under
strain because husbands were unable to talk out their experiences to
their wives.

Almost as soon as she got back to Haslar she knew that she
wanted to get out of the QARNNS as soon as possible. But the
only way she could do that before her contract was up was either

395

to get married or to get pregnant. There wasn't much hope of either.

About a month after she got back, she had a letter from her father. It had been written during the war and posted by a friend from Montevideo. He told her about his heart attack and said he would like to see her again before he died. Could she get herself to Montevideo? If so, he would move heaven and earth to come and see her. It was just the wrong moment for her to receive such a letter. She sat down and asked herself if she felt she owed him anything at all and the answer was no.

It was about then that she began getting seriously bad nightmares.

She knew that her problems of loneliness and depression and fear of authority could have been solved immediately if only Rob could walk back into her life. She ached for him. She had been to the Thanksgiving service in St Paul's and had seen him with Clare, and she had also read the reports of his award of the OBE for his part in the Falklands campaign. Now, without him, there seemed no way forward. When she had broken up with him the first time she had managed to immerse herself in work – first at university, then as a nurse and later at Misión Yuchán. After her detention, she had managed to come to terms with the experience by plunging straight back into nursing and joining the QARNNS. But now he was back with Clare and the experience of war was behind her: there seemed to be no future left.

At Christmas, she was invited to the ball at Haslar naval hospital by someone who had been let down at the last minute. She was a spare bird, one of a party of eight, but the only one who had been to the South Atlantic. Towards midnight there was a silly, champagne-assisted conversation about battle trauma during which a rugger-playing ENT specialist, being deliberately provocative, remarked that half the people who suffered from depression could probably be cured by a good boot up the arse. Nikki had to leave. She went back to her room and stared for a long time at a bottle of Mogadon.

Only a few days after that there was a cable from Johnny to say that her father had been found dead.

She had not replied to his letter. It was another reason to blame herself. He had been found at the bottom of a lift shaft and it was not known whether it had been an accident or suicide. Either way, he had died alone, frightened, ill and down and out. She was an orphan. She was thirty years old and there was no one she could throw her arms round and hug.

She had a minor breakdown and was diagnosed as suffering from post-battle trauma. She was taken off the medical ward and given a sinecure in the Medical Director General's office. She became a Case, complete with Case Notes and a Case History. She had sessions with a naval psychiatrist who encouraged her to talk about her Falklands Experience. He invited her to write down everything she felt and persuaded her to take part in group-therapy sessions. He was a big, gentle, Irish surgeon commander, and from the moment she sat down in his consulting room she knew that there was not the slightest hope of her being helped in any way by him. She didn't think she needed help. She needed Rob, that was all, and was unable to talk about him because he had been turned into a hero, and heroes weren't allowed to have secret loves.

So she pulled the wool over her psychiatrist's smiling Irish eyes. She told him about her dreams and talked about her time aboard the NOSH and made a conscious effort to get better. She had read enough medical histories of neurotic women to know what a ball-and-chain a history of neurosis could be (those referral notes that start, 'This lady has a problem . . .') and was determined not to end up in Knowle Mental Hospital, which, she discovered one afternoon during a group therapy session, turned into 'El Wonk' when spelt backwards.

And she did get better. She was pronounced cured and was sent back to the wards. Her case became a model example of psychotherapy and a television company approached her to appear in a documentary programme they were making about post-battle trauma. She declined their invitation.

It was about this time that her feelings about military service and war came into sharper focus. Margaret Thatcher had called a general election and the Defence argument raged. Already, people were more interested in what the Falklands War had done for the Conservative Party than the catastrophic effects it had had on thousands of individuals.

She also began to feel increasingly strongly about what she regarded as the insanity of nuclear deterrence. She had never accepted that nuclear bombs had kept the peace. Now, the thought that billions of pounds were still being spent on Trident missile submarines made her feel physically sick.

But thoughts like these did not get rid of the nightmares or disperse the recurring feelings of self-doubt or depression. If anything, they made matters worse. She was fighting a solitary battle, bottling things up all over again. Behind the neat, cheerful exterior, she was turning into that most hated of individuals in the armed services – the Loner. In off-duty time she went for long walks by herself. She turned down invitations to parties. Whenever possible, she put an empty place between herself and the next person at meals. In the mess, infuriatingly happy people would snap their fingers in front of her eyes and say, 'Smile! It isn't as bad as all that!'

Then one afternoon when she was sitting alone in the corner of the staff anteroom sipping a cup of tea, there was a telephone call for her. It was Johnny, speaking on a bad line from Buenos Aires.

'Finally tracked you down!' he shouted. 'How are you?'

She said she was fine.

'You know we've got a new President?'

'Yes –'

'Well he's kept his promise. He's set up a commission of enquiry into the Dirty War. I was speaking to Bishop de Nevares yesterday – he's one of the members of the commission – and your name was mentioned. He asked whether you might consider coming back here to give evidence. What do you think, Nikki?'

She knew straight away that this was something she must do, if only for the sake of Larry and Adriana. But it would be for her own sake too: she saw that this might be a way out of the dungeon of depression and self-dislike in which she found herself.

On Johnny's advice she went to Amnesty International, and with their help presented her case for early release from her QARNNS contract. Within eight weeks of Johnny's call she was a civilian, and travelling on a Lufthansa flight from Frankfurt to Buenos Aires with a typed deposition to present to CONADEP, the National Commission on Disappeared People, in her hand baggage.

From the moment the Commission started its first session on the second floor offices of 1550, Sarmiento, it was inundated with information and requests for information. Every day for weeks there were people – mainly wives and mothers – queuing and demonstrating outside. As the extent of the killings and tortures became known, a wave of horror and revulsion swept across Argentina.

Witnesses led members of the Commission to places of detention and torture. Evidence was given concerning the mass cremation of bodies at Chacarita. Unmarked graves were discovered; burnt and dismembered bodies were exhumed.

Gradually, it became apparent that members of the Argentine Navy,

Army, Air Force and Police had committed unnumbered murders and atrocities against many thousands of innocent people.

Nikki gave evidence to the Commission in March 1984. She told the whole story for the first time. The telling of it was an ordeal in itself.

She had been transferred by truck from Misión Yuchán to a helicopter base, and from there had been flown to another airbase and held with other prisoners for three days, during which time she had to remain seated during daylight hours on a concrete floor with a bag over her head. There were no toilet facilities. They sat in their excrement and urine. They were given two meals of stale bread and unsweetened maté per day. At the end of three days Nikki was hosed down before being loaded blindfold into a military aircraft. After a flight of about two hours the aircraft landed. She was able to glimpse air-force blue trousers from underneath the bag that was over her head. She was pushed down the steps from the aircraft and put into a jeep which drove fast along a perimeter track. On arrival at the detention centre she was allocated a number, stripped and forced to run the gauntlet between two lines of guards, who abused her verbally and sexually. She had been made filthy by the guards but was not provided with any washing facilities. She was handcuffed, blindfolded and gagged with sticking plaster. She was subjected to an examination by a man who the guards referred to as 'Doc'. This man told her that if she gave him oral sex he would see that she was granted special privileges. She refused and was then chained up in a cell with about a dozen other prisoners, young men and women, naked like herself. They were required to sit in total silence and without making any move for many hours each day. From time to time, prisoners were called out by their numbers, and after they had gone screams could be heard coming from an adjoining building.

One day she was called out with another prisoner and they were forced to dance with each other, naked, for the amusement of the guards. Another time, she was made to put her finger on the floor and spin round it, faster and faster, a game they called 'prospecting for oil'. When she fell over from giddiness, they kicked and beat her. On another day, after refusing to answer the questions of her interrogator, she was taken out, stood up against a wall and orders were given to a firing squad to load, and take aim. She heard the rattle of rifle bolts but the order to fire was not given. Instead, she was taken back to the room they used for torture and was made to lie on the concrete floor while the guards urinated over her. She was accused of working for the ERP and subjected to repeated interrogation and torture. She was strapped down on her back to a metal bed-frame and tortured with a cattle prod. They gave her a treatment they called the dry submarine. Her mouth was sealed and a clip put on her nose and the clip was removed only after she had lost consciousness. Her interrogators questioned her repeatedly about her work at Misión Yuchán. She was taunted that she had abandoned the Catholic faith and was questioned about Larry and Adriana. When she refused to give information, her blindfold was lifted and she was shown a photograph of Adriana lying in blood and vomit. She was returned to the cell and other prisoners were taken out for transfer or interrogation. No prisoner who was called out for transfer ever returned. Their places were taken by new prisoners. One day a priest came and said that if any prisoner wished to make a good confession it would be taken as an indication of a change of heart and would help to secure an early release. He said that obedience to the State was an essential part of Christianity, and that all they had to do was renounce their subversive views in order to win a clear conscience and freedom. The priest asked them individually if they would confess to him, but no one complied.

After her interview, she was able to obtain more information about Larry and Adriana from CONADEP. They had been last seen in the detention centre at the Naval School of Engineering, the headquarters of Admiral Massera's operation against subversive operations. Their names were included in the list of the Disappeared.

She stayed in Buenos Aires for two weeks. Most days she lunched with Johnny, who was no longer a military chaplain and was working among the poor on the outskirts of the city. He told her about his last meeting with Tito and showed her the photograph of Blanca's adopted son, Rui. He had been in touch with Blanca. She was living apart from Jorge now, and splitting her time between La Calandria and her luxury apartment on the Avenida Quintana. She had not been aware of her son's identity, but was now as convinced as Johnny that Rui and Daniel were one and the same person. Johnny had thought hard about what to do about it, and after a visit to Rui's school in Palermo, where he found the little boy well and happy, he decided that Blanca was the best person to look after him and that the best course to follow would be to use his relationship as uncle to keep in regular touch.

'Blanca's agreed to tell him about his parents when he's a bit older,' he said over lunch one day. 'There's no point in turning his life upside down now, just when he's settled. Blanca's calmed down a lot, you know. She's still angry, but so are a lot of people these days. She told me that since adopting Rui she has felt more at peace with herself than at any time in her life. Now she knows who he is and what happened to Larry and Adriana, she feels strongly that it's her duty to be a good mother to him.'

Johnny looked across the table. 'I could fix up for you to spend a weekend at Calanuria if you'd like that. Remember José Ocampo? He's taken over Casa Nova and says he'd be delighted to put you up for a night or two if you'd like to see the old place.'

'No,' she said. 'I think I'd rather not.'

'Quite understand,' Johnny agreed. 'You – never liked Ocampo, did you?'

'Not much.'

On her last day, they lunched at a steak house on the Avenida Costanera before driving out to the airport.

'So what will you do now?' he asked.

'I don't know.'

'No hope of your finding yourself a husband, I suppose?'

She shook her head and smiled.

'What happened to that guy you fell for up in Edinburgh?'

'I've no idea,' she said. 'Except that he went back to his wife.'

On the road out to the airport, they passed a dead horse lying at the side of the road. Its body was bloated by the sun and its legs were up in the air.

Johnny shook his head. 'Nothing changes,' he muttered.

She returned to Britain with a feeling of anti-climax. She had hoped that giving evidence would finally lay the ghosts of the past and that she would be able to start afresh, but however hard she tried, she still could not stop herself thinking about the past.

After doing a succession of temporary jobs, she applied successfully for work at Amnesty International. Gradually, as the months passed, she began to put the pieces of her life back together. She started work on a book and became active among expatriate Argentines who had been obliged to start new lives in Europe. She took on translation work and did research for the South American department of the BBC World Service. She rented a ground-floor flat in Islington in a house that backed onto the Regent's Canal and buried herself in work. She surrounded herself with books and music and a few carefully chosen friends, until the hot summer evening when she arrived home to find Rob waiting for her on her front doorstep.

'I'm on the cadge,' he said. 'For tea and sympathy.'

401

She closed the front door behind them. He looked round at the shelves of books, the piles of papers and manuscripts, the Indian poncho over the back of the sofa, the carved wooden ducks on the mantelpiece.

He smiled apologetically and shook his head. 'I don't know where to begin.'

'Begin here,' she said, and opened her arms.

He had been through a rough time since coming back from the South Atlantic. He had suffered from nightmares, depression and an inability to communicate with Clare. He said that she had treated him as if he were a sports trophy that she kept in a glass case and took out to polish once a week.

They had struggled for a long time to keep the marriage going. He had been to the edge of alcoholism and back.

'Things fell apart,' he said.

It had been the same situation as before, only this time Rob had been the invalid and Clare had been the one who was determined not to give up. They had been to a marriage-guidance counsellor. In a desperate attempt at repairing the damage, Clare had encouraged him to talk his way out of depression. Then Nikki's name had come back into their discussions, and as soon as that happened they began tearing each other apart all over again.

'It just couldn't go on. As soon as we both accepted that – that the damage was irreparable – things became easier. We separated, and soon after that I left the Navy.'

'So are you still married?'

He shook his head. 'The divorce was made final in March. I wasn't going to contact you, but – well, it gets a bit lonely, and I couldn't stop thinking about you . . .' He lifted his eyes to meet hers. 'I'm a divorcee, I'm out of work and I've had a drink problem. I love you, Nikki. I need you, I can't live without you . . .'

His tears came suddenly, shockingly. She held him for a long time. 'It's all over,' she whispered. 'It's all over. You're safe now.'

They talked into the small hours. She told him about her arrest and detention, but without giving many details.

'Will you go back?' he asked.

She shook her head. 'I doubt it. Not for a long time, anyway. When I was out there to give evidence I was frightened every time I turned a street corner of who I might bump into. I couldn't take a ride in a taxi without wondering what the driver had been doing five or ten

402

years ago.' She shook her head and shivered. 'The trouble is, an awful lot of people still condone what happened. They're still saying things like "something had to be done".'

'What *did* they do?'

She stared at him. 'You really want to know?'

'Yes. Yes – especially if it would help you.'

She got up from the sofa and went to her worktable and found a few sheets of paper. It was an article she had been writing for *Index on Censorship*. 'Read that.'

'Is it by you?'

'In a way, yes, but in another way, no. You'll see what I mean when you read it.'

'I'd rather you read it to me, Nikki.'

She sat with him on the sofa and he put his arm round her and she began to read in a quiet, matter-of-fact voice.

'How can we make you believe what happened to us, we who have no name, no grave, no death certificate, no witness to what we endured? We are nameless, faceless, un-numbered and numberless. We are silent, voiceless. How can we make you believe what happened to us?

'How can we measure the enormity of it? How can we measure the experience of a girl who is stripped, laughed at, fingered and prodded, forced to walk between lines of jeering soldiers? How can we weigh the agony of a little boy who is tortured with an electric prod? How deep runs the wound in a child of seven who has been forced to watch her parents being broken under torture?

'Why should you not know the names of our torturers? Why should there not be erected, alongside that monument in the park to the glorious police officers who died fighting the guerrillas, another monument, a monument of shame, a monument bearing the names and aliases and pseudonyms of those who made us suffer in filth and fear and agony? Why should you not know about the "Dog" and the "Parrot" and the "Witch"? Why should not the names of Menendez and Massera and Astiz be written in the Book of Death? Why should not every single one of our torturers be given a place in the halls of infamy?

'Why should you not know what they did? Why should you not know about the metal beds they tied us to, the electric corsets they made us wear? Why should you not know about the Telephone and the Machine? Why should you not know about the mock executions, drownings and electrocutions that made us shriek in terror, collapse in

403

convulsions, lose all sense of time and place and identity? Why should you not know that by the time some of us were slaughtered, there were maggots feeding on our encrusted eyes?

'Why should you be allowed to forget? Why should anything of what they did be suppressed or pardoned? Why should you not know that these things were often done in the name of Christ and with the approval of a bishop or a priest? Why should you be prevented from knowing that they gave absolution to our torturers, gave them the sacraments every week, took sides with them against us or kept shameful silence about the atrocities that were being performed? Why should you not know that many of us are Jewish and were taunted, tortured, mutilated and murdered because of our race? Why should you not be reminded that we were sometimes told by priests that we had brought our ordeal upon ourselves and had only ourselves to blame?

'How can we make you believe? How can we measure the enormity of it? Why should you not know the names of our torturers? Why should you not know what they did? Why should you be allowed to forget?

'To our tormentors and murderers and all their fellow travellers we say: We shall walk past you in an endless line, staring at you in silent condemnation as we go by. We shall never go away. We shall always be with you, night and day. You will be aware of us, come face to face with us at any moment of the day or night. In your everyday life. At work. In the conference room. At the athletics club. When you are with your wife or your mistress or your mother. In your dreams. Especially in your dreams. You will hear us whispering to you, whispering on the night wind when you are trying to get to sleep. Our faces will loom up before you, staring back at you.

'Come – look us in the eye, one by one, as we file past in our thousands. And remember, you who did it for your country and for your God, you ex-choir boys and altar boys and good little boys and smart boys and brave boys and tough boys and tennis-playing boys and football boys and boys who remember Mother's day and their aunties' birthdays; you boys that looked so clean and smart in your new uniforms when you joined the Police or the Army or the Navy or the Air Force – remember these words, the words of the Christ in whose name you performed your inquisitions and committed your atrocities: INASMUCH AS YOU HAVE DONE IT UNTO ONE OF THE LEAST OF THESE MY LITTLE ONES, YOU HAVE DONE IT UNTO ME.'

* * *

'But that isn't all, is it?' Rob said when she had finished reading.

'Isn't it enough?'

'It's more than enough. But what I mean is, that isn't all as far as you are concerned.'

'I've got a copy of my deposition. You can read that if you like.'

He shook his head. 'There was something wrong – something had happened to you – before all this. When we were in Edinburgh, you used to say that you bottled things up. And . . . I always felt that there was something you were keeping back. Something you needed to talk about but never dared. Well – is there anything else you need to talk about now? Anything at all?'

She felt the old fear come back. It was like a motor starting up inside her. It was as if she were being questioned by her mother about José Ocampo all over again.

Rob was holding her hands together under his chin. There were tears in his eyes. 'There is something else, isn't there?'

She nodded, compressing her lips tightly.

'Tell me,' he whispered. 'Please tell me.'

She took a deep breath and closed her eyes. When she opened them, she seemed to look straight through him.

'I was sexually assaulted. When I was eleven years old.'

She put her arms round his neck and clung to him. Slowly, painfully, tearfully, she went on to tell him what she had never told anyone before. She told him the whole story. Going back to the compartment on the train to Cadoret. The man in the blue suit who lifted the corner of his newspaper. Going the wrong way along the corridor. How he put his foot in the door of the lavatory. What he did. The telegraph poles. What he said. How he threatened her. How he said that he would send his soldiers to do it to her again. How that threat had dogged her ever since. How she threw away the necklace he gave her. How she had run away from him and lost Pollyanna. How her father had shot Pollyanna. How she had bottled it all up, kept it inside herself, year after year after year.

They talked through the night. They wept together, laughed together, visited heaven together; and very early in the morning, when the first sparrow was cheeping sleepily outside the window and a milk float was humming and jingling in the road, they dressed and went out for a walk along the canal path.

Dawn was just coming up; London was quiet and nobody was about. They walked along the canal bank arm in arm, still talking, still planning, still sharing.

405

'The sad thing is,' Nikki was saying, 'that the very people Argentina needs most have been driven out. That's the real tragedy. This obsession with being macho the whole time. Maradona worship. In Argentina, a first-class honours degree in history counts for less than a nine handicap at polo or a place in the city football team.'

Rob smiled wryly. 'That's not so very different from this country.'

'I remember Larry and Adriana ticking me off for being apathetic. Well, I'm not apathetic any more. I *do* give a damn. If there's anything I can do to help Argentina emerge from all this, I want to do it.'

'Is there much that anyone can do?'

'Not as individuals, no. But if people work together, perhaps Argentina can recover some of her self-respect. I'm only just beginning to look at things in perspective. What I lost when I was assaulted on that train was really the same thing that Argentina lost. And my father for that matter. Not property or power. Not Calandria or the Islas Malvinas. Property doesn't matter, does it? What matters is – the ability to love. Really love. Deeply. The ability to trust one's fellow human beings. To live without fear. To be innocent again. Like –'

'Like the person who taught me how to cook steaks?'

'Yes. Like I was then. Far away and long ago.'

'It's the same with me,' he said quietly. 'I never thought it would be possible, but I'm beginning to think that perhaps, with you, I'll be able to regain – I don't know – a sort of innocence. What I lost when I went into the Navy. What do you think. Would it be very old fashioned of me if I asked you to marry me?'

'Not in the slightest.'

'Then will you?'

She leant against him. 'Yes. Yes, I will.'

'No point in delaying things is there?'

'None at all,' she agreed.

'So . . . when are you free?'

She put her head back and felt the morning breeze cool on her face.

'I'm free now.'